Praise for

DIXIE BROWNING

"There is no one writing romance today
who touches the heart and tickles the ribs like
Dixie Browning. The people in her books are as warm
and real as a sunbeam and just as lovely."
—*New York Times* bestselling author Nora Roberts

"Dixie Browning has given the romance industry
years of love and laughter in her wonderful books."
—*New York Times* bestselling author Linda Howard

"Each of Dixie's books is a keeper guaranteed
to warm the heart and delight the senses."
—*New York Times* bestselling author Jayne Ann Krentz

"Dixie's books never disappoint—they always lift your spirit!"
—*USA TODAY* bestselling author Mary Lynn Baxter

"A true pioneer in romantic fiction, the delightful Dixie
Browning is a reader's most precious treasure, a constant
source of outstanding entertainment."
—*Romantic Times*

Dear Reader,

The editors at Harlequin and Silhouette are thrilled to be able to bring you a brand-new featured author program for 2005! Signature Select aims to single out outstanding stories, contemporary themes and oft-requested classics by some of your favorite series authors and present them to you in a variety of formats bound by truly striking covers.

We want to provide several different types of reading experiences in the new Signature Select program. The Spotlight books offer a single "big read" by a talented series author, the Collections present three novellas on a selected theme in one volume, the Sagas contain sprawling, sometimes multi-generational family tales (often related to a favorite family first introduced in series) and the Miniseries feature requested previously published books, with two or, occasionally, three complete stories in one volume. The Signature Select program offers one book in each of these categories per month, and fans of limited continuity series will also find these continuing stories under the Signature Select umbrella.

In addition, these volumes bring you bonus features...different in every single book! You may learn more about the author in an extended interview, more about the setting or inspiration for the book, more about subjects related to the theme and, often, a bonus short read will be included. Authors and editors have been outdoing themselves in originating creative material for our bonus features—we're sure you'll be surprised and pleased with the results!

The Signature Select program strives to bring you a variety of reading experiences by authors you've come to love, as well as by rising stars you'll be glad you've discovered. Watch for new stories from Janelle Denison, Donna Kauffman, Leslie Kelly, Marie Ferrarella, Suzanne Forster, Stephanie Bond, Christine Rimmer and scores more of the brightest talents in romance fiction!

The excitement continues!

Warm wishes for happy reading,

Marsha Zinberg

Marsha Zinberg
Executive Editor
The Signature Select Program

MINISERIES

DIXIE
BROWNING

LAWLESS LOVERS

Published by Silhouette Books
America's Publisher of Contemporary Romance

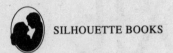 **SILHOUETTE BOOKS**

ISBN 0-373-21763-3

LAWLESS LOVERS

Copyright © 2005 by Harlequin Books S.A.

The publisher acknowledges the copyright holder of the individual works as follows:

THE PASSIONATE G-MAN
Copyright © 1998 by Dixie Browning.

HIS BUSINESS, HER BABY
Copyright © 1998 by Dixie Browning.

Visit Silhouette Books at www.eHarlequin.com

Printed in U.S.A.

CONTENTS

Dear Reader,

Most of my stories begin with a question. *What if*? In the case of *The Passionate G-Man*, I wondered what would happen if a tough guy were to hide out in the middle of a swamp until his injuries healed enough to face down the bad guys who were chasing him? What if something happened to him while he was there...say something that happens to most of us, sooner or later? What if he pulled a muscle in his back, and while he was lying there helpless and vulnerable, an unemployed actress came along with a face full of poison ivy?

And then there's Harrison, another of old Squire Lawless's descendants. They keep turning up, don't they? This guy is different from the others, though. Harrison Lawless has been called arrogant, controlling and coldhearted. When you're as brilliant as a rose-cut diamond and almost as hard, arrogance is definitely a risk. Being CEO of a successful company demands the ability to control. But coldhearted? No way. Harrison's warmth might be buried so deep I had trouble digging it out in *His Business, Her Baby*, but once I introduced him to Cleo, he gradually began to thaw. Cleo has her own set of problems, a few of which can't be solved by eating a pint of ice cream in one sitting. Once Harrison shows up, he can either become a part of the problem or a part of the solution.

You'll meet Travis, too. He's been on location all along, right in the area where it all started a century or so earlier. Trav has some baggage, but he'll get through it. He's been through far worse.

Now I'm beginning to wonder just how many other cousins there are—seconds, thirds and removes. Once we get beyond third cousin, twice removed, shall we stop counting?

See what you think...

Dixie Browning

THE PASSIONATE G-MAN

One

Lyon hobbled away from the truck stop with as much haste and dignity as he could muster, leaving the waitress staring after him, her tired blue eyes filled with sympathy. By all rights she should have clobbered him. Instead, she'd taken one look at his stricken face, another at his cane, and started in with the, "Oh, you poor man" routine.

Levering himself into the driver's seat, he brushed a crumb of fried oyster off his sleeve and shifted until he found a position that was bearable. He'd been warned against driving at all, much less driving for hours at a stretch.

Needless to say, he'd ignored the warning.

Dammit, he'd tried to apologize to the woman. It wasn't her fault he'd been in the process of extracting himself from the cramped booth just as she passed by with two big seafood platters.

Lyon was no good with apologies. Never had been.

He'd wanted to help her clean up the mess, but he knew better than to try, so he'd done the next best thing. He'd crammed a fistful of bills in her apron pocket and got the hell out of there, red face, grease-stained shoulders and all.

At least, with the help of a back brace, a knee brace and a cane, he could do that much. Walk away. There was damned little he was good at anymore, but he'd always been good at walking away.

Five weeks ago he had walked away from an explosion that had killed two other agents and three civilians. Crawled away, actually, after being blown clear. Miraculously, he'd suffered only minor burns, but he'd been thrown against the side of the surveillance van, injuring his back and one knee.

At least he'd survived.

Five days ago he had walked away from the hospital. He'd had a choice of lying there taped up like a mummy, waiting either to mend or to croak from sheer boredom—or for the bad guys to find him and put a permanent end to his career—or get the hell out.

He'd got out. Walked away. Because if the bad guys hadn't got to him first, the boredom would've done him in.

Although there'd been a couple of nurses who'd done their best to relieve it. One, a sweet-faced, middle-aged woman, had joked about adopting him.

Another one had been more interested in seducing him.

He might even have considered it—the seduction— if only to prove to himself that he still had a few working body parts, but the last thing he needed was to get involved with a woman.

It had been Lyon's experience that men and women viewed sex from widely different perspectives. Women—at least the few he'd been involved with for any length of time—used sex the same way he used the tools of his trade. As a means of achieving an end.

To all but one or two of the women he'd known, sex was bait. The female of the species was programmed by nature to latch on to the richest mate available. His old man had drummed that lesson into his head before he'd cleaned out the cash drawer where he worked and disappeared, leaving behind a bitter wife and an angry twelve-year-old son.

Lyon hadn't learned much from his father, but he'd heard that little homily repeated too often ever to forget it.

Cautious by nature, he'd learned to be even more cautious, both in his work and in his relationships with women. Not all women were dishonest. Not all of them were looking for commitment, but enough of them were so that he didn't care to take chances.

To a man, sex was relief. A basic requirement, like food and water and a couple of hours sleep out of every twenty-four or thirty-six hours, conditions permitting. For a man in his position, it didn't pay to think beyond that.

Back on the highway, Lyon tuned to a country music station and set his mind on automatic. There were too many things it didn't pay to think about. Not yet. Not until he was fully recovered, had a few answers and was ready to go back and deal with them.

He spotted the patrol car in plenty of time to ease his speed back to a safe and legal seventy. Not that he was afraid of getting pulled over. His ID, if he cared to use it, would get him past any branch of law enforcement. It was more a matter of common sense.

A matter of survival.

Common sense told him that a man in his condition had no business being on the highway at all. A well-honed sense of survival—which, admittedly had taken a beaten lately—told him that driving like a bat out of Daytona wasn't particularly smart, either. Especially as he'd quit cold turkey taking painkillers and muscle relaxants three days ago. As a result, he was hurting. As a result of something else, although probably not the pills, he was jittery.

The smoky lost interest. Lyon breathed a sigh of relief. Near the Virginia-North Carolina border he pulled into the visitors' center, parked and scanned the immediate surroundings out of habit. It was called situation awareness.

He took his time getting out of the pickup, not that he had an option. By the time he'd done three slow laps around the parking area, his muscles had loosened up enough so that he barely limped, even without the cane.

Mind over matter. His body might have been screwed over pretty thoroughly, but his mind was still in first-class working order.

Although there'd been some argument over that when he'd signed himself out of the hospital.

Following the road map, he left the interstate at Roanoke Rapids and took an east-southeasterly course, using two lanes and what was euphemistically called "other roads." There was no deadline. He had three months before he had to make up his mind whether to put in for early retirement or go back on line.

At least where he was headed there wouldn't be any reporters. Or any drug-runners, terrorists, or survivalists, any one of which was bad enough. When the territories started overlapping, things got spooky.

And when there was a leak from somewhere in the chain of command, things got even spookier. The wrong people started dying.

"How'd you want your burger, hon? We can't fry 'em rare no more, gov'ment rules. We got sweet onions up from Georgia, though. A thick slice, and even shoe leather'd taste good."

Lyon ordered two burgers, well-done with extra onion, extra cheese and a quart of coffee. When the waitress leaned across in front of him to realign the salt and pepper shakers, offering him a front-row seat in her balcony if he was interested, he said, "To go, please. And could you give me directions to—"

"Any old where, darlin', you name it. You here for the huntin' or the fishin'? I could show you some real good places."

"Yeah, both," he muttered. *I'll just bet you could, sugar, and I'd probably enjoy them all, but not today, thanks.* "Could you point me in the direction of the nearest hardware store, supermarket and the local tax office?"

Jasmine was depressed. All the way across the country she'd been pumping up her expectations. She'd managed to keep them high during the long drive from the airport to the nursing home, but there they'd collapsed like a wet soufflé.

Her grandmother didn't know her. Her only living

relative, whom she hadn't seen since she'd moved with her mother from Oklahoma to California eighteen and a half years ago, didn't know her from Adam.

Make that Eve.

And the worst part of it was, Hattie Clancy wasn't interested in knowing her. She was sweet and polite and a little vague—well, a lot vague, actually—but Jasmine could tell right off that she was more interested in playing cards with her friends and watching her favorite soaps and game shows than she was in getting to know the granddaughter who had flown all the way from the West Coast to see her.

Jasmine told herself it was probably for the best. Why get attached to someone who lives thousands of miles away, someone who's old and might die—someone who's probably set in her ways and wouldn't be interested in moving to L.A., even if Jasmine could afford to move her there?

All the same, it would have been nice...

She shook off the sense of depression. It hadn't been a total waste. She'd met her only living relative, after all. Now when she sent snapshots and letters and greeting cards, she'd have a face to attach to the name and address she'd found among her father's papers after he'd died.

Having barely known the man before he turned up one day on her doorstep, sick and broke, she'd been surprised to learn that his mother—her own grandmother—was still living, much less living in North Carolina. She would have thought Oklahoma if she'd thought at all, because that's where her parents had parted company.

Jasmine had written to Hattie Clancy immediately.

She hadn't heard back, but she'd continued to write. For an actress who was unemployed more often than not, she'd been too busy trying to pay off her father's medical bills, along with her own living expenses, to have much free time, but she'd made time to send cards and brief notes, and sometimes a clipping when she happened to land a part and her name was mentioned in a review.

Which was practically never.

To make ends meet she'd done a few commercials and taken a fill-in job in a dress shop. It paid minimum wage, plus a tiny discount on clothes she couldn't afford to buy anyway.

And now she'd spent money she didn't have to fly east to see a grandmother who didn't know her and didn't seem particularly interested in getting acquainted. She might as well have stayed home. It had been a total waste of time and money.

No, it hadn't. She'd earned herself a vacation. The last one had been—

Yes, well…that was another reason she'd needed to get away. Her last vacation had been with Eric. A week after they'd come back from Tahoe, Eric had started seeing her best friend. Jasmine had made excuses for him at first. She was good at that.

What was that popular song? *Cleopatra, Queen of Denial?*

Boy, was she ever. Her friends said she was easygoing. Laid-back. Which meant more or less the same thing—that she didn't blow her stack at the least little thing, which was a definite advantage in the dog-eat-dog world of acting.

All the same, she hadn't felt very laid-back when Cynthia had breezed into the shop one day last week and said, "Guess what! Eric and I are getting married. You've got to be our maid of honor, you've simply got to! After all, if you hadn't introduced us, it never would have happened."

Right. Smartest thing she ever did. Introduce the man she was in love with to her best friend, who was blond and beautiful and had a continuing, if minor, role in *Wilde's Children.*

"When?" she'd managed to ask. Actually, it had sounded more like a whine, but Cyn had been so wrapped up in her own euphoria she hadn't noticed.

"Valentine's Day. Isn't that just too, too perfect?"

Jasmine had agreed that it was just too, too perfect. And then she'd come up with the too-too perfect excuse. "Oh, but my grandmother—it's her seventy-ninth birthday. Actually, her birthday's on the fifteenth, but I promised to help her celebrate. You wouldn't want to wait until next year, would you?"

They couldn't possibly wait, and so Jasmine had been stuck with her excuse. She'd told herself it would be a lovely thing to do, to surprise her grandmother— her only living relative, unless her father had taken a few more secrets to the grave—and so she'd flown all the way across the country on a ticket she couldn't afford, and gone still deeper in debt renting a car to drive to the nursing home, which was hours away from the airport.

And now, here she was at loose ends for a whole week. She'd planned to stay near the nursing home, only there wasn't really any place to stay—at least no place she could afford. She'd asked for a weekly rate on her car, and planned to drive her grandmother around, just the two of them, and talk about her father and her grandfather, and any aunts or uncles and cousins she might have.

Family things. Things like, who else in the family had kinky maroon hair and legs that went all the way up to her armpits?

Things like who else in the family loved animals, hated insects and was allergic to cantaloupes?

Things that would have taken her mind off the fact that Cyn and Eric were at this very moment honeymooning in Cancún.

Instead, she'd spent a day at the nursing home, looking at pictures of grandchildren of people she didn't even know, watching soaps and seeing a few people she did know, but not Cyn, thank goodness—and being largely ignored by her own grandmother.

She'd played cards with three lovely old ladies, gradually coming to realize that they weren't all playing with a full deck. She'd strolled around the grounds once the rain had let up, exclaiming over straggly little flowers and squishing through the mud to pick a bunch of red berries for one of the residents who admired them.

She'd had to battle great swags of Spanish moss and several thick, hairy vines to get to the things, but when her grandmother had asked for some, too, she had gladly waded into the jungle again to oblige her.

What else were granddaughters for?

Feeling lost, rootless, she'd woken up the next morning and considered her options. If she went back now— that's if she could even exchange her tickets—she'd have to pay the daily rate for her car instead of the cheaper weekly rate.

Of course, she would save on her motel bill, but money wasn't her only problem, or even her biggest one. Eric and Cynthia would be back on Friday. Cynthia would insist on giving her a detailed description of the honeymoon. Cynthia insisted on giving anyone who would listen a detailed description of her entire life. It was one of her charms—her breezy openness.

And Eric, blast his gorgeous hide, would gaze adoringly into his bride's eyes the way Jasmine had dreamed of his gazing into her own eyes, only he never had, and she'd probably throw up or something equally embarrassing.

Dammit, he *knew* she loved him! She hadn't even tried to hide it. They'd met thirteen and a half months ago at a New Year's Eve party and it had been one of those magical, magnetic moments that come once in a lifetime.

They had everything in common. They'd both grown up in the Midwest in single-parent households, but they'd been happy, comfortable households. They both believed in love at first sight, in fate. They both liked vinegar on their french fries.

The first time they'd gone away for a long weekend together, Jasmine had thought of it as a honeymoon. She'd been waiting ever since for a proposal, being just old-fashioned enough to believe it was the man's prerogative. Which was a hoot considering she was an actress who had lived in L.A. for nearly five years.

And then she'd made the fatal mistake of introducing Eric to Cynthia.

After driving aimlessly for hours, she pulled into a service station, filled her tank, hoping her credit card wasn't maxed out, and splurged on a candy bar and a diet cola. Savoring the unfamiliar aroma of nature in the raw mingled with diesel oil, she studied the map in search of anything of interest between where she was and the airport.

She'd had to ask the attendant where she was. It seemed she was somewhere in the vicinity of Frying Pan Landing, not too far from Gum Neck, smack dab in the middle of that part of the map labeled Eastern Dismal Swamp.

Dismal. If she'd been looking for something that suited her mood, she couldn't have found a better place.

"I don't suppose there are any hotels around here?" she said hopefully. It was getting late. She'd been driving more or less aimlessly all day, trying to make up her mind what to do.

The motel catered to fishermen and hunters. The bed was more like a hammock, but it was clean and cheap, and Clemmie, the woman in the office, told her that the café next door opened at five every morning for breakfast and closed about dark.

Jasmine managed to stay awake long enough to eat a bowl of clam chowder before she fell into bed, too tired to think about tomorrow. A pale sun was shining in through the one small window when she opened her eyes the next morning. She stretched, scratched her left cheek and yawned. And then she scratched again.

Shower. Breakfast. Then maybe spend another day looking around before she went home. As long as she'd come this far, it would be a shame to go back without seeing anything other than a nursing home, a gas station and a cheap motel. She might as well soak up a little atmosphere as long as she'd spent money she couldn't afford to spend just to get here.

Jasmine had never been farther east than Tulsa. There was a different feel to North Carolina. For one thing, it was quieter. Unnaturally quiet, in fact. But that could be because, according to the map, the nearest city was miles away. Or maybe because it was the dead of winter, and here where they had real seasons, things like that made a difference.

By the time she had rinsed off under a trickle of lukewarm water, she felt marginally better. She might even write about it, she thought, idly scratching her face. She hadn't written anything in years, even though she had a perfectly good degree in journalism.

The Further Adventures of Jasmine Clancy. A Thousand Miles From Heartbreak? In Search of Family Ties?

Her stomach growled. How about in search of breakfast?

She was hungry, which was a good sign. Even heartbroken and suffering from acute disappointment, she wasn't bothered by a lack of appetite. In fact, she felt surprisingly good.

That is, she felt good until she looked in the mirror.

"For Pete's sake, what happened to you?" she whispered, touching her red, swollen face, which instantly began to itch like crazy.

Clemmie was alone in the office, thank goodness. The wife of the owner of the four-unit motel, she did the rooms, helped out in the café, and after one look at Jasmine, she told her to go back to her room.

Twenty minutes later she brought her a breakfast tray of scrambled eggs, sausage and hash browns, with a side order of calamine lotion and a handful of tourist brochures.

"We got these things—mostly nobody ever wants 'em, but since you're not from around here, it might give you something to do. Sort of take your mind off your troubles. If you don't think about it too much, you forget to scratch."

"I can't believe it," Jasmine wailed. "I haven't had poison ivy since I was a child."

"I used to get it real bad, every summer. My mama used to threaten to make me wear boxing gloves to keep me from scratching."

"But it's February!"

"Poison ivy don't die, it just hides out over the winter. Gets you just as bad, though. Now don't scratch, you hear?"

He'd been there for one full week. The first few days he'd nearly gone nuts without his cell phone, his laptop and all the other accoutrements of civilized living he'd grown used to.

Daniel Lyon Lawless, chronological age thirty-seven, physiological age one hundred and seven, rolled over onto his back after the last push-up and stared at a pair of buzzards circling overhead. Maybe they knew something he didn't.

"Not a happy thought," he muttered just to hear the sound of a human voice.

Closing his eyes, he listened to the hollow echo of birds deep inside the boggy forest. Nearby, a frog tuned up. First one, then a dozen. He'd have thought, if he'd thought about frogs at all, they'd be buried in the mud this time of year, but then, what did he know about roughing it in the wilds of the great Dismal Swamp?

Not much. Enough to know that he'd been right to come here, though. In a place like this, away from all distractions, a man could think. If thinking got a little too uncomfortable, he could concentrate on more immediate things, such as keeping the damned bugs from eating him alive. Such as working out until he dropped from exhaustion. Such as wetting a hook in a blackwater creek in hope of catching something to relieve a monotonous diet of tinned meat, tinned soup, stale crackers and black coffee.

He had a feeling it wasn't a healthy diet. On the other hand, he'd shed his knee brace three days ago and his back brace the day before that. His cane was no good in this boggy terrain. No good for walking. He carried it anyway, because he felt naked without a weapon, and foolish carrying one here in the back of beyond, where the most dangerous critter he was apt to encounter was a damned mosquito.

He carried a knife, though. It was useful in whacking through vines and opening cans of Vienna sausage. And he walked. He counted it in hours, not miles. He'd done four hours yesterday, on top of six miles rowed back and forth on the nameless creek that bordered his campsite.

Tomorrow he was going to row in one direction until he was exhausted, then he'd go ashore, give his knee a workout and then row himself back to camp. It was a good system. It was working for him. Except for a few minor problems, he was in better shape now than he'd been before the explosion.

He was a hell of a lot more relaxed. Couple of days ago, he'd actually found himself whistling. Another few weeks and he might even find something to smile about.

He wondered what was going on back in Langley. Madden had promised to find out who'd been turned. Who had leaked names, times and places so that two of the best men in the unit had been taken out in one night. Lyon's name would be on that list of expendables. Which was one more reason why he hadn't cared to hang around the hospital like a sitting duck.

A duck on the wing had a far better chance of surviving.

A camcorder. Even a disposable camera. Jasmine would give anything for some way to record what she was seeing. No wonder half of Hollywood had moved to North Carolina, with scenery like this. Moody, spooky, fraught with atmosphere—not to mention the exotic noises and all the different odors. Perfect for a remake of the *Creature from the Black Lagoon*.

At least there were plenty of black lagoons, if mercifully few creatures.

Away from the motel, there was practically no traffic. None at all once she'd left the narrow two-lane highway. Clemmie had told her about the old logging road, and she'd followed it, determined to stay out of public view until her face improved, but wanting to take something back with her after spending the better part of eight hundred dollars on a wild-goose chase.

She'd had sense enough to shove a notepad into her shoulder bag. Clemmie had provided that, too. Her writerly instincts had been stirring all morning. She was even considering doing a travel piece on spec to help pay her expenses.

She might even offer it to one of the two newspapers where she'd briefly worked as a special features writer before being laid-off, downsized or consolidated, depending on who was offering excuses.

At least it had led to her acting career, which paid at a better rate, only not nearly as regularly.

Fortunately, she was good at rolling with the punches. Going with the flow. Surviving.

The logging road ended at a hill, which turned out to be a mound of rotted sawdust, covered with creeping, crawling vines. Something was blooming somewhere nearby—something with a sweet, spicy scent.

There was enough high ground so that her feet didn't sink in the mud, so she followed an all but imperceptible trail deeper and deeper into the woods.

Red berries beckoned from the wild tangle of vegetation. Gorgeous, big fat red berries, like the ones she had picked for her grandmother. Uh-uh. Not again.

She scratched her face, careful not to dig too hard because poison ivy was bad enough without scars. Her face, after all, was her fortune. At five foot ten, her height and her long legs helped, but mostly it was her face. She would like to believe it was her acting ability, because then a few scars might not matter too much, but she was realistic enough to know better.

She had a modest talent and the kind of looks that were just different enough to land her a few parts. Until another kind of look came into fashion, and then she'd do commercials or even catalog work, and maybe some modeling.

Not that modeling appealed to her. The few models she knew were obsessed by diets, cutaneous laser resurfacing, ultrasound liposuctioning. One of them was actually growing her own collagen for when she needed a major overhaul.

Jasmine would much rather settle into a comfortable, low-key life with Eric and their children, and maybe her grandmother living together in a little bungalow somewhere. Fashion was fleeting. Film fame was fleeting. Family was forever.

Oh, yeah? So what happened to all of yours?

Somewhere up ahead she heard a sound that didn't belong in this mystical, moss-hung environment.

A splash. A bump, a yelp...

And then a groan.

Two

The boat looked out of place in the muted setting. It was painted a muddy shade of royal blue, the paint scuffed in places to reveal a previous coat of turquoise.

Idly, Jasmine scratched her right cheek with her left hand and her left ankle with the toe of her right shoe. When she itched anywhere, she was inclined to itch all over. Power of suggestion.

Either that or mosquito bites.

A canoe would have been good. A dugout canoe would be wonderful, but probably too much to hope for, even in this wilderness. At least it was wooden, not aluminum. It could still belong to a native hunter or trapper or maybe a fisherman with a rich lode of stories to share. Travel pieces with a human interest angle had a far broader appeal. Oklahoma had Will Rogers. North Carolina had...Daniel Boone? Blackbeard?

Well, surely they had somebody interesting. A place like this must have a fascinating history. She'd have to ask Clemmie about it before she checked out tomorrow.

"Hello-oo," she called out tentatively. "Anybody there?"

The sound that greeted her could, she supposed, have come from a hunter or a trapper. As profanity went, it was not particularly original. At least it didn't reek of filth and venom. She didn't mind a few damns and hells when the occasion demanded, but she hated filth and venom.

Whoever it was, he didn't sound as if he were in the mood for company. Carefully, she began to edge away from the creek, or stream or rivulet—whatever it was. According to the map, there was supposed to be a big lake with a name that reminded her of mosquitoes and a river called the Alligator somewhere around here.

What if he was an alligator poacher? She'd read somewhere that hunting alligators was against the law. Jasmine had been called laid-back. She'd never been called stupid.

"I'm leaving now," she sang out, in case he decided to cut the odds of getting caught. "I didn't see anything, so I think I'll just go on back now. Have a nice day."

"Dammit—hold on!"

She held on. It was the kind of voice that commanded obedience. Clutching the straps of her shoulder bag, she held on as if her life depended on it, thinking that in a pinch, she might use it as a weapon.

"I've, um…I'll send somebody if you need help, all right?"

"Need—help!"

He sounded as if he were in pain. Torn between cu-

riosity, concern and a healthy respect for hidden danger—
she'd been at an impressionable age when she'd seen *Deliverance*—Jasmine hesitated just a moment too long.

"Can't move. Need—a hand. *Please.*"

That last word was uttered too reluctantly to be anything but sincere. Whoever he was—whatever fix he was in—one thing was clear. He hated like the very devil having to beg for help.

"Sorry, but I'm on the other side of the creek."

That prompted more cursing, and then another, "Please?"

"It looks awfully deep. I can't swim." Even if it was only up to her knees, she wasn't particularly eager to step off the bank into that dark, sluggish stream. She couldn't see a glimmer of bottom. Even if she didn't drown, she might get eaten alive. Maybe not by piranhas, but there might be leeches. She'd seen *African Queen* three times.

"Follow bank—south—forty yards. Fallen tree."

Fallen tree. Uh-huh. "Which way is south?"

She peered through hanging branches, hanging vines and swags of gray-green Spanish moss, trying to catch a glimpse of the man behind the voice. If she was going to take the risk, she'd just as soon know what she was getting involved in.

"Toward sun."

Well, that was easy. As dense as the trees were, there weren't enough leaves to block out the pale, low-riding sun. "Well…all right, I'll try."

Her mind raced ahead as she picked her way along the narrow, winding creek. It could be a heart attack, snakebite—anything. He might even have tripped on one of his own traps and now he was lying there in agony, his lifeblood seeping into the muck while hyenas sniffed at his carcass.

There weren't any hyenas in North America, even she knew that much. That didn't mean there weren't scavengers. Predators.

"Where the devil are you?"

"I'm coming!"

Forty yards. How was she supposed to measure forty yards when every few steps she had to circle around a root or a fallen tree or a tangle of vines—none of them hairy, thank goodness, but some with wicked briars.

There was the tree he'd promised. It had fallen across the creek, blocking two-thirds of its width. Barely enough room to squeak past in a boat, if he'd come from this direction.

And he must have come from this direction, because he'd known about the tree.

Scratching her cheek—not actually scratching, but pressing into the itch with her fingernails—Jasmine surveyed the situation. If she could keep her balance, keep from falling in, she might be able to walk out far enough to jump the rest of the way. That's if she didn't lose her nerve first.

She lost her nerve, but it was too late. Teetering on the lower edge of the huge trunk, she faced two choices. Turn around on the mossy rounded slope and go back…or jump.

She jumped.

"Ow! Oh, shoot!"

"What happened?" His voice held an edge that could

have come from pain, or it could have come from anger. She'd like to think it came from pain.

Well, that didn't sound very nice, either. She certainly didn't wish the man any more pain. All the same, an angry man—an angry strange man, all alone here in the wilds of the jungle...

Not jungle—swamp. There was a subtle difference, although she wasn't certain just what it was.

No lions or tigers, only alligators and poisonous snakes?

Oh, God, why didn't I stay home? Being a bridesmaid couldn't be much worse than this.

At least this place was on the map. It had a name.

Dismal. Oh, great. She slapped at a mosquito and swore a mild oath. This probably wasn't the dumbest thing she'd ever done, but it was right up there near the top of the list.

"What happened?" he called again.

"Nothing happened! I landed on my knees in the mud," she yelled back.

She was filthy. No more scratching, at least not until she'd scrubbed her fingernails with soap and water. Unless she used a stick. A twig. Natural things were naturally sanitary, weren't they? Hadn't she read that somewhere?

Sure they were. Like natural poison ivy.

Lyon had plenty of time for second thoughts while he lay there waiting for deliverance, his face set in a grimace of pain. He'd tried ignoring the agonizing spasms in his back. He'd tried forcing himself to relax, muscle by muscle. He'd tried mind over matter, but pain was pain, and his mind wasn't up to the task.

Here she came. It would have to be a female. With
his luck, she'd be one of those environmentalists, ready
to land on him with both feet for disturbing the pristine
wilderness with his beer bottle and his Vienna sausage
can and his crass human intrusion.

He could have told her the possums would eat the
grease. The can would eventually rust away. They did
still make 'em out of tin, didn't they? As for the bottle,
he'd take the damned thing with him if she could just
help him get on his feet and back in his boat. Eventually, he'd drift back to the campsite.

Eventually. Like maybe, in a couple of weeks.

Either she was wearing snowshoes or she was leading a troop of cub scouts. He heard her thrashing
through the underbrush long before she came into sight.

Long. That was his first thought. That she was long
all over, especially her legs, which were pink and white
and muddy. That she was wearing a fright wig the color
of raw venison that stood out around her face like a halo,
only he'd never seen a halo in that shade of red, nor one
decorated with leaves, cypress needles and twigs.

She smiled. It was a surprisingly sweet smile in what
would have been a pretty face except that there was
something wrong with it. He wanted to tell her she
shouldn't go around smiling at strange men that way.
For all she knew, he could be dangerous, only she could
probably tell by the way he was lying here flat on his
back sweating bullets that he was no threat to anyone.

"Did you fall?" She had a nice voice when she wasn't
yelling; low, husky—no discernible accent. Even half
dead, his brain automatically noted and filed away such
details.

"Not recently." At her look of puzzlement, he added, "Bad back. Took off brace, rowed too far in one stretch." He sort of grunted the words, trying to keep from breathing too deeply because every breath he took was sheer agony.

She sat on her haunches beside him, her knees projecting over his chest. God, didn't the woman have a grain of sense under that fright wig?

A man would have to be dead not to react to all that satiny white skin, even when it was daubed with mud and laced with red scratches.

He drew a cautious breath, inhaling the scent of perfume, calamine and feminine sweat.

"Never wear perfume in a swamp," he grunted.

"I know. I only wore it to, um—boost my morale, but it draws mosquitoes. Is it sort of like a Charly horse?"

"Your perfume?"

"Your back."

He kept staring at her. Jasmine was used to being stared at; she was a minor celebrity, after all. A very, very minor one.

Somehow, she didn't think that was the reason he was staring at her. What did he expect her to do? She was no medical missionary. She'd never even been a Girl Scout. They'd moved around too much.

"Yeah, sort of," he said through clenched teeth. He had nice teeth. White, even, but not quite perfect. They showed to an advantage in a face that was covered in several days' growth of beard.

He closed his eyes. Without the distraction of a pair of intense periwinkle blue eyes, he looked tired and miserable. Logic told her she had no business being there. Instinct told her that he was harmless and that he desperately needed her help.

Jasmine always trusted her instincts. Every time she went against them—as in the case of Eric—she lived to regret it.

"So…what can I do to help you? Go for help?"

"No!"

He winced, as if speaking sharply hurt him. If she didn't know better, she might even have thought he was afraid of something.

Of course, she didn't know better. For all she knew, he was a criminal on the run. Might even have been injured in a shoot-out, only she didn't see any sign of blood.

"Are you a criminal?" she asked. Might as well get everything out in the open. He didn't appear to be armed, and she was pretty sure she could outrun him, if push came to shove.

"No way," he gasped. "Retired…cop."

"You're too young to be retired, and how do I know you're a cop?"

"Disability," Lyon said, not without a glimmer of humor. Damn, she was persistent. If he'd had to be rescued by a female, why couldn't she have been a physical therapist?

"Then you really are a policeman?"

He nodded, which was a mistake, the neckbone being connected to the backbone, et cetera, et cetera. He wasn't a cop and he wasn't retired, but it was close enough to the truth.

Close enough for government work, as the old saying went.

"Well. I don't suppose you can walk, but if we can get

you in the boat maybe I can take you back to the motel and have someone send for a doctor. It's right on the water. The motel, I mean. It might even be on the main river, I'm not sure, but if it is, this stream should get us there sooner or later. All we have to do is follow—"

"No way."

"No way, what? Everything east of the Mississippi flows into the ocean by way of streams and rivers. If we—"

"No, I mean—ah, hell, it hurts!" Lyon closed his eyes and willed himself to let go—not to tense up. "Get me back to my campsite and we'll call it even."

"I don't see anything even about that. I do all the work and you—"

"And I do all the bitching and groaning. Sorry about that. I'll pay you for your time."

"I don't want your money." She had dark eyes— brown with a hint of maroon, like her hair. They were shooting off sparks.

"Take off, then. Sooner or later someone else will come by." They both knew that was a crock. They were so deep into uncharted territory it was a wonder the buzzards could even find them. "How'd you get here? The road doesn't come anywhere near here."

"I followed an old logging road and then just kept on walking."

"Why?"

"Why not?"

"Lady, that's no answer, but if it's all right with you, I'd just as soon skip the dialogue and head on back to camp. You wouldn't believe how dark it can get this far from the nearest streetlight."

Jasmine was no judge of distance. There was a security light outside the motel, but that would be miles away. Miles and miles and miles. The trouble with long legs was that they covered so much territory, even at a leisurely pace. "If I can get you into your boat, can you do the rest by yourself?"

He gave her that "Duh" look.

"Okay, so maybe I'll paddle you as far as your camp—and even help you get out, but then I'll have to get back to the motel. I'm catching a plane to L.A. tomorrow."

She was catching a plane nowhere, no time soon. That much quickly became obvious. By the time she managed to get him into the boat, they were both practically in tears. He from pain; she from sheer exasperation.

Not to mention the fact that he was about a hundred eighty pounds of solid muscle and bone, and fighting her all the way. Or if not her, fighting the pain.

She'd have sympathized more if he hadn't cursed under his breath every step of the way. "Relax," she snapped.

"Lady, if I could relax, I wouldn't be here."

"Fine. Then don't relax. If I had a brain, I wouldn't be here, either."

The fighting didn't stop at the edge of the water. "It's not a paddle, it's a damned oar!"

"I know what it is, and stop cursing."

"Then stop jiggling around and sit down."

She sat. On the back seat, because he was sprawled out across the front seat, taking up most of the middle space. He was sweating. It wasn't really cold, even though it was February, but it wasn't warm, either. Especially not now that the sun was almost out of sight.

Jasmine wished, not for the first time, that she'd worn jeans instead of her white shorts. And a jacket instead of a long-sleeve yellow denim shirt. She was a summer person. She didn't own clothes suitable for a North Carolina winter.

"Don't you even know how to row a boat?"

"Of course I know how to row a boat." She'd seen it done plenty of times in the movies.

"You don't row from the stern thwart, you row from amidship."

"I know that."

"Then move!"

"You're there. Amidship, I mean." He was propped up against a seat cushion on the whatsis up front, but his legs stretched out so that his feet were under the middle seat.

"Straddle my damned feet!"

She'd rather straddle his damned neck. With her bare hands.

But she moved, rocking the boat, causing him to gasp so that she was thoroughly ashamed of herself. The man was injured. She didn't really want to hurt him any worse than he was already hurting, but if anyone deserved a bit of pain, he probably did.

Once settled on the edge of the wooden seat, she eyed him cautiously and reached for the oars. There were no oarlocks, only wooden notches that had been wallowed out until they were all but useless.

The oars stretched almost all the way across the creek. Cypress knees reached out from both sides. Lyon could have told her she'd need to shove from the stern until they cleared the fallen gum. Once past that point, the creek widened out.

He didn't tell her because the last thing he needed was a clumsy, clueless beanpole dancing around in the stern of his boat. They'd both end up overboard, and he'd sink like a stone.

She muttered enough so that he pinned down her accent. Bible Belt with a faint patina of West Coast, polished by a few diction lessons. He wondered what the devil she was doing here, and then he quit wondering about anything except whether or not he would survive the night.

If he could've gotten his hands on all those muscle relaxants he'd quit taking cold turkey, he'd have downed the lot. And then, if he was still capable of unscrewing a cap, he'd have started in on the painkillers.

She shipped the oars as they approached the fallen gum tree. One of them swiveled around and struck him in the shoulder. The other one rolled across his shin.

"Oops. Sorry," she said. "It's getting dark. How far is this camp place of yours?"

"About six and three-quarter miles."

Her mouth fell open. She had a nice mouth, well curved, full lower lip, but not too full. The swelling on her right cheek and eye was probably poison ivy. Even with most of his attention taken up by his own situation, he'd noticed her trying not to scratch. She'd reach up, hesitate, frown at her grimy nails and sigh. He'd have scratched it for her if his back had permitted him to reach out.

"I can't go that far, I have to get back to the motel."

"Fine. Pull over to the bank and get out."

"What about you?"

"What about me? I won't starve, if that's what you're worried about. I had half a can of Vienna sausage for lunch."

"How will you get home?"

"Not your problem."

"It is so my problem! I can't see my way back to the motel in the dark. I'll take you to your camp and you can lend me a flashlight and point me in the direction of the road, and…"

She gaped at him, her mahogany-colored eyes growing round. Even the one that was swollen half shut. "Did you say six and three-quarter *miles?*" she whispered.

The boat scraped against a cypress knee, and without even looking, she reached out, grabbed the thing and shoved off. Her survival skills were on a par with her rowing ability.

"Like I said, pull over to the bank and get out. Follow the creek to where you found me and then retrace your steps back to wherever you came from." If he'd known there was a motel within walking distance, he might have gone even deeper into the swamp.

Company, he didn't need.

Jasmine was having trouble making out his features. He was facing away from the rapidly fading light. His shoulders looked enormous in the baggy gray sweatshirt. She had a feeling they would look even more impressive without it. A surly man with shoulders the size of a refrigerator she didn't need.

With a heavy sigh, she retrieved the oars now that the creek had widened out. One of them scraped his hip. He caught his breath, she apologized, and told herself it would make a wonderful travel piece. Lost in the wilderness, surrounded by silence, Spanish moss, cypress knees and a perfectly splendid sunset that was reflected, now that she'd come around a bend, on the water.

So far she'd seen no signs of any predators, but she had seen a huge, graceful bird she recognized as a heron type. It lifted from the bank just as they'd rounded the bend and flapped right overhead. If she'd been standing, she could have reached out and touched it.

If she'd been standing, she would have probably fallen overboard. Heaven help her if that happened, because she couldn't swim a stroke and whatsisname wouldn't be able to pull her out.

"What is your name, anyway?" She slapped at a mosquito and winced when it set off her itching again.

He hesitated just long enough for her to wonder why he hesitated at all. "Lyon," he said.

"Oh, right. As long as it's not alligator."

"What's yours?"

She didn't hesitate. She, at least, had nothing to hide. "Jasmine. Jasmine Clancy," she said, just in case he was wondering where he might have seen her before.

"Great. That takes care of the flora and fauna."

"Ha-ha, very funny. How far is it now?"

"At a guess, I'd say about five and a half miles."

She groaned. She'd been rowing steadily ever since the creek widened. Thanks to his constant carping, she was beginning to get the hang of it, but her hands would never be the same. "I don't suppose you have a pair of gloves, do you?"

"I'm sorry." Actually, Lyon thought, she wasn't all

that bad. Her form was lousy, but what she lacked in physical strength, she made up for in determination. He should have thought about her hands, though. If he could have got to his knife, she could have hacked off his sleeves and pulled them over her hands like a mitt.

Jasmine felt tears sting her eyes. She hated pain, she really did. She hated itching, hated mosquitoes, hated noxious vines that hated her right back, but most of all, she hated being here in the middle of the wilderness, not knowing where she was or how she was ever going to get back.

She was a coward. She'd always been a coward. After her father left, she and her mother never stayed in the same place more than a year or two. She used to wake up in the middle of the night terrified that she would come home from school and find her mother gone, too, and strangers living in her house.

She leaned forward—from the hips, the way he'd told her—and bumped the oars against the wallowed-out wooden oarlocks. Dammit, she would get him there if it killed her! She refused to be put out in the middle of this damned swamp in the dead of night, without so much as a flashlight.

"Take a break."

"It won't help."

"Do it. I've got a handkerchief. Dig it out of my hip pocket, rip it in two pieces and wrap it around your palms."

She really didn't want to break her rhythm. And she had one, she really did. He had a lousy disposition. He'd fussed at her constantly, but he'd taught her the rudiments of rowing a boat.

Taught her enough to know that if she never set foot in one of the damned things again, it would be too soon.

"Do it, Jasmine. I don't want you bleeding all over me."

"Why, because you're afraid the scent of fresh blood might attract alligators?" She lost her rhythm. A blade caught the water and jerked at her arm, and she uttered a five-letter word. Tears trickled down her cheeks, making her rash itch all the more.

"At least when I hit the headlines—Actress Lost in Damned Dismal Swamp, Feared Dead—my grandmother won't recognize my name."

Three

The sky was beginning to grow pale when Lyon opened his eyes. Being careful not to move, he drew a shallow, experimental breath. He still hurt. Hurt like hell, in fact, and where he didn't hurt, he ached. The difference was subtle, but it was there.

He toyed with it as his senses came quickly alive. Mental exercises served a purpose when physical exercise was out of the question.

Like now. A fourteen-foot skiff was no place to spend a night. Especially not with a broken back and a knee that was still none too reliable.

Especially not an open skiff. In February. The warm spell was over. The temperature must've dropped into the forties last night.

They'd stopped for a rest. Her hands had been hurting. He'd been hurting all over. He'd known there was no hope of reaching camp before dark, and rather than risk taking a wrong turn, he'd let her sleep. And then he'd fallen asleep himself. Not a smart thing to do, but then, his options weren't exactly limitless.

"Ah, hell," he muttered, gazing bleary-eyed at the woman still huddled in the stern of the boat. She'd turned up the collar of her shirt, rolled down her sleeves and done her best to cover those long, naked legs with a few rumpled tissues and the flap of her shoulder bag.

"Wake up," he rasped.

She groaned and tried to draw her knees up to her chin. Her no-longer-white shorts weren't particularly skimpy. They'd been designed to come halfway down her thighs, but when a woman had legs as long as hers, there was still a lot of flesh left exposed to the elements.

Not to mention exposed to the eyes.

"Jasmine, look alive. We've got to get some heat going."

"Turnip therm'stat."

"Right. You do it—you're the closest."

She opened one eye. The other one was swollen shut. Shivering, she mumbled something that sounded like "Where Nell ama?"

"By my reckoning, you're approximately five miles north of Billy's Landing, about half a mile west of Two Buzzard Ditch, and a mile or so east of Graceland."

"Oh."

She scratched her cheek and then her ankle, and smiled. There was something dangerously disarming about a woman who woke up shivering, scratching, blinking one eye and still managed to smile.

She yawned, rearranging splotched remnants of calamine lotion. "Graceland? I thought that was in Tennessee." Her voice was early-morning soft. Husky. In another woman, under other circumstances, he might have taken it as an invitation.

With Jasmine he took it as merely easy on the ears.

"Bad joke. Think you can do a few warm-ups without falling overboard? We need to get your blood circulating."

"Too late. 'S frozen like a raspberry snow cone."

He yawned, too. And then, unexpectedly, he grinned. Couldn't recall the last time he'd smiled, especially before breakfast, but she seemed to have that effect on him.

Lyon had come here to be alone. If he had to have company, he'd have preferred a chiropractor or a physical therapist. Instead, he got Jasmine Clancy with her poison ivy and her blistered hands and her world-class legs. He wasn't sure just what breed of woman she was, but she didn't belong here. One way or another, he probably ought to get rid of her.

"How're you doing? Back still broken?" she asked in a voice that reminded him of late nights, rumpled beds and soft women.

"It's better." It was worse. A hell of a lot worse, but there was no point in giving her all the bad news at once. "Are you hungry?"

"Starved. I don't suppose this yacht of yours runs to a galley?"

"Chef's night out. If you can manage to get your hand into my left side pocket, you might find half a chocolate bar. It'll be messy, I'm afraid."

"I'll take it."

It wasn't quite as simple as it sounded. She eased herself up to a kneeling position, but in doing so, she was forced to straddle his legs. The boat rocked. She grabbed the sides, winced at the pain and waited for things to calm down again.

Lyon waited for her to recover her balance, grab the thing out of his pocket and get the hell off his lap. He would have dug it out himself if he hadn't been afraid to move anything connected to his back. Which included his arms.

Fine pair they were. He shifted slightly to give her access. Cargo pants had plenty of storage room. He didn't particularly want her exploring it all.

Cautiously, she dragged one knee alongside his legs and leaned forward to slide one hand into his left side pocket. Her hair tickled his face. It was wilder than ever—probably hadn't seen a comb in days—and it smelled faintly of…lilac?

Oh, hell, if there was one thing he didn't need it was a woman who smelled of lilacs. "Come on, come on, we don't have all day," he growled.

He was discovering—rediscovering, at least—things about himself that he'd just as soon have left safely buried for another few years.

Such as the fact that the male of the species was about ten parts brain to ninety parts testosterone. If there was one thing he didn't need screwing up his ten percent at the moment, it was that other ninety percent.

Her fingers fumbled against his groin. He could kick himself for not wearing a shirt with pockets. He could kick himself for not eating the whole damned thing instead of saving half for the trip back to the campsite in case he ran out of energy.

She dug out a knife, a pocket calculator and a shapeless lump that was half a chocolate bar that had melted and stuck to the wrapper. "Don't you want any? One bite, that's all I need. Just enough to wake me up. Chocolate has caffeine, doesn't it?"

"Nah, I don't want any. You eat it all, you're the one who's going to have to get us out of here."

So then he had to watch while she unwrapped the thing and licked it off the paper. Nearby, a small flock of fish ducks dived for breakfast. A great blue squawked a protest and lifted from the banks, long legs dangling gracefully.

He scowled at the birds and then he scowled at her long, graceful, mud-stained, briar-scratched legs. And then he scowled some more just on general principle. "We'd better get going. If you want to go ashore for a minute, there's a place just downstream from here where the bank's pretty clear."

"I'm thirsty. I don't suppose you have anything to drink, do you?"

"Warm beer?"

She shuddered. "I'll wait for coffee, thanks. You will offer me a cup of coffee before I head back to the motel, won't you?"

He shrugged, which was a painful mistake, but it was all the answer she was going to get. He'd offer her coffee, all right, but she wouldn't be going back. Not anytime soon.

As dainty as if it were a perfumed finger bowl, she dipped her hands over the sides, swished them around, then wet a tissue and daubed at her face.

Pity. He'd been admiring the rim of chocolate around her mouth. Shifting painfully into the most comfortable position he could achieve for the long trip ahead, he said, "You missed the spot beside your nose. No—left side. Got it."

And then he had to wait while she took a brush from her purse and set to work on her hair. "I won't be much longer," she said when she caught him staring at her. "It's just that I can think better once I've washed and brushed. I'd give anything if I had my toothbrush."

Closing his eyes, Lyon braced himself to endure the next few hours.

"This is it?" Jasmine shipped the oars. He'd used the phrase earlier and she liked the sound of it. It sounded...brisk. Decisive. If there was one thing she could use about now, it was a shot of brisk decisiveness.

He appeared to be waiting for further comment. When none was forthcoming, he began the painful, awkward business of getting to his feet. She offered to help.

"Just stand back, okay? No, don't touch me!"

She wasn't about to touch him.

Well, yes...maybe she had reached out to him, but that was purely instinctive. It would take someone really heartless to stand by and watch a man suffer the way Lion—Lion?—the way he was suffering. "Watch out for the wet place on the floor," she cautioned.

"Deck."

"I knew that."

The look he sent her would have blistered paint. "Hold the boat steady when I start to swing my left leg over the side, will you?"

She grabbed the sides. Her hands hurt like the very devil, but she grabbed and held on until something in the way he was looking at her tipped her off that this wasn't what he'd had in mind.

Crouched over, one hand on his back, the other gripping the scarred wooden trim that ran all the way around the edge of the boat, he glared at her over his shoulder.

Jasmine glared right back. "I'm doing the best I can. If you don't like it, hire someone else."

Under the heavy growth of beard, his face was roughly the color of wet plaster. He was sweating. The temperature had to be somewhere around zero minus ten. Personally, Jasmine had never been colder in her entire life than she'd been last night, and he was sweating.

"Pick up one of the oars," he said through clenched teeth.

She picked it up. He obviously read her mind, because he said, "If you're going to knock me in the head, wait until I'm on shore, will you? You don't want to show up at your motel with a dead man on board. Too much explaining to do."

She took a deep breath, puffed out her cheeks, which made her face start itching all over again, and said with deceptive mildness, "All right, I'm holding on to the oar. I'm pretty sure this one won't try to get away, but what about the other one?"

Ignoring her sarcasm, he told her what to do. "Jab it in the mud as far up on the bank as you can reach and hang on. If you feel the boat start to move away, pull it in again."

"Why not use an anchor?"

He closed his eyes. His lips were moving. *One, two, three, four…* "Because I don't have a damned anchor, all right?"

"Doesn't the Coast Guard require stuff like that in all boats?"

"Just jam the damned oar into the mud and hold on long enough for me to get out, will you? Then you can go find the nearest Coast Guard station and turn me in!"

Well. It wasn't her fault he didn't have all the required equipment. Selecting a place on the bank that looked relatively root-free and damp, she clutched the oar and lunged. The boat rocked. Lyon groaned. And then he swore.

"If you're going to jump out, hurry up. I can't hold us here all day." She closed her eyes against the fire in her palms. Both hands hurt all the way up to her armpits. She felt the boat lurch and opened her eyes just as the man landed on the shore. Mostly on shore. Parts of him hung over the bank, one foot touching the water.

"If this is the Alligator River, you're asking for trouble." And if her voice sounded funny, it was because she was trying not to cry. Itching was bad enough. Freezing was even worse. The way her hands hurt was worst of all, because it meant they were totally raw, and as dirty as she was, she'd get infected and everybody knew there were germs these days that thumbed their noses at antibiotics. Flesh eating germs.

Or was it viruses? Organisms?

Whatever.

"What the hell are you waiting for?" growled the man in the mud. He was lying belly down, making no effort to get up, but of course, he couldn't without excruciating pain.

If she wanted to get away, this was her chance. All

she had to do was walk off and leave him. He could hardly come after her.

On the other hand, she could hardly leave him here in this condition. It wouldn't be kind.

Besides, there was no sign of a road. No sign of anything except for a small clearing, a tiny fire pit, a metal trunk of some sort and a scrap of camouflage-colored tent hardly big enough for a small Boy Scout.

She'd seen better outfitted bag ladies, and said so, which elicited another groan from the shore.

"If you're going to go, then shove off. Go back the way you came, leave the boat on the bank. Chances are it'll still be there when I get around to collecting it."

"Oh, sure, just paddle off and leave you sprawled out for the hyenas and buzzards to finish off, right?"

"Don't forget the alligators."

"And the mosquitoes." Irritably, she waved off a swarm of the pesky things. She hated the whining sound they made almost as much as she hated the itchy welts they raised on her unprotected skin. Which was just about all of it.

Taking the piece of rope he called a painter, that was tied to a rusty eye in the front of the boat, she gripped it tightly between her thumb and fingers and jumped for the shore. This time she landed on her feet.

"If you're waiting for applause, forget it," he said after half a minute or so. "How about helping me to my feet?"

"Why not just lie around for a while? You probably need the rest."

"What I need is to use the can, if you'll pardon my indelicacy."

She blushed. She, who had heard more and seen

more of life before she was fifteen years old than some women did in a lifetime. She, an experienced woman of the world who'd had one-and-a-half lovers, blushed at the mention of a bathroom.

Thank goodness, what with the dirt and poison ivy and all, it couldn't possibly show. She'd have been laughed right out of L.A.

Getting the Lion into an upright position again was almost as bad as getting him into the boat had been, the only difference being that neither of them was likely to fall overboard and drown.

"Can you swim?" she asked. She was leaning against a tree, both hands cupped in front of her, examining them for signs of imminent infection.

Lyon was making his cautious way toward the swag of vines that separated the slit trench he'd dug just yesterday from the rest of his campsite. "Yeah. Why?"

He didn't like questions, even dumb questions from a gorgeous, lopsided, long-legged dodo bird.

"I dunno, I just thought I'd ask."

"Well, don't. I told you, if you want to clear out, feel free. Now that I'm back on familiar territory, I'll be fine."

"Is that where the bathroom is?" She nodded toward the tangle of vines and underbrush. "I need to freshen up when you're done."

Freshen up. Sure. "I'll put out a clean towel."

She blushed again, and this time he caught it. Caught it and grinned, in spite of the fact that he was sweaty, buggy, his bladder was fit to burst and with every breath he took he felt as if a dozen dull knives were excavating his spinal column.

"No point in waiting. Walk five yards in any direction and you're out of sight. There's paper in the locker, soap and a towel if you need it. You'll have to use the creek, though. City water doesn't come out this far."

She was already picking her way carefully across the clearing, still holding her hands as if they hurt like the very devil. They probably did. "Hey, wash your hands good with soap, and I'll fix 'em up for you, okay?"

Evidently, she took him at his word. Five minutes later, he heard a splash, a gasp and then a yelp. Soap and water on raw flesh was no picnic.

But then, what was?

And that reminded him that neither of them had eaten since yesterday, other than half a melted bar of chocolate. He washed his hands, using the rainwater he'd collected in a hollow stump, and surveyed his supplies, moving slowly, stiffly, smothering the occasional curse.

Brunch was Vienna sausage, cold, canned chili and warm beer. "Sorry I don't have any sodas. Never touch the stuff. Too many chemicals."

Jasmine wrinkled her nose, touched her cheek gingerly with a bandaged hand, and jiggled the gauze against the itch. "This is fine. I always intended to cultivate a taste for beer."

"The creek water's probably okay, but I don't believe in taking chances."

She nodded. Sitting cross-legged on a log, she forked out another sausage and bit it in two. A zillion calories and all of them fat, but don't drink the water. Some people were weird.

"So. You never did say what you were doing here in the jungle all by yourself," she ventured after a while.

"No, I never did, did I? How's your face? Still itching?"

"Not until you reminded me."

"Want coffee for dessert?"

"Made from warm beer?"

"I don't waste valuable beer. I only brought in a dozen six-packs."

"Why?"

"Why what?" They'd played this game before. The girl asking questions, trying to slip in under his guard and pry loose a few answers. He could have told her, but didn't, that he'd been interrogated by experts.

"Why'd you bring in so much beer?"

"Because I like beer."

She sighed. He liked to watch her sigh. She put more feeling into a single sigh than most women did a crying fit and two tantrums. He was inclined to believe she was on the level, not that it mattered. Once he got rid of her he'd move to a different location. He was good at covering his tracks.

While she was still here—and that would be longer than either one of them wanted—she couldn't contact anyone. Until and unless he caught her flashing mirrors or launching notes in a bottle, he'd keep her.

Slipping off the log onto the leaf-covered ground, she said, "Well," and patted her flat belly, white gauze mitts contrasting against her once-white shorts. "Thanks for the meal and the first aid. I'd better take a pass on the coffee and get started back if I want to get there before dark."

Lyon studied her without appearing to. It was a minor talent he'd honed to a fine art. God, she was a mess. That hair—the poison ivy. All the mud and the scratches.

He'd like nothing better than to lay her down in a bed of leaves and spend a few hours practicing another art.

Funny, the way she affected him. She wasn't at all his type. He liked his women short, busty, blond and temporary.

Jasmine Clancy was none of the above. And even if she happened to be willing, he sure as hell wasn't able. He could barely move. Bed-sport was totally out of the question.

Pity, though. There was something about her that could easily light his fuse under other circumstances. He didn't understand it. Anything he didn't understand became a challenge.

"Do I need to cross the creek to reach the road?"

"Huh?" He'd been thinking about something else. About fuses, and how uncomfortable a smoldering one could be when letting it burn to the logical end was out of the question.

"The road. I was just saying, I hope it's on this side of the creek or river or whatever, because I don't think I can row another stroke." She held up both hands. They'd been in bad shape. It amazed him that she hadn't complained, either about her hands or about sleeping uncovered in an open boat in February, even if it was the mildest February in years.

If he'd been any sort of a gentleman he'd have stripped off his sweatshirt and covered her up. Not that he could've moved to do it. Not that he'd even thought about it. Too many other things on his mind.

Anyway, he'd never pretended to be a gentleman.

Still, he mused, it might have been interesting to see how warm he could keep her.

His voice softened to a gravelly rasp, which was about as close to apologetic as it got. "Look, why not stick around awhile. I mean, I know you have a plane to catch, but you've already missed it by now, so why not relax and enjoy a wilderness experience? Once you're back in L.A. you can tell all your friends how you survived being lost in the Great Eastern Dismal Swamp all alone."

"Hardly alone."

"Makes a better story that way."

"Hmm." She looked thoughtful. He wondered what she'd look like without the poison ivy. He wondered what she was really doing here. First chance he got he intended to go through her purse. A guy in his position couldn't afford too many scruples.

"But I'm not lost, am I?"

She sounded so worried he nearly relented and told her she could go if she could find her way out. He didn't really need her. Hell, she needed him more than he needed her.

All the same, going back was not an option. Not just yet. "No, you're not lost. I know exactly where we are."

It took half the afternoon for full realization to sink in. Lyon didn't push it. It was better if she figured it out all by herself. Then she couldn't blame him.

"You knew I couldn't row myself back with my hands like this, didn't you?" she accused.

Without thinking, he shrugged and then winced as the knives attacked again. "Depends on your pain threshold."

"Why does it hurt worse now than it did before you spread that yucky stuff on me and bandaged me up?"

He started to shrug again and caught himself just in time. "Maybe because you're starting to heal? Healing usually hurts."

"Is that what's wrong with you? You're healing?"

"I'd damned well better be." He was wearing his back brace again. She'd had to help him get the thing on. Help him get his shirt off, and then reach around him with both arms and help him fasten the velcro straps. He'd been in worse shape when they'd finished than when they'd started, and not just his back.

"But if I took your boat, how would you get it back? And don't tell me to leave it where I found it, because I'm not sure I can even locate the place again, and even if I do, you're in no condition to walk that far."

"So you noticed that, did you?"

"Don't look at me like that, like I'm stupid. I'm not. Only, you knew exactly what you were doing, bringing me here, didn't you? You didn't even care if I was inconvenienced." She glared at him. She had a very effective glare. Funny, he'd never before noticed how many different shades of brown eyes came in. As a rule he was a noticing man. In his line of work, lives could depend on it.

"Yes, well—I guess I don't have to go back right away. My reservations are not until the end of the week, but that doesn't mean I intend to hang around here any longer than I have to. I don't even have a toothbrush, for goodness sake. Everything I own is back at the motel."

He nodded. "Duly noted."

"So, how far's the road from here?"

"I haven't a clue."

Her eyes accused him of lying.

"I haven't looked for a road. As far as I know, the nearest trail of any kind is about two, maybe three miles away." He'd purposefully looked for a place with a single access. No place was foolproof, but this one was close. He'd been here nearly two weeks, and flower girl was the first person he'd seen. Evidently, there wasn't a whole lot of traffic in the middle of the swamp this time of year. Too late for hunting—too early for fishing. The site he'd selected was located between a couple of wildlife preserves. Any tourists in the area would go there, not here. He was banking on it.

"Then what are you doing here? Are you sure you're not hiding out?"

"What if I told you I'm a celebrity hiding out from the paparazzi?"

"I wouldn't believe you. Besides, if you were a celebrity, I'd recognize you, and I don't."

"Okay, how about I'm a millionaire hiding out from the IRS?"

"Any self-respecting millionaire would have better camping gear. You don't even have a decent tent."

"This region's known for the hunting and fishing."

"So where's your gun and fishing pole?"

Lyon was amused. It had been a long time since he'd been amused. He could've shown her both items, but she might tumble to the fact that neither the Glock nor the Sig-Sauer 9mm would pass as hunting equipment. Instead, he said, "Okay, my turn. What's a woman like you doing in a place like this?"

"You brought me here?"

"Uh-uh. You brought *me* here, remember?"

By that time they were both grinning. It felt good.

Lyon couldn't remember the last time he'd flashed his pearlies twice in as many hours.

"About that coffee," he reminded her. "If you'll dip us a potful of water, I'll see what I can do about getting a fire going."

"Let me. I don't want you to strain your back. One way or another I plan to leave first thing tomorrow, and I'd feel bad about leaving you here hurting."

Four

"**S**top!"

Jasmine teetered on the brink, arms flapping wildly.

"Dammit, don't do that!" he yelled.

"Don't do what?" Exasperation sharpened her husky voice.

"Don't even think about stealing my boat. You'd never make it back to civilization."

"What's the matter, are you afraid I'll get lost and then you'd have me on your conscience?" Planting her bandaged hands on her hips, she gave him her best shot at scathing contempt. She'd never done scathing contempt very well. It wasn't in her repertoire, but she was working on it.

"Yes, you'd get lost, and no, I wouldn't have you on my conscience." He did scathing contempt exceedingly well. Academy award performance. "I don't have a conscience."

She snorted. "Everyone has a conscience. Every decent, normal person."

"Who said anything about being decent?"

Lyon watched her eyes widen. The swelling was coming down on the side of her face. Her eyes almost matched now. It was an improvement.

He didn't need any improvements. Not in her appearance, at any rate. She was enough of a distraction as it was. Wearing one of his T-shirts, a leather windbreaker and a pair of his jeans bundled around her waist, with six inches of elegant ankle hanging out the south end, she was driving him crazy.

"Help me get into this damned knee brace again, will you?"

She looked as if she might consider it. Then again, she might not.

"Please?" he added grudgingly. Even to his own ears, it sounded more like two big feet landing in a bed of gravel. Neither one of them was ever apt to center a stage at the Metropolitan Opera. He didn't know what her excuse was; his was having his larynx damned near shattered by a flying foot back in his training days.

"Stick out your leg then."

"Lady, if I could stick out my leg, I wouldn't need you." He was sitting on a stump, his back stiff as a poker, trying to figure out how he could get up without moving a muscle.

She waited a full minute, and then she stalked over to him like a stiff-legged dog in a yard full of cats. "I wasn't going to steal your old boat."

"I know you weren't." Gradually, clasping his thigh,

he eased his knee into position while she knelt in front of him and rolled up his pants leg.

She frowned. She had a nice frown. Puckers between her eyebrows, pursed lips. Yeah, she had a nice frown.

Holding the black elastic contraption in one hand, she reached under his knee, which brought her head close enough so that her hair brushed his skin. He stiffened, caught his breath as his back protested, and swore silently.

He'd almost rather be back in the hospital. At least there he hadn't felt like such a crock. Hospitals were full of crocks. And none of the nurses had tickled his knee with their hair at a time when he was in no condition to do anything about it.

"Why'd you accuse me of it, then?"

"Accuse you of what?"

"Stealing your boat."

For once in his life, he'd spoken without thinking. It wasn't the boat he'd been worried about, it was the woman. He'd been afraid she might slip on the muddy bank and hurt herself.

Yeah, sure you were. You were afraid she might leave you, weren't you? "Actually, I was afraid you were going to jump in the creek and try to swim back."

"I would've changed into my own clothes first. I wouldn't have stolen yours."

"I can't tell you how relieved I am," he snarled, and then damn near bit his tongue off when her fingers brushed over the sensitive place behind his knee.

"Besides, I can't swim."

"Good." With half his supply of sterile gauze wrapped around her palms, she was taking forever. He'd like to tell her to bug off, and do the job himself, but there was no way he could manage without either bringing his knee up within reach of his hands or bending his back. At the moment, neither option was viable.

Jaw clenched, he stared down at the top of her head. Sunlight filtered through the bare gum branches, spinning rainbows of color around every wild, curly strand of her hair. He concentrated on the colors instead of on the warm moisture of her breath against his naked thigh.

"There's nothing good about it," she grumbled. "All children should be taught to swim at an early age. How'd you get these scars, anyway?"

"Falling off the back of an elephant. Why weren't you?" He was on to her tricks now. She'd muddle along at a moderate speed just long enough to throw him off guard, and then without warning, she'd veer off in another direction. There was a slim chance it was a deliberate tactic, but he didn't think so.

Correction. He didn't *want* to think so. Which was even worse.

"Why wasn't I what? Going to steal your boat? I do have to get back, you know. And I do know something about boats. I helped drive those two posts in the bank to tie it up to, didn't I?"

"Right. And you know the pointy end goes first and the flat end follows. Why weren't you taught how to swim at an early age?"

She lifted her shoulders in an oddly elegant gesture and let them fall again. "I don't know. Mama said we lived too far from the pool and she didn't have time to take me, but we were probably too broke. We didn't have a lot of money. There, is that tight enough?" She sat back on her heels and tugged his pants down over the lumpy wad of his knee.

"Perfect. Thanks." It occurred to him that he'd said please and thank you more in the past twenty-four hours than he had in the last ten years. Not that he was necessarily rude. It was just that in his line of work, courtesy wasn't exactly commonplace.

With Jasmine, it probably was. He knew a lot more about her than she suspected, partly from observation, partly from deduction, partly from skillfully placed questions.

She was an actress. There was a slim chance that she was also a journalist. That was a risk he hadn't anticipated. But journalist or not, the lady was by nature open, impulsive, generous and far too trusting for any woman in this day and age. She was thirty-four years old. Old enough to know better. Most women learned caution by the time they started experimenting with lipstick.

Jasmine was about as cautious as a kid with a brand-new puppy. Besides, she didn't wear lipstick.

What kind of an actress didn't wear lipstick?

One who had a face full of poison ivy? One who was stuck in the swamp without her war paint? One who wasn't interested in impressing a man with her looks?

Jeez.

At the moment, they were stuck with each other. He could've told her about the outboard he had stashed away, but he couldn't afford to let her go back and leave him in this condition. He'd be a sitting duck for anyone who came snooping around, and if that was paranoid, so be it. Paranoia went with the territory. A solid case of preventive paranoia was better than a Kevlar vest when it came to keeping a spook alive.

And Lyon fully intended to stay alive. He had one more job to do. He owed it to Giotto and McNeil. But first, he had to get himself in shape, and while he was doing that he had to go over and over the pieces of the puzzle in his possession until he came up with the missing one.

So he'd keep her here a few more days, at least until he was able to move to a new location. It wouldn't be hard to do. It seemed he'd caught himself that rarest of all creatures: a tenderhearted woman. Would she go off and leave a helpless invalid out here in the wilderness?

Hell no, she wouldn't.

Besides, her hands were in no condition to row the seven miles it would take to reach a road. Even if she got to digging around and found his cell phone, it wouldn't do her any good. The only tower within five miles in any direction was an unmanned fire tower. Even with fresh batteries, the thing was as good as dead.

"Want me to help you walk around some?"

"I'm not a cripple," he growled.

"I know that. I only meant, if you want to move around some to sort of loosen up, I'll be glad to steady you so you don't trip over a root or a vine or something. It's not like we have a sidewalk."

"Yeah. Sorry. Sure, help me up and let's circle the clearing a few times."

She was too damned softhearted. With a little encouragement, he could probably have her leading him to the bathroom. Either she was a far better actress than he'd thought—in which case he was in trouble—or she was too naive for her own good.

In which case he was also in trouble.

They walked until he'd loosened up the parts of him that needed loosening. Other parts would have to wait. Carefully, he lifted first one arm and then the other over his head, bending sideways three inches. Stretching it another cautious inch more. He was improving, but it wouldn't take much to set off the spasms again.

Gingerly, he flexed his knee. He'd been well on the way to complete rehabilitation until he'd overdone the rowing, and on top of that, been forced to spend a night in that damned boat. The combination had set him back at least a week.

He couldn't afford a single day.

The sun, still riding low in the sky, reached its winter apex and began a rapid descent over the area designated on his map as Mattamuskeet Wildlife Refuge. He hadn't explored that far west yet, but he intended to. According to his information, the Lawless tract stretched at least that far, maybe farther. Some of the original tract was in the next county. Some was probably included in the refuge. In fact, from what he'd been able to determine in the tax office, the largest part had been claimed by various state and federal programs, the choicest parcels sold off for farming or logging. What was left was undivided and either inaccessible or useless or both.

"Does it still hurt?"

"Nah. It's just stiff. Thanks, though."

He patted her hand. Patted her hand! God, when was the last time he'd patted a woman's hand?

They had circled the small clearing five times. Jasmine was afraid he might overdo it and collapse, and she didn't want to have to go through the agony of getting him back on his feet. She'd heard enough profanity the last time she'd had to help him up.

Not filth and venom, though. She appreciated that, although she could do without quite so many damns and hells.

"Shall I fix us some lunch before I leave?" And she was going to leave today, she really was. She had to.

"If you're hungry."

"I'm always hungry. Mama said it was on account of I shot up so fast, I never managed to catch up."

"What else did Mama say?" She knew he was laughing at her in that solemn, tough-guy way he had, without even cracking a smile, but it didn't bother her. If he'd been Eric her feelings would've been hurt, but Eric never laughed at her. He was far too suave.

Suave was not a term that would ever be applied to this man.

She helped him back down onto his stump, which was stool-height and conveniently placed between his tent, his two metal lockers and the fire pit. Then she rummaged around in the largest locker, the one that was unlocked, and came up with crackers, a jar of cheese spread and more warm beer. The crackers were stale, the cheese spread was the Mexican kind, with salsa, and the warm beer tasted just the way it smelled.

It was probably safer than the water, though. Better safe than a bellyache or worse.

The air was cooler than yesterday, but warm enough so that before eating, she shed her borrowed coat. Before leaving she'd have to change back to her shorts and shirt, but she was in no hurry. "Is that really your name? Lion?"

"Yep."

"Like the animal?"

"Does it matter?"

She had dragged his bedroll out into the filtered patch of sunlight, and now she dropped down on it, sitting cross-legged while she attempted to spread cheese on crackers with her bandaged hands. "Not really. I only wondered what kind of mother would name her baby after an animal."

"She could have called me Dog, I suppose. Or Goat."

"Or Bear. Maybe if she'd known you better, she might have called you that."

"Actually, it's Daniel. Lyon is a family name. Spelled with a *y,* not an *i.*"

"Daniel." Jasmine handed over two crackers, stretched out her legs in her borrowed jeans and wrinkled her nose at the sight of her muddy cross-trainers.

Which started her face itching again, which made her twitch all over, trying not to scratch.

Taking a deep breath, she plunged into conversation, hoping to take her mind off her troubles, which were multiplying almost faster than she could keep up with them. "Daniel's a nice name. Strong. I can't remember any villain being named Daniel, can you? I was thinking just yesterday—" Had it only been yesterday? "—that Daniel Boone lived in North Carolina. Maybe your mama named you after him—unless it was a family name?"

"It wasn't."

"Mine wasn't, either. At least, Clancy is family, but Mama picked Jasmine out of a seed catalog she was reading when she went into labor. I used to think, what

if she'd been in the vegetable section? I could've been
named Spinach. Or maybe Cabbage."

"Cabbage Clancy. Has a ring to it, wouldn't you say?"

Jasmine looked up to find him smiling down at her.
She'd never seen him actually smile before. A quick half
grin or two, and that was it, but this was a genuine smile,
with all sorts of dancing little lights sparkling from
those blue eyes that looked so out of place among his
irregular features.

He was not a handsome man, she told herself, not for
the first time. The only reason she liked looking at him
was that he was…different. Rugged. Wicked looking,
actually, but in a nice way.

Well. That made about as much sense as anything
else in her wacky life had made lately.

"You know, I really should be thinking about getting
back." Funny how reluctant she was. Just yesterday—
just this morning, in fact—she could hardly wait to get
back to civilization. Maybe she'd been more stressed out
than she'd realized. Maybe she needed the break.

"Any particular reason to rush off?"

She thought about it. "No, not really. I mean, I could
probably afford to be gone for a few more days. I was
supposed to be gone all week, at least until after Cyn
and Eric got back from…"

"Cyn and Eric?"

She wanted to tell him. Of all things, she was actually tempted to pour out all her miseries on his shoulder. The only reason she could think of for such a crazy
reaction was that, first of all, she'd never told a soul
about Cyn and Eric and her own broken heart, or about
her grandmother and how absolutely crushed she'd been

to realize that her only living relative wasn't the least bit interested in her.

Besides, everyone knew you could tell a stranger things you could never tell a friend. It was like pouring your heart out in a letter, and then burning the letter. It happened all the time in movies. Wartime confessions that were supposed to end there, but never really did. Sometimes they led to true love. If the soldier wasn't killed in battle, he might show up years later on crutches, or with a patch over one eye, and the heroine, who'd been an ambulance driver or something in the war, had been faithful to his memory and welcomed him with tears and open arms. The door would close quietly behind them, and the theme would swell, and you'd know in your heart that they would live happily ever after.

There was no sex in the old movies, but that was even better. If there was one thing she had learned since moving to L.A., it was that, where sex was concerned, imagination was a lot more satisfying than reality.

And anyway, who needed sex when you could have all sorts of nice, warm, fuzzy feelings?

She loved old movies. The world had seemed a far safer place back in her mother's day. Which didn't even make sense, considering the fact that her father had walked out and left them when her mother didn't even have a job and Jasmine was only a child.

"Jasmine? Cyn and Eric?"

She blinked at him, noticing that he had nice ears— not too large, not too small. Just right. Ears were important on a man.

"Well, you see, my grandmother—"

"Your grandmother's named Cyn and Eric?"

"Of course not, Cyn and Eric are partly the reason I went to see my grandmother. Her name is Hattie Clancy. Cynthia Kerry is my best friend. You might know her from *Wilde's Children?* She plays Hannah? Right now she's supposed to be in a plane that crashed in New Mexico, because she's actually off honeymooning with my fiancé. At least, Eric wasn't actually my fiancé—we never got around to getting officially engaged, but…"

She sighed. When no comment was forthcoming, she peered up to see Lyon slowly shaking his head. "I talk too much, don't I?"

She did, but he said she didn't. The truth was, Lyon didn't know what to make of her. If she was genuine, she was either a total wacko, or the most innocent, guileless female left on the planet. He was beginning to believe she was genuine.

And it scared the hell out of him.

What scared him even more was that she was beginning to make sense.

"I do," she said dolefully. "I don't know what's wrong with me, I'm never like this. I'm a trained journalist, did I tell you? I know all about the what, when, where, why stuff, only sometimes when I start to tell something, I don't stop to organize it first. Telling is different from writing. Normally, I make lists for everything. In fact, I'm about the most organized woman I know."

Considering where she was from and what she did for a living, he didn't doubt it for a minute. He could have told her that the people he hung out with were usually pretty big on lists, too. Most Wanted lists. Evidence lists. Source lists. Suspect lists.

"Yeah, well…cut yourself some slack, honey. This is hardly normal circumstances."

To his astonishment, her eyes slowly brimmed with tears. "That's probably the sweetest thing anyone's said to me in—I don't know when."

Ah, jeez, he didn't need this.

"Mostly, people say things they don't mean because it makes them feel good—you know, like they're being magnanimous or something? They call you d-darling, because they don't remember your name. They tell you how good you look when you really don't, and they pretend they're all sorrowful because you didn't get a part, when you know good and well they'd cut your throat to get a shot at it."

She drew in a shuddering breath and expelled it in a long, soulful sigh. He'd noticed before how much she put into one of her sighs.

He tried to think of something comforting to say. "Well, hell, Jazzy, that's just life" was the best he could come up with. He had a feeling it didn't quite fit the bill.

"No, it's not. Life is *The Waltons*. Life is—is—"

"Not a movie. Not even a TV series. Honey, life is—"

She looked up at him with those big, trusting brown eyes overflowing with tears, the tip of her nose as red as her blistered, oozing cheek, and he lost it. Flat out, clean lost it.

He opened his arms. It hurt like the very devil, but he did it anyway, and as if he were the angel Gabriel or whoever the geezer was who was supposed to welcome poor souls through the pearly gates, and she took him up on it.

It nearly killed him. He couldn't manage to stifle a

gasp when the muscles alongside his spine seized up on him, but she was blubbering too hard to hear.

"Here now, it's not all that bad. Hey, poison ivy's not fatal."

"My g-grandmother didn't know me. I wrote all those letters and sent all those cards, and I even—I even sent her a picture of me with Charles Eastwood. I only had a small role in *Winds of Hell,* but he was real nice."

Lyon didn't have a clue who Charles Eastwood was, but he could understand any man being nice to her, small role or not. He only hoped the bastard hadn't taken advantage of her trusting nature.

"Shhh, so your grandmother didn't recognize you. Maybe her eyes aren't what they used to be."

Jasmine leaned back, not all the way out of his arms, because his arms felt too good, but far enough to look him straight in the face. "I'm pretty sure she has Alzheimer's disease. I never even met her before. I wouldn't have even known about her, but Daddy turned up one day and he happened to mention her before he died."

"Uh-huh. Want to go back and try that one over again? Who, what, when and where?"

So she drew in a deep breath and filled in the bare outline of her story, which no one had ever asked for before. Never been interested enough to ask. Eric always changed the subject when she mentioned her family, such as it was.

Lyon probably wasn't interested, either, but he was kind enough to pretend to listen, and she needed to talk to someone…she really did. They said a burden shared was a burden lightened.

Hadn't someone said that?

If not, someone should.

"I was born in a little town outside Tulsa. Daddy was a horse broker, but not a very good one. Actually, he only worked for a horse broker, but mostly, he drank. I don't remember a whole lot about him, but Mama said he was always good to her, only he'd wanted to be a big rodeo star and he wasn't. He never made it past the county fair, so he drank, and he brooded, and then one day he just up and walked out and never came back."

"You said he told you about your grandmother."

"That was later. He showed up one day—not that I recognized him, but he had this picture of Mama and me when I was four years old, and I recognized it because Mama had one just like it. He said who he was, and I could tell he was really sick, because his skin was yellow and he was way too thin."

She deliberately skimmed over those last few months. Discovering how very ill he really was, and how far down he was on the list for liver transplants, even if they could have worked out the insurance mess. But before she even got started on the paperwork he died. One day he was sitting in her living room, polishing his boots—he always took real good care of his boots—and the next day he was dead. Just like that.

"Well." She went to draw back in his arms, but he held her, and as it felt so good, she let him. "Anyway, I don't want you to get the wrong idea. Mama and I got along just fine. Mama cried a lot at first, but nobody had to tiptoe and whisper anymore. I could laugh and play music as loud as I wanted to, and after a while we didn't really miss him as much as we probably should have. At least, I didn't. Maybe I should have. Maybe if I'd loved him more…"

Lyon closed his eyes and held on, partly because it felt so damn good to hold a woman for reasons other than sexual—partly because he knew it would hurt like hell to move, even enough to let her go. One thing he'd discovered—it wasn't the position he was in so much as the getting there that hurt.

"Lyon?" she whispered. "I didn't mean to bore you with all this junk. About my past, I mean. Anyway, to make a long story short, Daddy told me about Grandmama, and I wrote to this nursing home. She didn't write back, but someone on the staff did, so I kept on writing. They said she didn't write anymore, but she enjoyed getting letters, and that she especially enjoyed getting gifts, so I sent candy and hand lotion and scented dusting powder and things like that. And once a lovely bed jacket I bought on sale. Yellow, with ecru lace. I guess she liked it, I never heard."

For a long time, neither of them spoke. The pale February sun quickly lost what little warmth it offered. Neither of them even missed the heat. A woodpecker drummed on a hollow tree, then squawked and flew off. A few feet away, a muskrat crawled up onto a cypress knee, took his bearings and slid silently into the water again.

Lyon moved his hands over her back, feeling the slight knobs of her spine. He couldn't reach any lower. Maybe it was a good thing. All she'd asked of him was a hearing and a little impersonal comfort. It was all he could offer.

Unfortunately, it was no longer all he wanted to offer.

Five

Staying was too easy. Physically, Jasmine had never been more uncomfortable in her life. Well, maybe once, when she'd had that awful case of flu and stayed in bed half out of her mind for three days, too sick even to call for help. Yet here she was, cold and grungy, dreaming up one excuse after another to stay one more day with Daniel in his cold, dank Lyon's den.

Not that she really needed an excuse. She could hardly board a plane full of people with her face in such a mess, could she? They wouldn't let her on. People were afraid of catching things on planes. Something to do with the air filtration system.

Besides, she had no intention of letting Cyn or Eric see her until she was completely healed over and looking fabulous.

Make that semifabulous. No point in being unrealistic.

And besides all that, Lyon needed her. He might pretend he could get along just fine without her, but he was probably the loneliest man she'd ever met in her life.

Not that he would ever admit it. He might not even be aware of it, but she was. She recognized loneliness.

Determined not to allow him to sink into a gray funk and ignore her, because it was obvious that's what he wanted to do, she asked him the names of all the birds that came around looking for the cracker crumbs she scattered for them.

He wasn't a whole lot of help. She didn't believe for one minute that the little brown bird with the rich, sweet call was a brown-speckled snuff-dipper, but she smiled, and so did he. Almost.

She'd noticed right off that when he was teasing her, one side of his mouth twitched. His eyes would go a shade lighter and crinkle at the corners. It was worth working at—prying him out of his lion-with-a-briar-in-his-paw mood, so she gave it her best shot.

He was hurting?

Tough. She was itching. Her hair was a mess, her face was a mess, her clothes, what few she had, were a mess. He thought she was a ditz, which might have hurt her feelings, but she refused to allow him to get under her skin. Instead, she played up to his expectations.

Or down to them. "Does this place have an address?"

She got "The Look." Semivillainous male chauvinist pig.

"Yeah, it's called The Ridge."

Which was a joke, because as far as the eye could see, which wasn't really all that far, what land wasn't under water was as flat as a pancake. Flatter. Her pancakes were usually lumpy. She put all sorts of healthy junk in them. Sunflower seeds, raisins, berries…

"The Ridge. I like it." At least he'd chosen to make camp on what just might be the highest spot in the entire Eastern Dismal Swamp, and for that she was grateful, because she'd woken that morning with her teeth and every bone in her body chattering, feeling as if she'd been sleeping on a block of ice. The dampness hadn't actually soaked through; it only felt that way.

She tried not to imagine how Lyon must have felt, because he'd insisted she take both his sleeping bag and his tent. She'd argued, for all the good it had done. His body might be temporarily impaired, but there was nothing wrong with his mule-stubborn will.

Once she'd thawed out enough to move, she had tied a line between two trees, following Lyon's instructions, and spread all their bedding so the sun could soak up the dew. Next, she'd put on as many layers of his clothing as she thought he could spare while he punished himself by marching in circles around the clearing, probably doing more harm than good, but you couldn't tell the man anything. He simply tuned out anything he didn't care to hear.

Still, she could hardly go off and leave him. Her conscience wouldn't let her do that, even if she'd had a way to leave, knowing that any minute now his muscles were going to go into spasms and he'd be utterly helpless again.

Once it warmed up enough, she tried fishing with the two-foot-long rod she found behind the two metal box lockers, one of which was padlocked. Against raccoons, he'd told her. She wasn't entirely sure she believed him, but it was his business, not hers.

He told her he'd brought the fishing rod for when his back was in good enough shape to cast, and she was welcome to use it if she wanted to. He suggested using a black plastic worm, which was just fine with her. She had no intention of using a live anything.

He told her how to throw it out. A dozen times, at least. Maybe two dozen. "No, don't close your eyes. That's right, nice and easy now—over your right shoulder. Aim for that floating leaf."

There were roughly ten thousand and seventeen floating leaves. She could hardly miss. All the same, she missed and hit a bunch of bracken growing on the bank.

Still, she was rather amazed at his patience. He even congratulated her when she managed to make her first decent cast. The plastic blob landed nearly four feet out in the water this time, but if there'd ever been any fish around they were long gone, scared off, no doubt, by all her botched attempts.

Lyon came and stood behind her. "Look, if you hold it this way…" He demonstrated. Reaching one arm around her, he covered her hand with his. "Thumb right here—that's it. Now, we swing—no, not like that, like this."

The worm draped itself over a cypress branch, but neither of them noticed for a while. Jasmine did notice the solid warmth pressed against her back. She noticed the arm holding her, and the callused hand covering her own. She noticed that her breathing had gone haywire.

And she noticed that hers wasn't the only set of lungs that had suddenly forgotten how to function.

"Well…" she murmured. "I hope you didn't hurt your back again."

He assured her he hadn't, but there was something

in his voice that made her think *something* was certainly hurting.

"Maybe if I went to work on those muscles, I could—"

"No way. What I mean is, no thanks."

She shrugged. It was his loss. She'd learned a lot about easing back muscles last fall when she'd stepped off a ladder in the stockroom. Stepped off the second rung thinking it was the first. The shop had been so afraid of OSHA they'd insisted on paying for her treatment.

So. It was crackers and cheese and warm beer instead of fish for lunch. Later on, seeing the way he moved— or rather, didn't move—Jasmine insisted that he lie down on his stomach and let her work on his back.

"I know what I'm doing, honestly. And the sooner you're well, the sooner I can—"

"Yeah, I know. The sooner you can leave."

She could tell he didn't want to, but he did it anyway. She spread the groundsheet in a patch of sunshine and he took his own sweet time getting down. He was tense. When she straddled his thighs so that she could work without straining her own back, he tensed up even more. What did he expect? That she'd tie his arms behind him and escape with his boat?

She really did know how to give a good back rub. Sort of...

"Not bad," he muttered about the time she'd nearly massaged her fingerprints down to the bone.

His head was turned to one side, his eyes closed, both hands flat on the ground, ready to lever him up at the first sign of...whatever.

Jasmine flexed her fingers and admired the prone

form beneath her. He was wedge-shaped. Broad shoulders, long back, several interesting scars. He had narrow, muscular hips, flaring into even more muscular thighs. She inhaled deeply, exhaled in a gusty sigh, and leaned into her task again, hammering with the sides of her hands, lifting with her thumbs, soothing with her palms.

He felt warm to her touch. Her hands slowed, lingering on the small of his back. Warm and silky, and slightly damp. He smelled musky, like the earth. And spicy, like the dried leaves she'd spread to pad his groundsheet. He had nice hands. Square palms, long fingers, with blunt tips. The scattering of hair on the backs was silky and dark.

"Jazz?" he murmured sleepily.

"Hmmm?"

"What's the matter, you fallen asleep?"

Dreaming maybe, but hardly asleep. Stiffening her arms, she pressed with the heels of her hands and then lifted with her thumbs. He groaned, sighed and groaned again, all without opening his eyes.

Mercy. Maybe this hadn't been such a great idea, after all.

When the sun dropped below the treetops, she folded their bedding and felt honor bound to lie and say she'd just as soon sleep out under the stars in the makeshift bedroll tonight and let him have his tent and down-filled sleeping bag back.

He didn't even bother to argue. Just changed the subject, asking if she'd mind laying a fire to heat supper.

"Sure, but I warn you, the only fire I ever laid was in the fireplace of a house we lived in for seven months when I was about twelve or so. It was going to be a surprise for Mama. I was going to have hot dogs already cooked by the time she got home from work. Instead, I smoked up the whole house and blistered the paint on the mantel, and made such a mess she made me scrape and repaint the thing because we couldn't afford to hire it done, and she was afraid the super would pitch a fit."

"Made a mess of that, too, I'll bet."

"Drips all over the floor. I forgot to spread papers."

She smiled, and in another of those odd moments of perfect understanding, he smiled back at her. "Don't worry about my floor, just don't burn down the woods, will you?" he cautioned. "Take a handful of dry leaves, a few twigs, a few of those splits of kindling over there and three of the smallest logs on the stack. I'll tell you what to do with 'em."

Lyon was on his stump again. Jasmine thought of it as his throne. From there he reigned over his small kingdom like a royal monarch.

She'd like to think she'd done his back some good earlier, but if he was better, he wasn't about to admit it. He never admitted anything unless he absolutely had to. She knew more about the exterminator who serviced their building than she did the man she'd actually slept with for three nights in a row.

Or if not actually with, then nearby.

After three tries, a few small, satisfying flames crackled and flared up. Jasmine stood back and admired her handiwork until Lyon suggested she open another can of chili and set it to heat for supper.

"I wonder if I'm too old to be a Girl Scout," she mused, bending over his diminishing supply of canned goods.

When he didn't reply, she glanced over her shoulder to see him staring at her backside, which, she'd be the first to admit, must look pretty lumpy under all the layers she was wearing.

She shivered. "It's getting colder now that the sun's beginning to go down."

"It's February. Just hope the rain holds off."

"Don't even think rain. Anyway, there's not a cloud in the sky." There really wasn't. Only a soft, golden haze wisping across the sky like layers of pale chiffon.

The chili was better warm than it was cold. She was getting a little tired of the stuff, but there wasn't a whole lot to choose from.

So they ate warm chili and stale crackers, Lyon on his stump and she on the plastic groundsheet, and they talked about this and that. Mostly, Jasmine talked. Lyon grunted the occasional reply. Sociable he was not, but he did thaw out enough to tell her the names of some of the trees and a few of the geographical features he'd seen noted on various maps in the tax office. Most of the boundaries, it seemed, were either ditches, creeks or canals.

"Little Alligator Creek doesn't sound too inviting, but then, neither does Buzzard's Point. If this place doesn't have an official name, we could call it Squatter's Ridge. There was this town in a spaghetti western I once almost had a part in called Squatter's Ridge. It wasn't really a town, only a big ranch and a water hole. The main conflict, of course, was the water hole. And the rancher's daughter."

He nodded, but didn't say anything. Jasmine had an idea he didn't see very many movies.

"Although I guess this place is more water hole than ridge. What about Squatter's Hole?"

Which was when he admitted that technically, he wasn't a squatter. The place belonged to him. He'd inherited an undivided interest in it, at least.

Jasmine gazed around with fresh perspective. In the fuzzy yellow sunset, with nothing but trees, water and vines, softened by gray-green moss and feathery stands of winter-brown bracken, it was almost beautiful. It would be a fascinating movie location.

"I never heard of anyone actually owning a swamp before. Why on earth would anyone want to? I mean, it's lovely, once you get used to it, but what good is it?"

"You want the environmentalists' spin, or the tax collector's spin?"

He came close to actually smiling. It made Jasmine's heart flop over, and she told herself it was because it meant he was feeling better. That he'd benefited from her treatment. Soon he'd be well enough so that she could go with a clear conscience.

"How about both?" she said. "Did I mention I'm thinking of doing a travel piece about this area? Do I need your permission?"

He grunted, stirred his chili, and avoided a direct answer. He did that a lot. Avoided direct answers. If there was one thing Daniel Lyon was, it was private. The longer she was around him, the more he intrigued her, more because of what he didn't say than what he did. Underneath that grouchy, shaggy persona he projected, she was beginning to sense vast areas of darkness.

Hidden depths, she mused, scraping the last of her supper from the sides of her bowl. If there was one thing that could capture a woman's fancy, it was a man with hidden depths.

She fairly itched to write a description of the man and the place, and of how she'd come to be there. It would make a fabulous story. Maybe even a screenplay.

Setting her bowl aside—he had only the one bowl, which he'd insisted she use, preferring the can, himself—Jasmine leaned back on her elbows and stared up into the treetops. A hazy premise began to take shape in her mind. Not a plot precisely—not yet—but she could definitely visualize a hero who looked a lot like Lyon and a heroine who looked a lot like—

Oh, sure. A wild-haired, long-legged beanpole with a face full of poison ivy. Some heroine.

"As I said before, I inherited the place, I didn't buy it."

She opened her eyes and blinked. He'd actually volunteered some information? Well, my mercy, would wonders ever cease?

Lyon had had about all he could take of innocence in disguise. If he had to spend much more time around a woman who looked like hell, who talked a blue streak—none of it particularly riveting—and who lay sprawled out before him like a seven-veil dancing girl offering herself to the head sheikh, he just might take her up on her offer.

Great. Now she even had him thinking in terms of movies.

All that saved her was that he was pretty sure she wasn't being deliberately provocative. They both knew that in the condition he was in, he was no threat to any woman. She might think she was no threat to any man, either, dressed like a scarecrow with her face broken out in a rash. The trouble was, none of that seemed to matter. He couldn't figure it. Physically, she was a mess. Mentally, she was a mess. Yet she turned him on more than any woman had in years.

He thought about it some. Not a whole lot. It didn't add up.

Lying back on one elbow with one long leg sprawled out so that the sole of her shoe actually touched the toe of his boot, the other leg bent at the knee, she continued to gaze up at him. "You inherited it? Who from? I mean, from whom?"

"Huh? Oh, the swamp." He was sorry he'd ever mentioned it. Didn't even know why he had, because he had no intention of telling her the sorry saga of his life. It was none of her business.

The lady asked too many questions.

But then, the lady was out of her element.

Which might explain why she talked too much. It was a recognized tool of his trade. Throw a person off balance and they talked. Toss in a little fear and they talked even faster.

Grudgingly, he relented. Hell, he was still human, despite a few doubts he'd heard expressed in certain quarters. "I dunno. Some old geezer who died a long time ago. I never knew him, never even heard of him until a few weeks ago when I got this letter from a lawyer saying I was an heir."

She sat up then, elbows planted on her knees. The way she moved reminded him of something he'd seen once in Africa. He and a fellow agent had been racing north toward the Sahara when they'd spotted a herd of giraffes just about the same time the giraffes had spotted their Land Rover. The guy with him—he was dead now, killed in an ambush—had laughed and called them great, gawking, ugly beasts.

Lyon had felt more like crying. To this day it embarrassed him, the way he'd reacted to a bunch of animals galloping across the plains. He'd never told a living soul. Never would.

"That's even better," she exclaimed with that sweet, guileless smile that slashed through his guard like a few rounds of armor-piercing ammo. "That you never knew him, I mean. Then his dying wouldn't be so sad. Who was he, your grandfather?"

He shrugged, and this time it hardly hurt at all. He was getting better. "Who knows? Great, maybe even great-great. Some relative a few generations back, I guess. First I knew I even had any relatives."

He didn't know if he'd been sorry or relieved to learn that somewhere in the world there might be a handful of cousins, however distant, who shared a few genes, some DNA and maybe even a few inherited traits. From what he'd experienced so far, family was something he'd just as soon do without.

Had done without for more than half his life. His parents had fought constantly. They'd split when he was about twelve. An only child, Lyon remembered too well lying awake in the night, hearing them argue over which one would take him. Neither one of them had wanted him, so they'd shipped him off to an uncle, who hadn't wanted him, either.

The next few years had been memorable, but not in a way he cared to remember. Two years later he'd walked out. No one had come after him, not even social services. He doubted if his uncle had even reported him missing. The school probably had, but evidently he wasn't high on anyone's priority list, so he'd stayed missing and stayed out of jail, not because he hadn't stepped over the line a time or two, but because he'd been smart enough not to get caught.

And he'd managed, through a series of breaks he sure as hell hadn't deserved, to get enough of an education so that he'd eventually become a cop. A few transfers, a few favors called in and he'd worked his way into a small, tightly organized, totally off-record arm of federal law enforcement where he'd built a reputation for being efficient and effective. A little too effective.

At least someone seemed to think so.

"I read this book once," Jasmine was saying, and he slammed the door shut on his past and pretended to listen while she talked about books she'd read, movies she'd seen and roles she'd played, just as if they were in a cozy drawing room somewhere instead of hunkered down in the mud in the middle of a swamp in February with rain on the way and a one-man pup tent between them.

Idly, he listened to the sound of her husky, Bible Belt, West Coast, diction-corrected accent, but his mind was on other things. She had skin like pale silk, at least where she wasn't covered with a rash. The skin under all those layers she was wearing—layers that would smell like her body after she left—was probably even paler. She had a redhead's skin, so fine it was almost translucent.

She bathed every morning, using creek water in the only pot he'd brought with him, and his only bar of soap. He'd figured the soap would last him at least a month

as he hadn't planned on bathing every day. No point in
it, a man living alone in the wilderness. But damned if
he wasn't getting almost as bad as she was. It wasn't
easy, either, bathing in a two-quart cook pot. Not when
privacy was a problem—when you were afraid your leg
was going to buckle under you and the slightest wrong
move could mean another week in a damned back brace.

He'd come here to get his body back in shape and to
find some answers. The information was all here, filed
away in his head in no particular order. It was only a
matter of fitting the pieces together. All it took was
concentration.

He'd destroyed all his notes before leaving Langley.
There was nothing on his computer that couldn't stand
scrutiny, because he knew damned well it would be
scrutinized. He was counting on it. There was no such
thing as a fool-proof encryption system, at least not in
the United States. In other, less regulated countries they
were miles ahead in that particular technology.

"Do you happen to have a needle?"

It took all of ten seconds to react. He was getting
rusty. "A needle?"

She held up her right hand, the palm pink but no
longer raw. "I must have picked up a splinter from the
firewood. I can't seem to grab it with my teeth."

"I've got a pair of needle-nosed pliers. Here, let me
see."

It was almost too dark to see, but she came up onto
her knees and held her hand up under his face. She
smelled of soap, and faintly of chili. Hell of an aphrodisiac, he thought wryly.

In the end, he used his knife on her. His pliers were

in the war chest with a few things he'd just as soon keep private. His knife was as good as any surgical instrument. Sterilized with a flick of his Bic, it did the job easily.

Lyon looked up at the face so close to his own and felt something crumble inside him. She was all puckered up, bracing herself against pain, all on account of a splinter no bigger than half an eyelash.

"Hey, that wasn't so bad, now was it?"

"Is it out?"

"Sure is. Probably won't even leave much of a scar."

She laughed and then caught her bottom lip between her teeth, and on an impulse that came at him like a sidewinder, he kissed the all-but invisible wound and then folded her fingers over it.

"Mama used to do that," she said, her soft, raspy voice doing things to his body he could've done without.

"I'll just bet she did." His own mama had never kissed him at all so far as he could remember. Whenever he'd come in bearing battle scars from a schoolyard brawl, she'd either blessed him out or ignored him.

She drank. So had his old man. It was one of the reasons why he didn't, other than beer. Even then, three a day was his limit. He'd always liked testing himself against limits. He usually won.

An hour after the operation, Jasmine could still feel the soft, fleeting brush of his lips on her palm. Amazing, the way something so insignificant could affect her. Like a high, fast roller coaster. Like seeing the ocean for the first time, bigger than all Oklahoma.

Like seeing her daddy again after so many years and realizing that he was desperately ill, and then realizing on the heels of that, that he was a stranger.

A little kiss in the palm of her hand. It felt bigger than that. It felt bigger than the first time she'd made love. Than any of the times she'd made love, which weren't so very many, after all. She was practical by nature, not passionate.

"Is it my imagination, or does the air feel damper than usual?" she asked a little while later, handing back the tube of toothpaste she used on her finger.

"Probably your imagination. Sure you don't want a smear of antibiotic cream on your wound before you turn in?"

She shook her head. "It'll be okay. I thought I'd head back tomorrow, anyway. I could take your boat and then find someone to tow it back to you right away, so you won't be—"

"Yeah, I know. Up the creek without a paddle."

It was a standing joke between them, the reason why she hadn't been able to leave. At least it was as standing as a joke could be after only a few days.

"You'll be all right now, won't you?"

One part of her—the decent, dutiful part—wanted him to say yes, but another part wanted him to say no.

Which was the very reason why she needed to leave.

At first she thought she was dreaming. Rain beat down on the roof, on the front walk and the driveway where her mother's old Chevy Nova was parked.

Something mumbled in her ear, and she froze.

"Whaa—?"

"Shh, go back to sleep, it's only me."

Lyon.

He was in her bed?

Not really. She was in his sleeping bag, which was a double because he liked to spread out when he slept. And he was in it with her.

He wasn't spread out now. He was curved around her backside, one arm over her waist, one leg drawn up between hers, while rain drummed down deafeningly on the flimsy canvas barrier overhead.

Six

Rain. Rain, and warmth, and the smell of earth and soap and that subtle, masculine essence that Jasmine recognized as his alone. Lyon's arm tightened around her. He murmured sleepily in her hair, but he wasn't asleep.

At least, not all of him.

He was curved around her back. Without meaning to, Jasmine pressed her hips into the heat and hardness swelling against her bottom. Her heart skipped a beat. Her lungs skipped several breaths.

"This isn't very smart," she whispered.

"Mmmm?"

"I said…" She wriggled. Just a tiny bit, because there was a lump underneath the sleeping bag. Because there was a steady drip coming off the edge of the tent and more than a hint of dampness working its way through the flap.

Because he was aroused and she was aroused, and she didn't even know the man. She certainly wasn't in love with him.

Because she couldn't help it. What she wanted to do—wanted desperately to do—was to press against him even harder—to turn in his arms and open herself, and feed this ravaging beast that was threatening to consume her from the inside out.

What on earth was happening to her? She'd never been what you might call passionate. With Eric she'd pretended, but she suspected he'd known. They'd never talked about it. They'd never talked about much of anything other than his enormous ambitions and her modest ones. Mostly, they'd talked about what he wanted, and what he was doing to get it, and what he thought his chances were.

Something warm and gentle closed over her breast. She shut her eyes tightly and cupped her shoulders to protect the sensation.

"You really shouldn't," she murmured, doing nothing at all to remove his hand.

"Yeah." His voice was early-morning gruff, his breath causing her hair to tickle her face. But he didn't remove his hand. With his thumb, he stroked gently over a peaked nipple, back and forth. With each pass, electricity streaked clean through her, setting off dangerous tremors in her belly, pooling like molten lava between her thighs.

Outside, rain beat down noisily on sodden earth, on water, on the canopy of winter-bare trees. The sound was deafening, shutting out the rest of the world. Lyons's thigh, the one wedged between her legs, shifted ever so slightly, and she thought wildly, *Oh, Lord, what if his muscles lock up? We'll never get untangled!*

He was breathing hard. So was she. Why couldn't she have been sleeping on her other side when he'd slipped in beside her? Then they'd have been lying front to front instead of front to back, and who knows what might have happened?

"Yeah," he said again, his voice as rough as the bark on that big old tree that was doing such a poor job of sheltering them.

"Yeah what?" She sounded a little like tree bark, too. She certainly didn't sound like Jasmine.

"Yeah, what you said. That this wasn't a smart move."

Funny, though, how smart it felt. As if she'd been programmed since birth to lie in this man's arms, in a tent in a wet, rainy swamp in late February, with rain beating down all around, drowning out past and future alike.

She shifted slightly and managed to turn over so that she was facing him. Not touching him—at least, not all over. Nothing was going to happen. Considering his back and his knee, not to mention her own broad streak of common sense, it couldn't.

She almost wished it could.

Wished she could have something besides a fading rash to take home with her. Something she could look back on when Lyon was only a memory and think, *Someday, with the right man, under the right circumstances, I'm going to discover what the big hoopla over sex is all about.*

She had wondered. Any woman would. Sex, money and power, otherwise known as SMP—or was it PMS?—was what drove the world according to Cyn, who might look like an airhead, but who was a very savvy woman.

Jasmine had never been quite convinced. Money and power, perhaps, but sex? She'd never been able to understand how something as ephemeral as sex could make fools of otherwise intelligent people.

But she was beginning to understand. When Lyon held her in a certain way—touched her in a certain way—the world suddenly came alive with sound and color and all sorts of special effects. Without even trying, this grizzly, grumpy bear of a man made her *feel* more, and *want* more, than any man ever had.

Including Eric, with his suave manners, his cashmere jackets and his three-hundred-dollar loafers. And she'd been head over heels in love with Eric, hadn't she?

Had she?

"I'm going to get up now," she declared in a firm whisper. And then, in a clear voice, "Why am I whispering?"

She thought she heard him chuckle, but maybe it was a belch. His face was inches from her own, every whisker, every line, every tiny scar clearly visible, even in the gray morning light.

It occurred to her that if she could see his flaws, he could see hers. At the best of times, she had a few. At the moment, she had more than a few. If she'd had a single brain cell, she would've unzipped the flap and crawled out the minute he'd crawled in.

She waited, staring at a star-shaped scar just underneath his left eye. He didn't speak. Not so much as a murmur. A muscle in his jaw twitched once, and then he closed his eyes and sighed.

She wished she could think of something devastat-

ingly clever to say, so that he'd think about how witty
she was instead of the way she looked early in the morning, all puffy-eyed, with finger marks pressed into her
cheek. The cheek that didn't have a rash.

"It's periwinkle, isn't it?" She had this thing about
silence. When she was nervous, silence made her even
more nervous, which is why she felt compelled to fill it
with words.

He opened his eyes, looking confused. Looking wary.

"That shade of blue, I mean. Your eyes? It's unusual.
I know three women who wear contacts that color, but
it's rare in real life, almost as rare as turquoise. I've
never seen turquoise."

Devastatingly clever? Try dumb.

Their knees were all mixed up, bumping together.
His felt rough because of the hair. She'd never realized
how sexy body hair could be on a man. Eric shaved what
little he had. So did the other man in her life. They'd almost made love once, but he'd been allergic to the perfume she was wearing. It was hard to combine sneezing
and wheezing with sexual intimacy.

"Lyon, are you allergic to—?"

It was as far as she got. His periwinkle eyes, embed-
ded in thick, stubby black lashes and a web of squint
lines, came closer and closer until she felt herself going
cross-eyed, and so she did the only thing possible.

She closed her eyes and let him kiss her.

It was everything a kiss should be, and a million
times more. Heat, electricity, gentleness—sort of hungry, but sleepy, too, as if they had all the time in the
world instead of no time at all.

Her arm, the one that wasn't curled underneath her

body, slipped around his waist. She stroked his back, her fingers lingering on the slightly puckered ridge of another scar.

He used his tongue. Not aggressively—not demanding entry, but seductively. Almost lazily, as if he had nothing better to do at the moment than explore her mouth.

Which might have been more convincing if his heart hadn't been beating so hard she could almost hear it. Plink, plank. Plunk, splat.

Plink plank?

That wasn't his heart, it was the rain slacking off. His heart was going *boom-kaboom,* like jungle drums in an old Tarzan movie.

Reluctantly sliding her mouth away, Jasmine buried her face in his throat, felt the throbbing pulse there and marveled at the physiological effect one human being could have on another. It had to mean something. Her own pulse was beating so rapidly she felt giddy, breathless.

Actually, she felt aggressive. For the first time in her entire life she was tempted to take the lead. A heady sense of power swept over her as she pictured herself easing him onto his back—gently so that he wouldn't hurt anything—and then moving over him, straddling his hips with her thighs, and settling slowly, gently...

Not slowly, gently, but fiercely!

Merciful saints alive, Jasmine, what's come over you?

Hearing the sound of her own rasping breath, she was suddenly filled with panic. Her eyes popped open. She flapped a hand behind her and fumbled with the zipper while struggling to extricate herself from the cocoon of arms and legs and fiber-filled, weather-proof nylon.

He didn't do a thing to stop her. Didn't say a word.

Silence again. "The rain's stopped," she blurted. "I'd better—it's time to—"

"I'm sorry."

On her hands and knees, she glanced over her shoulder, wondering what *he* had to be sorry about. That they almost had?

Or that they hadn't.

"I am, too. Sorry, I mean. I hope you didn't hurt your back."

He told her in three short words what she could do with his back, and it sounded interesting, but not as interesting as a few other possibilities that occurred to her.

"Don't laugh," he said, his voice more like crunching gravel than ever.

She wasn't laughing, she was hysterical. She always did hysteria as a glassy-eyed smile.

And then, wonder of wonders, he was smiling, too.

"Yeah, well…you can probably come up with a movie that covers a situation like this if you think about it for a few minutes."

She crawled the rest of the way out, hardly a graceful exit. *Crimes of the Heart?* Sissy Spacek descending the staircase trailing that chandelier?

No, that had been funny. This was merely pathetic. "Coffee," she muttered.

"Wet wood."

"Oh." She sighed. Who needed movies? What had just happened to her hadn't even happened, not really. As a romance, it would have been perfect for one of those old Carol Burnett skits.

Outside the tent, she got to her feet. Her brittle smile fell away, leaving her feeling vulnerable and a little sad. The trouble with being an actress was that one tended to overdramatize things. Even casual sex. And it hadn't even been that. Not casual, at least. Not even sex.

Jasmine wasn't foolish enough to believe she'd fallen in love at first sight. A week ago, she'd thought she was still in love with Eric. Correction: she'd tried to convince herself she was still in love with Eric. The truth was, she'd probably never loved him, she'd only wanted to be in love, and he'd been the likeliest candidate. God, what a pathetic wimp she was.

It was that old belonging thing again. Ever since she'd heard her first happily-ever-after fairy tale she'd longed to belong to someone special. Her mother had. For a little while, at least, until her father had run out on them. After that, her mother had "belonged" to any number of men, some nice, some not so nice.

The trouble was, Jasmine hadn't belonged to anyone. Sometimes she thought that was the only reason she'd ended up in Hollywood. She was still trying to recapture the fairy tale.

So far, it hadn't happened. If there was one thing in short supply in the world of Hollywood make-believe, it was Prince Charmings. Or Princes Charming. Eric had looked like a prince, but he was too self-centered ever to share himself with anyone. He liked ambition in a woman. Jasmine's ambitions were too modest.

Peter, who was allergic to her perfume, hadn't even been a contender, but he'd been nice, and she'd thought maybe…

Well. And maybe not.

Standing outside the tent, she lifted her face to the

chilly morning dampness. Feeble rays of a lemony sun slanted down through the trees. Wisps of fog trailed across the still water. Before she knew it, she was slipping back into a world of illusion, where anything could happen.

From practically under her feet, a heron croaked and flew away. She yelped, and the spell was shattered.

You want to belong to someone? Fine. Belong to yourself. Get it together, Clancy. You're the captain of your own fate. Or ship, or whatever.

Jasmine didn't know much about Daniel Lyon, but she did know he was a loner. He might need her at the moment, but he resented that need. He would quickly come to resent her, too.

And that wasn't going to happen. She would leave first. Then maybe when he thought of her—if he thought of her at all—he would miss her just a little bit.

"Jasmine? Come back inside."

"No, thanks. I've really got to think about—"

"We need to talk."

"No, we don't, I need to—"

A high-pitched whine cut through her thoughts, and she wondered distractedly if bees swarmed in February. Just her luck. Poison ivy wasn't enough, she had to have bees. Talk about the *Perils of Pauline*.

She tugged at the waffle-weave longhandles she'd borrowed to sleep in until the placket was back in front where it belonged, trying to recall if Indiana Jones had had to deal with bees, wondering if airplanes—

Airplanes?

"Airplanes! Lyon, get out here quick, someone's coming!"

Cramming her feet into her shoes, she burst out into the clearing and scanned the sky, searching for what she'd just heard.

She had heard it, hadn't she? It hadn't been a part of some wild, science-fiction, time-travel dream. Hadn't the Wright brothers done their big gig not far from here?

"Get inside," Lyon commanded softly. She hadn't even known he was behind her.

"I was right, it is a plane! Look, here it comes again!"

"Jazzy, get back inside the tent."

"There it is! It's coming right up the creek, see?"

It was small, the single engine sounding more like a lawnmower than a real airplane. Lyon reached for her just as she pulled away and raced down to the edge of the creek, waving both arms and yelling.

There was no place for a plane to land, not even a small one. One of the reasons he'd chosen this place was that it was all but inaccessible. All the same, if the pilot spotted Jasmine, he could radio their location. A fast boat could get here in well under an hour.

The plane made a slow pass and headed south. Searching? Hard to tell. There was only one thing Lyon could think of that anyone would be searching for in this particular location.

Him.

Spooks were a close-knit bunch of loners. Trust had to be earned. Even then, it was never taken for granted. When one of them turned, no one was safe.

One of them had turned. Lyon didn't know for sure which one, but he'd narrowed it down to two men. The trouble was, one of those two was the Director of Operations himself. Lyon had a feeling he was in way over his head. Of the three men in the outfit he trusted, only one was still alive.

At least, he hoped to hell Madden was still alive.

Moving closer to the woman, he watched the plane grow smaller. How long would it take him to pull up stakes and move to a new location? Would he have time?

Would it do any good?

Sunlight shafted through the low-lying bank of clouds, glinting off her hair. Momentarily distracted, he reached out and touched a wild, corkscrew curl. It was warm. Alive. Unable to check the quick response, both physical and emotional, to all the things she was and he wasn't, he swore silently.

He was still thinking of all the reasons why he had no business getting involved when the plane banked and headed north again.

"Oh, look, it saw us!" She started down toward the bank again, waving wildly.

"Dammit, Jasmine, come back here!"

A look of surprise on her face, she turned just as he launched himself. They landed flat in the mud, Jasmine on her back, Lyon sprawled on top of her. It took several moments before she could gulp in enough air to speak.

"What are you trying to do, kill me?"

"What are you trying to do, get me killed?" He glared at her.

Jasmine glared right back. "Who do you think they are, poachers? Ivory hunters? Get real."

There was mud on his face. He looked like one of those armed and dangerous commando-types who was always slipping through jungles with a helmet and gun and a grim look on his face.

"I told you not to signal." His voice was so taut it vibrated. Eyes that had been periwinkle blue only moments before were suddenly black, with only the tiniest rim of blue.

It dawned on her then that he was naked. Strip, stark naked.

She fought to reclaim her common sense. "Well, what did you expect me to do...pass up a chance to get back to civilization?"

"You want to go back? I'll get you back." He was growling. Her wounded Lyon—her muddy, naked, wounded Lyon was growling.

"What I *want?* Well, what do you think I want, to spend the rest of my so-called vacation out here in the jungle? You didn't give me a choice, remember?"

"No?"

"No!" At least it hadn't seemed like it at the time. She could have insisted. They both knew she'd have been well within her rights to simply take his boat and row herself back if her hands could've stood the pain, and then hire someone to tow the thing back to him.

"Jasmine?"

"What?"

"I'm cold."

No, he wasn't. He was hot. She could feel his skin burning right through the single layer of waffle-weave cotton between them, setting her on fire again. You'd think a cold, wet drizzle and even colder mud would have a dampening effect on desire, but it didn't.

It was really sort of funny, only she didn't feel much

like laughing. "You'd better get some clothes on. If whoever's in that plane happens to look down here, they'll get an eyeful."

"I'm not sure I can get up."

"Let me help." She wiggled. It didn't help. Lyon was tempted to ask her to close her eyes. Damned if he wasn't embarrassed. He couldn't remember the last time he'd been embarrassed. Maybe when he was about five or so, when he'd wet his pants in a supermarket because his old man had been so steamed at having to do the marketing he'd ignored the whining kid tagging along behind him.

She had to know what was happening to him. Unless he was way off base, it was happening to her, too. Crawling into the sack with her last night had been a world-class mistake, and Lyon wasn't a man who made mistakes. In his business, mistakes could be fatal.

This one might not be fatal, but it was going to be a doozy. And he was going to make it. Lying on top of her, his bare backside in plain view of any surveillance plane passing overhead, he made what just might turn out to be the biggest mistake of his entire adult life.

He kissed her again. Kissed her hungrily, thoroughly, taking his time about it. Doing with his tongue what he intended to do with his body. Plunging, thrusting into her hot, sweet depths. Deliberately driving them both dangerously close to the edge, because there was no time to linger, to savor.

"Come on," he rasped. Dragging his mouth away, he came to his feet in a smooth, balletic movement that, if he'd allowed her time to think about it, might have made her wonder.

Overhead, the plane made another slow pass. He hoped to hell they weren't armed. If they were, he was a dead man.

They made it to the tent just as the plane came directly overhead and droned off upriver. Which meant he had a small window of opportunity. More like a porthole. Lyon couldn't believe he was doing what he was doing instead of getting the hell out while there was still time, but he was doing it, all right. With full knowledge and aforethought, as the legal types would say.

The condemned man ate a hearty meal.

She was muddy. So was he. Most of hers was on the backside of his long underwear. Most of his was on his hands and knees. Neither of them was thinking about mud. At this point, neither of them was capable of rational thought. It was a wonder steam wasn't rising from their bodies.

He hadn't come prepared, and he knew damned well she hadn't because he'd gone through her purse. He also knew it would kill him to stop now, but he had to give her one last chance to bail out. He owed her that much.

"Jasmine, listen, if you'd rather not—I mean, there are certain precautions, and I didn't come prepared to—"

"Please? Lyon, I won't hurt you. I mean—well, you know what I mean."

"I know, sweetheart. I'm okay in that respect, too, but there are other considerations."

She began to shake her head. Oh, hell, if it came to that, he could marry her.

Yeah, sure you can. Marry her and fight over the kid, the way your parents fought over you.

He had a feeling she'd be a good mother. He wasn't

cut out to be a father, but at least his kid, if he had one, would know what love felt like. And he'd see that they didn't lack for anything in the way of support. Hell, he'd sign over his life insurance. Lacking anyone else, he'd named a certain charity as beneficiary.

The scent of rain and wet vegetation, of sex and soap mingled in the warm confines of the tent. Suddenly, he was trembling with need, torn with indecision, the ten percent of him that was rational fighting a losing battle with the ninety percent that wasn't.

And then she touched him. Reached out and closed her hand around him, and that was it. Head back, eyes closed, he started counting under his breath, knowing he wouldn't last past single digits.

But he'd make it good for her. As close as he was to the edge, he would do that much if it killed him.

It probably would. "Easy, easy," he cautioned, laying her down on top of the sleeping bag. Wanting to rip her clothes off, he forced himself to move slowly. Unbuttoning the union suit, he folded it back, exposing her small, coral-tipped breasts.

He'd been right about her skin. She was smoother than a rose petal, whiter than a magnolia, and so beautiful his brain had obviously turned to mush. He'd been called a lot of things in his life. Poetic was not among them.

Reaching up, she touched the scar under his right eye where he'd been caught by the butt of a sawed-off shotgun.

And then her hand drifted down over his jaw, past his throat where a pulse was throbbing out of control, to trail over his chest. When her fingertips raked across a nipple he caught his breath, hoping she wouldn't notice his obvious—his very obvious—enthusiasm.

She noticed. Her eyes widened. Lyon had long since passed the stage when boys liked to brag about such things. All the same, he wished he could turn out the lights. Wished they were somewhere else, where there was soft music and plenty of uninterrupted time.

Clean sheets and a little heat would have been nice, too.

Back, don't play tricks on me now.

He touched her. Explored. She was hot and wet and tight, and that alone nearly catapulted him over the edge. Slowly, he positioned himself and eased inside her. Eyes closed, fists knotted, he braced himself to hold out for as long as it took to bring her along with him.

It was going to be a close race. He was determined to make it good for her, but it had been too long. Slowly, carefully, he withdrew. She clutched his shoulders and made a small sound of protest.

Slowly, carefully, he thrust again, shaken to his very depths by the avalanche of fire that threatened to consume him. Lowering his head, he tasted her lips again and then risked disaster by arching his back enough to suckle her breasts.

By then he was trembling hard with the effort to control his own need.

She was trembling, too. She was surprisingly awkward, the way she moved under him. He suspected that she hadn't had much experience, and that inflamed him still more.

He felt her tighten around him, felt the beginning of her spasms, and he went out of control. Gripping her shoulders, he drove harder, faster. She met each thrust, clutching him with her thighs. Her eyes widened on a look of dawning wonder. In a tremulous voice, she said his name. "Lyon? *Lyon?*"

He bit his lip to keep from shouting aloud as wave after tidal wave of mindless pleasure swept over him.

Never before...

Never like this—!

Seconds, or maybe centuries passed, and they collapsed together. Bearing the full weight of his body, she clung to him, refused to let him roll away. Still inside her, he could feel every beat of her heart, every hot, raw rasp of breath—feel the small aftershocks that threatened to set him off all over again.

Slowly, reluctantly, he drifted back to earth. He'd have given anything he possessed to be able to freeze time, rewind, and replay the last five minutes in *slo-o-ow* motion.

But time was the one luxury he couldn't afford. "Sweetheart, we have to go," he said.

"Too late," She smiled that slow, sweet smile of hers without even opening her eyes. "I'm already gone."

It was too late, all right. Too late for second thoughts. He glanced at his wrist and gauged the time elapsed. Too much. They'd have to hurry.

The ten percent was just beginning to override the ninety percent when his gaze fell to the vulnerable hollow at the base of her throat. Without stopping to think, he kissed the fluttering pulse there. She was damp with sweat, sweet with the scent of his own soap and Jasmine.

One last kiss, he thought, wondering if she realized that it was over. Hoping she did.

Hoping she didn't.

Hell, he didn't know what he hoped anymore. The lady had royally screwed up his mind.

Seven

The way Lyon saw it, he had two choices. He could uncover the outboard and move them farther downstream, which would only be a delaying tactic—or he could pack up just enough to get by with and move them deeper into the swamp. Another delaying tactic.

Either way, a move was imperative. If he was right about that plane, time was rapidly running out.

"Lyon? Is something wrong?"

That husky voice of hers caught him halfway across the clearing. He froze, but didn't look back. Looking back was a luxury he couldn't afford. He'd wasted enough time pulling on his pants and boots.

"Rain's stopped," he said gruffly. "Time to move camp."

"Move what?" She sounded breathless. Getting dressed in a one-man pup tent wasn't easy. Crawling

out, when your legs were as long as hers were, was no
cinch, either.

Dammit, Lawless, don't look back!

"You think the river's going to rise that fast?"

He bent over to unlock the chest and grabbed his
back for effect. His physical condition had improved far
more these past few days than he'd let on. A smart man
didn't lay all his cards on the table. A smart man who
wanted to survive learned how to use every advantage,
and the element of surprise was always good.

Not that he thought Jasmine would, or even could,
use his weakness against him, but after all these years
the habit was too deeply ingrained to forget. Trust had
killed many a good man.

"Lyon? Is it the rain? Are we going to be flooded out?"

"Nah, the water's not going to rise," he said gruffly.
"All the same, it's time to move on. I've got a better
place in mind."

He was going to shoot for the house. According to
the woman in the tax office it was still standing at last
report. He knew the approximate location. Even had a
pretty good idea of how to get there, but if what he suspected turned out to be true, they were in for some rough
going between here and there. Maybe he could leave her
here to make her way back the best way she could.

No way. There was a sixty-forty chance, odds
against him, that he'd been followed. What he couldn't
figure out was why they hadn't come in after him right
away instead of waiting a week. Unless finding someone who didn't want to be found in the middle of several thousand acres of swamp wasn't quite as easy as
checking out a street address. Something he'd counted

on when he'd chosen to look into old man Lawless's legacy.

If he was right, then Jasmine would be in almost as much danger as he was. They wouldn't think twice about using her to get at him and then offing her when they discovered she didn't know anything.

It wasn't going to happen.

When Lyon had first gone into law enforcement, protecting the public had been only an abstract concept. Now it didn't seem quite so abstract. Not at all abstract, in fact.

After scraping away a layer of concealing debris, he whipped the tarp off the small outboard and battery. They'd save time by taking the first leg by water. He'd done some exploring. The way was clear as far as he'd gone. Once the creek veered eastward they'd have to hide the boat and cut across country for a mile or so, but as long as they got away in the next ten minutes, they stood a good chance of—

From behind him came a soft gasp. He groaned and then he swore. "Save it for later, will you? Roll up the sleeping gear and take it down to the boat."

"Lyon, will you please tell me what's going on? I'm starting to get scared."

Oh, hell. "Nothing's going on. Nothing will go on as long as you do what I say without wasting time on questions." He made his voice flat, unemotional. There was no room in his life for emotions at the best of times. This wasn't the best of times.

He'd hurt her feelings. He was a master at intimidation when it served his purpose, and right now, it served his purpose, but he didn't feel good about it. In fact, he felt lousy.

She had that look on her face again. Leading with her chin. Mad as hell, but too stubborn to argue. Lyon unlocked his war chest, grabbed the fanny pack, the cell phone, the 9mm and a spare magazine, and strapped it on. He wouldn't need the Glock where he was going. It was good for getting through airport security, but that wasn't a problem at the moment.

Jasmine dumped all their clothes—clean and dirty—together in the middle of the sleeping bag, rolled it up and tied it, using granny knots. They might hold long enough to get them into the boat. Might not. He didn't have time now to worry about it.

Even as he checked out the battery and the outboard, he was conscious of every move she made. Long legs flashing, heels digging into the mud, she stomped back and forth, bristling with indignation and questions as she bundled up armloads of soft gear, dumping everything into the boat.

Why, he wondered fleetingly, had he never before noticed how graceful a long-legged woman could be? Maybe not all of them were. Maybe it was only the woman named Jasmine Clancy—a mahogany-haired, patchy-faced woman with a raspy voice, gentle hands and all the survival skills of a newly hatched chicken.

He watched her snatch up half a dozen cans of chili and Vienna sausage and hurl them into the boat on top of everything else. Hard, as if she was trying to hole the bottom. Moving fast, he grabbed the beer before she could throw that, too, and stowed it carefully under the stern thwart.

She was scared—he couldn't much blame her for that—and trying hard to pretend she wasn't. He wanted to take her in his arms and tell her everything was going to be all right, but there was no time.

Besides, he was in no position to offer any guarantees.

All the same, sooner or later he was going to have a big chunk of explaining to do. He was no good at explanations. Personal ones, at any rate.

On the other side of the clearing, Jasmine clamped her jaw shut so tightly it hurt. She refused to ask another question. Refused to look at him. Refused to allow him to frighten her, because that was obviously what he was trying to do. Some men got a large charge out of scaring women. She could have sworn Lyon wasn't one of them. But then, what did she know about men?

Not much. As for what had brought on all this frantic activity, she hadn't a clue. It had started when that plane had flown over, but then they'd both forgotten about the plane.

If he was worried about what had happened back there in the tent, she could have told him he didn't have to go to such lengths to make his point. She might not know much about men, but she wasn't stupid.

Damn Daniel Lyon, anyway. Did he think she was out to entrap him? She hadn't asked for any commitment, nor did she expect it. Just because she'd been stupid enough to hop into bed with a man she'd only just met— If she'd taken time to think first, she would never have done it.

And she wasn't going to think about it now. Maybe later, when she wasn't feeling quite so frightened and confused. And, of all things, sad.

She snatched the smoke-blackened cook pot off the fire

pit and hurled it into the boat on top of all the rest of his grubby old junk. The stuff looked as if it had been through the wars. The thing bounced, hit the side of the boat with a satisfying clunk, and fell overboard. Crossing her arms, she spread her feet and glared down at spreading ripples, savoring a sense of righteous indignation.

Indignation that faded almost instantly, leaving her even more tired and discouraged. Things were *not* going according to script. What had been intended as a combination family reunion and vacation, not to mention an excuse to avoid an awkward social obligation, was turning out to be one big, wretched mess.

Her mother used to tell her whenever she asked when her father was coming back, that they were better off without him. That Jasper Clancy had a rare talent for doing the wrong thing at the wrong time. The man couldn't even make a simple mistake without botching it.

Evidently, it was genetic.

"Ready? Climb aboard." The command was given softly, but there was no mistaking its dead seriousness.

"No, I'm not ready, I have to use the bathroom." She lifted her chin in defiance.

He uttered a word that was short and to the point. And then he said, "Well do it, but be damned quick about it, will you?"

Her chin lost its authority. It quivered. Her eyes filmed over. Where was the man who had made such sweet, urgent love to her less than an hour ago? Where was the man who had turned her world upside down with a single earth-shattering experience that registered about eight-point-five on her personal Richter scale?

He was standing right here before her, that's where

he was. Wearing nothing but boots and a pair of cargo pants, with a big ugly gun stuffed into his little black fanny pack and a Dirty Harry look on his face.

She took a judicious step back. "I think if it's all the same to you, I'll just…um, stay here?"

"Get in the boat, Jasmine."

"No, thanks." Her smile might not win her an Academy Award, but it was the best she could do under the circumstances.

The smile faded. She shivered. It was cold. It was February. She was trapped in a scene from *Deliverance* with an armed, half-naked madman. She felt like crying, but crying wasn't going to get her out of this mess, so she glared at him instead.

Lyon didn't have time to argue. Faced with two choices, he didn't know whether to leave her here and find some way to rescue her later, or pick her up, throw her into the boat and spend the next three weeks in traction. His back was better; it wasn't first class.

Suddenly, he tilted his head. His eyes narrowed on the spot where the creek disappeared around a brush-hung curve. "I'm afraid we just ran out of options."

He spoke calmly, as if making a casual observation about the weather. When she opened her mouth to question him he cut her off, deliberately using the kind of words he knew she hated. The kind she called the filth and venom words. Seeing her wince, he felt a momentary twinge of remorse, but it was too late for remorse. Or regrets. It was also too late for retreat. His only hope now was to scare her into following his orders without question.

"Get behind the bushes and stay there," he snapped.

"Don't say a word and whatever you do, don't come out until I give the all-clear, you got that?"

Judging by sound alone, the boat was in no great hurry. A lot of horsepower pushing a heavy load, approaching slowly, probably on the lookout for hidden snags. It would be on them before he could even get his own boat cranked up. Even if he managed to get underway, a trolling motor would be no match for that kind of power.

There was no way he could disguise the fact that he was armed. His jacket was balled up in the sleeping bag. He hadn't even taken time to put on a shirt.

He knew she was still there. Hell, he'd know if she was within five miles. Talk about instincts, she'd really done a job on his. "You still here? What are you looking at?" She stood rooted in place, her big dark eyes staring at him as if he'd suddenly sprouted horns. "Go!" He clapped his hands. She jumped, and then turned and loped away, back stiff, head high, elbows pumping indignantly.

At least, with those long legs of hers, she covered ground. By the time their guest rounded the thick stand of wax myrtle that hung over the bank, she was out of sight.

Assuming his best dumb-jerk attitude, Lyon flexed his shoulders a few times, then relaxed his stance and waited, his mind automatically registering data. The boat, about a twenty-two-footer, was built for hauling, not for speed. A workboat, she was square-ended, flat-bottomed and cheaply finished. Hardly a rich man's toy. At the moment, she was loaded with what appeared to be a bundle of twelve-foot poles, some sections of PVC and half a dozen concrete monuments.

Trojan horse, he thought while he waited for the man

at the controls to make his move. Nobody welcomed strangers too freely these days, not without checking them over pretty carefully.

The stranger cut the throttle and glided in toward the shore. The two men sized each other up. Lyon filed away more data. Mid-sixties, wearing camouflage, duck and denim, all pretty well-worn. Braves cap, new. Waterproof work boots. Touch of arthritis. A heavy drinker, either that or he was fighting allergies.

The workboat nosed up behind Lyon's rental and the gentleman tossed the painter ashore. Deftly, wordlessly, Lyon caught it and flipped it around the mooring stob he'd sunk into the bank. Unless the old guy was a lot smarter than he looked, he figured he could take him without firing a shot, if he had to.

Don't let me down now, back.

Trojan horse, he reminded himself again. He'd been fooled before. The last time he'd damned near bought the farm.

There were three rules in the game he was playing.

Keep your mouth shut.

Keep your options open.

And don't forget the damned rules.

"Some rain we had last night, huh?" the stranger said by way of greeting.

"Sure was. Real frog strangler."

Frog strangler? He hoped Jasmine was listening. He was beginning to get into the part.

"Figgered it was you I spotted down here."

A tingle of adrenaline raced through him, but his good-ol'-boy grin never wavered. "Hey, was that you up there in that airplane? I thought maybe it was a crop duster. I was getting ready to take cover. Heard you guys used some rough chemicals."

"Wrong time o' year. Won't even get the 'taters in for a month. Nah, I ain't no duster, I was just up there takin' pitchers. Best time o' year to see the lay o' the land. This warm winter we had, trees didn't even shed till near 'bout Christmas. Next thing you know, they'll be leafin' out again, then it'll be too late."

If he was playing a game, he was damn good. Lyon hitched up his britches, which were sagging on account of his knife and the spare magazine stashed in his back pocket. "Care to come ashore and have a beer? Afraid I can't offer you much of anything else."

"Moving out?"

"Yep. Thought I might." If he had a straw, he'd have poked it between his teeth. While he might not be up to Jasmine's standards, he was pretty damned good. He hoped she'd cooled down enough to appreciate his performance.

"Going up to the house?"

Silent alarms went off. "The house?"

"Old Lawless place. You're him, ain't ye?"

"Lawless? I understood he was dead."

The guy stepped ashore. He couldn't weigh more than a hundred pounds, from his brand-new Braves cap to his muddy waterproof boots. If he was armed, it didn't show. Which didn't mean a damned thing except that he was good.

"Maggie down at the tax office said you was askin'. You're the second one that's showed up in less than a week. Leastwise, the other feller didn't show up in person. Had his sec'etary call my office."

"Your office?"

"You said sumpin' about a beer?"

Where the devil was the beer?

In the boat.

Lyon sauntered over to the boat, conscious of the weight of the 9mm within easy reach of his right hand.

"That there thing good for snakes?" The old coot was staring at the pack that held his gun.

"Hope so. Haven't seen any so far." Lyon hooked three bottles between the fingers of his left hand just as Jasmine stepped out from behind the swag of vines.

The stranger whipped off his cap and grinned, revealing one gold tooth, five yellow ones and a few prominent vacancies. "Well, lardy, lardy, I didn't know ye brung yer woman wi' ye."

He pronounced it *woo-mern*. Lyon hoped Jasmine wasn't one of those PC conscious ladies who got all bent out of shape if a man used the wrong designation. He could do without any more complications.

"Jazzy, this is…I didn't catch your name?"

"Folks around here call me Catfish. Name's Wilburn, though. Wilburn W. Webster, at yer service, ma'am."

Wilburn W. Webster made himself right at home. He took the stump, leaving Lyon and Jasmine to find the driest spot available and hunker down.

Lyon's knee, while it hadn't so much as twinged in the last day or so, didn't take kindly to hunkering after its recent workout.

Remembering the workout, he cut a glance at Jasmine, taking in the way his flannel shirt hung from her shoulders, just grazing the tips of her breasts, and the way his best pair of jeans creased at her thighs when she spread her knees apart and crossed her ankles.

She was staring up at the old geezer with a look of open fascination.

Which was a decided improvement, Lyon thought wryly, over the way she'd looked at him only moments earlier.

"You're from around here, aren't you?" she asked, giving him the full force of her husky voice and her big, mahogany-colored eyes. "I'll bet you know lots of good stories."

"Well now…" Wilburn W. Webster pronounced it "Waal," and Lyon barely kept from snorting. The guy was spreading it on with a front-end loader. "I reckon I know 'bout as much as most folks, more 'n some. Man in my perfession, we know where folks buries their skeletons."

Jasmine hauled out the grimy little notepad she was seldom without, wet the tip of her pencil and gazed up expectantly.

"Now you take old man Lawless—"

"Lawless?" She jotted down the name.

The storyteller nodded toward Lyon, who waited for the bones to start rattling. He'd deliberately avoided mentioning his full name, figuring that what she didn't know couldn't hurt him.

"His old man, I reckon. Few generations back, though."

"Lyon's?"

"That yer name, son? That'd come from the Arkansas branch, I reckon."

"Arkansas branch? Is that one of the creeks around

here? Thank God they didn't name me after Two Buzzard Creek."

The old fellow slapped his knee and cackled. "Jest like yer great-grandpappy, ain't ye, son? Always pullin' a feller's leg. Squirrel, they called him. Name was Squire. Squire Lawless. Famous man in these parts."

Jasmine scribbled rapidly. Lyon opened another beer and handed it over. He checked the sun, glanced at his watch and thought, what the hell, I'm not going anywhere now.

Squirrel Lawless, it seemed, was a professional man. A maker of fine beverages. "They say he was the best shiner east of Wilkes County. Before my time. Before my pappy's time, near 'bout. They say he traded it for cows, pigs, horses, boats—whatever a feller had to trade. Squirrel weren't a greedy man, but he died rich, all the same. You see, back there in them days, they had 'em this here thing called pro-ee-bition. Best thing that ever happened to gentlemen in Squirrel's perfession. Got so successful he even branched out into the importin' business. Had boats running all the way up to Canada. That was cash money dealin's. Big money. Yessir, he was right famous, yer great-grandpaw. There was even talk a few years back o' putting up some kind of monument, but the church ladies didn't think it'd be fitting."

Jasmine couldn't believe her luck. She'd give anything to have a tape recorder. Wisps of steam rose from the wet earth. Her stomach growled audibly, reminding her that it was time for lunch and she'd never had breakfast.

She could eat later. Right now she was getting material she could easily stretch into a feature piece. Maybe even a short series, depending on the way it turned out.

"What happened to him, Mr. Webster?"

"Squirrel? Died o' the lead poison, they say. Some said it come from wrongfully soldered copper tubin'—others said it come from a revenuer's gun."

Wilburn W. Webster, who invited her to call him Catfish, graciously accepted another warm beer and continued his tale of Squirrel Lawless, Lyon's distant ancestor, who evidently fathered a slew of children, one of whom built a mansion right here in the middle of the swamp.

"That'd be Laurel Lee. She married Billy Lancaster. Folks come from over near Dead Mule Pond. Billy, he was a logger. Cleared more acres than a herd o' beaver before he give it up. Made him a bunch of money, what with one thing and another. Built Laurel Lee this fancy house right on the river. Only thing is, the ground weren't none too solid, and she started sinking before she was even finished."

"Laurel Lee?" Jasmine gasped, scribbling frantically.

"Naw, not Miss Laurel. The house."

"Oh, this is wonderful," Jasmine murmured, wetting her pencil stub and covering page after page with cryptic notes.

Openly peering over her shoulder, Lyon didn't think it was all that wonderful. This was his heritage they were talking about. And while he didn't need it and sure as hell hadn't asked for it, as long as he had one, he'd just as soon it involved something more respectable than moonshining and bootlegging. The guys over at BATF would have a field day if this ever got out.

"Getting late," he drawled, easing his cramped muscles by stretching first one leg and then the other. His butt was wet, his back was tired, and it was time he either fished or cut bait, as their guest would say.

Had said, in fact. "Yessirree, old Squirrel, he built hisself a real fine empire, like they say on the TV. Young'uns scattered down as far as Arkansas, clean up to New York, all the way out to Texas. Reckon you got more kinfolk, boy, than Carter's got little liver pills."

Jasmine blinked. "Who's Carter?"

Catfish was embarked on a description of the patent medicine mogul when Lyon cut him off. "How do you know all this?"

"Waal now, like I say, a man in my perfession—"

"Which is—?"

"Surveyin'. Yessir, been a legal, registered surveyor since the year '76. Maggie down at the tax office, she's my cousin. She give me a call when old man Squirrel's chickens started comin' home to roost."

If there was a plot to the rambling tale, Lyon had long since lost it. "You mean the law finally caught up with him? But that would've been—"

"Sixty, seventy years ago by my count. No sir, what I meant was, once the town o' Columbia started talkin' about declarin' a historical district all over the place, and all them wildlife and environmental folks started lettin' loose red wolves and findin' all kinds o' endangered plants and critters, lawyers started crawlin' outta the woodwork. They set in to track down ever' one o' old Squirrel's descendants. I reckon you got one o' them letters. Maggie says she give this lawyer feller a whole list o' names. Had the devil's own time trackin' 'em down. Spent so much time bent over fam'ly Bibles an' deed books, she had to go to the chiropractor."

Lyon could sympathize. With his crossed arms resting on his knees, he gazed up at a snake shed dangling from an osprey's nest in the branches of a bare cypress tree, his mind turning over the new data. A whole list of names? All his *kinfolk?*

A week ago he didn't have any family. He was used to being on his own. He liked it that way. No complications, nobody demanding answers and explanations. The last thing he needed at this particular point in his life was a flock of shirttail cousins digging into his past.

"I think that's just about the most wonderful thing I've ever heard," Jasmine said reverently.

He scowled at her, not liking the soft glow in her eyes.

Absently, he noticed that her rash was almost gone, except for one cheek being pinker than the other.

"Oh, this will make a marvelous story. I can't thank you enough, Mr.—Catfish. May I use your name? Oh, I'd give anything for a camera and a tape recorder!"

Lyon had had enough. He got to his feet without so much as a twinge, and dusted off his hands. "Getting late," he observed. "I guess if we're going to move downstream, we'd better get started."

Jasmine didn't budge. "Who are you working for?" she asked the grizzled old surveyor.

Lyon should have been the one to ask that question if anyone asked. If the guy wasn't on the level, he'd lie. If he was genuine, then Lyon didn't particularly want to know the answer. He wasn't in the market for family connections.

"Feller by the name o' H. L. Lawless from New York. Real big shot, accordin' to Maggie. She talked to the man he sent down half a dozen times."

"And you say Daniel's branch of the family, the Lyons, are from—?"

"Waal now, the Lyons, that'd be on your grandmama's side, wouldn't it, Lawless?"

Lyon looked at the old surveyor. He looked at Jasmine.

"Lawless?" she echoed.

"Right," he growled. "Look, do you want to go check out this dump, or don't you? If we're going to find it before the sun goes down, we'd better get moving."

"Waal now, why'nt you folks jest foller me? That's where I'm a-going. This New York cousin o' yours hired me to survey him out a section, centerin' on the house. Land's never been divided. Each one o' the original descendants inherited equal shares. Three, four generations down the line, I reckon it all depends on how many young'uns they all had. The New York gent was the first to speak up for the house, but that don't mean you can't challenge. That goes on all the time, especially when you got all them wildlife folks hornin' in on things. I know plenty o' folks's that's got land that's been tied up in court for years, not doin' nobody no good 'ceptin' fer the tax man."

Lyon took a deep breath while his mind raced over his options.

The old guy was genuine. He had to be. Nobody was that good. In which case, he could gamble and stay here, or…

"Okay, let's go check out this house of ours. New York can have it, but as it's the closest I'll ever come to an ancestral mansion, we may as well look it over."

Eight

Catfish left them at the eastward bend of the creek, after telling them that there was a drainage canal a quarter of a mile farther south that would lead them directly to the house.

"Billy had it cut back in the forties to get his logs out. State keeps it open for access. All kinds of environmentalists poking around in here these days." The old man accepted two more beers after offering to share his wife's packed lunch of cold collard greens, side meat and cornmeal dumplings. They declined. Although Jasmine was a little curious about the cornmeal dumplings.

With collard greens?

Mercy.

"I'll be headed back up the creek about dark. If ye think of anything ye need, I can collect it and bring it out tomorrow. I'm jest hauling material in today. Job'll take up'ards of a week, I reckon."

They both watched until he was out of sight. Jasmine sighed. "What an utterly fascinating man. I wonder what he was like as a young man. I wonder what his wife is like. I wonder—"

Lyon scowled and cranked up the outboard. "I wonder what the hell I'm even doing here," he muttered. He'd come close to forgetting the reason he'd signed himself out of the hospital and gone to earth.

Sam Madden was one of the few men he trusted, but not even Madden knew exactly where he was. Somewhere in North Carolina, that was all Lyon had told him. That left a hell of a lot of territory to search, if he hadn't been followed.

And it was just possible that he hadn't. That his suspicions were unfounded. That once he put together all the pieces he would discover that it had all been a fluke. A simple case of bad timing. That no one had turned. That no one was out to get him.

Occasionally, things got screwed up even in the most tightly run organizations. An innocent bystander turned up at the wrong time and the whole house of cards came tumbling down. It happened.

He'd like to think that was what had happened back at the warehouse, but all his instincts said they'd been deliberately set up. There was damned little in this life he trusted, but he trusted his instincts.

At least he had until this morning. Until that plane had flown over, and he'd tackled Jasmine and ended up taking her to bed at the worst possible time.

Not that there would ever be a good time. He wasn't

in the market for anything like that. Men in his line of work couldn't afford ties. Besides, if genetics counted for anything, he'd be a lousy bargain for any woman. She deserved better. She deserved a hell of a lot better.

Suddenly, she stood up and pointed. The boat rocked wildly. Lyon grabbed the sides. "I see it!" she screeched. "There it is, right through those trees!"

"Sit down, Jazzy, before you dump us both overboard."

"But there it is, right there!" A squad of winged insects caught their scent and homed in on them. It was a sign of how excited she was that she, who abhorred all insects, ignored them.

So much for his legacy. "Look, it's just an old house, nothing to get excited about." His voice was gruff, but not stern. He hoped she appreciated the difference.

"Oh, my, it looks like something out of a Faulkner novel, doesn't it?" she breathed reverently as he cut the motor and glided toward the overgrown bank.

This had been a mistake. In less than a single day, he'd used up a year's allotment of mistakes. However, as long as they were here… "Grab that bush and hold us while I see if I can find something to tie up to."

Five minutes later they stood shoulder to shoulder and stared up at what must have once been considered a mansion. There was just enough paint left to show that it had once been white. One of the four columns had fallen out into the yard and was buried under a mound of vines. There was a single pane of glass left in one of the windows. The rest appeared to have either fallen out or been shot out. Of the four chimneys, one was left standing. The roof, what was left of it, sloped gently to the southeast.

Actually, the whole house sloped to the southeast.

"Come on, let's explore." She was like a kid at an amusement park.

Lyon caught her hand. "Let's don't."

She looked at him as if he were missing an ear or something. "But it's your heritage. How can you not want to see every inch of it? There might even be family portraits."

"Yeah, and there might be a liveried butler waiting to open the door. Jazzy, the place is a mess. Even if you could get in, the floors would be rotten. It's probably overrun with rats and snakes. There's sure to be termites," he added hopefully. Animals she liked. Bugs were another matter. He wasn't sure how to classify snakes, but he figured he'd better cover all bases.

They'd be lucky if that was all they encountered. He'd seen enough evidence outside to know that it had probably been used by generations of hunters and trappers as a sort of home away from home.

In other words, the place was a garbage dump.

She looked so woebegone that he half relented. "Okay, let's walk around it and see what we can see through the windows."

Way to go, Lawless. Take the sucker away from the kid, but give her back the stick.

They picked their way through the bushes, dodging boggy places and briars—which didn't leave much foot room. A one-story section on the back had separated from the rest of the house. Either that or it had been built that way.

Jasmine sank down onto a fallen tree trunk, shoulders slumping. Lyon settled beside her, absently rubbing his knee. "This is a waste of time," he grumbled.

"No, it isn't. At least now you know where your folks lived. The longest I've ever lived anywhere, at least since I can remember, is fourteen months. It was an apartment. We had a window box. Mama tried to grow tomatoes there, but they turned yellow and died."

"We'd better head back." He was tired. He didn't need this. He didn't need her and her Hollywood notions of decaying southern mansions, either.

"Do you remember that scene in *Gone With the Wind* where—"

"No."

"But I didn't tell you which one."

"I don't watch movies."

She looked so stricken he nearly lied and said he did, but then she'd ask questions, and he couldn't remember the last movie he'd seen. Something about aliens. The extraterrestrial kind.

"All the same, can't you just picture this place with magnolia trees and live oaks, and maybe a peacock or two strolling around the grounds?"

He sighed. "Jasmine, how old are you?" She told him. She'd told him before. "Aren't you too old to play house?"

She just stared at him, another stricken look in her big, mahogany-colored eyes. "Too old to dream, you mean? I guess not."

"Damn," he said softly. Rising too quickly, he clutched his knee, but it was all right. So was his back. It was his brain that was falling apart, and he wasn't going to get it together again as long as she was around. "Come on, we're going back. When Catfish comes through tomorrow you can leave with him and go back to la-la land where you belong."

"What will you do?"

"Go back where I belong." Sooner or later.

"Where's that?"

He nearly shrugged, but caught himself in time. "Wherever I happen to be."

He didn't belong anywhere. He wasn't a settling man.

But she was definitely a settling woman, and the last thing he wanted her to do was settle on him. He was about as stable as a mansion built on the mud.

Untying the boat, he handed her in and turned for one last look, trying to visualize an old couple standing out on the front porch, their arms spread in welcome for the return of the prodigal son. Grandson. Great-grandson.

"Ah, hell, let's go." There was nothing for him here. Not that he'd been expecting anything.

By the time they reached camp, Catfish had already come and gone. There were three empty beer bottles lined up on the bank. Lyon collected them, along with their own trash, and dumped them into the hole he'd dug away from the camp. The water table was so high he had to fill the bottles with water before he could cover them with a shovelful of mud.

"Chili again?" Jasmine called from the makeshift pantry where he kept his canned goods.

"Your choice."

"Hmmmm. In that case, why don't we celebrate and have chili?"

"What are we celebrating?"

"I'll be leaving tomorrow. I guess you'll be glad to see me go."

If she was waiting for him to deny it, she would wait

until hell froze over. Sure he wanted her to go. He wanted her gone retroactively. He'd be a damned sight better off if he'd never laid eyes on her patchwork face and her big brown eyes, her long legs and wild hair and that smile that could cut through his armor faster than an acetylene torch.

They were still sipping coffee, bitter and black, when a gold and lavender dusk gave way to darkness. A few stars managed to shine through the mist that drifted up as night air chilled the sun-warmed waters of the swamp.

The air smelled of wood smoke and something faintly spicy. In the distance he could barely make out the lights of Columbia, the nearest small town, reflected on the night mist. Lights and distances played tricks out here in the trackless swamp.

Imagination did, too.

For instance, Lyon could imagine standing, stretching, reaching for her hand and leading her silently to the tent.

Where they would silently undress each other and then silently make love.

Or maybe not so silently.

All he knew was that there was nothing to say. Whether he took her to bed again or not, nothing either of them could say would change things between them.

She was the kind of woman who needed a husband, a home and children. She was a nester. In spite of the movie thing and the writing thing, it stuck out all over her. It was there in the way her face softened when she talked about her father and her grandmother, and the places they'd lived.

Hell, he even knew where she'd been living when

she'd had her first kiss. Some little town called Minco in Oklahoma.

"Getting late," he observed, his voice scratchy, even gruffer than usual.

It was barely nine o'clock.

She made a production of gathering up cans, spoons and the bowl. He handed her his cup. "Save 'em until morning."

"I might as well wash them now, I'm not really sleepy."

Neither was he. That was the trouble.

They watched the fire burn down to a few glowing coals. From the creek came the occasional splash. Something croaked. For the life of him, he couldn't say whether it was fish or fowl. Probably a frog.

She sighed. They still hadn't had the nightly argument over who would sleep where. Considering who had slept where last night—and what had happened— he didn't even want to think about it.

Which was probably why he couldn't seem to think of anything else.

"It's not going to rain. I'll sleep outside," he said.

"Don't."

"Don't what? Don't sleep?"

"Don't pretend. If you don't want to sleep with me again, just come right out and say so. I'll understand. I mean, my poison ivy and all—and I've been wearing the same clothes for three days, and they're not even mine."

He started to swear. Softly, virulently. "Dammit, do you think that makes any difference? Jasmine, grow up. You don't know anything about me. Look, you're a nice lady, but—"

"I *beg* your pardon."

"Huh? What'd I say?"

"A *nice lady?* Is that what you think I am?"

What the devil—?

"I'm a woman, Daniel Lyon Lawless. A fully grown, reasonably intelligent woman. I've been earning my own way for more than half my life, and making my own decisions, and—and—"

"And?" he prompted softly.

"I have a—a college degree."

He nearly burst out laughing at that. "So? That qualifies you to jump in the sack with any man who asks you?"

All injured dignity, she said, "If I'm not mistaken, you're the one who jumped into the sack with me. I was already there."

"I'm not talking about the first time, I'm talking about—"

"I know what you're talking about, and I don't want to talk about it. If you're worried that I might—"

He leaned forward, so close he could see her in the flickering coals reflected in her eyes. "I'm not worried about a damn thing, I just don't want you to get your hopes up. I'm not looking for any ties, and even if I were, I wouldn't look—"

"Hush. I don't want to hear any more."

Closing his eyes, he tilted his head back and wondered how he'd gotten so far off track. He'd come into the swamp with a simple mission. Sort through the details of the last job, figure out who knew what and when they knew it—and who had what to gain and what to lose by selling out.

Instead, he found himself mired up to his chin in in-

terpersonal relationships, and if there was one thing he
didn't need—one thing he had successfully managed to
avoid since he was fifteen years old—it was interper-
sonal relationships.

"You want to go to bed?" he demanded harshly. "Fine.
Take off your clothes. I've got nothing better to do."

Hearing the sharp intake of her breath, he hoped to
hell his ancestors weren't hovering overhead haunting
their damned swamp, listening in on his conversation.
And he'd been ashamed of his great-grandpappy, the
bootlegger?

The old man would've disowned him.

He'd been asleep long enough for the chill to creep
into his bones when something woke him. The cold?

Sleeping cold was nothing new. He'd survived far
worse conditions than this.

Quiet sobbing. Sniffles. It was coming from the tent,
and he stared up into the thick darkness and waited for her
to fall asleep again. He wasn't going to make another mistake. No way. The last few had damned near killed him.

"Jasmine?" he called out quietly after several minutes had passed.

Sniffle. Hiccup. "What?"

"You okay?"

"Of course I am."

"Sorry if I woke you. I just thought you might be cold."

"I'm not c-cold."

Of course she wasn't cold. She had the sleeping bag.
He had two sheets of plastic and a few scraps of canvas.

"Then how come you're crying?"

"I'm not crying."

"No?"

"No. I'm—I'm allergic."

Yeah. Sure she was. Just like he was allergic. Allergic to sleeping five feet away from a woman he'd made love to, and wanted to make love to again.

Not that it was love they'd made together. Sex. That's all it had been. Simple, no-strings-attached sex.

"Want company?" he called out softly, hopefully.

Silence. He wondered if she'd shrugged her shoulders. Picturing her lying there inside his sleeping bag—his warm, soft, waterproof, wide-enough-for-two-people sleeping bag, he thought, oh, what the hell.

Tossing off his meager cover, he rose and made his way over to the tent, leaned down and called her name. "You still awake?"

He heard a muffled sound. It was all the encouragement he needed. Going down on his hands and knees, he crawled inside, where the air was at least ten degrees warmer, and dark as pitch.

"I thought we might talk a little if you're having trouble sleeping."

Jeez, would you listen to him. Lawless, give up the spook trade. You've got the makings of a first-rate con man.

He fumbled with the zipper, and when it stuck, she reached out an arm and helped work it loose. "Just talking, though," she warned.

"That's what I said, isn't it? I mean, you're leaving tomorrow. I thought there might be a few questions you wanted to ask—stuff for your article. I picked up some information from the tax office, and there's a welcome center in Columbia where you could collect a few brochures. Maybe get a phone number to call if you run into a snag."

She exhaled with a shuddering little sigh. "That's a good idea. I think I have to go through there to get to the airport, I'm not sure. I left my map back at the motel. I know I had to drive for hours to get to the nursing home."

She edged away when he slipped in beside her, but there was no way they could keep from touching. Her foot brushed his. His hand came down on her hip. The warm scent of soap and sex and Jasmine swirled around him, clouding his senses. That and the memory of what they'd done the last time they'd shared this same space, was enough to set him off.

He'd promised himself no more sex. No more mistakes. Just a little quiet conversation, a little companionship. He'd read somewhere that men living alone reverted to a primitive state and had trouble rejoining society.

Not that he intended to rejoin anything any time soon. He'd never been very social.

"I hope nobody messed with my things. Do you think they're safe? I mean, Clemmie might think I'd run out without paying my bill."

"Nah, she wouldn't think that. You left your baggage there, didn't you? And your car?"

She nodded. Her hair brushed his chin. He was already so hard he ached. He got harder.

"I don't itch anymore," she confided.

He did, only he had an idea that wasn't the kind of itch she was talking about.

"It was Clemmie who gave me the calamine lotion. She's the one who told me about the old logging road. Do you think it could've been your ancestor who built it?"

"Billy?" He eased closer, turning onto his side so that he could curve his body around hers. "Who knows? Anyhow, I doubt if he was even mine. Maybe New York can claim him. I'm from the Arkansas branch of the family."

"You're all connected."

He knew what he wanted to be connected to, and it wasn't any long-dead logger, or a New York hotshot. He slid his arm around her waist and hauled her closer, fitting curve to curve, hill to valley. This hadn't been such a great idea.

"Go to sleep, Jasmine."

"I thought you wanted to talk."

"I think you know what I want to do, and it isn't talking."

More silence. He'd promised himself not to. That is, unless she wanted it, too. If she did—well, hell—he'd be a fool to deny himself. Two single, healthy, consenting adults. It wasn't like he'd made her any promises.

"Jaz?" he whispered.

"Mmmm…"

"Are you—comfortable?"

"Mmm-hmm."

"Is there…anything you want?"

He could almost see her smile. She had the kind of smile that could melt a glacier. He wasn't a glacier. Hard as one, but not as cold.

"Cold pizza and a peach milk shake," she murmured. He could tell by the sound of her voice she was smiling. He could almost picture it. Funny, how knowing a woman could sneak up on a man when he wasn't looking.

"Go to sleep," he growled, drawing her even closer.

You're a fool, man. No wonder you nearly got caught...your brain's shot. You're starting to think like a civilian, one of those nine-to-five, suit-and-tie, station-wagon types you always despised.

She was snoring softly long before he ever closed his eyes. His libidinous ninety percent finally subsided enough so that his rational ten percent came into play. He remembered thinking just before he fell asleep that maybe it was time he got out of the business. He'd definitely lost his edge. A man who'd lost his edge didn't last long, and for the first time in about a million years, Lyon wanted to last. Wanted to do something with his life besides cleaning up messes other people had made.

Nine

At first she thought it was a mosquito. Considering it was the dead of winter, there were a surprising number of the pesky little devils around. She hated bugs, always had, but there were some things in life she couldn't change. Life was buggy. You either accepted it and moved on, or you dissolved into a quivering mass of...whatever.

Lying there in a warm tangle of arms and legs with Lyon purring into her hair, Jasmine tried to make plans for her immediate future. Time to get back to the real world. If she left today, she could be home sometime tomorrow. She could start organizing her notes on the cross-country flight.

You will *not think about him. You do* not *love the man. You're in lust. It's a temporary, not a terminal, condition.*

Right. She would concentrate on her future. No more
stockroom work. No more cattle calls or walk-ons. No
more dreams splattered all over the floor like a carton
of busted eggs. She would write.

And this time she would make it as a writer because
this time she had something to write about. There was
her grandmother, for starters. Intergenerational relationships and the effect of broken families on the elderly.
Had it been done?

Probably. She would do it better.

*One-night stands, the dangers of. Enforced intimacy,
dangers of, etc., etc., etc.*

Shut up, Clancy.

Lyon rumbled in his sleep. It wasn't really a snore,
it was more like a purr. Like a big, slumberous jungle
cat. When his hand moved so that his fingers brushed
her nipple, instant heat pooled low in her body. Drums
throbbed along her veins.

Had he done it intentionally?

No, he was still sleeping. All the same, she reached
up, clasped his wrist and eased his hand back to her
shoulder. Concentration wasn't easy for a woman who'd
been referred to as "that flaky redhead" more times than
she cared to remember.

But all that was about to change. Getting into the
role, she pictured a computer screen and tried to read
the words written there. Something with Jasmine and
jungle. She liked alliteration.

Swamp. Not steamy tropical jungle, but dark, brooding swamp. Forget *Creature from the Black Lagoon*, think
Edgar Allan Poe. Think ravens quothing "nevermore."

How many people even knew such a place existed

only a few miles off an interstate highway, right in the middle of farmland and small towns and all sorts of wildlife refuges? For diversity there was even a bombing range not too many miles away.

What effect did living in such a place have on the native population? Talking to Catfish was almost like stepping back in history. Evidently, time moved at a slower pace in parts of the country where people stayed in one area for several generations. They spoke of things that had taken place more than a hundred years ago as if they'd happened only yesterday. Something to do with the storytelling tradition. She'd taken a course in the tradition of storytelling back in her junior year. Now she had actually experienced it in the raw.

Oh, this was so exciting. She had so much material, so much research to do, she could hardly wait to get started. She would have to buy a computer. She would have to—

Lyon rolled over onto his back, carrying her with him so that she was sprawled halfway across his body.

With her face tucked into the hollow of his shoulder, she drew in a deep, intoxicating breath, savoring the essence of healthy masculinity.

Where was she? Oh, yes—she would have to get herself a computer and—

He slept in his briefs. Which meant that everywhere she touched she felt skin.

Concentrate, Clancy! You have plans to make.

There was just one small flaw in her plans. A flaw that, at the moment, was quietly purring in her left ear. A tough, lonely, sexy, enigmatic, irritating flaw named Daniel Lyon Lawless. No mere matter of three thousand miles between them was going to cure what ailed her. After knowing the man for less than a week, she was more attracted, more intrigued, and definitely more aroused than she had ever been in her life.

Which was a problem, because a lion, no matter how you spelled it, was not a domestic animal.

She should have known better. At her age, considering where she lived and the people she associated with, she should have known far more than she did about men. She wasn't naive. No woman in this day and age could afford to be.

Stupid—now that was something else. She had seen in Eric only what she'd wanted to see, blindly ignoring his flaws. They'd met at a cast party. Eric had hovered around her, even though he'd come with a client. He had taken his "client" home, and Jasmine had thought that was the end of it.

She'd been eating her yogurt and wheat germ the next morning, mentally rewriting editorials, when he'd called to ask her out. She'd been flattered. Eric was handsome. He was successful. He worked for one of the most prestigious agencies in town, and besides all that, he'd just ended an affair with Karen Lakehurst, who'd once been married to Scott Walton, who'd been nominated for best supporting actor three years in a row.

Three dates later her imagination was soaring. She'd pictured them shopping for houses, nothing too large, but nice—maybe something near a school. She'd pictured herself wearing designer originals instead of thrift-shop specials, being a presenter if not a nominee.

Forget all that, Clancy. From now on, we're thinking in terms of Pulitzers, not Oscars.

She had invested nine years in earning a degree in journalism, which was a darned sight more than she'd invested in her acting career. It was time to stop pretending and start living.

Outside the tent, the day grew steadily noisier. Raucous birdcalls ricocheted off dew-wet trees. Insects, or whatever that high-pitched sound was, continued to buzz in the distance.

"Lyon? Lyon, wake up."

No answer. Not so much as a twitch. She didn't know if he was shamming or not, she only knew that if she was going to get serious about her future, it was time to stop spinning dreams out of thin air. Things like this didn't help. Things like the feel of Lyon's arms around her, his warm breath stirring her hair, his legs tangled with hers, and his…

Well. That, too.

At least they hadn't made love again. She didn't know whether to be sorry or relieved. She did know it was time to get out of here, before he realized that he was the one with all the control. That hers had melted like a snowman in August.

Go now, and don't look back. If there was a defining cliché in her life, that was it. She tried not to, but sometimes she forgot and did it anyway. This entire episode in her life had been a looking-back thing. She'd like to think she could look back one day without feeling as if something valuable had slipped through her fingers, but it would take a while. Like maybe forever.

Another cliché came to mind. Been there, done that.

"Lyon?" She knew very well he was awake by now.

His breathing was different. No faster, no slower, but more controlled.

She wondered what he was thinking. If he was thinking along the same lines she was, they were in trouble.

"Stay here for a minute, will you?" he murmured even as he lifted her arms from around his waist.

So much for a meeting of minds. "But I have to—"

"Stay here. Let me check something out first."

"Check out what?"

"Jasmine."

"All right, all right!" she whispered fiercely.

Rising to his knees, he peered through a slit in the tent flap. He grabbed a pair of jeans, tugged them up over his briefs, reached for his boots and slipped outside.

"Well...darn," she muttered.

The buzzing grew louder, like a swarm of angry bees. More irritated than frightened, she considered zipping herself inside the sleeping bag and staying there until the danger passed.

And then suddenly the buzzing ceased. A man's voice called out, "Lawless?"

It wasn't Catfish. It definitely wasn't bees.

Oh, God, Lyon was out there alone. She didn't know if he had his gun with him or not, didn't even know why he carried one in the first place.

What she did know was that Daniel Lyon Lawless was no ordinary businessman on a brief back-to-nature holiday. He was obviously on the run. Maybe hiding out. He might even be in the witness protection program.

And now they'd found him.

She had to do something, only what? She wasn't armed, wouldn't even know how to use a gun if she had one. For heaven's sake, she didn't even know how to use a fishing rod!

The old fake-gun-in-the-pocket routine. It would have to serve. She grabbed a pair of his cargo pants and the rope she'd used as a belt. Wearing only that and the long-sleeve undershirt she'd slept in, she eased the tent flaps open and peered outside.

Not a soul in sight. One cold, dead campfire, one sooty aluminum pot they'd recovered from the creek. Last night's dishes, washed and stacked on the metal box near the edge of the clearing.

She opened her mouth to call out, and then she heard them. Two male voices down by the creek, speaking quietly. Against a background of what passed for silence in the swamp, but was not really silent at all, Lyon's voice was distinctive for its gravelly sound. She couldn't make out what either man was saying.

If there was only one intruder, they were in luck. Lyon could take him, easy. With her as backup, they could take down Arnold Schwarzenegger, Chuck Norris and Don Johnson, easy.

"Jasmine, come out here."

Her jaw dropped. Her armed-and-dangerous finger faltered.

"Jazzy, come on out, your chauffeur's here."

Her chauffeur? Suspiciously, she peered around the corner of the tent. Her first thought, when her brain came back on line, was that if she lived to be a hundred, this scene would be indelibly etched on her memory.

Shafts of pale sunlight slanted down through the high branches, sparkling on every wet surface. Misty veils drifted just above the surface of the creek, moving as if propelled by an offstage fan. Rising from the early-morning mist stood two men, one a lanky, half-grown boy in a red shirt.

And Lyon. Lyon in his last clean pair of jeans, boots flapping at his ankles, a gun rammed in his waistband.

Lyon with his hair standing on end, with a chin full of stubble, with an expression on his face that defied interpretation.

"My chauffeur?" she repeated, gawking at the grinning boy standing at the wheel of a boat that was painted a garish, glittery shade of fuchsia.

"Meet Horton. Clemmie sent him."

The boy spoke up. "Clemmie from the motel? She's my aunt. She got worried when you didn't come back, and called the sheriff. Catfish was listening on his scanner, and he called Clemmie, and she called me. You ready to ride?"

Lyon waited a full ten minutes before making up his mind. He could still hear the whine of the outboard in the distance. The kid was doing about a knot and a half, probably afraid of scraping his fancy new boat on a hidden snag.

Taking time only to secure the camp and toss a few things into the boat, he set off upstream. Not trying to catch up, but being careful not to fall too far behind.

Why?

Hell, how did he know why? He didn't even want to think about why.

Because he was running short on supplies, that was why.

Because he'd stocked up for one man, for two weeks,

and then she'd come along. If it hadn't been for her, he'd have made out just fine. Part of his early training had included being dropped in an inaccessible mountainous part of Colorado with only his 'chute, a compass and a pocketknife. Eight days later he'd walked out, a lot thinner, a lot tougher, having learned that while ants were sour, mice weren't half bad once you got past the initial revulsion.

He followed the twisting creek, his mind working feverishly. This was twice he'd nearly been caught off guard. He'd let himself be distracted, and that was the one thing he couldn't afford. There were risks...and then there were unacceptable risks.

Jasmine Clancy came under the latter heading.

Eventually, the creek widened out to encompass a bay of sorts, complete with a rickety marina and a four-unit motel. He spotted the kid's boat tied up at the base of a finger pier and eased in behind it.

There were two vehicles parked outside the motel. One was a rust-eaten 4x4 with a local license, the other a rental. He headed for the rental parked outside unit number three.

The door was open. Shielded from view, he listened as two women carried on a raised-voice conversation. The shower was running, but evidently the bathroom door wasn't shut all the way, either.

"I got a dryer. I'll have these things done up inside an hour. Want me to bring you something to eat?"

"Sure! Anything. And Clemmie—thanks."

She didn't have to sound so damned pleased to be rescued. He'd have brought her back. In a day or so. All she'd had to do was ask.

The woman called Clemmie stepped outside, lifted her eyebrows in his direction and asked, "Was you looking for me? I'll be in the office directly, just let me stick these things in the washer."

Jasmine took her time under the shower. She didn't want to think about how long it had been since she'd had a real bath. Washing in lukewarm creek water in a two-quart cook pot didn't quite do the job.

She dumped another handful of Clemmie's shampoo into the palm of her hand and applied it, working up a wonderful, coconut-scented lather. The motel didn't run to toiletries, but Clemmie didn't mind sharing. She'd said it was so rare to have a woman stay there, it was almost like having company.

Which was sweet, Jasmine thought. All the people she'd met since she'd come east were really nice. She would try to include them all in her article, which was already taking on epic proportions in her mind.

She would play the starring role, of course, with Lyon the male lead, but Clemmie and Catfish, and maybe Clemmie's nephew, Horton, would definitely be the supporting cast.

Oh, shoot. She was doing it again. Treating life as if it were a film script. As if Jasmine Clancy was no more than a fictional heroine, part adventuress, part saint. She'd been doing it for so long it was second nature. First Cinderella and Snow White, and then Nancy Drew. Somewhere along the line she had eased into a make-believe life that had taken the place of reality.

The reality of having a single parent who was almost never home because it took two jobs to support them.

The reality of always being the new girl at school, of exploring tentative new friendships only to have them cut short when they moved again. The reality of losing a mother to cancer and rediscovering a father, only to lose him, too—and finding a grandmother who didn't even remember her own son, much less the granddaughter she'd never known.

"Jasmine Clancy, you're a blooming basket case," she told the blur in the steamy mirror.

Wrapping the towel around her, she shoved open the door, yelped and clutched the ends of the skimpy towel together. "What are you doing here? You're supposed to be back in the jungle."

"Swamp. I came in for supplies."

"Here? I don't even know if there's any place to buy supplies around here, you'll have to ask Clemmie."

"I left my truck in town. How about hitching a ride with you?"

She rolled her eyes. "Here we go again. If I drive you back to Columbia, or wherever you left your truck, what are you going to do with your boat? Leave it here? How're you going to get back to your camp?"

Instead of answering, he leaned his shoulders against the wall, crossed one booted ankle over the other and regarded her steadily from those startling blue eyes that looked so out of place in a face carved from eroded granite. He'd combed his hair. He hadn't shaved. He didn't look like anybody's hero, yet she was as certain as she'd ever been of anything in her life that he was hers.

Or rather, that he could have been hers if things had been different. "You know, Lyon, you never did tell me anything about who you are, what line of work you're

in and why you're living out in the swamp." Her tone
was commendably casual. Conversational.

"Sure I did. Digging up roots, remember?"

"You didn't tell me that, Catfish did. Remember?"
she added, openly mocking him.

He shrugged without even wincing, and she wondered how long since his back had bothered him. He
hadn't been fooling that first day, but after that...

"You know my full name."

"No thanks to you," she reminded him.

"I don't have any permanent address. As for what I
do for a living, I'm currently between jobs."

"I don't believe you."

He cocked an eyebrow. "Your prerogative. I don't lie."

She didn't argue. What good would it do? All men
lied. Her father had. Eric had. Either with words or ac-
tions, or by omission, they all lied.

Lyon probably did all three. He even lied about lying.
Worse, he didn't care if she knew it.

"All right, I'll drive you to wherever you left your truck,
but I'm not bringing you back here to get your boat."

As if he were reasoning with a child, he said, "Once I
have my truck, I can get back here under my own power."

It was the last straw. Since she'd first opened her
eyes this morning, snug in Lyon's arms, to hear that irritating, high-pitched swarming-bee sound, things had
moved so fast she hadn't had time to think.

Well, now she did, and suddenly it was all too much.
Why was it that when she tried her very best not to
screw up, she did it anyway? Even when she thought
things through first, she handled everything all wrong.
Everything. Her entire life!

What had made her think she could change now?

Glaring at him, she felt her eyes slowly fill and spill over. She snorted and wiped a wet cheek with the corner of the towel. The same moment she felt the draft on her damp body, she heard the sound of a door clicking shut.

Actually, it was more the sound of wood scraping against a sandy floor and the protest of rusty hinges, but the finality of it did her in. With all the grace of a tired and hungry two-year-old, she began to wail.

Two strides and she was in his arms. She'd been so sure he had left.

He held her, settling into the room's only chair and pulling her down onto his lap. Whoever thought sitting in a man's lap was romantic hadn't tried it with a woman who was almost as tall as the man. Her head was higher than his. She needed a chest to hide her face in while she cried her heart out.

Instead, tears dribbled off her chin onto his hair. He patted her awkwardly on the back, which was naked on account of the towel coming undone.

"There now, there now," he rumbled, and she wondered, choking back a bubble of laughter, if he'd ever said those two words in that same tone of voice before she'd blundered into his life.

"It's all right," she said, comforting the man who was trying to comfort her. "I've made a mess of your shirt."

"No problem, I'll send it out."

"I could ask Clemmie to throw it in with mine." She managed a watery chuckle. He eased her off his lap and somehow, they were both on the bed, with her hands still holding the towel in front of her. She shivered as a cold draft struck her naked backside. When they film the story of my life, she vowed silently, I'm going to be wearing a chiffon negligee in this scene instead of a rust-stained motel towel. And it'll be a four-star hotel instead of a four-unit motel.

"I really did come in for supplies," he said.

"I know."

His face was so close her eyes nearly crossed trying to focus, so she closed them. That business about out of sight, out of mind was a crock.

Lyon's hand smoothed the towel over her hip. "Goose bumps."

"It's cold."

"It's February."

They were talking all around the subject on both their minds. Jasmine reached back and drew a corner of the bedspread over them both. "Nearly March. That's almost spring."

"You asked what I did. I work for the federal government."

"As what? Postman? Tax collector?"

"Sort of an all-around troubleshooter, I guess."

"You were out there in the swamp shooting trouble?"

"Look, there's no need for you to know all the sordid details of my life, Jasmine." His hand was moving slowly over her back, sliding the bedspread over her naked skin, moving down over her hips.

No need. In other words, butt out. "I know that," she said sadly. "Thanks for humoring me."

His hand fisted. She could feel his muscles tense, and she wanted to warn him not to forget his back, but then he said, "Dammit, Jazzy, I'm not trying to humor you. I'm trying to explain why there's no future in this—this—"

"Right. You don't have to explain, I understand."

Lyon groaned. His arms tightened around her as if he would like nothing better than to shake her.

What he wanted to do was to make love to her until he couldn't move, and then he wanted to lie here and watch her talk, watch the expressions come and go on her face, listen to that soft, husky voice while she told him about the stray dog she had wanted to keep but hadn't asked for because they couldn't afford to feed it, and all the goldfish that had died and been buried with full honors. About books she had read and dreams she had dreamed, and all the other ordinary, day-to-day details of her life.

He wanted to make it all a part of his life, retroactively. He wanted to share her past, which seemed so full in spite of certain obvious lacks.

They'd both been products of broken families, subject to more than a few of life's sharp edges. He wanted to know why she'd turned out the way she had—warm and impulsive, generous and open. Full of dreams, as opposed to the way he'd turned out. Bitter, suspicious, a man who chose a line of work that only reinforced what he already knew about life: that it held damned few rewards outside the satisfaction of doing a job well.

And right now, he didn't even have that satisfaction.

"Honey, we'd better move out."

"Honey?" she murmured. She was too close, too warm, and entirely too accessible.

"Figure of speech. When in Rome…"

Her hands were playing games with the hair on his

chest. He could have sworn his shirt was buttoned up when he'd come in here. Maybe he should've kept his leather jacket on instead of leaving it in the boat.

"Jazzy, you're asking for trouble," he warned.

"I know. Usually I'm pretty sensible, but not always."

He caught her hand at the equator as it began to explore his southern hemisphere. At the moment, his south pole was extremely vulnerable. "You want to get dressed and head for town?"

"Not particularly. Do you?"

He swallowed hard. Why lie, when the proof was right there between them? "Not particularly."

The scent of arousal was thick and intoxicating. Lyon thought briefly that what he was about to do wasn't fair, not to either one of them. What he saw in her eyes, what he heard in her voice, told him she was already emotionally involved, and he couldn't afford emotional involvements. Especially not now, when his whole career, if not his life, was on the line.

"Jazzy, are you sure you want to do this?" he rasped.

Her face lit up like a Christmas tree. "Yes. Oh, yes."

If she'd said no, he would've backed off. It wouldn't have been easy, but it probably wouldn't have killed him outright.

But she'd said yes, and suddenly he was paralyzed by a rush of unfamiliar feeling. Part tenderness, part protectiveness, part something that defied description, it was unlike anything he had ever experienced.

Luckily, it was swept away almost immediately by a feeling that was even more powerful. Trembling with conflicting needs—the throbbing need to be inside her, the aching need to make it last—he kissed her, taking his time about it. Savoring her textures, her flavors, the scent that was uniquely Jasmine.

Eventually, he lifted his head to stare down into eyes dark with passion, lips that were swollen with desire. Dimly aware of a feeling of masculine triumph in its most basic form, he kissed her again. Long and hungrily. Wondering in a brief burst of reason why he had never before considered kissing as a part of making love.

Because he'd never made love before. Sex was different.

This was different.

Great. Now that it was too late, he finally recognized the difference between having sex and making love.

Ten

Lyon's olfactory sense, like all his senses, was acute and well trained. She smelled of soap, toothpaste, coconuts and Jasmine. A hell of a combination. The last time he'd made love to her she'd smelled of insect repellent, coffee, wood smoke and Jasmine. Regardless of the blend, she was lethal.

He'd never had any trouble defending himself against feminine wiles. As for perfume, which was supposed to be some sort of aphrodisiac, he was immune to it. From the dollar-a-pint stuff to the pricey French kind. It came as something of a surprise to discover that he was vulnerable to a woman who wore no scent, no makeup, unless you considered calamine lotion a cosmetic; a woman who didn't possess a single wile and probably wouldn't know how to use one if she had it.

He wondered fleetingly if Clemmie kept a supply of

condoms on hand. Once without was a gamble. Twice was asking for trouble. Jasmine wasn't the kind of woman who needed trouble of that sort, especially with a man who wasn't cut out to be a husband, much less a father.

Lyon prided himself that since the age of fifteen, when he'd faced homelessness, joblessness, and the usual battle with raging hormones, he'd done a pretty good job of staying on track. It hadn't always been easy, but he'd managed.

This time he'd been blindsided. Hadn't even had time to duck. If he had a preference in women it was for small, busty, flashy-dressing blondes who weren't looking for intellectual stimulation.

And then along came Jasmine Clancy with all her stealth weapons. Legs up to her shoulders. A face full of poison ivy. Maroon corkscrew curls. An artless way of asking questions that could pry answers from the sphinx.

As for her figure…

To put it diplomatically, she was built for speed, not endurance. No curves to speak of, other than a tush that made a man want to fit his hand over it. Something that could get him slapped, if not slapped with a lawsuit.

The woman was a walking, talking conundrum. She didn't wear a bra. Didn't need one. So how come he couldn't keep his eyes off the front of her shirt, watching to see if her nipples would peak under his gaze?

His hand slipped between them and he brushed his palm over her small breast. "I want to see you," he whispered. "The trouble is, I don't want to stop holding you long enough to look."

She stared at him mutely. The scent of arousal, escalated by body heat, mingled with the fragrance of coconut, soap and wood smoke.

Lyon groaned. And then he kissed her again while he teased the turgid peak between thumb and fingers. She gasped, shuddered, and started tugging at his shirt. Lifting first one shoulder, then the other, he shrugged out of it.

Her hands moved to his buckle and he sucked in his breath. Between them, they managed to get him out of his jeans and his briefs. He'd already shed his boots and socks. Thank God he wasn't wearing his gun. He'd have felt pretty damned foolish wearing nothing but a vacant grin and a fanny pack.

Her palms slid down his sweat-filmed torso, lingering on his own nail-hard nipples, tracing a scar on his rib cage, circling his navel and…

The last vestige of his rational ten percent shut down, and the remaining ninety percent took over, ending all possible hope of salvation. Without lifting his mouth from hers, he rearranged her so that she lay on top of him, and then had to shift again to accommodate his…

Enthusiasm.

"Oh, my," she gasped, lifting her head to stare down at him. A hectic pink flush spread over her throat and her face, adding a lambent glow to her dark eyes.

Arching his back, he captured her mouth again, engaging her tongue in a rhythmic duel that sent reciprocal fireworks streaking through his body. He cupped her buttocks, squeezed, shaped, and then slid a finger down to curl between her thighs. She was hot and damp and ready. When he touched her in a certain way, her sharp gasp and low, throaty moan nearly sent him over the edge.

"Sweetheart, I still don't have protection. It's not too late—"

"I don't care."

"There are other ways—"

"Please. Make it happen," she begged.

He made it happen. And then, he made it happen again. He'd never known a woman to climax so sweetly, so explosively. If he hadn't known better, he might have thought she'd never before experienced an orgasm from the wondering way she looked at him.

Lifting her to sit astride him, Lyon positioned her over his rigid shaft and lowered her slowly, bracing himself to endure the exquisite torture. Determined not to miss a single nuance of expression, he watched her eyes widen again. He watched her lips part, her head fall back. In the end, he had to shut his eyes. It was too much. Sensory overload. He felt her tighten around him and pulled her down until he could reach her nipple with his tongue.

She quivered. He thrust once, twice, holding her in place with both hands, and then they both went wild. Rolling over in a tangle of limbs and bedclothes, he rode her fiercely. Dimly, he was aware of something knocking—someone calling her name. And then everything came together in a soaring, blazing, pulsating climax that engulfed them both.

Eventually—a year, maybe a decade or so later—they collapsed, wet, panting and throbbing. He could have sworn there wasn't a bone in his body.

Jasmine came reluctantly to her senses. *We can wait.*

Had one of them actually spoken those words, or had she only imagined it?

Of course they couldn't have waited. This had been the last time. Whatever was between them ended here, ended now, and they both knew it.

Her face crumbled, but she didn't cry. Instead, she allowed the ache of loss to flow through her, the pain of it mingling with the tide of slowly receding rapture. Maybe in time she would forget the pain and remember only the pleasure.

Then again, maybe not.

Jasmine stepped back under the shower. Lyon was sprawled out across the bed, asleep. At least she thought he was asleep. If any man deserved his rest, he did, but with Lyon, she could never be sure. He was unlike any other man she'd ever known.

Unlike any man she would ever know in the future. Getting over him was going to be a long, painful process. She wasn't sure she could.

Wasn't even certain she wanted to. An aching heart was better than an empty one, wasn't it?

"Your turn," she said a few minutes later, fully dressed, but feeling defensive.

Without moving, he opened his incredible periwinkle blue eyes and gazed up at the ceiling. "If I'd known I'd have a shot at a shower I'd have brought along a change of clothes."

"I borrowed your clothes. If you'd like to borrow something of mine, you're welcome."

"Yeah, sure." He looked at her then, and smiled. Not a grin, but a genuine smile, one that kindled in his eyes, deepening the crow's-feet and those trenches that bracketed his mouth, that weren't really laugh lines because he never really laughed, but were irresistible, all the same.

"I'm going to call the airline and see if I can get a seat on a plane out, and then I'll see if Clemmie has my clothes dry. We can leave after that if you're ready."

"I need to make a couple of calls, myself."

"You want to go first?"

"No, thanks, I'll use mine." Land lines were easier to trace. Lyon was pretty sure he'd be long gone before anyone could track him down, but it didn't pay to take chances.

And you're not a guy who takes chances, right?

Go to hell, Lawless.

Swinging off the bed, totally at ease with his nudity, he retrieved his cell phone from the fanny pack he'd brought inside and tossed onto the dresser. He gave her a pointed look, and she edged toward the door.

"Um, maybe I'll check on my clothes first."

He nodded, already punching in a number. Madden had set up a series of relays that should be safe. He was on the point of collecting any messages when he heard the sound of clattering crockery, heard her swear.

"What?" He was at the door in a split second, his gun half drawn.

"Food. Clemmie brought a tray and left it outside the door, and I nearly stepped in it."

He frowned down at the rusty, flower-painted tray containing a thick white bowl covered with a plate, a matching cup covered with a saucer, an assortment of stainless-steel cutlery and something wrapped in a napkin that had already attracted a trail of ants.

Jasmine said slowly, "I wonder why she left it out here."

Lyon's silence spoke for him. Her gaze lifted slowly, taking in everything there was to take in. He could tell exactly when realization set in. A fiery blush stained her cheeks. "Oh my," she murmured, and then hurried away.

Lyon lifted the tray, flicked off the ants and took it inside. While he punched in a set of numbers, he unwrapped a chunk of buttered corn bread and bit in. He was starved. Still naked, needing that shower, needing even more to find out if he was still a target, and if not, why not.

At least one of his appetites had been satisfied. For the moment, at least.

It had turned cold just since morning. What had happened to the early spring weather they'd had for the past few days? Jasmine wasn't used to all these changes; she'd lived in California too long.

Clemmie didn't beat around the bush. "Is he going to be staying long?"

"No, I—that is, we'll both be leaving in an hour or so. If I need to pay extra, I can do it."

"No need. I'd have brought two trays if I'd known you had comp'ny." She gave Jasmine a piercing look. Seemingly satisfied, she went back to folding clothes. Evidently, the office served as the laundry room, too.

Jasmine sorted through the stack for her own things, then said, "If you could do my bill, I'd appreciate it. I need to call the airport in Greenville, but I've got a phone card. Don't forget to add on the cost of my laundry and the food—oh, and the calamine lotion."

"No charge for that. Face healed up real fast, didn't it? You're lucky. Some folks gets scars."

Two men came in just as Jasmine was leaving. Hunters, from the looks of them. She'd noticed them down by the pier on her way to the office, evidently admiring Horton's flashy fuchsia boat.

Lyon was in the shower. The bathroom door was open about six inches, which was as far as it would shut. His clothes were spread neatly on the chair, but his fanny pack was missing. Did the man actually wear his gun in the bathroom?

"You used all the hot water," he accused.

"Sorry. How'd you know it was me?"

"How many people use your bathroom?"

She hadn't meant that. She'd meant, how did he know Clemmie hadn't come back to collect the dishes.

But then she noticed that the medicine cabinet door was open so that the mirror reflected the door of the unit. He could see anyone who came in. A feeling of unease came over her. What did she really know about him?

Nothing.

How could she possibly be in love with a man she didn't even know?

Her brain told her she couldn't. Her heart told another story. It whispered of all the things she'd sensed underneath his gruff exterior. The loneliness, the basic integrity, the offbeat sense of humor that she'd glimpsed now and then when he'd dropped his guard. The feeling that he was searching for something just as she was, and that together, they might find it.

Oh, for goodness' sake, Clancy, when are you going to pack your bags and move back to the real world?

* * *

They headed north from the motel. He let her drive. That implied trust, didn't it? She could still remember hearing her mother complain because her father refused to allow a woman to drive him anywhere, even when he'd been drinking, which was most of the time.

"It's the long way around for you," he told her. "You could've headed south, picked up 264 and probably make better time."

"I told you I'd take you to wherever you left your truck."

"Thanks."

They might as well have been two strangers instead of a man and a woman who had been trapped together in the wilderness for days, who had slept together and made love together and talked about hopes and dreams and early childhood memories.

At least she'd talked and he'd listened.

So much for getting back to the real world. Given a choice, she'd rather go back to playing Tarzan and Jane in the Great Goopy, Buggy, Southeastern Dreary Swamp. Or whatever the place was called. On some maps it wasn't called anything. On others it was.

"The airport said if I could make it by three, I could catch a flight out today with only four stops and three changes between here and LAX."

He grunted.

"I don't know what happened to the weather. I guess it's a good thing the cold front waited to come through until I got back to my clothes." She was wearing a pair of jeans and a yellow cable-knit sweater.

This time, he didn't even bother to grunt.

He did point out the visitors' center and remind her of the material she could pick up on her way out of town. "Hang a right here," he instructed.

Her stomach growled. He glanced at her then. "Hungry?"

"Why no, I had half a can of chili just yesterday."

"I think we'll pass a place not far from here. Pull in. We'll grab a burger."

She was tempted to keep on going, but it probably wouldn't bother him at all, so she watched for something that looked as if it might be open and pulled into the unpaved parking area.

The place was deserted. There were four tables, three booths and a counter. The specials of the day were written on a mirror that looked as if it could have come from a Wild West saloon. She was trying to decide between the bean soup and the barbecue plate when the door opened behind them and two men entered.

The same two hunters she'd seen back at the motel.

Lyon didn't move a muscle, but she knew he saw them. By now he probably knew what brand of underwear they were wearing. Little escaped those periwinkle blue eyes of his.

"Barbe—" she started to say when he cut her off.

"Couple of coffees and a bag of chips to go."

She glared at him, hunters forgotten. "Why did you even bother if you weren't—"

"We don't want to miss our plane do we, honey?"

Something in his manner kept her from arguing. All the same, she didn't much like it and refused to pretend she did. The bearded proprietor slid two foam cups across the counter. Furious, Jasmine grabbed both. He

tossed a handful of creamers, sugars, napkins and stir-
rers along with the chips into a bag and swept up the
bills Lyon laid on the scarred surface.

Without waiting for change, Lyon took the bag and
ushered her out the door, not even glancing at the two
men in the third booth on the end. The door had no
sooner shut behind them than she turned on him.
"Would you mind telling me what that was all about?"

The grip on her elbow tightened so that, if the cups
hadn't been covered, she would have sloshed scalding
coffee all over her hand. She opened her mouth again,
took one look at his grim face and shut it.

This time he drove. Not a word was spoken, but she
could sense that something had changed drastically.
And that something didn't concern her, except that she
was here, involved up to her neck through no fault of
her own in whatever game he was playing.

There was little traffic. It was easy to spot the navy
blue sports utility vehicle when it pulled out of the parking lot behind them. They'd been headed east before.
Now they were heading west.

"I thought we were going to get your truck."

"Change of plans."

"Would you mind telling me what's going on? It had
something to do with those two hunters, didn't it?"

He was silent for a long time. She waited, fear bat-
tling anger as she noticed the way his gaze kept moving between the road ahead and the rearview mirror.

"You seen many hunters wearing a gold earring?"

"What?"

"Seen many hunters wearing a watch that costs at
least two grand?"

"How do you know all that?"

He shot her a look that told her to wise up.

Her eyes widened. She drew in a breath that caught in her throat, and he reached out and touched her thigh in a gesture that was meant to be reassuring.

At least she thought it was. Right now, she didn't know what to think. For all she knew, she was being kidnapped.

No, she wasn't. Whatever else she didn't know about the man, she did know he'd never hurt her. Not intentionally. "They're not really hunters, are they?" she whispered.

"You got it."

"Then why were they dressed that way?"

"Protective coloration. Hunters don't exactly stand out around here, in case you hadn't noticed. This is big hunting country."

"That pair did? Stand out, I mean?"

He shrugged. She figured it out for herself. She was learning. "Their clothes were too new, right? And like you said, the jewelry. Who'd risk losing an expensive dress watch when you can buy something cheap and expendable for practically nothing?"

"Good going."

"Was that all? Was there something else that made you notice them?"

This time he took so long to answer that she felt like screaming. He might look relaxed, but he was doing almost eighty. There was no sign of white knuckles, but the grim set of his mouth didn't bode well for anyone who dared tangle with him.

"Maybe the fact that they checked out our license before they came in. Maybe the fact that they were watching us in the mirror. Maybe the fact that they just happened to turn up at the motel, and then they showed up in town. Maybe the fact that they're staying a steady quarter of a mile behind, not trying to catch up, but not dropping out of sight."

It never even occurred to her to take notes. There was a quality of unreality about this whole episode. The sun was shining. There were brash yellow flowers blooming here and there. A man was burning stumps at the edge of a newly harrowed field. Everything looked so normal.

Indiana Jones, eat your heart out.

Traffic picked up near Plymouth. Lyon reduced his speed to seven miles over the legal limit. He passed two fast-food places, pulled into a third and ordered two burgers, two coffees and two orders of fries at the drive-through window. "You need to go inside?"

She shook her head. "What about—you know?" She jerked her head toward the rear window, keeping her voice pitched just above a whisper.

"They stopped at the drive-in we just passed. They'll catch up."

"Oh, my Lord," she whispered. "What will you do? Can't we find a police station somewhere? Can't you call somebody?"

He unfolded the road map, scanned it briefly, refolded it with mathematical precision and then pulled up to the window where he paid for their food. All without answering a single question.

"Eat. Unwrap mine and hand it to me once we get out of town, okay? Salt on my fries, but don't open my coffee yet, I don't want to get scalded."

He glanced at her then, and added, "Please?"

Not until they were out of town, passing miles of farmland, a few tiny roadside communities and some logging traffic did he speak again. The sports-utility was still following, maintaining the same relative position.

"I'm going to take you to the airport and put you on the plane. I'll give you a number to call when you get home. I won't be on the other end, but leave a message, will you? I need to know that you're home safe."

Eleven

Not until she was in the air did Jasmine allow herself to think about those last few hectic minutes. It was a small airport. There weren't many passengers waiting for the feeder airline. While she'd stood at the counter and showed her photo ID, assuring the ticket agent that no one had meddled with her luggage, Lyon had taken care of matters with the rental agency.

She'd probably looked like a fugitive on the run, the way she kept glancing over her shoulder, wondering about the two men who'd been following them. Wondering if they were waiting outside. Wondering what Lyon intended to do, and if he'd even thought about how he was going to get back to Columbia, or wherever it was he'd left his truck.

She'd grabbed her stamped ticket, raced across to the plate-glass windows that overlooked the parking lot, and there they were, leaning against the hood of the dusty navy blue vehicle.

By the time Lyon had appeared at her side, she'd been frantic. He'd handed her a folded receipt and steered her away from the window. "What's your gate number?"

"Gate number? Lyon, listen, they're outside waiting for us. You've got to get help! You've got to—"

"Shh, easy now. I want you to listen to me."

A voice over the loudspeaker announced the last call for her flight. "But I can't go off and leave you like this!"

"Jazzy, listen to me. You're going to get on that plane. You're going to go home, and the first thing you're going to do when you get there is call that number I gave you and leave a message telling me you've arrived. Right?" He waited for her to nod, and under the compulsion of his steady regard, she did. Gulped and nodded.

"Right. And then, in a week or so, or however long it takes to be sure that—ah—that—nothing happened. I mean, that—"

"That I'm not pregnant."

"That we're not pregnant," he said, correcting her, his eyes never once faltering. "You're to give me another call. Promise?"

"Will you be there?"

He hesitated just long enough for her to know the answer.

"Last boarding call for Flight 1332 to Atlanta," had come the tinny voice over the speaker.

Jasmine had felt the tip of her nose turn red. Her eyes had begun to burn. Lifting her chin, she'd said, "If I were you, I'd grab a security guard and—"

"Yeah, sure. Listen, honey, you've got to go or you'll miss your flight. I'll be okay. I know what these guys are after, and it'll be just fine, believe me."

The image of his face had blurred. He'd grabbed her by the shoulders, kissed her hard and then turned her around and pushed her away. By the time she'd looked back he was gone.

On Monday morning, Jasmine was back at work tagging inventory in the stockroom at Marcelle's. At ten o'clock she took a break and called her agent, who was away from her desk. She left a message saying that she was back in town and available.

Not that she expected anything to turn up. She'd finally faced the fact that the odds against making it in the acting world were astronomical. It was time to grow up.

She borrowed a portable typewriter because she couldn't possibly afford to buy a computer yet, not even a secondhand one. She told herself it was excellent discipline. Using a typewriter instead of a computer would force her to think ahead.

In one respect, at least, she'd already thought ahead. She would do the swamp piece on spec, shooting for the high-end market. Once she sold that, it would be easier to sell the relationship piece on proposal. By the time her baby was born, she should be launched on her new career. She could move into a cheaper place, maybe fill in by writing ad copy for one of the small weeklies, and eventually, if she was lucky, get into something syndicated.

But then, one of her dreams had died. She wasn't pregnant. Which was certainly good news, because she could hardly support herself, much less a baby.

All the same, she was so disappointed she cried.

She waited three days before calling the number Lyon had given her. After waiting through a series of mysterious hums and clicks, she reached his answering service and left her message. "This is Jasmine. You can stop worrying."

It was with a vast sense of accomplishment one Sunday morning in early April that she put a new ribbon in her borrowed portable typewriter, rolled in a sheet of her best twenty-pound bond and started on her finished copy. At three that afternoon, she stopped long enough to massage her aching fingers, to admire the growing stack beside her, and to read over what she'd written.

It was good. Not to brag, but the piece was really, *really* good. Clean prose, action verbs—a smattering of carefully chosen adjectives, just enough to lend atmosphere. Two pages into her story and she could see it all over again—the muted shades of winter-bare trees, all that dark, slow-moving water. She could smell the distinctive fragrance of fertile earth, of spicy dried leaves, of mud and wood smoke and—

Lyon. Oh, blast. The trouble with reliving her brief sojourn in the primeval wilderness was that, no matter how objective she tried to be, Lyon was always there. At the very heart of it all.

He *was* the heart of it all.

She had honestly thought he would call and at least let her know he'd survived whatever it was that had been going on when he'd left her at the airport. He knew she'd been frantic. How was she supposed to forget the wretched man when she didn't even know if he was still alive?

Yes, she did, too. If he'd been killed, or even badly hurt, she would have felt it in her bones. After all, she was part Irish, and everyone knew the Irish had more than the allotted five senses.

But just on the off-chance that she'd been shortchanged in the sensitivity department, she'd spent hours at the library searching the major eastern papers for some lead.

She'd found several stories about another Lawless who might be related but probably wasn't, unless he was the New York connection Catfish had mentioned.

Which was too big a coincidence. Evidently, H. L. Lawless was some fancy international hotshot who'd suddenly dropped out of sight. The stock market had dipped a couple of points on news that he'd divested himself of something or other. She hadn't bothered to read past that point, knowing that whatever else he was, the chances of Lyon's being an international tycoon were slightly below her chance of landing a lead part in a major film and going on to win an Oscar.

Thanks to pints of Wite-Out and the frequent use of her spelling dictionary, she was almost done when her buzzer sounded. "Oh, shoot. Not now, Cyn, please," she muttered, rolling a fresh sheet of paper into the machine. Cyn had called three times yesterday and twice this morning wanting to come over and talk about her honeymoon, which evidently hadn't lasted much longer than her suntan.

Jasmine's friendship with Cyn had suffered, but in the end, she'd decided Eric wasn't worth losing a friend over. She'd known Cyn since her first week in L.A. They'd been through a lot together. They were as different as night and day, but it didn't seem to matter. On some levels they would never be able to communicate, but they'd shared a lot. Hopes, a few dreams—some disappointments.

And Eric.

Jasmine would have taken the phone off the hook, but there was always that one-in-a-million chance that Lyon would call.

Sighing heavily, she raked a hand through her hair, stretched and realized that she'd been sitting in the same hard-bottomed chair too long. If she took a break now, she could find a pillow, make herself a peanut butter sandwich and do a few stretching exercises while she listened to Cyn's latest tale of woe.

"Hi, have you had lunch?" she asked, swinging the door open. "I'm getting ready to make a peanut butter sandwich, so if…"

Lyon. Her mouth opened and closed. She blinked, tried to think of something intelligent, or even faintly coherent, to say and failed.

"Are you going to invite me inside?"

"I—oh—won't you come in?" She stood back and held the door, staring at the well-dressed, clean-shaven man who stepped past her.

He'd had a haircut. There was more gray showing than she'd remembered. He was wearing neatly creased khakis, a black T-shirt and a well-cut Harris Tweed jacket. Her gaze dropped to his narrow waist, and he held up both hands in mock surrender.

"I'm not armed."

"I didn't—I wasn't—Lyon, what are you doing here?"

"We had some unfinished business, remember? I thought it was time to wind it up."

Oh, for heaven's sake, just when she was beginning to get over him—or at least, if not to get over him, to relegate him to that portion of her mind where she stored fairy tales and all those old happily-ever-after movies.

"If you'd let me know you were in town, I would have—"

"You'd have what? Run out on me? Not answered your door? Taken your phone off the hook?"

"Don't be—" She crossed her arms in an unconscious defensive gesture. "I might have. Or I could have gotten an answering service to screen my calls."

She tried to interpret his expression, his mannerisms. The trouble was, he had no mannerisms. As for his expression, it was a cross between wary and hopeful.

She was the one who'd dared to hope. What did he have to be wary about?

Lyon moved past her into the room, automatically scanning and storing information. This was a mistake. He didn't belong here. It wasn't a high-end rental. Far from it. But there were rugs on the floor, pictures on the wall, plants on the windowsill. This wasn't just rooms; this was somebody's home.

Her home. She was wearing a pair of white tights with a flowered sweatshirt. Barefoot. No jewelry, but a pencil in her hair. And makeup. There was a smudge of white on her chin and her cheeks were as red as those crazy trees he'd seen on the way from the airport. All trunk and flowers, no leaves at all. "You look…different."

"So do you."

She hadn't sat down, nor invited him to have a seat. So they stood, scoping each other out like a pair of guard dogs thrown together for the first time.

"I was about to make myself a peanut butter sandwich. Would you like one?"

"What, no chili?"

Her eyes started to itch. The tip of her nose began to
tingle. In about thirty seconds it would turn red and
she'd be bawling her eyes out.

So she hit him in the chest.

"Ow! What the hell was that all about?"

"You c-c-could at least have told me you were all
right," she wailed.

"I did. I am. What do you think I'm doing here?" He
took her by the arm and steered her over to a white love
seat. It wasn't as comfortable as it looked.

"What are you doing here?" She sniffled and he
pulled out a handkerchief, wiped her eyes and told her
to blow.

She did, and he noticed that there were no mascara
stains, no rouge stains, no lipstick stains. She was just
naturally…colorful.

Lowering himself beside her, he turned, one knee
practically dragging the floor, and studied her silently
while she got control of her emotions.

Some things at least didn't change. She was a mess.
That incredible redhead's complexion, reflecting her
emotions like a mirror. Those eyes, red-rimmed now, but
every bit as big and as beautiful as he remembered.

"Are you sure?" he asked.

"Am I sure of what?"

"That we're not going to have a baby."

Her eyes widened still further. "You weren't going
to have a baby, I was. At least, I hoped I was—or I
thought there might be a chance. I told you that. I left a

message with your service. And by the way, your service stinks. It's slower than molasses and noisy, and—and—Lyon, why did you come here?"

Oh boy. Here goes. "I had to know if I'd been wrong about something."

"Wrong what?"

"About what I read in your eyes before you left. At the motel. At the airport. Even before that."

"I don't know what you mean."

"I think you do." He watched her intently, but didn't touch her. For now this was enough. Being close enough to reach out as soon as he saw some sign that he hadn't been wrong. "I think you know exactly why I'm here, Jaz. What's more, I think you've been expecting me. Tell me you haven't, and I'll go. Tell me you don't want me here and—"

"Lyon?"

He could almost feel the sizzle of electricity in the atmosphere. He didn't know what to say—was afraid of saying what was on his mind, so he didn't say anything; he just looked at her.

"Why don't you stop talking so much and kiss me?"

Hours later, Jasmine put the phone back on the hook and turned on a lamp in the living room. Lyon had showered, folded their clothes and made the bed. He was surprisingly neat for a man who admitted that his home was a room and a bath, a bed, a telephone and a packing crate that held his books and computer.

"What about your acting career?" he'd asked her during the first intermission. Right after the standard missionary thing, just before the…well, whatever.

"I'm a writer, not an actress. I've given Hollywood every opportunity to discover me, and they didn't. Their loss is the publishing world's gain."

He came into her minuscule kitchen and wrapped his arms around her from behind. She tipped her head back onto his shoulder. "Do you want scrambled eggs or an avocado omelette?"

"Surprise me."

She had already surprised him. Even now that it was all settled, she didn't know where she'd ever found the courage to propose.

They'd been lying in her bed, not a stitch of clothes between them. The stash of condoms was still on her bedside table, untouched, right where he'd left them.

So she'd asked him and before she could even finish telling him all the reasons she thought he needed her, he'd said yes. "Hell yes," and "Yes, sweetheart," and "Right now, today, before you change your mind."

As if she ever would.

"Do you know, I still don't know exactly what it is you do. I know you're some kind of government worker, but that's all. Does that mean we have to live in Washington? I mean, I can write anywhere, but there's probably a lot of pavement in Washington, and I sort of liked living in the woods."

"How about Virginia? You haven't seen swamps until you see the main body of the Great Dismal. Not that I've ever seen it, but we could check it out together."

"Back up. All the way to question one. What do you do? You're not a politician, are you? I'm not going to have to go to fund-raisers and rallies and things like that?"

"God, I hope not. How about living somewhere in the

country, spending as much or as little time as you want to with your writing, getting away on weekends, maybe in a few years going to a few Little League games? Omelette, if that's all right."

"What omelette?" she cried, laughing. "Lyon, you're as disorganized as I am, do you know that? Mine comes with a disorganized mind, but yours—" She broke off and shook her head. "I'm doing it again, aren't I? Would you mind answering my first question? Are you a mailman, a bureaucrat, or what?"

Dragging a chair out from the tiny table, he straddled it, crossed his arms over the back and watched her move around the kitchen, which was all of seven square feet. "I guess I fall under the heading of bureaucrat. I'm new at it. The desk part, that is. The kind of work I was doing before—what can I tell you? I was in a line of work where we're not allowed to talk about our successes, but the press sure as hell likes to talk about our failures. Which aren't as frequent as they'd like you to believe."

"And those two men who followed us?"

"Business associates."

The unofficial type. There was a lot of gray involved in the counterintelligence world. Those two were a paler shade of gray than some he'd been forced to do business with. They'd been helpful in winding things up. For a price.

An egg in each hand, Jasmine dropped into the opposite chair and stared at him. "Are you saying you're some kind of an—an undercover operator? A spy?"

He laughed at that. "I wouldn't call it that, exactly. Let's just say that what I was doing before entailed things I won't be doing in the future. As a matter of fact, I just got a promotion."

Yeah, sure he had. His D.O. was about to be indicted. Both he and Madden would have to testify at the hearing, which wasn't going to be pleasant, but he'd do it. It was part of the job.

Once he took over as the new assistant Director of Operations, he'd be in a position to help sort through the wreckage and rebuild something that would function effectively in the post-cold-war world.

And while he was at it, he would build himself something that would make all those bleak years worthwhile. A life. A home, a family—something to serve as an anchor.

"Lyon, tell me again," she whispered when his silence lasted a few beats too long.

His face crinkled in a smile. He'd smiled more with her in a few hours than he had in the past twenty years.

"What, that I love you? That's old news. That you're going to be the mother of my son and win a Pulitzer Prize for literature and learn how to fish and darn socks and operate a riding lawnmower and maybe even learn to like warm beer?"

"Don't push it, Lawless. How about two out of three?"

"How about three out of six, my choice?"

"You're on."

* * * * *

HIS BUSINESS, HER BABY

One

Stress was a killer. Dump it or die. For weeks on end, those words had been ricocheting through his mind. Harrison Lancaster Lawless, founder, chief stockholder and, until recently, CEO of Lawless Inc., had been called a lot of things, including arrogant, stubborn and hard-nosed. He'd been called a bloody-minded, cold-hearted pirate as well as a domineering control freak.

The one thing he had never been called was stupid. So, if he had to move out of the fast lane, after having led the pack for years, he would do it.

But he'd damned well do it his way.

And this, he thought, surveying the sprawling log house—three spacious wings, each with its own deck, surrounding a tall central portion, tucked away in a hidden cove on the shore of the Alligator River—was the way he intended to do it. In style, comfort and privacy.

Once he was settled in he could have a few pieces of equipment shipped down, take his time setting them up, and before long, he'd have another company up and running.

Single-handed. In less than a year. Three years from now he'd have it on the stock exchange. Nothing like a challenge to get a man's juices flowing.

Right. Nothing like going flat out, twenty-two hours a day, year after year, maxing out your stress levels before you even down your fourth cup of morning coffee.

Swearing quietly, Harrison shoved his sunglasses to the top of his head. The trouble was, after thirty-seven years, he knew himself too well. Some kids inherited red hair. Some inherited flat feet. He'd inherited a competitive streak a mile wide. Cutting down was not an option. It was a case of cut loose completely, get out of range of temptation or end up back in the coronary care unit.

Or six feet under.

Okay, so he'd take the time to smell the damned roses.

Turning his back on the log house, he watched as two yachts, a yawl, a houseboat and another sailboat—part of the annual snowbird migration—headed north along the Intracoastal Waterway. He had friends who sailed. He'd always wondered how any man with a functioning brain could be content to do nothing but drift with the wind.

He had a feeling he was about to find out.

Swinging open the door of his dusty new Land Rover, he forced himself to watch until the last boat had passed. Forced himself to breathe deeply of the fresh, resinous air. Sooner or later he'd have to get used to it, but right now he'd give a big block of his own stock for the familiar stench of exhaust fumes, the blare of taxis and the hordes of humanity moving in restless eddies along city sidewalks. There was an energy in New York, in London, in Hong Kong. Here, there was nothing.

Correction. There had to be something. No place was completely devoid of energy. It was up to him to tune in to it, harness it and learn to use it appropriately if he was going to thrive. Or even survive.

And genetics or no genetics, he was damned well going to survive, if it killed him. A man who couldn't control his own stress levels didn't deserve to control a multibillion-dollar enterprise. Harrison had always prided himself on being in control of every aspect of his life, right up until the gods had decided to knock him off his throne.

So here he was. And here he damned well intended to stay. In the land, supposedly, of his roots. The land of peace and harmony.

The land of lethal boredom.

He'd almost missed the unmarked dirt road after miles of nothing but trees, swamp and farmland. Acting on sheer instinct, he'd veered off Highway 64 and followed it.

He might have missed the house completely, so well did it blend in with its surroundings. But two things had caught his attention. A blue-and-white For Sale sign and a yellow-print nightgown flapping on a clothesline. A *big* nightgown, more in the style of Pillsbury Mills than Victoria's Secret.

Eyes narrowed against the brilliant, late May sunshine, he studied the sprawling log house surrounded by weeds, the nondescript sedan parked out front, the lack of any attempt at landscaping. Mentally collecting, collating and filing away data, he reached the conclusion that, overgrown and undermaintained or not, it was just what the doctor ordered.

For one thing, it was far enough off the beaten track that he wouldn't need to worry about nosy reporters. He'd given all the interviews he intended to give concerning the rise and fall of H. L. Lawless. What was that old song? "If they could see me now, dah-dah-dah-da-dadah," he sang tunelessly. Boat watching from the front deck, bird watching from the back. God, how would he stand all the excitement?

And yet…for the first time in over a year, since his whole world had come crashing down around him, Harrison Lawless was conscious of a small undercurrent of optimism.

Cleo wandered out from the kitchen, a bowl of ice cream in one hand, a book of names in the other. For a full week now she'd been thinking about names instead of concentrating on what she'd come here to do. What had happened to the organized, capable, competent woman who had mailed out all those résumés and set forth to sell the lodge, find a new job, establish herself in a new home and get started on building a new life?

Lately she'd had trouble remembering her own name, yet here she was, trying to decide on a name for someone else. As for deciding what to do with the remains of her past, it was simply beyond her.

For three weeks, ever since she'd driven down from Chesapeake and signed all those papers in the real estate office, putting the lodge on the market, she'd been drifting along in a warm pink cloud of prepartum euphoria, unable to concentrate on anything.

What to take, what to leave behind? How could she

decide that when she didn't even know where she'd be going? So far, she hadn't had a response to a single one of the résumés she'd mailed out.

Of course, she'd discovered yesterday that her phone wasn't working. No telling how long it had been out of service. No one could have reached her, even if they'd tried.

Cleo had had a plan when she left Chesapeake. Not a particularly well-thought-out plan, but a plan all the same.

Part of the trouble was that she'd never had an enormous amount of self-confidence, even before she'd married Niles. Some women were born knowing who they were, where they were going and how to get there. Not Cleo. She'd always been sort of hazy. A dreamer. An artist, to put a kinder face on it. And then, between Niles and her in-laws, what little self-confidence she'd once possessed had been systematically destroyed.

"Get moving, friend," she murmured. "Time's passing. Nothing's getting accomplished."

So she stretched, rubbed her back, savored another spoonful of rocky road and thought about names and about all the junk she'd found stashed away in various drawers, closets and Niles's wall safe. She'd started boxing it up, but what on earth was she going to do with it?

Thank goodness no one had inquired about the house. The rest of her life wasn't ready. Funny, no one had thought to tell her that pregnancy affected the brain.

Once the phone was back in service, she was going to have to get back on the ball, starting with her tire. Being alone and pregnant, miles from the nearest neighbor, with a flat tire and a phone out of service was no laughing matter. Not that she was laughing.

And of course, her tire hadn't been flat when she'd driven into town to report her phone out of order.

She sighed, licked off her ice-cream spoon and murmured, "Mabel." She'd known a Mabel once a long time ago. It was a nice name, but somehow it wasn't quite right.

Madelaine? Magnolia?

Magnolia, daughter of Niles and Cleopatra Barnes. Oh Lord, wouldn't her mother-in-law just love that?

Cleo scraped the bottom of the bowl, closed her eyes in a moment of ecstasy and considered going back for seconds.

Better not. She'd gained too much weight already. Either her hips had spread or the baby had dropped. She could barely waddle, and she still had six weeks to go.

"Marcia? Margaret?" She sampled the sound of two more names. Margaret was a pretty name. Old-fashioned. Nice and ordinary. After being christened Cleopatra Evangeline by a couple of hippy art students who'd been nowhere near ready to take on the responsibility of a family, she'd learned to appreciate nice, ordinary names.

Laying the name book facedown on a packing crate, Cleo eased herself awkwardly onto the leather-covered sofa and hoisted her legs one at a time. With a sigh, she placed both hands on her swollen stomach and closed her eyes.

Oh, shoot. Someone was at the door. Why couldn't he have come three minutes ago, before she'd sat down? She was tempted to pretend she didn't hear him, but it had to be the telephone repairman, and she needed the blasted phone.

She struggled to rise, a process that didn't grow easier with practice. The knock came again, and she grasped the back of the sofa and managed to get to her feet. "I'm coming, I'm coming," she grumbled, clasping a hand to her back.

Swinging the door wide, she said, "It's probably mice. They chewed through…" Her voice trailed off as she stared up at the large fist raised as if to knock again. Conditioned reflex took over before common sense could step in. Flinching, she flung up a protective hand.

"What the devil?" The man looked puzzled, not quite so threatening now that he'd lowered his fist.

Hormones. It had to be her crazy hormones, because she really wasn't paranoid. "I'm sorry." This was embarrassing. "You're not the telephone man, are you?"

"Do I look like a telephone man?"

He didn't. For one thing, he didn't have a name on his shirt. For another, she'd never seen a repairman dressed the way he was dressed, in casuals that cost more than her entire winter wardrobe. For still another, he had The Look.

Cleo knew all about The Look. She'd been drilled on it first by her late husband and then by her mother-in-law. It was what set The Haves, uppercase, apart from the have-nots, lowercase. It was the unspoken password, the subtle membership badge used by people like her in-laws to separate The Right People—again, uppercase—from the wrong people. Tiny, almost invisible lowercase.

She'd obviously been the wrong people.

Someone had introduced them at a party. She'd been wearing a borrowed scrap of sequined georgette and feeling worldly and beautiful. "You two have got to meet. Cleopatra, meet the Nile."

It had been Niles, not Nile. Close enough, though, after a few glasses of white wine. Their mutual friend had told them they were meant for each other, and Cleo, silly, romantic, impressionable fool that she was, had believed it.

They'd been married a week and a half later, after a whirlwind courtship. Before her honeymoon suntan had even faded, Niles had set about changing her into someone more acceptable to his parents.

Cleo blinked her way back to the present. "What do you want?" she demanded now, trying to sound more courteous than she felt.

"I saw the sign. I believe I'll take it."

"The sign?" She blinked again.

"The For Sale sign."

"You want my For Sale sign?"

He looked at her as if she were not quite bright. At the moment, she felt every bit as bright as a burned-out forty-watt bulb. "I want your house," he said patiently.

He didn't look quite as patient as he sounded. There was a twitch at one side of his jaw, a glint in his eyes that made her step back. Evidently, he took it as an invitation to enter and moved past her.

"Look, whoever you are, I don't—" she began, but he was too busy gazing up at the vaulted ceiling, at the moose head, the bear head, the coatrack made of antlers and all the rest of Niles's trophies. So she raised her voice. "I think you'd better go," she said firmly.

Evidently, the firmness didn't quite offset the faint quiver in her voice. The look he turned on her made her think of granite viewed through a layer of ice.

"I beg your pardon?" he countered mildly.

The massive rock fireplace, every rock trucked down from Virginia, had always struck her as slightly pretentious. He looked right at home standing there, under the mounted head of a black bear that was said to have been taken locally.

"I hate trophies," she said, and then was embarrassed because the remark was totally out of context. Not quite a month of living alone and she couldn't even carry on a coherent conversation.

"This is it," he said softly, almost reverently. Almost as out of context, but she knew what he meant. It was there in the possessive way he was gazing around her living room.

"No, it isn't." She crossed her arms, resting them on her protruding shelf. She wasn't exactly afraid, but it paid to be cautious. He was big. Not massive, but tall, lean and powerful. He didn't look particularly mean, but then, sometimes meanness didn't show until it was too late. Sometimes it was disguised by expensive clothes and nice manners and a smile that was…

She shivered in spite of the warmth of the early afternoon sun slanting through the windows. "I should have taken the sign down, but I forgot." He turned so quickly she flinched again, but held her ground. "You see, I've decided—"

"It's already sold?"

"Well, no, not exactly."

"Are you the owner? It's still for sale, then?"

"Yes, I am, and no, it's not. I told you, I've changed my mind."

"No, you didn't."

"Well, I would have if you'd given me a chance. This isn't a good time. For me, I mean. I'm, uh, I'm expecting a baby."

"I noticed," he said dryly.

She detected a slight thaw in those blue-gray eyes.

In an ordinary man it might even have passed for amusement. But he was no ordinary man, and she wasn't about to take chances.

Besides, if he was amused, it was at her expense, and that she could do without. "I'm sorry for your trouble. Driving all the way out here, I mean. Did the real estate agent send you? I need to call her as soon as I get the phones hooked up again. Anyway, I'm sure she'll be able to find you something else."

"But you see, I don't want something else," he explained gently, almost as if he were speaking to a child. "I want this place."

Harrison watched the words register and gauged their effect. She stared at him helplessly, her arms unconsciously cradling her bulging middle, anxiety and something that looked oddly like fear in her clear, honey-colored eyes.

She was a mess, he told himself. A genuine flake. Or maybe all pregnant women were this way. Never having been around one before, he couldn't say. But it wouldn't wash. She'd put her house up for sale and he'd decided to buy it. When it came to a straightforward business deal, he wasn't in the habit of backing down.

"What kind of a contract did you sign?"

She stared up at him in mute misery. He was almost tempted to back off, but then, he hadn't got where he was by backing off.

Wrong. That's precisely what got you where you are—the inability to back down from a challenge.

"Was it a thirty, sixty or ninety-day contract? How long ago did you sign it?"

"Five days ago," she whispered.

"Then the place is obviously still for sale. I've decided to buy it."

"But you haven't even seen it."

God, she really was a mess. Piles of straw-colored hair, half of it pinned up on top of her head, half spilling down over her shoulders. Clear brown eyes. Too clear. And a damned sight too revealing. Her chin was small, but she used it effectively. He summed up the parts and came up with the total.

Proud, determined and...vulnerable?

Vulnerable.

Oh, hell.

Reading the opposition was an art, one at which he excelled. Right now, he almost wished he didn't. "How much are you asking?"

A shadow flickered briefly in her eyes. He could practically hear the wheels spin. She would come up with a figure that was twice what she was really asking, thinking he'd turn it down and that would be the end of it.

She named a figure. It was half what he'd expected. Either the lady was loco or property values down here were at rock bottom. "Sold," he said, his voice devoid of the jubilation he was feeling.

Jubilation? Hell, you'd think he'd just pulled off a major coup instead of buying himself a log cabin that for all he knew was full of termites, damp rot and God knows what else on an unmarked dirt road in a jerkwater place that didn't even have a name. And all on an impulse that didn't even make sense.

"No, it's not sold," she snapped. "I told you I'd changed my mind. Look, I need to sit down. When I stand too long, all the iced tea I had for lunch runs down to my feet and ankles, and I can't get my shoes on."

Without waiting for a response, she plopped down onto the sofa.

Without waiting for an invitation, he took the matching chair. It fit him as if it had been custom designed for his six-foot, two-inch, one-hundred-and-ninety-seven-pound frame.

At least that's what he'd weighed when he'd gone into the hospital. Since then, subsisting on the boring diet prescribed by some witch doctor at the hospital and religiously followed right up to his last day in New York by his own chef, he was probably considerably less.

"Do you need to consult your husband first?"

"I don't have a husband."

He looked pointedly at her third finger, left hand. Following his gaze, she covered her bare fingers with her other hand.

"My fingers are too swollen to wear my rings, and anyway, it's none of your business whether or not I'm married."

"You're right. All the same, the place was obviously built and furnished by a man. I just assumed—"

"Well, don't."

He lifted both hands in a gesture of surrender.

Surrender, hell. Crazy or not, the place was beginning to grow on him. He had two other properties outside New York, both professionally decorated with custom-made furnishings and an art collection that had been chosen by a friend.

Chosen by an ex-lover, actually. She'd made a hell of a commission off him, too, not to mention all the gifts over the year and a half of their relationship.

He glanced at the window facing onto the river. "A van just pulled up out front."

She groaned and closed her eyes.

"Want me to handle it?"

He watched her struggle to rise, knew the exact moment when she surrendered to the inevitable. Her eyelids were shadowed. She looked tired. Tired and defeated, and vulnerable.

That word again. It made him feel uncomfortable. The women in his life were, without exception, about as vulnerable as sharks. He preferred strong, challenging women.

"Looks like the telephone company. Stay there, I'll show him in. If there's anything he needs to know, you can direct me from there."

So she did. Feeling guilty. Feeling like a coward for allowing a stranger to take over. She was just so tired. Her feet ached. She hadn't seen her anklebones in weeks. Her back hurt, and half the things she ate gave her heartburn. And now, in desperate need of relocation money, she had turned down the first offer she'd received for the lodge.

Or tried to turn it down.

Not even to herself would Cleo admit that for once, it was nice to leave things to someone else. Back in the early days of their marriage, she and Niles had decided to build a private hideaway somewhere within a day's drive of Richmond but well off the beaten track. It had been Niles who had chosen the architect. Niles who'd had final say on the design, who'd driven to High Point to select the furniture while she'd stayed behind to help his mother with one of her charity drives. She'd resented being left out, but by then she'd already been well on her way to becoming a doormat.

Niles had bought the trophies already mounted,

claiming they'd impress the clients he intended to entertain here so that they could depreciate the lodge on their taxes.

Her watercolors, the ones she'd done when they'd vacationed here between clients, had been relegated to one of the guest rooms. She'd been allowed to furnish only one wing—two small bedrooms and a bath. Mrs. Barnes, on her one and only visit, had criticized Cleo's taste in decor as well as her ability as a watercolorist. In retaliation, Cleo had dashed off a scathing caricature of the older woman.

Of course, she'd ripped it up immediately, but it had given her a small sense of power that had lasted until they'd returned to Richmond, to the huge Victorian mansion they shared with Niles's parents.

Now, lying on the vast leather-covered sofa, which was hot and sticky against her bare skin, she sighed, listening absently to the low rumble of masculine voices from the kitchen area.

It was probably a mess. She'd started to make a sandwich, changed her mind and dipped into a bowlful of ice cream instead. And then he'd shown up. She didn't even know his name.

Not that it mattered. Not that anything seemed to matter much lately. She spent half her time traipsing back and forth to the bathroom, the other half floating along on a dreamy mirage, just as if everything were under control.

Nothing was under control. In six weeks she was going to have a baby. She no longer had a home, much less a job. She'd left Richmond to move in with a friend without telling her in-laws she was pregnant because they would have taken over her life and her baby. Niles's baby. And wrong or not, she couldn't bear to move back into that stately mausoleum, her every thought subject to Vesper's approval.

Vesper Barnes was the kind of woman who, if she met God face-to-face, would have looked down her nose and asked Him who His people were, and if they weren't among the First Families of Virginia, heaven help Him.

Niles's father, Henry, was even worse. He had to be in control. What he couldn't control, he destroyed. In the end, he had destroyed his son by demanding that Niles be someone he was incapable of being.

"All done," Granite Eyes said, coming in from the adjoining kitchen.

Cleo blinked up at him. For a large man, he moved too quietly. "Thank you. How much do I owe?"

"No charge."

"Certainly there's a charge. Oh—I suppose it'll show up on my phone bill."

"There's food out on the table. Would you like me to do something with it?"

"Would I like *what?*" She struggled to sit up.

His smile was a work of art, but he wasn't taking her in with it. She'd been taken in by experts. "It looks like I interrupted your lunch," he said.

"You didn't. Thank you for taking care of the phone thing. Drive carefully." When he didn't react, she added, "Have a nice day," and felt even more like a fool.

With his long-fingered hands bracing narrow hips, he reminded her of a pirate ruling from his poop deck, or wherever it was pirates ruled their ships from.

"You're not going to leave, are you?" She experienced a sinking feeling, more like resignation than fear.

Neither of them said a word about the lodge. About the contract she'd signed with the real estate people and whether or not he could force her to honor it. Her stomach churned. Now even ice cream was giving her heartburn.

Well…shoot.

He just smiled. Stood there in his expensive shoes, with his thumbs hooked into the hip pockets of his expensive pants, and smiled.

And she lay there in her mail-order tent dress, with her bare, swollen feet propped on a red-and-white cowhide pillow, and burst into tears.

Two

That night in his motel room, Harrison considered checking out and heading back to New York. It had been a long, eventful day and he was tired.

After years of chauffeured limousines and private jets, he had quickly come to enjoy being in control of a powerful, well-engineered vehicle, free to go when and where he pleased. The sense of freedom was new.

The urge to control was not. But it was one of the things he was working on. Learning to ease up. To let go. To relax, if he had to do it one muscle, one gray cell at a time.

Cutting down hadn't worked. He'd tried limiting his hours, but there was no way he could shut off his brain. He'd drawn the line at meditation, yoga and biofeedback. One of his personal assistants had suggested aromatherapy, whatever the hell that was.

He'd spent three weeks examining his options, and then he'd placed a call to the West Coast, to a highly innovative competitor who had approached him two years before about a possible merger. He'd laid out his terms. They'd spent a month negotiating and arrived at a mutually satisfactory deal with a minimum of hassle. The details had been left to their respective legal departments and directors.

He'd been able to block off second thoughts right up until the end, but then it had struck him. Now that he had been relieved of any possible source of stress, what the devil was he supposed to do with the rest of his life? Hang out in Central Park feeding the pigeons?

He'd made himself get on with the tedious business of dividing his assets among various trusts, endowments, annuities and a few large charitable bequests. Under the circumstances he figured it couldn't hurt to be on the right side of the angels.

By the time he'd headed south, there was only one loose end that hadn't been taken care of. Marla.

Marla Kane, good friend, ex-lover. She'd been out of town when he'd left, and he couldn't deny he'd been relieved. Funny how a man who made business decisions involving hundreds of millions of dollars on the basis of a hunch could go to such lengths to avoid making certain personal decisions.

Although he was improving on that score. The decision to buy the log house was personal. A snap decision based solely on instinct. But then, what was instinct besides a knack for absorbing information subliminally and reaching a conclusion? Nine times out of ten, his instincts were right on target. In the rare instance when he was wrong, he cut his losses, analyzed his mistakes and, as a consequence, never made the same one twice.

He hoped to hell this wasn't going to be one of those learning experiences.

Standing before the open window of his riverside motel, he watched the stars come out and thought about snap decisions in general, about today's decision in particular. And about the woman.

Her name was Cleo Barnes. Something about her intrigued him, and Harrison couldn't remember the last time he'd been intrigued by a woman. Much less by a woman like Ms. Barnes, who was not only pregnant and untidy, but about as sharp-witted as a bowling ball.

Fortunately, she wasn't part of the deal. If at some time in the future he changed his mind about the house, he could always put it back on the market. A house was a commodity, no more, no less.

As for the woman, she wasn't quite as easy to classify. Something about her didn't add up. He probably should have hung around, at least until she'd calmed down. She'd started to cry. He'd panicked. He'd felt obligated to do something, or at least say something, but was afraid anything he did or said short of bowing out completely might be construed as taking advantage of an opponent's weakness.

But what if she was in some kind of trouble? A woman didn't burst into tears for no reason, did she?

He hated tears. He was always embarrassed when a woman cried. Emotions, especially the messier emotions, were either a sign of weakness or a signal that the woman wanted something from him.

On the other hand, for a woman in her condition, it could have been a simple matter of hormones.

All the same, he'd been embarrassed, so instead of trying to comfort her, he'd found her a box of tissues, mumbled something about not seeing him out and left her there on the sofa.

Left her pregnant, alone and crying. Closing his mind to all that, he had driven straight to the real estate office, signed an option to buy and felt guilty as hell all the way back to the motel.

"What the devil have you done to feel guilty about?" he muttered. The house was for sale. He was buying it. End of story.

It had to be this crazy diet he'd been halfheartedly trying to follow. Cutting out everything that made life worthwhile was bound to affect a man's thought processes.

He removed a cigar from the case in his jacket pocket, inhaled the rich aroma of Cuban tobacco and put it away again. How the devil could he kick back and enjoy his one cigar of the day when he kept seeing her the way she'd looked when she'd first opened the door, her face tanned, flushed and innocent of makeup. Before she could utter a single word, the look in those clear brown eyes had told him two things.

One—she was frightened. And two—he was about as welcome as a bad case of food poisoning.

Once inside, he'd considered offering her one of his business cards by way of introduction, but decided against it because it no longer defined his identity. As for his new identity, that was a work in progress.

He took out the cigar again. This time he clipped the end, lighted it and took one draw, blowing out a cloud of aromatic smoke before stubbing it out.

The process of redefining his identity had actually begun a couple of years ago, when he'd received a letter informing him that he was one of several heirs to an undivided tract of land somewhere in northeastern North Carolina. In a battle to fight off a hostile takeover at the time, he'd turned over the letter to his personal lawyer and promptly dismissed it from his mind.

Not until a few months later, when he was flat on his back in a hospital bed, hooked up to a bank of monitoring machines and wondering if he would ever walk out of there alive, had he given the matter a second thought.

On being told that unless he wanted to die at an even earlier age than his father had, he was going to have to make some drastic changes, he'd come face-to-face with his own mortality.

It had scared the hell out of him.

"Is this everything you know about your medical history?" his cardiologist had asked, scanning his notes. "A few broken bones, sports related. The usual childhood stuff. Hmm, insomnia, tension headaches, occasional dyspepsia—that's it? No vices?"

"No more than you'd expect in a man my age. I don't take chances, if that's what you mean."

"Good. Then I take it you don't smoke, don't drink—"

"Cigars. I like a good cigar after meals."

"Cut down to one and then phase it out. Drink?"

"Not a lot. Actually, more beer than anything else."

"Better not. New study out. Switch to red wine, but don't overdo it. Your cholesterol's pushing four hundred. Your blood pressure's a time bomb waiting to go off. I'm going to put you on medication for the time being, but I'd like to see you tackle this thing another way. So tell me, what kind of exercise do you do?"

Thoroughly disgruntled but scared enough to hear the

man out, he'd stuck pretty close to the truth. "I used to ski. Haven't had time lately. I was on the swimming team in my undergrad days. Now it's mostly walking." With a tendency to pace and an office the size of a gymnasium, he figured he got in enough mileage to qualify as exercise.

"What about genetics? Anybody in your family other than your father have a history of heart problems?"

"My father didn't have a history, he had a single heart attack and died."

"At age forty-seven, I believe you said. And you're…what? Ah, thirty-seven. Right. Well, son, I'm going to send a dietitian in to talk to you about your diet, among other things. Meanwhile…"

Meanwhile, he'd been poked, prodded, explored and wired up like a Christmas tree. He'd been warned against everything that gave life meaning and released with orders to unload a lifetime accumulation of stress and learn how to relax.

Once released, he'd gone home, taken the phones off the hook, given orders that he wasn't to be disturbed and locked himself in his study. He'd clipped a cigar and left it unlit, poured himself a drink and left it untouched. He had stared out at the familiar skyline until the first streaks of dawn began to dim Manhattan's glitter. Grudgingly, reluctantly, he had faced his choices. He could sell out and leave town, or he could hang around the same scene, seeing the same people, and try to modify his behavior. He'd never been good at compromise, at half measures, but he could give it a shot.

Less than a week later, one of his closest friends had dropped dead in the middle of a board meeting. Suddenly, all the warnings he'd been given had hit home. That was when he'd set the wheels in motion.

It was the questions about his medical history that had first touched off a mild curiosity concerning his inheritance. Family had never been more than an abstract concept. He'd grown up as the only child of a distant, overachieving father and a neurotic mother, and when he'd thought of family at all, it had been as something to avoid whenever possible. It had simply never occurred to him to wonder what sort of people he'd sprung from. Whether or not any of them had blue-gray eyes and a tendency to chronic insomnia. Whether or not any of them liked Mexican beer and Cuban cigars. If any of them had been allergic to champagne or cashew nuts.

Acting on impulse, he'd sent Perry Edwards, one of his three personal assistants, to North Carolina with instructions to locate the property, check out the possibilities and get back to him ASAP.

The first report hadn't been long in coming. Timber. Large presence in area by major producer. Also corn, cotton, soybeans and potatoes. Possibly other crops. No industry.

Since he'd invested in timber, cotton and soybeans on the commodities market, his interest had perked up. The report also mentioned a dwelling located somewhere on the property.

He'd filed the information away in the back of his mind while he wound up his affairs. By the time he'd headed south, his mind was already working on plans, contingency plans and backup plans.

He wasn't exactly sure which plan he was working on now.

On day one he had checked into the motel Perry had

recommended and spent hours poring over surveys, tax maps and old deeds. A few of the deeds, written in the descriptive style of the period, had read almost like an old diary.

On day two he'd hired a guide to show him over his legacy. By the time he'd returned to the motel, he'd been tired, discouraged, all but ready to admit defeat. It seemed that his legacy, while it might once have included hundreds of acres of valuable timber and farmland, had shrunk over the years. After previous generations skimmed off the gravy, and various green groups condemned large portions for the sake of whatever wildlife happened to live there, all that was left was swamp.

If there was a commercial use for swampland, it had yet to be discovered.

As for the house, it was little more than a ruin. Whatever elements of grandeur it might once have possessed had long since fallen victim to time, mud and generations of hunters and trappers who used it as a convenient camp.

At least he now knew who he was and what kind of people he had sprung from. The surveyor, a character called Catfish who fancied himself a raconteur, had regaled Harrison with a detailed history of dozens of previous Lawlesses. It seemed his father's heritage was somewhat less than illustrious. No wonder he'd never mentioned it. Moonshiners? Felons? Bigamists?

Harrison had fully intended to leave the next morning, but for some reason, he hadn't. Instead, he'd started thinking about all those earlier Lawlesses who had grown up in the area. Most had been farmers. A few had been fishermen or guides. There'd been a couple of boat builders and a state senator. One Lawless had died in prison, another had gone into law.

And one—his own father—had founded a small investment house and a major chain of resort hotels.

Learning that he was a direct descendant, several generations removed, of a man whose given name was Squire Lawless, who had operated an illicit distillery right in the middle of the ancestral acres, took some getting used to. He'd always assumed, if he'd thought about it at all, that he was a product of generations of men just like his father.

Evidently, there was a strong strain of ambition in the Lawless stock. Old Squire had been an entrepreneur, and a damned successful one, from all he'd been able to discover. There'd been a few notable failures over the past generations, but Harrison thought on the whole, the old man had passed on some pretty potent genes.

He wondered if his own father would have felt the same way. King had believed in following both the letter and the spirit of every law on the books. It was a wonder he'd been as successful as he had, in today's business climate. Harrison would like to think he'd inherited the best from both men. Time would tell.

Meanwhile, he had some time to kill.

Fully intending to head north again, he'd found himself walking around the small, sleepy town of Columbia, built in a curve of the winding Scuppernong River, with a tiny marina, hundred-year-old cottages and turn-of-the-century gingerbread homes.

He had spent the entire day exploring, unconsciously absorbing the slower pace of life. On the way back to the motel, tired, hungry, but more relaxed than he could remember being in years, he'd followed his nose and ended up at a barbecue place. Before he'd remembered the doctor's orders, he was halfway through a plate of the best barbecue he'd ever tasted.

Sated, he'd gone back to his room, smoked a cigar and decided that moderation made more sense than austerity. Cutting down, not out. A moderate diet. A moderate program of exercise. Walking, maybe even running, but no competitive sports. No more of his favorite Mexican beer. Beer, it seemed, was contraindicated for heart patients.

Wine, then. He could live with a decent cabernet.

East Carolina barbecue was lean pork. Pork was white meat. He could live with that if he had to.

Meanwhile, the natives seemed friendly. On reflection, he'd decided he could do a lot worse than hang around here in the land of his beginnings until he decided what to do with the rest of his life.

Not that he hadn't had plenty of offers before he'd even left the hospital. He'd been invited to spend as much time as he needed recuperating on a certain ranch out in New Mexico. Ditto a villa in the south of France. Ditto a cozy palazzo in Florence.

The trouble was, all the offers had come from women with whom he'd been involved at one time or another, and all came with strings attached. Even at death's door, he was considered prime husband material, thanks in large part to a monthly piece in *Prominence Magazine* naming him one of the world's most eligible bachelors.

What was it they'd called him? The pirate prince?

He was no pirate. Not that he didn't know a few. Professional CEOs who moved from company to company, skimming off profits, looting assets, moving on to the next victim. But he wasn't among them. He liked to think of himself as a builder, not a plunderer.

As for being a prince, while it was true that his father, Kingston Lancaster Lawless, called King by his enemies and even his few friends, had inherited a few million and parlayed it into billions before dying of a massive coronary, the analogy ended there. King had left a rich widow who'd gone through the motions of grieving for all of three weeks and a son who'd been determined not to follow in his father's footsteps.

Or at least not to ride his father's coattails.

Instead, he had transferred from Harvard to MIT, earned a couple of degrees and built his own empire, and now, here he was, starting all over again.

Somehow, the idea didn't seem quite as discouraging as it had only a few days ago. The barbecue had helped. So had being free to drive as long and as far as he liked, with no deadlines, no boundaries—no secretaries reminding him of meetings, commitments, appointments.

Feeling relaxed and energized at the same time, Harrison stretched out on the motel bed, which was both too small and too hard, and began revising his plan of action.

First on the list: buy the lodge. That was already in the works. He'd agreed to the asking price and the house was now under option—to him. He was pretty sure Ms. Barnes wouldn't have the legal gumption to contest the signed contract. And he wasn't going to point out the legal possibilities to her.

Next item: send for the things he'd put in storage. Better yet, find out from the Realtor what furnishings, if any, were included with the sale and then fill in with whatever was needed. As long as he had a king-size bed with a good mattress and a place to set up his computers, the rest could wait.

Next on the list: hire a housekeeper-cook. The doctor had said simplify. He'd said nothing about starving in squalor.

On to Marla. Item four. He would call and invite her down to look over the house. Ever since he'd left the hospital, he'd been reading up on stress reduction. In the process he'd learned that married men had a far greater survival rate. The statistics alone were enough to triple the marriage rate and wipe out divorce altogether. Divorced men, according to one expert, were twenty-one times more likely to enter psychiatric hospitals. Their death rate was twice as high for heart disease, four times as high for pneumonia and seven times as high for suicide.

Ergo, the need for a reliable, stress-free wife. Of all the women with whom he'd been involved, Marla was the best candidate. She was intelligent, resourceful and beautiful. She wasn't tied down to a career in New York. If she was hardly the most exciting bed partner he'd ever had, all the better. Too much excitement was probably bad for a man in his condition.

Mental note: find out about risks involved with sex.

Marla had a son from her first marriage. Richard…Robert… Something with an *R,* anyway. Harrison had never met the boy, who spent most of his time either away at school or with his father, but that was no problem. Children were number five on his list. A son first. A daughter approximately three years later, if all went well. With little Radley or whatever, that would give him his allotted two-point-something-or-other children.

Mental note: have a personal assistant check out schools in area.

Mental note: man, you don't have a PA. You're on your own now, remember?

So be it.

He yawned. A good sign. All in all, he felt pretty damned good about the whole crazy situation. It was sheer coincidence, the way things had turned out. The legacy, which he'd all but forgotten. The coronary, which had precipitated a drastic change in his life-style. The fact that the house on the property he'd inherited was uninhabitable. The fact that, with time on his hands and nothing better to do, he'd spent a day exploring the area.

The fact that he'd happened to turn off onto an unmarked road, happened to glance up at the right moment, happened to notice the For Sale sign....

Pure coincidence, nothing more than that. He'd once read some statistics on coincidences. It seemed they happened far more frequently than was generally thought.

Interesting, he mused, and yawned again.

On with his agenda. Next item: prying a pregnant woman out of her nest. Not something he looked forward to doing, but it had to be done, for her own good. She'd been the one to put the place on the market, after all. Which meant she either wanted to sell or needed to sell or both. If she was having second thoughts now, it was probably because he'd caught her at a bad time.

Or maybe it was just a pregnant-woman thing. Like pickles and ice cream.

Whatever her problem was, he could afford to take it slow and easy now that he'd signed that option and handed over the good faith money. Timing was everything. He was in no hurry.

Next item...

Mid-agenda, Harrison Lawless, insomniac ex-tycoon, drifted off to sleep.

Cleo was in the shower the next morning when someone pounded on the front door. Whoever it was had probably been knocking for ages. With the water running, she hadn't been able to hear.

Might not have answered even if she'd heard. She still hadn't gotten over yesterday's encounter, when she'd been forced to come to terms with reality.

Hastily, she blotted her face and those parts of her body she could still reach, then slipped on a faded denim tent dress and padded barefoot to the front door.

"Sorry. I didn't mean to disturb you." He was leaning against the door frame, silhouetted against the glare of sun glinting off the water.

Inhaling the scent of freshly laundered cotton and a brisk aftershave, she stepped back. She'd been expecting him. Dreading it, wanting only to slip back into her nice, safe cocoon. Knowing she was caught in a trap of her own making.

The agency had called yesterday to tell her they had a sale for the lodge, and it was a sure thing. The buyer had accepted every single one of her terms. After hanging up, she had cried some more, and then cursed, and then cleaned out the last of the rocky road. None of it had helped.

"You didn't disturb me," she said with a sigh. "You might as well come in…."

Three

Harrison allowed his opponent to take the lead. As a tactic, it was often advantageous. It took her a few tries, but once she hit her stride, he sat back and let her run, confident of the outcome.

She shot him an accusing look. "Tell me the truth, you wanted to buy my house no matter what I was asking for it, didn't you?"

"Your asking price is reasonable."

"Yes, but you didn't know that. Besides, it's got mice."

He nodded thoughtfully.

"And—and maybe even termites. Well, maybe not termites. I think Niles had an exterminator, but I'm pretty sure there're a few powder post beetles. It takes centuries for them to eat up a house, but even so…and there's only one nest of mice. And with cross ventilation, I don't even have to run the air conditioner until July."

Bless her little heart, didn't she realize what she was doing? The more she talked, the more she undermined her own position. It was enough like taking candy from a baby to make him feel mildly guilty, but not enough to change his mind.

"Mrs. Dunn at the agency said she'd never even heard of you before you walked in yesterday afternoon and said you'd take it."

He waited. Not a tense bone in his body. Piece of cake.

"You did it deliberately, knowing I had changed my mind."

"So you said. I don't believe we settled it yesterday. There was the matter of your contract? Giving the Realtor the ability to okay a deal?"

She nodded slowly, then frowned. It occurred to him that even when she was scowling at him, her face had a glowing, dew-kissed look that no amount of cosmetics could have achieved. Conditioned to avoid anything that could possibly be construed as sexual harassment, he refrained from mentioning it.

"I believe you said you listed the place five days ago." His gaze fell to her belly. The inference was clear. "May I ask why you left it until the last minute?"

"No, you may not," she snapped, and then told him anyway. "My baby's not due for six weeks. That's plenty of time. It—it took longer than I expected to clear up the estate."

The estate. He lifted an eyebrow, silently encouraging her to explain. Husband? Father?

Husband. She was a widow, he'd lay odds on it.

He murmured something that could conceivably be taken for sympathy and waited. Ten seconds. Twenty. Right on the count of thirty, she took a deep breath, throwing certain portions of her anatomy into further prominence. "Yes, well, you see…"

He'd thought big, really huge, when he'd seen that yellow nightgown on the clothesline. But except for one area, she wasn't a large woman. Small bones. Hands and feet that were probably long and narrow under normal conditions. At the moment they were a bit puffy.

She was saying, "You'd think a lawyer would have known better. I guess he thought he was too young to have a will, but even so…"

Even so, Harrison prompted silently. Come on, lady, cut to the chase.

"Well, there was the prenuptial agreement. But of course, the lodge is marital property."

He nodded gravely. "Of course."

"It's just that everything takes so much longer than I expected."

"By everything, I take it you're not talking about your, uh, the baby."

"Not the baby. My résumés and all this." She waved a hand in the general direction of several half-filled cartons scattered around the room.

Don't ask, Lawless. If she starts making sense, just get the hell out.

"Things just sort of slipped up on me, and now I'm not sure I'll have time to finish what I started. Sorting everything out, deciding what I want and what I don't, packing it all up and then finding another place to move into. It's not as simple as it sounds. And besides, there's a mallard nesting near a pond behind the house, and I have to try and guard her against snakes."

That's it. He started to rise and make his excuses.

Ducks and beetles he could live with. Even mice. Snakes he didn't even want to hear about.

"They eat eggs and baby ducks, you know. Well, of course, snakes have to eat, too, but I've been watching that nest ever since I've been here, and I'm pretty sure she's the same duck that used to nest in the same spot back when—" She sighed, momentarily looking as if her train of thought had been derailed, and then she managed to get it back on track again. "Well, anyway, I couldn't bear it if something happened to her babies while I was here to prevent it."

Harrison settled back into the chair. Sorting chaff from wheat, he selected a promising nugget. "You don't live here full-time, then?"

"Certainly not. I haven't been here in nearly three years, which is probably why the place was such a mess. We used to come several times a year, but Niles—that is, my husband—needed it more and more for business."

"I see," murmured Harrison, seeing all sorts of things she'd probably prefer him not to see. Things she might not see herself.

"Well, anyway, now you understand why I can't sell it just now."

"Because you're afraid a snake will eat some eggs."

"You're being deliberately obtuse, Mr. Lawless. I am not—"

"Harrison. And it's Chloe, isn't it?" He knew exactly what her name was. It had been on the option he'd signed.

"It's Cleo! And I didn't change my mind because of a snake, I changed my mind because there's a lot more to do than I expected, and because I have to think about what to keep and what to throw away—what's important and what's not—and all of it takes time and energy and I'm running out of both, and there's a lot of bending involved, which I don't do so well anymore."

She shoved her hair out of her face. On anyone else, her expression might be called pugnacious. With a heart-shaped face, a pair of lucent brown eyes and a soft, vulnerable mouth, it was…

Something other than that.

Her cheeks were flushed. She was breathing hard. "Are you all right?" he asked, suddenly uneasy. He leaned forward to touch her face. She looked feverish.

Judging from the way she flinched, she was as startled by the gesture as he was. It wasn't the sort of thing he did as a rule. Touching. Certainly not with strangers.

"I'm fine," she said, but obviously she wasn't. She sounded tired and discouraged. "I think it must be the heat. I never turn on the AC in May, but maybe just this once…" She bit her lip, drawing attention to it. Harrison shifted uncomfortably. "And I'm not sleeping well, either. I can't seem to stop thinking at night, and I can't seem to focus on anything during the day, and—" She broke off with a rueful smile. "I'm whining, aren't I? I can't stand people who whine. I never used to do it, but then, I never used to run out of energy, either. Lately all I seem to want to do is lie in the hammock on the back deck and watch the birds."

Harrison knew all about escape, all about denial. He also knew that denying a fact didn't change it. "Boat watching from the front deck, bird watching from the back. I'll probably be doing both once I move in."

"You're not moving in."

He didn't bother to argue. It wasn't necessary. All he had to do was give her enough rope.

"Look, I already told you I've changed my mind. I'm nowhere near ready to move out."

"I'm afraid it's not that simple," he said gently. "Let's see if we can't negotiate a—"

A mutually satisfactory arrangement, he was going to say, when she flung out her hands, grimaced and clutched her swollen sides. Alarm bells went off in his mind. *Don't go into labor on me, lady. Don't fight dirty.*

"Is there, uh, a problem?" He indicated her lump. Her pregnancy? What the devil did you call the thing at this stage?

She caught her breath and then smiled. "She's going to be a ballet dancer. They have to start training early."

"Is there someone you can call?"

"I don't need to call anyone. I told you, I'm not due for another six weeks."

"Six weeks sounds like enough time for us to get things settled between us." He leaned back again in the large oak-and-leather chair and waited for the next move. This was hardly the first time he'd dealt with a woman on a matter of business. Some of them were sharper than their male counterparts, possibly because they'd had to be to get where they were.

This one, though, was totally outside his experience, both businesswise and otherwise. He didn't know how to handle her. She didn't react the way any sensible woman would react. Against all reason, he found himself relishing the challenge.

He tried a diversionary tactic. "Does the fireplace draw?"

"The fireplace? Oh, um... Well, it used to. I suppose it still does. Did you ask at the agency about other properties? I'm pretty sure Mrs. Dunn can find something with a wonderful fireplace. Maybe even something on the beach. Had you thought about that? A beach cottage, a fireplace...lovely."

Oh, hell. So much for diversionary tactics. "Thanks, but I've already found what I'm looking for." He waited for the message to hit home. She didn't need stress any more than he did. What she needed, he told himself, was a hassle-free sale so that she could go somewhere and have her baby, free of mice, snakes, ducks and termites. Actually, he was doing her a big favor by not letting her wiggle out of the contract.

"Ms. Barnes, you don't seem to appreciate the fact that I'm doing you a favor. I've agreed to your asking price. I've agreed to your terms. I'll pay whatever additional costs are involved."

Her eyes snapped open again. She glared at him. "And that's another thing—why didn't you try to bargain? What kind of man just walks in off the street like that?"

One, two, three, four, five.... Take a deep breath, Lawless, you're on the home stretch. "I saw your sign, remember? If you'd put up a No Trespassing sign instead of a For Sale sign, I wouldn't be here." Having regained the advantage, he watched her take in the words and mull them over. Pucker of brows, gnawing of lower lip. "Cleo?" he prodded gently when a full minute had passed with no comeback.

"Where was I? Oh, yes—what kind of man just strolls in out of the blue and says, I'll take it, without even asking the price? And you didn't, did you? You said you'd take it before I even told you how much I wanted, and that's crazy! You shouldn't do that. I might have come down on the price, for all you know."

"Would you have come down?"

She picked at a loose thread on her pocket. She was wearing faded blue denim that lent her skin an incandescent glow. "Maybe. I don't know. I suppose it depends on whether you'd shown up right after they put up the sign, before I decided not to sell."

"The thing is, you didn't take down the sign. You didn't notify your agent you'd changed your mind." Her gaze slid away and he pressed his advantage. "Tell me something, Cleo, do you know the ramifications of signing a contract?"

"My husband was a lawyer. My father-in-law is a lawyer. My uncle-in-law is a lawyer. Of course I know about contracts."

"And yet you're willing to risk a breach-of-contract suit on a mere whim?" As if he would take things that far.

"It's not mere, and it's certainly not a whim! It's—I simply can't—oh, why don't you just disappear?"

"Better yet, why don't I go fix us something cold to drink? You look like you could use a refresher. Juice? Milk?"

"Well…maybe a glass of iced tea." She was horizontal again. He knew her pattern now. Sit, then lean, then ease one leg up and then the other…and then close her eyes, cross her hands over her belly and sigh.

He also knew that with her center of gravity as distorted as it was, she had a hard time getting up again. "Iced tea sounds perfect. How about something to eat? Did you have breakfast yet?"

"I had some ice cream."

Levering himself easily out of the deep, oversize chair, Harrison headed for the kitchen and paused to glance over his shoulder. "Breakfast is important. You're eating for two now, remember?"

God, would you look who's spouting platitudes. Was this what happened when a man was forced to give up beer and red meat and settle for pasta and red wine?

"What are you, a doctor?" she muttered. "Some kind of a health nut?"

"Everybody's a health nut these days, to some degree or other. I believe it's a government mandate. Now, how about some cereal?"

"With ice cream on it?"

He winced. "Why not?"

"Left side's the freezer, cereal's in the third cabinet on the right over the chopping block." She managed to look anxious and eager at the same time. He wished she wouldn't. It made him feel like a brute. "Bowls are in the dishwasher. I think they're done, but I'm not certain. Yell if you can't find a clean one."

He ought to be ashamed of himself, using food to undermine her defenses. Not that he hadn't wined and dined his share of women with a view to, in the vernacular, having his way with them.

But this was different. Sex wasn't even a consideration. The woman was not only extremely pregnant, she was a certified ditz. A disorganized, unsophisticated flake in dire need of a keeper.

Funny how a man could suddenly come face-to-face with his true nature when he least expected it. Maybe that pirate business hadn't been so far off track, after all.

Harrison took down both boxes and scanned the labels. The dietitian had advised him what to look out for. Brown-sugar-added versus honey-dipped. Here we go, apples, dates and nuts. Nuts were fat but unsaturated. Fruit was good. Eat enough of the right stuff and you live forever, barring traffic accidents.

"Help yourself if you're hungry," Cleo called out from the next room.

He picked out a fragment of varnished pecan, tasted it and shuddered. And then he spied the coffeemaker, red light beckoning, pot still more than half-full.

She probably shouldn't be drinking the stuff, but there was no reason why *he* shouldn't. *He* wasn't pregnant.

He carried her breakfast in on a tray and helped her into a sitting position, trying not to react to the scent of soap, shampoo and talcum power, and then he headed back to the kitchen for his coffee.

Talcum powder? An *aphrodisiac?*

No way. That part of his anatomy was evidently as screwed up as everything else.

Filling a mug with reheated coffee, he strolled back into the living room in time to see her lick her spoon and roll her eyes. An assortment of impressions kicked in. He dismissed them as irrelevant, not to mention highly inappropriate.

"Feeling better now?" he queried with the kind of heavy-handed cheeriness he'd come to despise during his convalescence.

"Mmm." She smiled. It was the first genuine smile she'd offered him. For about half a beat it threw him off stride, which was probably the reason he scowled at her.

Or maybe it was the coffee that made him scowl. It was weak, flat, scorched and decaffeinated. "Then let's get down to brass tacks, shall we?"

"Let's don't."

Calmly, he took out the checkbook he'd brought along, uncapped his pen and waited. *Dangle the bait and wait, Lawless, don't try to flog the poor fish to death with it.*

An assortment of emotions flickered across her face, and he thought there ought to be a law against eyes that revealing.

"You're not supposed to pay me, are you? I think you're supposed to arrange all that with a bank, or at least do it with the agent. I've never done this before."

"Naturally, I'll go through the agency. We can handle this any way you want. Lump sum—there'll be tax implications, of course—or monthly payments? Annual payments with adjustable rates? Fixed rates? Your choice." He smiled, hoping he didn't look as much like a shark as he felt. "I just thought a little extra earnest money up front might come in handy, with the baby coming so soon."

You're a low-down, dirty rat, Lawless. That's really hitting below the belt.

He was right, though. She was worried about money. Some women needed help managing their business affairs, others didn't. At a time like this, Cleo Barnes obviously shouldn't be trying to do it all alone. Her father-in-law was a lawyer. Why wasn't he looking after her business interests? Maybe he should suggest it.

And maybe he should shut up. If her timing was lousy, that was no fault of his. He was a businessman and this was a straightforward business deal. She had something he wanted; she'd put it on the market; he'd agreed to buy. End of story.

"Could I have some more?" She held out her bowl. He had a feeling duck watching wasn't her only means of escapism. Ice cream evidently ran a close second.

"There's not much left in the carton. Why not save it for lunch? We need to get matters settled between us so you can get on with your packing and I can get the ball rolling." He hated red tape. Over the years he'd waded through enough of the stuff to circle the globe.

Or rather, his legal department had. He was coming to realize just how many things he'd taken for granted.

Cleo placed her empty bowl on the cluttered coffee table beside his untouched coffee mug, wishing she could at least have offered him a decent cup of coffee. Hers was pretty bad. It was one of the things Niles used to complain about.

For God's sake, Cleo, can't you do anything right? I knew you were no rocket scientist when I married you, but any dunce can learn to make a decent cup of coffee!

Remembering, she felt the old familiar burning in her esophagus. It had started about a year into her marriage, gotten better when they'd separated, worse when she'd come back, and better again, to her everlasting shame, after Niles had been killed.

Now it was back. This time it wasn't fear, it was nature's way of telling her she'd screwed up again.

"I'll have to drive into town. I'm almost out of bread, too."

"Fine. We can stop in at the agency and sign whatever needs signing while we're at it."

"We're not going anywhere. I am. If you want to leave your name and address with the agent, she can get in touch with you when I'm ready to sell if you still haven't found anything."

Harrison allowed her a few moments to savor her triumph before he played his ace. "Is that your car with the flat tire?"

At her stricken look, he nearly relented. "I can call a garage for you. They probably charge by the mile. What is it, about fifteen, twenty miles? I guess that's just one of the trade-offs for living so far out in the country."

Cleo hauled herself to a sitting position again, wishing pregnancy wasn't so darned undignified. "I do know how to change a tire."

"I'm sure you do."

"I happen to have three-fourths of a college degree, and until three weeks ago I held an excellent position with one of the better galleries in Virginia."

Her three-fourths of a degree was in art. Her excellent position was as a glorified gofer. The gallery was a tiny hole-in-the-wall place that barely paid enough to live on, and no benefits at all. Even if she wanted to go back to Chesapeake, she'd have to find a better job, and so far, not a single one of her résumés had drawn a response.

"Well, say something," she snapped. "I know what you're thinking. You think I'm one of those helpless women who can't do anything for herself. For your information, I'm perfectly capable of taking care of myself. I've been doing it for years. I expect to go on doing it, so thanks for the offer, but no thanks."

He waited until the steam cleared. Waited to see if she had anything more to say on the subject. She usually did, and it was the addendum that was most revealing.

"It just so happens that I haven't gotten around to fixing my flat tire, but it's not because I don't know how."

"I'm sure it's not," Harrison murmured. "Look, I have in mind a deal that might save us both some inconvenience."

He'd thought it over the night before. Never go in without a plan, a backup plan and a fall-back plan, that was his motto.

Tilting her head, she sent him a suspicious look. Before she could launch another attack, he said, "As long as we're going into town anyway, you might as well clean out the last of the ice cream."

Offering her a smile worthy of one of the world's most eligible bachelors, he left her there on the sofa, one leg up, one down, both hands on her belly and a look of sheer frustration on her face.

"So, here's the deal," he said a few minutes later, handing over a bowlful of rocky road, premium-grade, high-fat ice cream with a generous drench of chocolate syrup on top. As a bribe, it couldn't begin to compare with his usual offering, especially as it was her ice cream and her syrup. "Number one, you need a flat changed. For my part, I need a certain amount of exercise every day, and I'm pretty sure tire changing qualifies."

It might if he could figure out how to do it. One of the drawbacks of having a large staff was that there were too many things he'd never learned to do for himself.

"That's it? You change my tire and we're even?" She looked calmer already. Evidently, rocky road worked something like Prozac.

"Uh—there's more. Now, we both know a woman in your condition shouldn't be doing a lot of heavy lifting. Those cartons might not be all that heavy, but they're bulky. You could fall, and being here by yourself, that would be dangerous."

"So if I let you give me some money—your earnest money, as you call it—I can hire somebody to pack my stuff and load it into my car and—"

"Not exactly. What I had in mind was more on the lines of a trade. I'm paying for a room about the size of your coat closet, with a bed that's been around since the Crimean War. With no kitchen facilities, I have to take what's available in your local dining establishments, and while it's tasty, it's not exactly what the doctor ordered."

"You're on a diet?" She let her gaze roam at will, down, then up, then back down again. There was nothing at all sexual about it. All the same, he was uncomfortably aware of his masculinity and surprisingly aware of her femininity.

"Cholesterol's a bit high, that's all," he admitted gruffly.

It was really none of her business. No man wanted to admit to his physical shortcomings.

"And you want to share my kitchen?"

Go ahead, take the bait, lady. Once I get my foot in the door, I'm in like Flynn. "You'd be doing me a big favor. The doctor says all I need is a stress-free regimen of exercise and healthy foods, and I'll be back in shape in no time."

She was nibbling. He could tell by the frown on her face. If she'd been going to shut him out, she wouldn't have waited.

He topped off his offer. "I can do your heavy lifting for you. No point in having to hire someone else."

"How long would you want to stay?"

"We don't have to decide that right now. Anytime you want me to leave, all you have to do is ask."

"You're not going to insist on going through with the sale?"

"Not until you're ready."

"What if I'm never ready?"

He shrugged. "Then you stay and I go."

The phone rang. Outside, the sounds of an outraged duck arose. Cleo struggled to rise, and Harrison handed her the phone. "You get the phone, I'll take care of your duck."

Four

The call was from Tally Randolf, longtime friend, one-time college roommate and, until recently, employer. Tally owned the gallery in Chesapeake where Cleo had worked as bookkeeper, show hanger, salesperson, artist liaison and anything else she could do to earn her keep.

"Hi, how ya doing, babe?" Hearing the familiar breezy greeting, Cleo sagged in relief.

"Oh, Tal—I meant to call you, but…"

"I know, I know, your line's been out of order. I tried to call earlier but nobody answered. I thought maybe you'd already sold the place and moved on."

"Mice chewed through some wires."

"Treat yourself to a few traps. Clee, why I called was, there was this guy who came in the other day looking for you. He said it was personal, but I figured that under the circumstances, you wouldn't have any personal business with a lawyer from Barnes, Barnes, whatsit and Barnes, even if he was a certified hunk. He gave me his card and said to call him as soon as you get back from vacation. I told him you'd mentioned the Virgin Islands."

"Tally, you didn't."

"Would I lie? I distinctly remember you mentioning you spent your honeymoon on Saint Croix. A mention is a mention."

"Did he say what he wanted with me?"

"Nope. I offered to let him tell me all about it over dinner, but I guess he likes skinny blondes better than Rubenesque redheads. Not that you're all that skinny these days. Hey, you think it might be trouble?"

Cleo swallowed a sudden surge of heartburn, glanced to see that her unwelcome visitor was still out of range and said, "I doubt it. He was probably in town on business and just decided to look me up before he went back to Richmond. I know who he is."

"Lucky you."

Or not so lucky. Pierce Holmes was the fair-haired boy at Barnes, Barnes, Wardell and Barnes. He'd been bootlicking his way to a junior partnership long before Niles had been killed.

"I've got his number. You want me to call him and tell him you've taken a job as lighthouse keeper somewhere in the Caribbean and can't be reached?"

"Lovely idea. D'you know of any good openings?"

They both knew she wouldn't be returning to her old job. She could barely support herself, much less a baby, on what Tally could afford to pay her. Tally had been the one she'd turned to when she'd had to leave Richmond. Friends since their college roommate days, Cleo had told her everything. Tally had offered her bed, board and a job. Swallowing her pride, she'd taken all three. In today's job market, there wasn't much demand for women with three-fourths of a degree in art and no work experience.

The job was a hodgepodge, but somewhat to her surprise, she'd turned out to be good at finagling free publicity and a whiz at hanging exhibits so that each work showed to an advantage, which was an art in itself. During the five and a half years she'd been married to Niles, she'd almost forgotten she'd ever been good at anything.

"Hon? You all right?"

Cleo shook off a slew of bad memories. "Sure, I'm fine."

"Look, if you need me, I can shut up shop and be there in a few hours."

"Tal, I'm fine, honestly. But thanks. Thanks for everything."

"Well, you know me. Randolf the Ready, at your service."

"I know. She keeps on going and going and going."

Another few seconds of silence, then Tally said, "You can do it, babe. Haven't I always said you're tough as old boots? Now, repeat after me 'I, Cleopatra Larkin Barnes, am one tough broad, and I can handle anything that comes my way without even breaking a fingernail.'"

Closer to tears than laughter, Cleo dutifully repeated the familiar mantra, promised to keep in close touch and replaced the phone.

To Harrison's relief, the duck handled the threat all by herself. Before he even located her nest, he saw a nondescript snake slither into the pond and glide across to the other side. At the same moment, something small and brown whizzed past his left ear. A tiny bird, obviously startled by his presence, had ejected itself from a faded and misshapen hunting cap someone had hung on one prong of a rack of antlers.

Bird watching and snake watching. How was he going to handle all the excitement?

Allowing Cleo a few minutes of privacy with her phone call, he surveyed the surrounding woods, which were neither magnificent nor particularly exotic. He'd seen more impressive trees in Central Park. Still, there was something oddly satisfying about the collection of pines, cypresses and nondescript hardwoods.

Could it be hereditary? His roots were supposed to be here somewhere. The particular tract of land in which he'd inherited an interest was a few miles farther west. Even so, this might be considered his ancestral stomping grounds. According to the old surveyor, there'd been Lawlesses behind every third tree not too many generations back.

Not that he put much stock in such matters. He'd simply happened across a place that was attractive, available and far enough off the beaten track to make his mandatory retirement easier to manage. His decision had nothing to do with genealogy. It had still less to do with the woman.

Sure, she was needy as hell, but she wasn't his problem. Nor had he ever been burdened with an obsessive need to be needed. Until a few months ago, thousands of men and women had depended on him, either directly or indirectly. And while he modestly accepted the fact that he was a major creator of jobs and a producer of a healthy portion of the GNP, not a one of his business decisions had been influenced by a burning need to be needed.

Except for the handful who had worked for him personally—his secretaries, his chauffeur, his chef, his housekeeper and three personal assistants—the thousands of people who'd once worked for him probably hadn't even noticed when the signature on their paycheck changed.

So much for the massive ego of the so-called pirate prince.

Cleo was still sitting right where he'd left her when he stepped back into the room. Uh-oh. She had that look again.

"What's wrong?" No reaction. He'd seen the same look on the faces of an old couple in the hospital waiting room. "Cleo? Who was on the phone?"

She blinked and came back from wherever she'd been. "What? Oh, the phone. It was a—a wrong number."

Yeah. Right. And he was the queen of England.

It was none of his business, he reminded himself as he collected her bowl and his mug. "Your duck and her eggs are fine, in case you're still interested. You were right, it was a snake. Ugly devil. She handled it without my help. Are all expectant mamas so self-sufficient?"

"Mmm-hmm."

"Looked to me like a python, about sixteen feet long."

"Mmm-hmm."

"A purple python. Probably a local subspecies." He waited. And waited some more. "Look, I just had a brilliant idea. Why don't we drive into town? You get dressed and I'll change your tire, and we can drop off the flat to be repaired while we're there."

"Mmm-hmm."

She was no ball of fire at the best of times, but this was something else. Harrison told himself it wasn't irritation he was feeling, it was concern, and realized somewhat to his surprise that it was true. "Cleo? Listen to me. If you've got a problem, I'm a pretty good troubleshooter. Try me."

He didn't know if he was or not. Up until recently he'd had a well-trained team of troubleshooters ready to leave at a moment's notice for any spot on the globe where there was even a potential threat to the interests of Lawless Inc.

She took a deep breath and then flashed him a smile that was obviously meant to be reassuring.

He was not reassured. Just the opposite, in fact. "Cleo? What's up?"

"Nothing's up. Stop worrying, I'm fine, but thanks, anyway."

He studied her for a moment longer, waiting to be convinced.

The smile stretched wider. She was trying too hard. "I'll just go change into something presentable," she said, sounding as chirpy as that small brown bird nesting out on her back deck.

He'd spooked the bird. Someone else had done the job on her.

By the time she finished changing into her coolest maternity dress and her oldest pair of sandals, did something neat, but probably temporary, to her hair, Cleo had her emotions under control again. "You can handle it," she muttered, erasing the glow from her nose with powder that would disappear within minutes. "You're tough as old boots, remember?"

When it came to tearing down self-esteem, Niles had been an expert. Along with his charm and good looks, he'd inherited his father's ruthlessness, his mother's snobbishness and a sly brand of meanness that was all his own. It was a wicked combination, one that could lie dormant for months at a time, then spring forth with terrible consequences at the least provocation.

The Barneses knew about her job in Chesapeake, not that they had even pretended to care what happened to her or where she went. They probably knew she'd be selling the lodge—Henry had been furious about losing it, trying to claim it for the firm, but by then she'd had her own lawyer.

There was no way they could have found out about the baby. She'd been too careful. She'd even gone to a drugstore across town to buy the test kit. Three of them, just to be sure. Shortly after the funeral, when all three had confirmed her suspicions, she had quietly set about making plans.

Still in deep mourning for their only son, neither of her in-laws had pretended to want her to stay. They still blamed her for tricking their boy into marriage—not that she had—and for leaving him less than two years later. That, she couldn't deny. They'd even blamed her for coming back to try to patch things up.

Not that it had done any good. Niles had refused to seek help. He'd been more abusive than ever when he was drinking, and by that time, he'd rarely been entirely sober.

Cleo tried not to think about it now, because she was carrying his baby. Perhaps if she'd realized in time that she was pregnant, it might have made a difference.

Then again, perhaps not. Nothing she could do had pleased Niles. He blamed her for his drinking. Blamed her for the fact that he'd botched one case after another, until even his own father didn't trust him.

She had left him for the second time after a terrible fight late one Sunday night. Niles knew where she would go, because she'd gone there before. A cheap motel just off 250. He'd come after her. Drunk as a lord, he had sideswiped a row of parked cars and plowed down a security light before crashing through a storefront.

All her fault, of course. Not that either Henry or Vesper Barnes had come right out and said as much. It wasn't necessary. They blamed her for stealing Niles away from the woman they'd planned for him to marry.

They accused her of driving him to drink, of not staying with him when he'd needed her and of not having the decency to give him a divorce when he'd begged her for one.

She hadn't even bothered to correct them. Niles had begged her for only two things during their relationship. He'd begged her to marry him when his mother was hounding him to marry the daughter of one of her blue-blooded friends. Like a romantic fool, she'd believed him when he said he loved her.

Later—much later—he had begged her to come back to him, promising never again to touch a drop of alcohol. And she'd believed him all over again, even though by then she knew he'd been an alcoholic ever since his university days, maybe even before that. She'd believed him partly because he could be so very persuasive, but mostly because she couldn't bear to think she'd been so wrong about him in the first place.

But she had. And his parents had to have known what was going on right under their own roof. They couldn't have failed to hear all those late-night fights. The house was large, but it wasn't that large. More than once they'd seen her come down to breakfast with bruises on her face and arms. They'd pretended to believe her when she told them she'd run into a closet door or stumbled against a dresser.

If Niles hadn't been killed, she didn't know how it would all have turned out. Maybe the baby would've changed him. She would never know.

Cleo still had a scar from the first time he'd struck her, but it was the internal wounds that had come closest to destroying her—that had nearly robbed her of her self-respect, her confidence as a woman.

"It's over, let it go," she whispered. She took a moment to organize her thoughts, something she'd been doing altogether too little of lately. She'd forgotten how to think, for heaven's sake. It was so much easier just to let her mind drift along like cloud shadows out on the river, believing that once she heard from a few of her job inquiries she'd have plenty of time to choose, finish packing and leave.

Taking a deep breath, she gave her image in the mirror a critical review. "You can do whatever you have to do, Cleo Barnes. You did it for your father, you did it for yourself—now you'll do whatever you have to do for your baby. Chin up, friend, you're tough as old boots!"

Collecting her shoulder bag, keys and sunglasses, she stepped outside. "I'm ready," she called from the front deck. "Do you need to come inside and wash your hands before we go?"

Mercy, he looked as if he needed more than a hand wash. Her car was jacked up like a dog at a fireplug, the wheel hanging by a single lug. Every tool she possessed and dozens more were scattered around over the ground.

"Almost done," he called back, wiping his dripping brow with a greasy forearm.

She was already beginning to wilt under the direct blast of a late May sun. Harrison looked as if he'd not only wilted and melted but had been rolled in the mud for good measure.

She took the three steps down from the deck, carefully holding on to the railing. "It might be rusty. The wheel, I mean. I've noticed signs of rust around the door frames. Around here, that usually means either salt water or fertilizer."

He shot her a baffled look.

"What I mean is, they'll both cause rust, but people don't usually haul fertilizer in sedans, so I think mine must have been a storm victim. I bought it a few months after that big hurricane last fall, and then later, I saw this piece on TV about the dangers of buying secondhand cars in the Tidewater area after a bad storm."

"Right. Sure. Makes sense." Regarding her as if he expected smoke to start coming from her ears any moment now, he pulled a filthy handkerchief from his pocket, glanced at it and put it back. "I guess I'd better finish up here before I clean up."

From the shade of a lacy cypress, Cleo watched him frown at her tire tool as if he'd never seen one before. Under several streaks of grease and a liberal coat of sweat, his face was flushed.

Heatstroke? Apoplexy? He'd mentioned his cholesterol level, but what if he was hypertensive? He seemed the type. Uptight. Inflexible. Tense. He probably shouldn't be exerting himself in the hottest part of the day.

"I've got a better idea," she said as he bent over to tackle the stubborn lug again. Standing several feet behind him, she admired the flawless cut of his khakis, and then admired the flawless cut of his rear end.

Woman, you are out of your ever loving mind! The shape you're in—the situation you're in—the last thing you need to be thinking about is a man's behind!

All the same, if the G-stringed male models in her first life class at VCU had looked anything like Harrison Lawless, she'd probably have flunked the course.

He fit the lug wrench over the nut and gave it a few hard twists. Nothing happened. Not because he lacked strength, but because the thing was obviously rusted in place.

He cursed and then apologized, which she thought was rather sweet. "Cleo?"

"What?"

"You were saying?"

"I was?"

He shot her a grin that expressed both exasperation and amusement. "I'm pretty sure one of us was saying something. Look, can this job wait until the sun goes down? I've got a perfectly good vehicle with four good tires."

She took pity on him. Sweat was already making her scalp itch and dripping down her neck. What in the world would she do if he had a heatstroke? Call 911?

She didn't even know if they had a 911 this far out in the country. Great. *Now* she worried about it. What if she'd gone into labor out here alone, with a flat tire and a dead phone?

"Fine. You go wash up and I'll make iced tea to go. You're not one of those people who frown on eating or drinking in cars, are you? My mother-in-law said it wasn't done, which is silly, because people do it all the time."

"Iced tea sounds great," said Harrison. He watched as a worried look came over her face, and waited for whatever non sequitur came next. One usually did.

Forking back his hair, he wiped the sweat from his eyes with a greasy handkerchief and thought about the bar in the back of his limo. Before he'd left New York he had given Nick, the retired wrestler who'd been his driver for nine years, the keys and the title, along with a year's salary as bonus.

He'd give five thousand dollars right now to hear the ex-fighter say, "Here, man, gimme that thing before you tear up a fine piece of machinery."

Not that her car was a fine piece of machinery. It was a piece of crap. If she wasn't broke, she wasn't far from it. Why else would anyone drive a clunker like this? Why else would she put a house she obviously didn't want to sell on the market at a price that guaranteed a quick sale?

There were still a few questions he'd like answered. Not that the answers were any of his business, but with too much time on his hands, he might just make it his business. A man had to do *something,* he told himself, until he learned how to do nothing.

It hadn't sounded all that difficult, cutting back on work, learning to relax, how to enjoy life. The trouble was, he'd enjoyed just what he was doing. The hard-driving, cut-and-thrust world of big business. Seeing opportunities before his competitors did, making opportunities where none existed. Winning every race he entered, not for the money but because he'd never learned how to be a loser.

Cutting back wasn't an option. It was like telling an alcoholic he could drink in moderation. An invitation to disaster.

"And maybe peanuts," she finally said, thoughtfully. "The unsalted kind."

Yes, ma'am, one non sequitur, right on schedule.

Once they hit Highway 64, the drive into Columbia didn't take long. With the air conditioner going full blast, the woman beside him silent and no traffic to speak of, Harrison pulled up his mental file and scanned the list of things to accomplish.

The fact that she had trouble getting in and out of the high chassis turned out to be an advantage. He left her in the car with the AC going full blast and a CD playing Sibelius while he checked out of the motel. Not that she'd offered to help him pack.

"Next stop, garage. I'll just be a minute, do you mind?"

She shook her head and gave him a sleepy smile, and he wondered how a woman who was all that pregnant could look all that appealing. Not sexy—something far more feminine than that.

File and forget, Lawless. Better yet, delete the file.

He arranged for the garage to collect Cleo's car, fix the flat or replace it, give the thing a thorough inspection, repairing anything that needed it. Wherever she went from here, she was going to need a reliable set of wheels. He'd hate to see her stranded out on the highway in her condition.

A few minutes later they pulled into the parking lot of the town's only supermarket. "Want to go in with me? I might need some supervision here."

She was sucking on a milk shake. He'd never known a woman to have such a love affair with ice cream in all its various forms. "I probably could use the exercise, if I can get out of this thing without a parachute."

Grinning, he came around and opened her door, and she braced her hands on his shoulders and then gave up and let him lift her down. Harrison told himself it was the heat that made his body react the way it did, not the feel of her moist, silky skin, her soap-and-talcum scent or the sharp little gasp she uttered when her belly pushed against his.

It wasn't the first time he'd noticed it lately—this latent streak of tenderness that affected him at odd times. He hoped to hell it wasn't a symptom of anything serious.

There were fewer than a dozen customers inside. Mostly women. A few men. Every single one seemed to know exactly what they were doing. Harrison had never been in a food store in his life.

Talk about survival skills.

He insisted on pushing the cart, not because he knew a damned thing about supermarket protocol, but because it seemed the gentlemanly thing to do. Cleo plucked things off the shelf and dropped them in. Ice cream for her, fresh fruit and vegetables for him. A package of frozen boneless, skinless chicken breasts.

In other words, a lot of raw material that he hadn't a clue how to prepare.

She picked up a carton of fresh crabmeat from an ice-filled washtub. "You like crab cakes?" she asked, peering at the price.

"My chef used to, that is, there's this thing with crab and noodles and cream and—"

"Alfredo. You probably shouldn't if you have a cholesterol problem."

They bought more chicken, this one already cooked, and a few more vegetables.

"Hedonist," he taunted when she went back for another gallon of triple-chocolate frozen yogurt.

"My cholesterol's one-sixty-three, what's yours?" she inquired innocently when he picked up a package of filet mignon, gazed at it longingly and regretfully replaced it in the cooler.

By the time they rolled up to the checkout counter they were joking like old acquaintances. They hit a slight snag when she dug out her billfold. Harrison shoved it back into her bag, telling her they'd settle up later, over drinks. "Ice-cream soda for you, black coffee for me." He'd bought the beans and ground it himself. Another first. It was half decaf, half high-test. He'd already discovered the downside of cutting out caffeine cold turkey. Headaches that wouldn't quit.

Next stop, a hardware store, not because they needed any hardware, but for the simple reason that he'd never been inside one, and he was fascinated. He was beginning to realize there was a whole world out here he'd never even bothered to explore.

Cleo teased him about being a kid in a toy shop and reminded him that her ice cream and his chicken breasts were melting. He was studying a display of salt licks.

"The last thing either one of us needs is salt. Besides, those are for cows."

"Yellow salt?"

"I think there're some minerals in it, too. I'm no expert, either."

He couldn't leave empty-handed, so he contented himself with buying a low step stool to help her in and out of the Rover.

Predictably, she protested.

Predictably, he insisted. "Would you rather I lifted you up bodily and put you on the seat every time? I don't mind." He'd never met a woman who resisted a man's help more than Cleo Barnes. Or one who needed it more.

"I'd rather be driving my own car. At least it's built for normal people."

"Are you insinuating that you're normal?"

She shot him a look that started out scathing, but he caught the quiver at the corner of her mouth. It was a nice mouth. One made for smiling. Funny thing—he had a hunch she hadn't been doing too much of that lately.

Come to think of it, neither had he.

"I don't suppose I could interest you in barbecue before we head back to the ranch, could I?" He shot her a leering look.

"I have only two words to say to that. Saturated fat."

"What, pigs are saturated?"

"To the gills. Look, Harrison, if you're going to be staying with me for a few days, maybe you'd better give me your diet list. I don't think mine would do you much good."

A few days? Think again, lady. One of us is staying permanently. And I don't plan on leaving anytime soon.

But then he caught that worried look on her face and deliberately set himself out to be charming, entertaining and distracting. It was a social skill he'd learned so long ago it came as second nature. By the time they turned off 64 onto the dusty two-lane road that led to the one-lane road that led to the lodge, they were both laughing.

It felt good. *He* felt good. A hell of a lot better than he'd ever felt working some boring social event with a glass in his hand and a phony smile on his face.

Cleo gave him his choice of rooms. Hers was the master suite, which took up the entire north wing. Each of the other two wings contained two bedrooms and a shared bath. Harrison chose a western exposure, facing the woods. The room was airy, light, not overtly feminine, but neither was it self-consciously masculine. The dark logs and paneling had been washed with a thin coat of white, and there wasn't a single trophy to be seen.

He liked it. Not that he was any expert on interior decorating. If any of his properties needed attention, he hired the best talent available and offered a minimum of guidance, insisting only on comfort, quality and no jarring colors.

This room qualified on all three counts.

Light, clean and unobtrusive. Solid pine furniture. White cotton curtains, white cotton rugs. The bed was only a queen-size, but it would do until he could have his own bed shipped down.

It was the artwork that held his eye. Art was something else he could take or leave, yet there was something about these works that held his attention. They seemed personal. Almost intimate. One was of a woman reading, her face in shadow, the details merely suggested. There was a lot of white paper showing, and some pencil lines that seemed to hint at more just out of range of the viewer.

He liked it. Damned if he didn't like all the works. The watercolors were more or less in the same style, obviously done by the same artist. Impressionistic landscapes, riverscapes, some with figures, some without, but all with the same hint of mystery, of lightness—of something just out of range of the viewer.

Harrison knew as much about art as he did about interior decoration, but he'd attended enough openings—usually under social duress—to suspect that these hadn't carried a large price tag. Yet oddly enough, they appealed to him far more than any of the expensive, showy works in his other properties.

He glanced at the signature, a tiny, penciled squiggle half-hidden under the mat. Not that he'd have recognized it, anyway. All the same, he made a mental note to ask if he could buy all five pieces along with whatever other furnishings she cared to leave behind.

Naturally, he would pay extra. Whatever she asked, which probably wouldn't be enough.

Cleo had gnawed one set of fingernails down to the quick and started in on the other by the time Harrison showed up in the kitchen. Wearing fresh khakis and a collarless shirt, glints of silver barely visible in his shower-damp black hair, he made her feel dowdy and dumpy, even though her gauzy floral tent dress, purchased on sale, had been billed as resort wear.

He'd picked up a layer of tan today, making his eyes look bluer than ever. She told herself that there was something reassuring about steady blue-gray eyes and a square jaw.

Or maybe it was just that she so badly needed reassurance.

"Nice," he said, nodding at her dress. At least she hoped it was her dress.

Or maybe she didn't.

Woman, you have lost it. Flat-out lost it! Now, behave yourself and get serious while you still have a window of opportunity.

"You're awfully quiet," Harrison noted. "Thinking?"

She shook her head. "Just gestating. It takes a lot of patience. I dished up the chicken and made us a salad."

"I was going to do that."

The look she gave him might have shaken the self-confidence of a lesser man. "I'll do it tomorrow," he conceded. "By the way, after dinner you'd better make out a list of numbers and names and leave it by the phone, just in case."

"In case of what?"

"In case of…well, you know. The baby."

"Plenty of time. Sit down. I'm starving, aren't you?"

He eyed the skimpy meal set out on the table, trying to look interested. His chef would have walked out in disgust.

"Harrison, did you ever have trouble focusing?" she asked after he'd cautiously sampled the salad, which was dressed with some thin watery stuff instead of the thick blue cheese dressing he preferred.

"Can't say that I have."

"I think it must be something to do with hormones. Nobody told me I was going to have to prop my eyes open with toothpicks to stay awake, or that I couldn't eat cucumbers, melons or radishes, or that I'd cry over nothing and practically take up residence in the bathroom."

"Do you?"

"Do I what?"

"All of the above."

She nodded and then dredged up a deep sigh. "Could I ask you a personal question? What do you do when the questions you ask don't have any answers?"

"No answers at all, or just none you want to hear?"

"I'm not sure. I guess that's one of the questions that don't have an answer."

"Oh, I suspect it does, only you're not ready to hear it."

She made a face at him, and he had to stop himself

from reaching across the table and smoothing out the faint pucker between her eyebrows with his thumb. Which was odd, because he'd never been prone to physical gestures.

Harrison studied the top of her head as she toyed with her salad. The last rays of a setting sun spilled in through the window, highlighting shades of copper and bronze among the tarnished gold of her hair. Her lashes, surprisingly dark for a blonde, cast shadows on her cheeks. He found himself wondering all sorts of things about this woman who had so unexpectedly stepped into his life.

Or he into hers. The results were the same. As if he didn't have enough on his mind, he had to take on a pregnant woman with no husband and no visible means of support.

"Here's a question you can answer. How far away is your obstetrician?"

She glanced up and he watched as she pulled herself back from wherever she'd been. Brown eyes on a blonde—especially clear, pale brown eyes—were strikingly attractive. "As the crow flies? Maybe a hundred miles, give or take. Longer if you go by road. Why?"

Shaking his head, he swore softly. "I knew I should never have driven down this road, much less stopped to read the sign. Much less come inside."

The look she sent him was totally guileless. "It's not too late to leave. I can give back any money you put down, so there's nothing to keep you here."

"That's where you're wrong. Walking away might have been possible yesterday. Today it's not even an option."

He didn't know what the hell had prompted the statement, he only knew it was true. Without knowing why, he knew he could no more leave now than he could skip over the past year and go back to where he'd been before his entire world had suddenly converged into an endless ordeal of pain.

Five

Lying in bed that night, Harrison gazed unseeingly at the impressionistic riverscape on the wall as his mind roved over his past, his present, and struggled to come to terms with the future. He missed being in the thick of things. Probably always would. The subtle excitement. The feeling of power. It was an addiction.

He'd be the first to admit that most of the glitter had worn thin as far as his social life was concerned. The playground might vary, but the players were much the same. He knew, without really wanting to know, who was sleeping with whom, who was about to declare bankruptcy, who was selling out to whom. That was one part of his old life he wouldn't miss.

But the rest—the building, the achieving—that never grew old. It was what he did. What he'd always done. All the years of seeing his ideas turned into reality...of giving the best of himself, expecting the best from others and usually getting it…of being respected by his peers, even those who hated his guts, and sought after by some of the world's most beautiful women…

Sure, he'd miss it.

But he could handle it. Considering the alternative, he would damned well have to. His cardiologist had compared his old life-style to being constantly at battle stations. He'd been so addicted to adrenaline that even in purely social situations he was on edge, never quite able to relax and enjoy where he was for looking forward to where he was headed.

More than one woman had accused him of being an impatient lover. In too much of a hurry to get on to the main course to enjoy the appetizers. But then, the women whose favors he enjoyed seldom had much to offer besides their elegant, pampered bodies. If he'd thought about it, he might have concluded they were far more interested in having those pampered bodies sufficiently appreciated than they were in having sex.

Actually, until quite recently, he'd never spent much time thinking about women as individuals. For the most part he'd divided them into three groups. The ones he slept with, the ones he did business with—more than half his immediate staff was female—and the wives of his male associates.

So what had changed? Could his brain have been affected by what had happened to his heart?

Even unpregnant, Cleo Barnes would never come close to being his type. While not always strictly beautiful, the women whose company he enjoyed most were invariably either brainy, shrewd and sophisticated, or polished, amusing and elegant.

Cleo Barnes was about as polished as a pinecone.

Yet he couldn't deny that there was a glowing quality about her he'd never noticed in any other woman. Whatever it was, he was beginning to realize it was more than skin-deep. The remarkable thing was, he liked being with her. He was comfortable around her, which was damned peculiar, since often as not she was chewing him out.

He had a feeling she wasn't too impressed with him. Women usually were. Maybe it was the novelty that appealed to him.

Or maybe not.

He forced a yawn, hoping the power of suggestion would send him over the edge. No such luck. He was like the AVUS Quattro a car-collecting friend owned. Five hundred horsepower, V-12 engine, permanently up on blocks.

"Va-room, va-room," he uttered softly.

She was afraid of something.

Or of someone.

Harrison told himself he was being overimaginative simply because he had nothing better to occupy his mind. That wasn't even the worst of it. He felt like a pervert for admitting it, even to himself, but that slow, sleepy sexuality of hers was beginning to fascinate him.

Amen and good night, Lawless. What you need is a shrink, not a cardiologist.

The birds were raising hell outside. Had he actually thought it was quiet out here in the country?

Harrison had spent another restless night. The bed was too small and not his own, but then, he seldom slept well in any of his own beds, either. Unless he dulled the edge with alcohol, which he did only on rare occasions—or exhausted himself with a woman, which he also did only occasionally.

Mostly, he lay awake thinking of new ventures and new ideas and how to put them into motion. Some people counted sheep—he went over profit-and-loss statements in his head.

When the woodpecker started hammering, he got up and showered, quietly put on a pot of coffee to brew, after guessing at the measurements, and went outside to collect the tools he'd left scattered around the day before.

The tow truck arrived shortly after he'd separated his tools from hers and replaced his in the Rover. He didn't even know the names of most of them, much less how to use them. He talked to the driver, who obviously did, about cars and about kids these days, and about what was going on in Washington, the gist of which seemed to be a pox on both their houses. The fellow was a font of wisdom.

Harrison made a few more adjustments in his opinion of life in the slow lane.

Her car was just disappearing around a bend in the road when Cleo wandered out onto the deck, drying her hair, wearing another of her shapeless tents, this one yellow with big, splashy white daisies. Barefoot, she made her way cautiously down the steps, looking freshly scrubbed and delicate despite her ungainly figure. "What's going on?"

"Just putting away the tools I left out yesterday. Ready for breakfast? I made coffee."

"Harrison, where's my car going?"

She was frowning. Not a good sign.

"You might say it's going in for a physical. I made arrangements yesterday to have it picked up."

"I had it inspected in March. It's not due for another inspection yet."

"Yeah, well, turns out your spare was bald, and what with the rust, I thought—"

"You have no right to think anything about my car."

"Cleo, be reasonable. As long as you're still here, you need dependable transportation."

"As long as I'm still here? What do you mean, as long as I'm still here?"

"Look, I probably should have mentioned it to you first. If I'd known you were going to object, I'd have told you about it, but—"

"Object! *Object?* You hijack my car, and you expect me to sit back and meekly accept it?"

"If it's a question of money, I owe you the first week's rent. That should cover it."

"I want you out of here." Her eyes were glistening with unshed tears. He didn't know whether to take her in his arms and offer comfort or clear out before she blew. "I've changed my mind about letting you stay."

"Now, Cleo, we've been over all that. The contract you signed, remember? And the offer to purchase I signed with the agency, agreeing to all your stipulations? You don't want to get all upset. It's not good for the baby."

"I am not upset! Stop patronizing me!"

Her eyes were too bright. Her chin was trembling. The tip of her nose was white, and her cheeks were flushed.

The shrill of the telephone cut through the twitter of birds and the soft swish of the river washing against the shore. They stood there for a full thirty seconds, glaring at each other. At least, Cleo glared. Harrison, doing

his best to summon up all the negotiating skills he had
honed to a fine edge over the years, was his normal reasonable, tactful, patient self.

"Don't you want to answer your phone?"

"No, I don't want to answer my phone. What I want
is my car back."

"It might be important," he suggested in a placat-
ing tone.

"I'm not expecting any important calls."

"Sometimes nice things happen when you least expect them."

"Did you make that up, or is it something you read
on a bumper sticker?"

"I'm trying to keep in mind your delicate condition,
but you're not making it easy for me." His patience
slipped a notch. She was hard as hell to reason with—
he'd noticed that before.

Her chin quivered. A tear spilled over.

"You're going to cry again, aren't you?"

"I am not going to cry. Stop looking at me like that."

The phone rang several more times and cut off ab-
ruptly, the ensuing silence deafening.

"How do you want me to look at you?" he asked, a
quizzical smile tugging at the corner of his mouth.

"From a distance. Over your shoulder. In your rearview mirror. On your way out."

"I think you need a dose of ice cream."

"And I think you need to call the garage and tell
them to bring back my car."

"Yes, ma'am. First thing after breakfast."

Clutching her belly, she turned and stalked away,
bare heels digging into the carpet of pine straw and cypress needles. He watched her go, wondering how a

woman could manage to look so militant and so feminine at the same time.

She was steamed. Royally steamed.

He dumped her tools in a deck chair for the time
being and followed her inside, a gleam of anticipation
in his eyes as he thought about the negotiations ahead.

"Yuk! What is this supposed to be, roofing com-
pound?" She glared at him across the hatch-cover
table in the kitchen, obviously not at all placated by
the big bowl of cereal-covered ice cream he'd served
her. He'd even topped it off with a sprinkle of unsalted peanuts.

"You don't like my coffee?" He hadn't quite got the
measurements right yet, but for a first effort he thought
it was pretty good. Of course, some people preferred
tinted water to real coffee.

"Now, about my car—"

"About the rent check. I was thinking five hundred a
week for room and board."

She dropped her spoon. "Five *hundred?* You mean
five hundred *dollars?* A *week?*"

"Not enough?"

"It's too much, you—you looby!"

"Looby?"

Her shoulders lifted and fell in an expressive gesture,
and he couldn't help but notice how delicate they were
compared to her breasts, and then he got to wondering
if her breasts were larger than normal. He'd heard that
at a time like this, a woman's breasts could grow a
whole cup size.

"What are you looking at?"

"Your, uh, neck?"

"What's wrong with my neck." It was a challenge, not a question. She had a way of framing questions that way.

"Nothing. Nothing at all. It's a nice neck. Long, but not too long—just right, in fact." He'd lost his flipping mind. Harrison Lawless, a man who could negotiate his way through a corporate minefield without even breaking into a sweat, had flat-out lost it.

She took a deep breath, throwing into further prominence the portion of her anatomy visible above the table. The portion that he was trying his damnedest not to notice. He finished his coffee, grimaced and refilled the mug with milk.

And grimaced again. "What the devil is this stuff? Are all the cows down south anemic?"

"It's skim, and stop trying to change the subject."

"I don't drink skim. Where's the milk?"

"Where's my car?"

Easy, easy. No stress, remember? "It's getting checked out so you won't break down on your way to the hospital. You don't want your son born on a back road out in the sticks, do you?"

He could see her trying to get a grip on herself. She was doing a better job of it than he was, and he was supposed to be the expert.

"Harrison, would you please just call and tell them to bring my car back? I'll buy a new tire if I have to, but they can probably stick one of those little pluggy things in the hole, and it'll be good as new. I'd really prefer not to—"

"What's a little pluggy thing?"

Regarding him steadily, she dug her spoon into her breakfast. "You've never changed a tire in your life, have you? Admit it. I knew all along by the way you were dressed—I knew for sure when I saw the way you had that jack rigged. It's a wonder you didn't break something."

"Now, wait just a minute there, madam. Nobody goes through life without the occasional flat tire."

"Ha!" With a smug, disbelieving look, she swallowed the whole spoonful of cereal-covered black-cherry ice cream. Suddenly, a stricken look came over her face. A look of acute pain.

"What's wrong?" He was around the table like a shot. "Cleo, what is it? What hurts?"

She moaned, her eyes closed tightly. Harrison placed a hand on her stomach. Something was wrong. Something down there felt almost as if it were moving.

It *was* moving.

The thing—her son, her baby—was getting ready to move out!

He eased around behind her, his mind racing. Call 911? No, get her into the Rover, put on the emergency flashers and head for the hospital.

The hospital. Hell, he didn't even know where the nearest hospital was. "Cleo, listen to me. No, maybe you'd better lie down first. I'll get the phone book and—"

"It's my head."

It was her head. "Oh. Right."

Her *head?*

He knelt beside her, one hand on her shoulder, the other trying to avoid touching anything vital. Anything personal. Was she too warm? Feverish?

She took his free hand and placed it on the dome, lifting her smock. He stopped breathing.

"There," she whispered. "Did you feel it? She's practicing her arabesques again."

He felt it. God, he could *feel* it!

"Is it—are you—is he all right?"

She smiled at him. If the sun had risen inside her, she couldn't have been more radiant. This close, he could see the fine lines fanning out at the corners of her glowing eyes like a delicate carved design on a piece of Chinese ivory. One of her front teeth had been chipped and never repaired. Lauren Hutton, eat your heart out.

She smiled, and he forgot to breathe. A pregnant stranger. A ditzy, flaky, bad-tempered woman he'd known for less than a week.

"Look, maybe you'd better lie down for a while. I've got some phone calls to make. Later on, when you're feeling better, we can make a dry run to the nearest hospital. One of us needs to know the route in case—"

"Stop worrying, I'm fine. I've still got nearly six weeks to go. By then, who knows where I'll be? I might even decide to go back to Chesapeake."

"All the same, I think you'd better lie down."

"What I'd better do is finish my ice cream, only this time I won't take such big bites. I never could figure out how it works."

"How what works?"

"You know—ice? Ice cream? Headaches? I think she noticed, don't you?"

He didn't have a clue what she was talking about, but that was nothing new. Just as long as she wasn't going into labor.

Cleo finished her breakfast, taking tiny bites, then swallowed her vitamin pill and a few more supplements, all under Harrison's watchful eye. He didn't know what he was watching for. All the same, he felt responsible. Not because she meant anything to him, but because it was his nature. It was one of the reasons his employees—his ex-employees—had one of the best benefit packages available, including paid family leave, health and dental care, auto club memberships, health club memberships and a fully vested retirement program.

He might be a pirate, but dammit, he was a caring pirate.

As soon as she was settled in the hammock on the back deck with a glass of iced tea and an old issue of *Art in America,* he got down to the business of renewing acquaintances and calling in a few favors. Some years ago he'd established and endowed a satellite children's clinic in an inner-city neighborhood. His name was not entirely unknown in medical circles.

By noon he'd managed to secure appointments with both an obstetrician and a cardiologist at Chowan Hospital in Edenton, about thirty miles out of Columbia on the other side of the Albemarle Sound.

Feeling invigorated by his successful negotiations, he made sandwiches. Lettuce, tomato, fat-free cheese and fat-free mayo. It was hardly worth eating, but if Cleo insisted on watching his cholesterol for him, he might as well humor her.

Actually, it was kind of nice, having someone who wasn't being paid to do it worry about him. Back in New York he'd had three personal assistants who did everything from sending out his dry cleaning to scheduling his dental appointments to ordering morning-after flowers sent to the lady of the moment.

This was entirely different.

"Hey, you're getting too much sun." He placed the

tray of sandwiches on the railing and touched her arm. The single shaft of sunshine filtering through the lacy branches had shifted until it fell across her face, turning the tips of her lashes translucent, highlighting a handful of freckles scattered across her nose.

"Cleo? Wake up, darling." *Darling? Where the devil had that come from?*

Without moving, she opened her eyes and gazed up at him. "This is nice," she murmured drowsily.

"Hammocks aren't very stable. You probably ought to stay out of them until after the baby comes."

"I'm not going to fall."

"Nobody ever intends to fall. You're, uh, that is, your sense of balance might not be—"

"You mean I'm big as a blimp and about as maneuverable."

"Yeah, well. Now that you mention it…"

He grinned. So did she. His sense of accomplishment underwent a subtle shift, from the gritty triumph he'd felt on securing quick appointments with two specialists in a strange town to something gentler, far less easy to define.

"What have you been up to?" Her voice, like her smile, was drowsy, unfocused.

"Nothing much," he said modestly. "A little bit of networking. I made lunch. No salt, no fat, no taste."

"I could've done it."

"You need your rest."

"What I need is exercise. Do you think swinging in a hammock qualifies?"

He chuckled. "Probably in the same range as changing a tire."

They ate tasteless sandwiches and he told her about

his Scottish chef, who was sensitive about his profession. "It's probably the reason I hired him. When the agency sent him around to be interviewed, the poor guy was so defensive. He's highly qualified, but he'd been cooking in an all-night diner in Jersey because nobody would hire a chef named MacDonald."

"He could have called himself Pierre."

"Not with that accent, he couldn't."

"Was he a good cook?"

"The best. His beef Wellington is world class, and no one can beat him when it comes to oysters Alfredo. The only thing I draw the line at is haggis."

"Harrison, what are you doing here?"

He pretended not to know what she was getting at. "Having lunch. Getting ready to drive you to the nearest hospital to interview an obstetrician, just in case."

"That's not what I mean, and you know it. Who *are* you?"

"A retired businessman from New York."

"At your age?" Her eyes widened. "Oh my. You're not an undercover agent, are you? Or someone in the witness protection program?"

"Is that what you've been thinking?" It might explain the hint of wariness he'd noticed before.

No, it wouldn't. She'd been wary the first time she'd laid eyes on him. It seemed to come and go. Phone calls made it worse.

"Answer my question. Are you?"

"I am not, nor have I ever been, an undercover agent. Nor am I presently under any type of government protection. You watch too much television."

"No, I don't. Are you a detective? Did someone send you here to—"

"Cleo, what the devil's going on? If you really believe all that, why did you let me in? Why didn't you slam the door and call the police?"

She looked confused. Maybe a little embarrassed, but mostly confused. He wanted to hold her, comfort her, sort out her problems so they could both get on with their respective lives. "Listen to me, I don't know who you think I am, or who you're afraid of, but take my word for it, I'm as harmless as anyone you're ever likely to meet. Now…isn't it about time we leveled with each other?"

"All right, then who are you?"

"I told you who I am. You want to see my driver's license? Harrison Lancaster Lawless, six foot two, one-hundred-and-ninety pounds, plus or minus, black hair, gray eyes, organ donor."

"That doesn't tell me anything new."

"You know the rest of it. Retired businessman, primary residence until recently, New York City. Your turn now. What are you so afraid of?"

She waited two full beats before saying, "I'm not afraid of anything."

Regarding her steadily, he said, "Take your time. I'm not going anywhere. But if you need help…"

She opened her mouth, hesitated, and then said, "I need help. Harrison, would you kindly get me out of this thing? I have to go to the bathroom again."

The appointments were for two-thirty and two-fifty, respectively. They argued over his choice of hospitals. "There's more than one hospital in the area. According to the map, there's one in Little Washington, one in Plymouth and something in—"

"I talked to your doctor in Chesapeake. The number was in your address book."

"You had no right—"

"I apologize, but as long as I'm responsible for you—"

"You might be responsible for someone else, but I assure you, you're *not* responsible for me."

"Cleo, be reasonable."

"No, you be reasonable! Just because I allow you to stay in my house until we clear up this thing about the contract or the option or whatever—just because you bought a few groceries—and by the way, I owe you for those."

She started fumbling to open her purse, and Harrison swore under his breath. "Don't cry. Just don't start crying, will you?"

"I *never* cry!" She glared at him, tears spilling over her lashes. "It's—it's this blasted air conditioner of yours. It blew dust in my eyes."

"Hey—truce, okay?" He adjusted the fan control, glanced at her to see if she needed his handkerchief and saw her eyes widen as she stared straight ahead.

Quick reflexes were all that kept him from slamming into the logging truck pulling out of a side road. But even superb reflexes weren't enough to keep him from veering off into a drainage ditch.

Six

Harrison paced the floor outside the examining room. He had already sent word to the cardiologist, canceling his appointment. The cut on his forehead, which had been the least of his worries, had been dealt with in the emergency room.

He grabbed the arm of a nurse's aide hurrying past with a covered tray. "Mrs. Barnes—is she all right? Can you find out what's going on in there?"

The woman looked at him, looked at his hand, which he promptly removed from her arm, and then seemed to relent. "I'll check again, but if she's not gone up to delivery, she's probably okay. You sit down and stop worrying, y'hear? You look worse'n she does."

He sat for all of two minutes, and then he began to pace again. While he paced, he made mental lists of things to do and things to buy on the way home.

Or maybe it would be better to take her home and come back—

No, he couldn't leave her alone until he was certain there would be no repercussions.

Flowers. He'd buy her flowers. And low-dose aspirin. That was for him. He hadn't been taking them regularly, but after giving his heart such a jolt, maybe he'd better start again.

An answering machine. She'd mentioned yesterday that she was supposed to walk every day. This way she wouldn't have to worry about missing a call. A couple of cellular phones would come in handy, too.

What else did a woman need when she was about to give birth? All he could think of was hot water. In the movies someone was always told to boil water. He had a feeling that no longer applied.

What she really needed was to move into town, where she'd be closer to the hospital. Not much chance of that. He'd settle for a few more phones. And while he was at it, he'd better take down the hammock and buy her a chaise longue for the deck. A wide one. Something with strong, steady legs. Better yet, he'd order one for each deck and have them delivered first thing tomorrow.

And he might as well stock up on ice cream.

Ice cream. Lounge chairs and ice cream? Was this the same Harrison Lawless described in *Prominence Magazine* as one of the world's most eligible *bachelors?* An international wheeler-dealer seen in all the world's plushest watering holes with some of the world's most sought-after women?

By the time the piece had come out, months after the interview, he was being described by a few hacks as the world's most elusive bachelor. Whether that was because he was skilled at eluding marriage or skilled at eluding the media, he didn't know.

Thank God there was no press around now. When word had leaked out that he'd been admitted to a hospital, his PR people had spun it into a routine insurance physical, with an added few days of therapy for a pulled muscle. Interest had died down. But once he'd started the process of liquidating his assets, the speculation had sprung up all over again. Wall Street had rumbled a couple of times before his people had managed to get a handle on it.

Now he no longer had to worry about spin control. For the most part, the media had moved on to the latest political scandal, the hottest new bachelor, the most recent Hollywood gossip. But he'd just as soon keep a low profile. If word got out that one of the world's most eligible bachelors was shopping for ice cream and deck chairs for a flaky blonde with a slow smile and a big belly, a few eyebrows might lift.

The aide helped her get dressed again. Cleo was grateful. She'd been given a clean bill of health, but she was still shaken. If it hadn't been for Harrison's quick reaction, she might've been—

She refused to think about "might've-beens."

"Think positive thoughts." She'd read that somewhere. On a maternity T-shirt? Or maybe it was Norman Vincent Peale.

Tally had said, Think pink. Tally wanted a baby girl.

Cleo didn't care what her baby was, as long as it was healthy. She eased down off the examining table, instinctively cradling her precious excess cargo in her arms. The doctor had told her not to be surprised if a few bruises showed up over the next day or so. He'd advised her to expect a certain amount of stiffness, too, because she'd clenched every muscle in her body.

But the baby was fine. Just fine. *Thank you, God.*

"Right across the hall," the aide directed her. "Dr. Jane wants to give you some pamphlets and maybe a prescription. I reckon you've already read everything there is to read about babies. Most women have by the time they get this far along, but humor her. She's only been working here a few months."

Cleo listened dutifully to a brief lecture, accepted the pamphlets, promised to walk at least half an hour a day, preferably early mornings or late afternoons. She promised to call if there was the least indication of spotting or any unusual pain, and to come back in two weeks.

Feeling like an armored tank that had just come through a battle, partly because Dr. Jane was tall, slender and beautiful, not to mention insufferably cheerful, she waddled out of the doctor's tiny cubicle and practically barged into Harrison, who was standing there with the gray-haired aide who had helped her dress and undress.

There was a strip of adhesive on his forehead. He looked worried. He looked awful, in fact. "If I was you," the aide advised, "I'd take 'im home and put 'im out of his misery. He wore out a good pair of shoes pacing the floor."

Harrison kept cutting worried glances at her on the way back across the bridge until she told him he was making her nervous and to please watch where he was going.

He said something about excellent peripheral vision. She said, "Huh!" but then had the grace to add, "I don't know about that, but at least your reaction time is good. Thank you for that, Harrison."

"Don't thank me," he said tersely. "If it weren't for me, this wouldn't have even happened." For the past few hours he'd been fighting a load of guilt, anxiety and this crazy tenderness that was beginning to worry him.

"You're right. If it weren't for you, I'd probably have drifted along in my nice pink funk until I went into labor, and then it would be too late. My tire would still be flat, and I wouldn't know whether to bribe a taxi to drive me all the way to Chesapeake or to start looking through the yellow pages for the nearest midwife."

"You'd have handled it just fine," he assured her, but Cleo knew better. She'd really, *really* been in a funk when he'd turned up the other day. It wasn't like her. The last time she'd been like this had been the first time she'd left Niles, after he had knocked her down and then kicked her.

Actually kicked her!

Niles, with his fancy pedigree. With his degree from the University of Virginia and another one from Yale Law School. Niles, who had criticized her for the way she dressed, for the way she wore her hair, for chatting with clerks and deliverymen and treating his mother's staff as if they were family.

She might have lacked what Niles had called class, but he had lacked something far more important. When things had reached the point where she'd feared him more than she loved him, she had walked out. Not just once, but twice. By that time, she'd already reached the conclusion that in cases where there weren't any answers, it was easier not to ask questions.

"Are you comfortable? Not too warm?"

Put it behind you. You're a survivor, remember? Tough as old boots. She shook her head. "I'm fine."

"How about the air conditioner? Want me to turn it up or down?"

"No, I'm just fine, honestly. Couldn't be better. This is really a lovely drive, isn't it? Have you ever walked around Edenton and looked at all the old houses? It's ancient. Dates back at least three hundred years. They say Blackbeard had a house there." She reached behind her to jab a hairpin back into what had started out as a french twist.

"Does your neck hurt? Did the doctor examine you for whiplash? It's not too late to go back."

She didn't know whether to laugh, cry or get out and walk. At the rate he was creeping along, she'd get there faster. "Will you please relax? From the looks of it, you're in far worse shape than I am. What about your head? Does it hurt? Did you have to have stitches? Are you seeing spots before your eyes? Do you think we'd better pull off the road and let you rest? I'd offer to drive, but I've never driven a stick shift. Actually, I'm not even sure I could fit under the wheel, but I'm willing to give it a try if you're feeling faint."

He grinned, and then he started to laugh. "Okay, okay, you win. I'll let up if you will. Since you're in such terrific shape, would you mind if I stopped in town to pick up a few things?"

"Not at all. And by the way, whiplash doesn't show up right away." He suddenly looked so concerned, she relented. "I've never experienced it personally, but my husband was a lawyer, remember? I've heard every lawyer joke in the book."

He parked in the shade of a sprawling live oak tree

and Cleo waited in the car while he went inside. With the air conditioner on low and a CD playing something weird but soothing, she forced herself to stop drifting and face up to reality.

Reality being that with no job in sight, she couldn't afford to keep the lodge even if she wanted to. She could hardly expect any employer in his right mind to hire her until after the baby was born. What on earth had she been thinking of? Tally had tried to warn her, but she'd refused to listen.

She still had a roof over her head as long as she stayed here. But her chance of finding a job in the area, even if she dared risk staying in a place where the Barneses could easily find her, was practically nonexistent. Without a job, she couldn't afford to pay property taxes, couldn't afford to buy groceries. Not to mention the fact that she couldn't afford health insurance.

Catch-22. Too many questions, no answers.

She simply hadn't bothered to think things through until Harrison had showed up, threatening to take away the very roof over her head. Much less think about how hard it would be to give up the closest thing to a home she had at the moment. Her last link to Niles at his best, in the early days of her marriage.

She supposed it could've been worse. What if the purchaser had been one of those cigar-chewing, hard-drinking, poker-playing jerks who called all women "little lady"? The type who would use the lodge for drunken orgies and then go out and shoot up everything in sight?

At least Harrison would never do that. He was bossy and stubborn—couldn't even change a tire. He'd had her car towed without consulting her first because he'd been too ashamed to admit he didn't know diddly about changing tires.

But to be fair to the man, he'd thought he was doing her a favor.

He couldn't make coffee, either. He'd wasted half a loaf of bread trying to make a decent piece of toast. If he could do anything at all, she had yet to discover what it was. The truth was, he was useless.

Ornamental, oh my, yes. But utterly useless.

At least he was nonthreatening. In her present hormonal state, she was even beginning to think of him as a protector, if not a provider. He was certainly of no sexual interest, in spite of his obvious virility, she told herself as she watched him stride along the sidewalk carrying a stack of boxes and a fistful of shopping bags.

It occurred to her then that, in spite of everything, she instinctively trusted him. Which was more than she could say of most men. For too long she had believed in fairy tales and happily-ever-after endings.

But that was before reality had shattered her last few illusions.

It was a new experience, playing Santa Claus and nursemaid all rolled into one. Harrison, priding himself that he was getting pretty damned good at both roles, made Cleo slip off her sandals and lie down on the couch while he fixed lunch.

"Did you know you can buy iced tea already made?" he called out from the kitchen. "One percent. That's okay, isn't it?"

"One percent *tea?*"

"One percent milk. Still tastes like ditch water, but it's better than scum."

"Skim," she called back, and he could hear the undercurrent of laughter in her voice.

He began to hum as he put away the groceries. He'd made another run at the supermarket on the way through town. This time, an old hand, he had braved the task alone.

Nearly alone. With the help of a friendly clerk, he'd stocked up on frozen foods, packaged foods, instant this and ready-made that. Mac would have a fit if he could see him now, Harrison thought, humming the theme from *Finlandia* as he followed the instructions on a couple of frozen entrées.

It was a cinch. So was operating a microwave. He had a degree in electronics, after all. He poured the tea, which wasn't as good as hers, but it was passable.

What he'd really like to have was a Reuben sandwich and a tall, cold Dos Equis. Fat chance of either. According to the experts, wine was in, beer was out. "If fruit and vegetables are supposed to be so damned good, what's the difference between grapes and hops? Answer me that, Dr. Crackbone," he muttered, arranging things on a serving tray.

She was lying on the sofa, her eyes closed and the mound of her belly pulling her skirt halfway up over her thighs. She had nice legs. Not terribly long. She wasn't a tall woman. Exceptionally nice knees. Pretty feet, even if they were a bit swollen. Nice toenails.

Toenails? Jeez. You're breaking my heart, Lawless.

He bent over to place the tray on the coffee table, and it hit him all over again. Instant replay. He'd taken his eyes off the road for one single instant. In that one moment, the logging truck had pulled out onto the highway. Three lives could have been snuffed out. Maybe four.

Sweat filmed his forehead. He felt a slight twinge in

his chest and thought, *Not now, God—please. This is* not
a good time.

Take a deep breath. Stay calm. Inhale, hold, exhale.
Do it again. And again.

Whew. Another crisis averted. "Here we go, can you
sit up? Need some help?" He slid her tray closer and decided against slipping an arm behind her to ease her into
a sitting position. Touching her had a peculiar effect on
him. He was feeling shaky enough without any additional stress.

Stepping back, he took another deep breath, inhaling
the mingled scent of talcum powder, shampoo and stale
herbs. "It was billed as chicken cacciatore," he apologized. "I followed the instructions, but I'm afraid it
doesn't look much like the picture on the box."

Nor did it taste even faintly like Mac's version of the
dish. He wished it was better. Wished Mac was here to
cook for them. Wished he'd never come here in the first
place, never heard of the legacy that had brought him
here, never had the heart attack, never...

But then, look at all he would have missed.

"The tea's not bad," he said encouragingly.

It wasn't good, either, but it was better than the
chicken. He'd bought bagged salads and bottled dressing. They were no better than the rest of the meal. God,
he missed Mac. He wondered if he could lure him away
from his present employer and bring him down here to
the lodge. He was going to have to hire staff pretty soon,
anyway. He could make a bed, do the simple stuff, but
he had an idea there was more to housekeeping than that.

They ate in silence. Harrison wondered what Cleo
was thinking about, and then wondered if she was wondering what he was thinking about. He glanced up once

or twice to see her watching him. She'd duck her face and pretend to be fascinated by an overcooked noodle.

He insisted on cleaning up, which meant stashing the remains of their dinner in the raccoon-proof garbage container out by the pan where she fed the crows and putting their few dishes in the dishwasher.

"Where does the soap go?" he called out from the kitchen.

"What soap?"

In the end, she had to show him how to operate a dishwasher. He couldn't believe how many things there were that he didn't know how to do. Didn't know, because he'd never had to know, never even had occasion to wonder about them. Harrison Lawless, product of Exeter, of Harvard and MIT, a man who had built entire companies from the ground up. A man who was on a first-name basis with royalty on two continents.

Life was full of new experiences, he told himself. Feeling stupid was just one of many.

Later on, he brought a stack of boxes inside and opened them. The first was the answering machine. Bottom of the line. There hadn't been much choice. She asked him to record the message, giving only the phone number.

He gave her one of the two portable phones he'd bought, and after she retired for the night, he took the other one to his room.

An hour and a half later, he leaned back in the bed that was too short, too narrow, too soft, and smiled a smile that more than a few of his former adversaries would have recognized.

He'd been called a prince, a pirate and, on rare occasions, a predator. This was his predator smile.

* * *

Early the next morning, after a surprisingly restful night, Harrison woke to the sound of a ringing phone. He reached out and then reconsidered. It was still her house. He'd given the number out to several people last night, but he owed her the courtesy of allowing her to answer her calls.

It rang four times and he heard his own voice cut in with a brief message. And then he heard another voice, one he didn't recognize, saying, "Cleo, this is Pierce Holmes. I've been trying to reach you. I called several times yesterday, but either you were out or you weren't taking calls. At any rate, I need to see you, so how about returning my call at your earliest convenience. And, Cleo—this is personal. It has nothing to do with Henry, I promise you."

Henry? Who the hell was Henry?
Who the hell was Pierce Holmes?

They had breakfast together. Neither of them mentioned the earlier phone call. She'd glanced at the machine with its blinking red light when she'd passed by but hadn't bothered to retrieve the message. Which meant that either she'd already heard it, or she didn't want him to hear it.

They ate a boring, healthy breakfast. Harrison thought longingly of Mac's omelettes, with bacon, cheese, salsa, sour cream and mushrooms.

He thought about the twinge he'd experienced yesterday and the momentary breathlessness that had accompanied it. It had passed so quickly he'd barely had time to react. All the same, it was time to get back to the prescribed regimen. Low fat, low stress, regular exercise and the dozen or so servings of fruit and vegetables that were supposed to bring his cholesterol down to a relatively safe level. With medication, he'd got it down to three hundred. Which wasn't good, but it was a damned sight better than where it had been. He was shooting for two-twenty without medication, once he learned to stick to his damned diet.

With no more expression than if she'd been commenting on the weather, Cleo said, "I've decided to let you have the lodge."

Harrison choked on his coffee and grabbed another napkin. "You've what? What brought that on?"

"You can't be all that surprised. You're the one who keeps reminding me of the option you signed."

He waited, knowing she reacted to silence the way iron filings reacted to a magnet.

"Well, anyway, it's not going to happen right away. Closing takes anywhere from thirty to ninety days. There are all the inspections."

Inspections. That would be to satisfy bank requirements. He had no intention of telling her that inspections weren't necessary. That he never involved his bank in minor purchases. "Fine. Whatever you say. I'm not at all demanding."

"Ha! And I'm not at all pregnant."

He chuckled. "Point to you." Rising, he rinsed out the dishes and stacked them in the dishwasher the way she'd shown him the night before, taking pride in having to be shown something only once. And then he heard her sigh. "What? Now what am I doing wrong?"

"You don't put in dirty dishes without first unloading the clean ones."

"I knew that. I was just waiting to see if you'd notice."

They settled a few domestic issues, and then Cleo confronted him with that brass-tacks expression that made her pointy little chin look almost aggressive. "Harrison, yesterday at the hospital the nurse's aide told me that my handsome friend had decided not to see the cardiologist until later. Would you care to tell me what that was all about?"

"Your handsome friend, huh? You think she mistook me for your, uh, significant other?" His gaze moved pointedly to the most prominent portion of her anatomy.

"Oh, stop it. What I want to know is, why would you be seeing a cardiologist? Does it have something to do with your cholesterol? Just how high is it, anyway? Is there something you're not telling me?"

Cleo told herself later it was as if a door had been shut in her face. One minute they were joking about his not knowing how to operate a dishwasher, the next minute that glacier look was back.

"As a matter of fact, there are several things I haven't told you. Go to the bathroom, then put on your walking shoes. We'll start out with half a mile in each direction, and I'll tell you what you want to know."

"You're not going to tell me what I want to know, you're going to tell me what you want me to know, and no more."

"You're right. Now, go get your walking shoes on."

"My walking shoes don't fit anymore, and stop trying to boss me around."

He glanced at her feet and then back at her face. "Then put on your sandals. We'll take it easy."

"Look, just forget it, all right? I don't need any answers, and I certainly don't need a keeper."

"Are you sure about that?"

God, he was smooth. Niles at his best couldn't hold a candle to this man. She'd once heard a certain Virginia politician described as a velvet-covered steamroller.

Harrison didn't even bother with the velvet covering.

"All right, all right, I'm going," she snapped. She felt like crying. Felt even more like kicking something. Her emotions were all over the place these days. It was like PMS, only a hundred times worse.

She put on her sandals and went to the bathroom again. If her baby dropped any lower, she might as well take up permanent residence there.

He was waiting on the front deck, staring out at the river. He turned quickly at the sound of the door, almost as if he hadn't been expecting her. As if he'd been lost in thought. A million miles away. For just an instant she caught a look in his eyes that was so bleak she almost reached out to him.

"I'm ready," she said, her irritation of a moment before gone. Vaporized.

It occurred to her then that for all his bossiness, all his uptight, inept, maddening ways, Harrison Lawless was one of the loneliest men she'd ever had the dubious pleasure of knowing.

Seven

Neither of them spoke for several minutes. They walked as far as the place where the river cut in closest to the road. Harrison checked his pace to match hers. His every instinct was to stride out ahead, as if he could outdistance his irritation. He might have known she would pick up on his impatience.

"You go on ahead," she said, already panting. "I'm too slow."

But he wasn't off the hook yet. That much was implicit in the look she gave him. Sooner or later he was going to have to answer a few questions. He owed her that much. "I'm in no hurry," he lied. "I thought we'd both start out easy, maybe half a mile in each direction with a bathroom break in the middle."

She caught his hand and gave it a shake. "Oh, for heaven's sake, stop being so darned understanding. It makes me uncomfortable."

"Uncomfortable?"

"Yes, uncomfortable! But then, everything lately makes me uncomfortable, so don't take it personally. At least you don't give me heartburn."

He chuckled at that. Briefly. And then he concentrated on the pace. His normal walking stride was roughly thirty inches. Hers was about sixteen.

They strolled. It drove him up the wall. He was a strider by nature, not a stroller. He had too much pent-up energy to waste time meandering down country roads. After almost a week, the novelty of the slower Southern pace was beginning to wear off.

Dammit, he wasn't ready to be put out to pasture yet. To be dry-docked, at his age. He'd almost sooner shoot for the moon and die trying to reach it.

"Stop clenching your fists, Harrison. It makes the veins in the side of your neck bulge."

She was right. He could feel it. Feel the pressure building. He made a deliberate effort to relax. Breathe in, breathe out. Smell the damned roses. She stepped on a pinecone, flung out her arms, and he caught her by the shoulders. "Careful there—we don't want a calamity."

"No wonder I can't stand up, I'm shaped like a lop-sided top!" She clung to his arm just long enough to catch her breath, muttered some dire threat against trees that littered, shook off his arm and waddled forth. "This is disgusting, Harrison. Pray you don't ever get pregnant. You don't have the temperament for it."

"It may come as a surprise to you, my dear, but that's not all I don't have."

She shot him a cheeky smile, and he could feel the tension begin to ebb. She was a comfortable woman. That is, she was when she wasn't chewing him out.

Or turning him on.

They were halfway back to the lodge when a delivery truck rattled past on the rutted dirt road, kicking up a cloud of dust. "Now, where on earth do you suppose he's going? There's not but one house on this road, and that's mine."

He didn't bother to correct her as to whose house it was. They'd had that argument too many times. Harrison knew where the truck was headed. He'd ordered three deck lounges from a furniture store in Manteo that had promised quick delivery. "Why don't I run on ahead and check it out?"

"He'll be back as soon as he realizes he's taken a wrong turn, but go ahead. You're dying to run, anyway."

His broad grin told her she was right on target. Cleo watched him round the bend, admiring his easy, long-legged stride. He wasn't a showy runner. No pumping elbows or fancy running clothes. He simply looked… good.

He looked good doing whatever he happened to be doing or trying to do, whether aligning the things on the mantel with mathematical precision or rearranging her cereal boxes in alphabetical order, from bran to Cheerios to Fruits 'n' Nuts to oatmeal—or even changing a tire.

He was an attractive man.

Correction—he was a strikingly handsome man with an aura of power and authority, even though he was a complete klutz when it came to actually doing anything useful. Efficient, he was not.

Cleo trudged along down the rutted road, shaking her left foot now and then to try to dislodge whatever it was that was sticking her in the foot.

In no particular hurry, she stopped to watch a couple

of local fishermen tending crab pots. She watched a chunky yacht bristling with outriggers and pennants go past and wondered idly where it was bound. She thought about baby names again. She was up to the *R*s now, torn between Ramona and Rebecca.

Or Robert after her father if it was a boy.

Breaking off a stem of tall grass and using it to shoo away insects, she plodded on toward the lodge, thinking about Niles, feeling sad for what might have been, for what he'd ruined.

She thought about Harrison Lawless and felt—

Oh, she didn't know. Irritation? Aggravation? Admiration?

A combination of all those and more.

Back at the lodge, she hobbled over to the steps and sank down on the middle one, winded. There'd been a time not too long ago when she'd climbed up and down ladders five dozen times a day, unhanging and rehanging heavy framed paintings.

The delivery truck was still there, pulled up behind Harrison's car. Truck. Whatever the thing was. From somewhere at the back of the house, she could hear the low murmur of male voices. For the past three weeks she'd hardly seen another soul. Now all of a sudden, the place was running over with visitors. Tow trucks. Delivery vans. What next, a parade of door-to-door salesmen?

She kicked her foot, but whatever was in her sandal refused to budge. She couldn't bend over far enough to go in after it with a finger. That was a new development, too. Either she'd gained a pound in the last half hour, or something had shifted.

She took the line of least resistance, something she'd become remarkably good at lately, and settled back to catch her breath. Maybe she could apply for a job as a bridge tender. That shouldn't require too much exertion.

And maybe, if she didn't snap out of it, she'd find herself right back where she'd been before Harrison had turned up. Drifting along in a totally nonproductive fog, waiting for all those wonderful job offers to start pouring in.

Two men came around the corner of the house, Harrison and a red-faced stranger in dark green coveralls who looked as if he could use a glass of something cold to drink.

So could she. She was about to suggest it when Harrison slipped the man a bill, dismissed him with a casual nod and turned to where she was sitting. Sprawling. Graceful, she was not.

Planting his fists on his hips, he assumed a familiar king-of-all-he-surveyed attitude. "All finished with your walk?"

"I've got something in my left shoe. Besides, the road needs grading. It's too rutty to walk on. Once it rains, it'll flatten out some, but then it'll be too muddy."

"Hmm."

"What did he want? Did he have the wrong address? Why did you give him money?"

"Left shoe? Right shoe?"

"Left." He was impossible to distract, whereas she found it impossible to stay focused for more than five consecutive seconds. Two more different personalities would be hard to find.

He knelt and lifted her foot off the ground. It wouldn't go very far without toppling her backward. She braced her elbows on the top step while he dug out a broken holly leaf, dusted off the sole of her foot and slipped her sandal back on. At the touch of his fingers on her arch, heat sizzled all the way up her leg.

He studied her a minute, making her uncomfortably aware of her damp, flushed face, her rumpled smock, the hair that had started out pinned neatly on top of her head but was now sliding out from under its restraints.

She was a mess. He was far too polite to mention it, and she didn't know why she cared anyway, but she did. Maybe because her ego had taken such a beating over the past few years, she was desperate for the slightest measure of reassurance.

Only it wasn't reassurance he was offering. All he was offering was money and an impersonal sort of kindness out of consideration for her awkward situation. Which should be more than enough, only somehow, it wasn't.

"Want to walk some more, or would you rather stretch out in the shade with a tall, cool glass of tea?"

"You have to ask?"

With a grin that looked suspiciously smug, he pulled her to her feet, held her by the shoulders and turned her toward the deck.

It was then that she saw it, half-hidden by the redwood deck chairs and matching cross-legged table. The frame was yellow. The cushions, still covered in clear plastic, were a splashy red, lime and royal blue tropical print. It looked totally out of place in the muted rustic setting.

"What is that thing?"

"A hostess gift?"

"Harrison, what's going on here? Have you already started moving in?"

"You could say that."

"Yes, but—*look* at it. It doesn't even *look* like you."

"I sincerely hope not," he said dryly. "But wait till you see how it feels. It's not too low, easy to get in and out of. You couldn't tip it over if you tried. Come on, you can be the first to try it out."

He'd bought it. For her. Not for the world would she hurt his feelings, but given a choice, she'd have suggested something in redwood, with cushions in a muted earth tone or maybe a fern print.

"It's a little gaudy," he admitted, "but the manager said it was more stable than anything else he had in stock. I told him it was for a woman who was eleven months pregnant with triplets." She choked off a giggle. "Hold on while I get the plastic off." Using a monogrammed silver penknife, he ripped through the protective covering, pulled it aside and then watched as she carefully lowered herself onto the thick cushions.

"Well? What do you think?"

Cleo looked up at him and sighed. How could a man be so darned overbearing and so irresistible at the same time? He watched her like a hawk. "It's…nice. Soft."

"But not too soft. Just right, huh?"

He looked so anxious she took pity on him. "Harrison, it's perfect. It's wonderful. It might be a little, um, bright—"

"Gaudy. I expect it's more suited to a beach cottage than a log cabin in the woods, but it's sturdy. And the back's adjustable." He was still towering over her, looking as if a single word of criticism would burst his balloon, so she tried one of his tricks. Distraction.

"Do you suppose I could have a glass of iced tea?"

Heaven help her, what was she going to do with the man? This whole situation was getting out of hand. The idea of paying rent on a house he was in the process of buying. Of sharing it with the former owner while they settled the details. If she let him, he'd wait on her hand and foot, and it was obvious he couldn't even take care of himself.

He was a drifter, whatever he'd been in the past. A businessman who'd lost his business? A husband who'd lost his wife? A man who'd lost his memory?

An escaped lunatic?

An escaped convict? She'd heard on the radio about some man escaping from a road gang just yesterday....

But then, Harrison had turned up before that.

Whoever and whatever he was, someone around here—she refused to name names—was definitely a candidate for the butterfly-net brigade.

There were three of the things, one for each deck, all equally colorful, all sticking out like enormous sore thumbs in the muted wooded setting.

Niles would have had a fit. He'd had the redwood deck furniture custom-built. It was exactly like furniture she'd seen for sale in practically all the better outdoor furniture places, but he'd insisted on having it built to order and paying twice as much as it was worth. Typical Niles. It was an ego thing.

Harrison had taken the hammock down and hidden it away. Darn it, she liked that hammock. It was one of her favorite spots to nap. However, knowing how hard it was for a leopard to change its spots, or for a control freak to change his bossy ways, she let it pass without comment.

Over the next few days, Cleo allowed a lot of things to pass without comment, including the plumber who came to inspect the plumbing, the electrician who came to check out the wiring. Something—squirrels or mice—had chewed through a couple of places, but other than the fact that the outside lights on the west side didn't work, it was in good condition. As for the rest, the roof didn't leak, there was no buildup in the chimney, no nests. The foundation had settled slightly— sooner or later it would need attention, but there was no immediate danger.

Still, it was a good thing she'd agreed to sell the place. She had a feeling repairing a settled foundation would cost a mint. Fortunately, Harrison didn't appear worried. Whatever his problem was, it didn't seem to be money.

Amazingly, it turned out that he had relatives in the area. Or at least, some of his ancestors had lived here at one time. Most of the workmen spent as much time chatting as they did inspecting. Harrison had encouraged it, listening to tales that sounded suspiciously tall to her, and with the meter running, no less. Still, he seemed to enjoy it, and as he'd already informed her, he was footing the bill for the inspections and any work done as a result.

It irritated her that the bigger and clumsier she grew, the mellower he seemed to become. These days he was so relaxed he grinned almost as often as he frowned. Several times she even heard him laugh.

They still argued. Sometimes she even won. It was a new experience, one that made her feel confident even though she was physically miserable, what with the heat, the heartburn and her constant trips to the bathroom.

After jeering at her for feeding crows in an old skillet in the backyard, he bought new bird feeders and put them up with no more damage than a few bruised thumbs, a few dozen bent nails and a generous supply of swearwords. They watched eagerly for the first visitors, watched the newly hatched baby ducks' first swimming lessons and commiserated with each other when Mama Mallard and her seven children left the pond and waddled down to the river.

She wouldn't have believed a man could change so much in such a short time. He was even drinking decaffeinated coffee and skim milk and fussing when they ran out of grapefruit.

Of course, he was still unbearably bossy. Once he discovered where she kept her few yard tools, he insisted on trying them all out. He whacked down the weeds around the house so that she wouldn't worry about it and try to do it herself.

She never had. Weeds were nice. Some had berries, some had flowers, some had interesting seeds. Most were lovely in the fall. She'd once done a series of weed studies in pen and ink.

But he had energy to spare and she had none at all. It was easier to let nature—and Harrison—take its course.

He'd been there a little over two weeks. It seemed like two months. Seemed almost as if they'd lived there together for years. They'd given up even pretending that she was leaving. At this point, the only logical thing to do—and she'd known it instinctively all along—was to stay right where she was until after the baby came.

Once she was on her feet again, Harrison could micromanage her relocation the same way he did everything else. All she would have to do is give him a list of specifications—small town, preferably one with an art gallery and good schools. North or South Carolina or even Georgia. Not Virginia. Henry Barnes had too many sources of information in Virginia.

But all that could wait until later. Meanwhile, Harrison refused to let her lift a finger. He made her walk a mile a day, made her drink milk, take naps and vitamins, and hummed while he was doing it.

She couldn't stand a cheerful dictator. She hummed right back at him, only she couldn't carry a tune, and seeing him wince didn't help her case at all.

At least she refused to let him smoke his stinky old cigars, which he'd mentioned once he was trying to give up. She saw that he ate five servings of fruit and vegetables each day, took his low-dose aspirin and ran at least three miles every morning.

Actually, they took care of each other. When she thought about it, it made her feel like crying.

But then, everything these days made her feel like crying.

Equipment began to arrive. A computer, fax machines, various exercise machines. Harrison worked out while Cleo read aloud from books on nutrition and stitched baby clothes. She'd forgotten the pleasure she'd once derived from designing and sewing her own clothes. There'd been a time when she'd had a real flair for it, but that was before she'd married into a family that considered anything with flair ill-bred.

They listened to the news, local and network, and discussed getting a satellite dish. As if she'd be here long enough to benefit. The prisoner was still on the loose, according to the local news report. Harrison warned her to keep the doors and windows locked while he was out running.

"It's too hot, and besides, no escaped convict with half a brain would hang around here. He'll be long gone by now."

"Then I'll stay home. Who needs to run in this heat?"

"You do. Go earlier, while I'm still asleep."

"This place is far too isolated. I'll see about having the AC checked over and a security system installed."

"I thought that was what you liked about the place—its isolation and all the fresh air. You could breathe air-conditioning in New York."

"I'm not going to argue, Cleo. Just remember, until I get a security system installed, I want you to stay close."

As if she could waddle very far in her condition. She told him so, and they shared another laugh. A nice, comfortable, no-tension, stress-free chuckle.

"I'm beginning to believe you're good for me," Harrison told her.

"I'm beginning to believe you're bad for me. You make it entirely too easy to procrastinate."

"Hey, I can't take credit for that. You're a natural."

She threw a pillow at him. "Actually, you're good for me, too. You make me feel almost competent, which makes me feel more confident. I needed that."

He looked as if he'd like to ask questions, but didn't. Instead, he said, "Mutual benefit. You make me feel calm, lazy, a lot more comfortable than I ever thought I could be in the slow lane. It's a new experience."

"I'll just bet it is. You never did specify what line of business you were in. Are you sure you aren't a race-car driver? How about a jet pilot? No, I've got it—you're European royalty hiding out from the latest palace scandal." He was such fun to tease. She had a feeling he wasn't used to it, which made her even more curious about his past. "No, not that—the accent's wrong." Tilting her head, she regarded him with a slight frown. "The accent, maybe, but not the attitude."

She let him drag her out to walk twice a day, early mornings and late in the evening, after the sun went down. They were down to half a mile each time now, which was more than she wanted to do, but she did it for Agatha. Or Arrowsmith. If her parents had had a son, they'd probably have called him that, or maybe Apollo. She'd got as far as Wilhelmina and started back at the beginning.

Harrison insisted on accompanying her, although she could practically hear him gnashing his teeth at her snail's pace. He was sweet. He was also arrogant, inept, bossy, kind and generous. She was halfway to being in love with the man—another symptom of hormones in chaos— when he announced that he'd invited a friend to visit and would be meeting her at the airport in a few days.

She couldn't believe the crushing disappointment she felt at the thought of someone else—another woman—invading their private world. It had been so peaceful, so perfect with just the two of them.

"Fine. That's wonderful. There's certainly plenty of room. In fact, I've been thinking, I really should move out of the master suite and take one of the smaller guest rooms. Or maybe even look for a place closer to the hospital. Now that I think about it—"

"Cleo. Kindly shut up a minute, will you? Her name is Marla Kane and you'll like her."

"Fine. That's just marvelous. It's a wonderful place to invite your friends. Is she…just a friend, or a very *good* friend? No, don't answer that. I shouldn't have asked. I'm just a little…surprised, that's all."

Was that kindness she saw in his eyes? Or, heaven forbid, pity? God, she was so gauche! Vesper Barnes was right about one thing, at least. She had absolutely no breeding, none at all. "Why don't I go air out another bedroom? In fact, why not the other room in your wing? Not that I—that is, maybe you'd prefer to share a—"

Her shoulders sagged. "Harrison, don't mind me. I'm running a twelve-volt mouth on a two-volt brain. You mentioned hiring a housekeeper? This might be a good time to start looking around."

The limousine arrived late that afternoon, just as they were setting out on their postprandial stroll, Cleo undertaking the excursion under duress, as usual. As limousines went, it was fairly modest. Certainly not one of those pretentious Hollywood models, but it was unmistakably a limousine.

"Harrison," she whispered, clutching his arm.

"Nick? What the devil—" He patted her hand absently, and then he began to grin. "Nick, you old son of a gun, what the devil are you doing down here?"

The front passenger door swung open. Something—or someone—was ejected. There was a cry of, "Oh, wow, a real log cabin, just like camp!" and then Cleo's attention was drawn to a long, *long,* elegant leg, in navy slacks that were obviously silk, emerging from the rear door.

Five-inch heels. They had to be all of five inches high.

"Darling, we decided to surprise you. What on *earth* are you doing in a place like this? Do you have any idea how long it took us to get here? God, I'm dying for a drink! Nick wouldn't let me open the Bollinger."

Eight

Life was far from boring, Cleo told herself as she brushed her teeth and prepared for bed that night. In fact, if it got any more *un*boring, she wasn't certain she could handle it. If she had to share her house with three strangers, she could have done with a bit more warning.

Not that she knew what she could have done with it. Put out the welcome mat?

Hardly. She might have cried a little more, eaten a little more ice cream, thrown a small tantrum.

The trouble was, she was getting entirely too comfortable in her cozy little rut. The intrusion of a woman, a child and a tough-looking, flashy-dressed man had come along just in time.

Harrison had been every bit as surprised as she was when the limo had pulled into the yard. He was good when it came to covering his feelings, but she was learn-

ing to read small signs. The tightening of his jaw. The
lines between his eyebrows. That flicker of surprise that
registered the instant before he could disguise it with a
broad smile.

Oh, yes, she was coming to know him well.

He had mentioned meeting a woman at the airport.
He hadn't said a word about the boy who'd scurried
from the front seat like a flushed quail, or the swarthy
man who'd climbed out from under the steering wheel.

What bothered her most—and the fact that it bothered
her at all bothered her even more—was Marla Kane. Exactly where did she fit in Harrison's life? Were they kin-
folks? Business acquaintances? Friends? Lovers?

So far she'd seen no sign of sexual interest on either
side, only a dry peck on the lips when he'd helped her
out of the car.

The boy had rolled his eyes and said, "Yuk."

Cleo had been too busy struggling to overcome surprise, curiosity and resentment, not to mention a few
other emotions that didn't bear close scrutiny, to say
anything.

And what about Nick Sebastiani, the driver? There
was obviously some sort of relationship between the
two men. They'd done that male thing—handshakes
with the extra clasp. Grins and a few backslaps. He
seemed pleasant enough. His clothes were a bit flam-
boyant—fitted purple shirt, lizard-skin belt on black
jeans and matching boots with silver-capped toes—but
then, he had the sort of good looks that could carry it
off. She'd like to paint him, only it had been so long,
her paints had probably all dried up.

Young Reynolds Kane was something else. He'd
burst out of the car like a frisky spaniel puppy, sizzling

with energy, brimming with curiosity. "Hey, Nick, what are those things in the edge of the water? They look like dinosaurs crawling up out of the prime—the primorbital ooze."

"Primordial," Marla corrected. "Sweetie, I told you, never preface your remarks with 'Hey.'"

"Yes, but what are they?"

Cleo had stepped in then. "Actually, they're—"

Cypress knees, she was about to say, but by then the boy was on to another question. "What's that man doing out there in the water with that cage? I bet he's a smuggler, don't you?"

"That's a—" She started to tell him about crab pots, but he was off again. What's this? What's that? Man, what are those big floppy birds?

She caught him staring at her stomach and hoped he wouldn't ask her about *that*. Helplessly, she glanced at Marla Kane, but the tall, reed-thin brunette in the navy slacks, lime green silk shirt and white blazer appeared to be arguing with Harrison about something.

Reynolds didn't ask. "I know what that is," he informed her smugly. "It's a baby. I know all about that kind of stuff. They told us in sex class how to get 'em and all." His audacious grin, complete with braces, indicated that he also knew precisely how close to the edge he could skate without getting into trouble.

Before Cleo could come up with a proper response, he'd spotted her family of mallards. "Hey, look—ducks! Can I feed 'em? We had ducks at camp last year, and we fed 'em corn. Do you have any corn?"

More questions followed before she could tell him that no, she didn't have corn but she did have birdseed, and yes, the river was really named the Alligator, and no, she'd never actually seen any alligators there her-self, but from time to time they were reported in the area, and no, she didn't really know what made alligators different from crocodiles.

Her head had been spinning by the time Nick stepped in. "Round up your gear now, Rip. Your mama's tired."

Marla hadn't looked tired, Cleo remembered think-ing. Irritated, perhaps, but hardly tired. No woman should look so good at the end of a two-day drive.

She heard Nick say quietly to Marla, "Has he taken his pill?"

Reynolds piped up, "Nah. I forgot it."

"Bat ears." Nick ruffled the boy's hair. Marla lifted her shoulders in a gesture too elegant to be called a shrug, and then Nick told the boy he might as well hold off until morning. "But slow down, okay? Find your blazer, hang it up and tie your shoestrings before you trip."

Judging by the amount of luggage they'd brought with them, Cleo thought they might be planning to stay all summer. Harrison reached for the two largest bags, but Nick waved him off. "I'll handle this, sir. You show Marla and the kid to their rooms."

Sir?

Cleo glanced at Harrison. "Sir?" she echoed softly.

"Yes, what is it?" he snapped without even looking at her. He was too busy looking at Marla Kane. Cleo, feeling dumpy and dowdy by contrast, decided she wasn't quite as skilled at reading faces as she'd thought.

But then, reading Harrison's face was like trying to read someone else's locked diary. It might hold a wealth of fascinating material, but unless you had the key, you'd never know what it was.

She waddled along after the parade, wondering if

she had enough food on hand, wondering where to put the two additional guests. She'd aired out the only remaining trophyless guest room, the one next to Harrison's. She had an idea young Reynolds—or Rip, as he preferred to be called—would adore trophies, the more ferocious the better. She only hoped Nick would be as easy to please.

Would he be staying? He was only the driver... wasn't he?

"Oh, man, look at those antlers!"

Cleo made it up the steps, huffing and puffing, just as the others disappeared inside. "You like those? Wait'll you see your bedroom."

"I've got antlers in my bedroom?"

She lowered her voice conspiratorially. "Honey, you've not only got antlers, you've got a bear and the skull of a longhorn bull with horns as wide as a pickup truck." She stretched her arms and wiggled her fingertips.

"Oh, man, this place is cool!"

If trophies were any indication of cool, then the place was frigid. Personally, she detested the things, but Niles had insisted on having them. Said they completed the image. Image had been important to Niles.

As far as Cleo was concerned, they were something else to be vacuumed, only not the birds. Those had to be wiped down with a damp cloth. She'd learned that the hard way, when she'd stripped half the feathers from a ring-necked pheasant. That was when they'd had their first big fight. Over a few feathers on a dead bird, of all things.

At least she no longer had to get dressed every morning under all that glassy-eyed surveillance. Niles, claiming he'd developed an allergy to them several years ago, had moved the ones from the master suite into one of the other wings.

Nick managed everything. While Reynolds explored and Harrison gave Marla the grand tour, he made her sit down. "My mama had eleven kids, Ms. Barnes. I was number six. You shouldn't be trying to do too much at this stage. Ma always said in the last few weeks, even breathing took too much energy."

If he was curious about who she was and what she was doing in Harrison's house in this condition, he was too polite to ask. He dug out the spare bed linens when she pointed out which carton she thought they were in. They weren't, but he eventually located them. He insisted on making up the beds in the south wing and assured her that he didn't mind sharing a bath with Reynolds, and that, no, the trophies wouldn't bother them at all.

Harrison shaved for dinner. He'd gotten out of the habit of shaving twice a day. It was only one of many things that had changed since he'd come south. It occurred to him a few minutes later as he joined the others that his life had been totally structured for as long as he could remember.

Was it possible that he could have mistaken structure for substance?

Marla had brought along a Bollinger '89, which he accepted with every evidence of pleasure. He wasn't much of a champagne drinker. White wines, even good wines, gave him a hellacious headache. Either she'd forgotten, or she'd never noticed.

Nick had brought him a box of his favorite double coronas. Don Jivan Los Lectores. At the rate of one a day, they should last him about six weeks. Naturally, he wouldn't smoke them inside, not until after Cleo had gone.

Gone. Funny thing—he had trouble picturing the lodge without her. He could picture diapers and other baby paraphernalia hanging from the antlers—he could even see cribs and playpens on the decks. But no Cleo?

No way.

Tilting his champagne flute, he watched the bubbles rise and wondered how the devil he'd got himself involved in this crazy situation. More to the point, he wondered what he was going to do about it. If he'd needed an example of just how far off course a man could swerve once he lost control of his life, he couldn't ask for a better one.

Conversation was desultory, mostly between Nick and Marla. The boy had gone to bed soon after a makeshift meal they'd all pitched in to prepare. Even Marla. She was a good sport. But then, that's why she was here.

They were all tired. Cleo was having trouble staying awake. She was usually in bed by ten. Tonight, in honor of the guests, she was evidently determined to stick it out.

Observing her without appearing to, Harrison thought about reminding her that they were his guests, not hers, and that she was under no obligation to play hostess.

But then, if he did that, either her feelings would be hurt or she'd climb back up on her high horse. Neither one of them needed the hassle. It was a battle they'd already fought to a draw. By silent mutual consent they had postponed a resolution until after the baby came.

Harrison watched her eyelids sag, fly open and then sag again as she tried to keep up with the conversation. Bless her, none of it was worth losing sleep over, especially as she'd be up at least half a dozen times during the night to go to the bathroom.

"Harrison? Harrison, wake up. Did you hear what I said? You knew I was doing the Rothstein benefit again this year, but did you read in the *Times* that we cleared nearly seventy thousand? That's net, darling, not gross. We had all the biggest corporate donors there, thanks to the latest flap about corporate welfare. The first hint of scandal and little ole Marla is off and running. I've learned to skip top management and go directly to public relations. You can't believe what a bit of bad press can do to open corporate vaults."

Harrison managed an appropriate murmur. Her tactics were no secret to him. It was one of the things he'd always admired about her, the talent for knowing what she wanted and how to go about getting it, even at his expense.

"Melba begged me to take on the children's thing next spring. They're in the middle of a nasty audit. I told her to ask me again after I've spent a few weeks at Elizabeth's, soaking in warm mud like a lazy pig. I'm flying out to Phoenix Thursday of next week."

She held out her glass for a refill. Nick reached for it, the fragile stemware incongruous in his hamlike fist. When he poured her a scant inch and a quarter, Harrison thought, amused, that if ever a man had been cut out to be a mother, it was Nick Sebastiani. When Harrison had left New York, it was with the understanding that Nick was going to use the limo and his severance pay to set himself up in business. Harrison didn't know— nor did he want to know—if this trip with Marla was strictly business or something more personal.

He did know that his perspective, and with it his

plans, had undergone a change. Thank God he hadn't actually proposed. Marriage, even the kind of marriage he'd been considering, was a serious step. The health implications for a divorced man were even worse than those for a man who had never married.

Early morning mist still blanketed the opposite shore the next day when Harrison quietly let himself out of the house. He stretched, flexing one set of muscles after another. He hadn't slept well, which was nothing new. Too much on his mind—also nothing new.

At least he hadn't woken up with a monster headache. There was something to be said for this moderation business after all.

"Hey, where ya going?"

Midstretch, with one foot up on the deck railing, he glanced around. Young Rip was strolling up from the water's edge with an empty birdseed sack in one hand, a stick in the other. Wet, muddy and grinning, he would have been a perfect model for Huck Finn if it weren't for the braces and the two-hundred-dollar shoes.

"Out."

"Mom says that's not an answer."

"Your mom's right. I'm going to run a couple of miles before breakfast. If you want to come with me, that's fine, but I warn you, I don't talk when I'm running."

"Why not? Because you're out of breath?"

"Because I'm thinking, da—darn it."

"You can say dammit. My dad says it a lot. He says worse'n damn sometimes. Mom doesn't curse. She says it's a sign of a weak vo—vocallary or something. I think it means you don't know enough good words."

They jogged along in silence while Harrison

concentrated on regulating his breathing. He wasn't in quite as good shape as he'd thought, but he was getting there.

"Mom said I had to call her 'Mother.' I wanted to call her Marla. Billy Schumer calls his stepmother Rosemary. That's cool, don't you think so?"

"Not particularly. Mom's fine. Or Mother."

"Yeah, I guess." They jogged along for another few minutes before the boy peeled off with a casual salute. "Hey, I'm starved. I'm gonna go grub up, okay?"

Harrison had a feeling Marla was in for quite an education before she returned the boy to his father. She'd mentioned that her ex-husband was supposed to have had him between school and summer camp, but a business delay in Belgium and an epidemic of head lice at school had played havoc with their well-planned schedule.

Picking up the pace, he ran as far as the graveled road and turned back, thinking that there was something wrong when a child's life was so damned structured that even time-out depended on someone else's schedule. Funny, he'd never stopped to consider it before, maybe because as far back as he could remember, his own life had been tightly regimented. He'd been taught at an early age that time was far too valuable to waste playing. Every minute must be used constructively, either to achieve or to acquire, with emphasis on the latter.

Amazing, he mused, how a simple change of perspective could open a man's eyes. Nothing had turned out the way he'd planned it, and he was a man who'd always planned carefully and then followed those plans to the letter.

Marla had been number three—or was it four?—on his list. The stress-free wife. Had he honestly thought she'd be content to settle down in a modest log cabin at the end of a dirt road?

If he'd chosen to relocate on Sanibel Island, or even Kennebunkport, it might've worked. But then, if he'd done that, he'd have been right back in the same old circle. Within a year—two years, tops—he'd have been right back on the old familiar treadmill. He didn't know a single soul who owned property within five hundred miles of this place, and that suited him just fine. If the time ever came when he grew bored with the pace—and he didn't rule out the possibility—he could move. For now, though, he was surprisingly content.

Granted, he hadn't thought beyond his own selfish interests. When he'd made his plans, he'd been so sure Marla would leap at the chance to snag one of the world's most eligible bachelors. What an arrogant ass he'd been.

Still was, for that matter. Thank God he'd come to his senses in time. Marla deserved far more than he'd been prepared to offer. She was a hell of a fine woman. Beautiful, intelligent, yet smart enough not to flaunt it. She was an expert when it came to dealing with people, singly or in groups. He'd seen her bring order out of chaos with the lift of a finely arched brow and the tap of a teaspoon on a microphone. It was one of the reasons she was called on so often to organize charity bashes, the other being that her own tax-deductible donation was usually in the vicinity of five figures.

It occurred to him that in some ways they were a lot alike. Polished on the surface, tough as steel underneath. She wasn't particularly good with the boy, but then, close relationships had never been his forte, either, although he liked to think he was improving in that respect. Growing, learning—a work in progress as opposed to being washed-up. Finished. Over the hill.

By the end of his run, Harrison was winded and sweaty, but invigorated. Not at all a bad way to start out the day. At least the muscles at the back of his neck weren't frozen into knots.

Nick Sebastiani, wearing green shorts and a leopard-print shirt along with silver-chained loafers and no socks, was busily polishing the limo when Harrison jogged into the yard again. He was beginning to understand why the man had occasionally griped about having to wear a uniform.

"You're keeping her in great shape," he remarked.

"She's never been on a dirt road before. Shock to her system."

"I thought by now you'd be hiring staff and looking into expanding your fleet."

"Thinking about it. Still checking out the territory."

"Sure, no point in rushing into anything. Join me for breakfast?"

"Nah, I want to check her levels before we head back."

"Plenty of time. You just got here."

Nick nodded and went back to caressing the right front fender with a chamois.

Halfway to the deck, Harrison spotted Cleo stretched out on the chaise longue, a glass of iced tea in her hand and a book on snakes in the other. The boy knelt beside her, cradling a snake shed in his hands.

"Harrison, back me up on this, will you? I say it's a rat snake. Rip insists it's a copperhead." Cleo gazed up at him, admiring the way his T-shirt clung to his sweaty body. For a man with an admitted health problem, he was a living, breathing picture of masculine fitness.

"Give me five minutes to shower and grab a cup of coffee first, will you?"

"Take all the time you need," she murmured, realizing somewhat to her surprise that she meant it. If he'd asked her for the next ten years, she would have agreed just as easily. Either her nice pink prepartum fog was clouding her judgment, or she was experiencing a few even more alarming symptoms. Such as the nest-building urge.

There was no point in calling it dinner when it was only a tray of assorted sandwiches, made and served by Nick on the front deck. He was turning out to be a real jewel. Cleo had learned that he'd once been Harrison's chauffeur, which had prompted a fresh set of questions, none of which she had voiced. What kind of man needed a full-time chauffeur? A millionaire? A politician? An international criminal?

No way. Not Harrison. And anyway, whoever he was—whoever he'd been—it was none of her business.

"There goes a sloop like the one Chad Williams bought last season." Marla waved a hand in the general direction of the river.

"More iced tea?" Nick asked Cleo.

"Thanks. You're spoiling me."

"Women need to be spoiled at a time like this. Pop said a woman's highest calling was—"

"Nicky, where's Reynolds? He didn't finish his sandwich."

"I'll check up on him. We forgot his pill again. I figured it was too late by the time I remembered it."

Cleo rubbed her aching back and wondered idly why Nick was the one to keep up with the boy's medication…and what the pills were for. He certainly appeared healthy. By the middle of the afternoon he'd gone through three changes of clothing in the process of capturing a box turtle, a mud slider and a bullfrog, all of which he'd brought to show her. She'd told him where there was a nest of baby mice, and then explained that they were too young to be separated from their mama, even if Marla would have allowed him to keep one.

Harrison, enjoying his cigar *du jour,* leaned back in a deck chair, both feet propped on the railing, and listened to the drone of insects, the soothing sound of water lapping against the shore, the buzz of a distant outboard motor and the soft murmur of voices behind him.

Contentment. It had nothing whatsoever to do with money, power or position. Funny, a man could live thirty-seven years without learning a damned thing about life.

He gave Marla two more days, tops, before she'd be out of here. He could always tell when she was growing restless. She stroked her right thumbnail. Tapped a toe. Drank a little more than usual.

Until recently, he'd probably exhibited his own set of signals. Now, perfectly relaxed, he blew out a stream of aromatic smoke and watched it drift off to disappear in the light fog floating a few feet above the still surface of the river.

Something was bothering Cleo. He didn't think it was Marla. Considering the little they had in common, the two women got along surprisingly well.

It occurred to him that Cleo could get along with anyone. She had her own way of dealing with things. She and the boy had a mutual admiration society going between them, mostly because she took time to listen as if she were genuinely interested in what he had to say. If she hadn't been so pregnant, she'd probably be wading, fishing, climbing trees and searching for arrowheads, enjoying it every bit as much as Rip did.

His own mother, Harrison mused, would have said Cleo had no sense of propriety. She'd have been right. It was one of the things he liked about her, the total lack of pretension. One of a growing number of things.

As for his father, he wouldn't have given her the time of day. Kingston Lawless was one of the most ruthless men he'd ever known. It scared the hell out of him to realize just how much like his father he was. In another few years...

Thank God for the warning. He only hoped he'd got out in time.

It was just after midnight. Something had aroused him from a sound sleep. He checked his watch, knowing that if it was anywhere near 4:00 a.m., he wouldn't be able to go back to sleep. Four was his personal witching hour. If for any reason he roused anywhere near four, he might as well get up, shower and start his day. At his desk. With the pot of coffee Mac always had ready and waiting, knowing it would be needed.

But something had definitely brought him out of a sound sleep. If it was that damned owl he'd heard last night, the bird was history. Endangered or not, it'd be one more trophy before it ever pulled that trick again.

Tap-tap-tap. Not whoo-whoo.

Okay, it wasn't the damned owl, it was the woodpecker. Whatever it was, it was dead meat if he got his hands on it.

The hesitant sound came again. From the door?

From the door. Someone was knocking on his door. Marla.

Marla?

Oh hell, what if she wanted sex? In spite of what he'd read about sex after a coronary, he wasn't sure he should. Wasn't even sure he could.

He knew one thing. If he did—if they did—there went another set of plans down the drain.

"Aw, hell," he muttered, throwing back the covers and reaching for his robe. He might as well give up and stop making plans, for all the good it ever did. He forked his hair back, tightened the belt on his navy silk robe and opened the door.

"Harrison, I need you. Please?"

Nine

"What's wrong? Come inside—sit down. Lie down. No, don't do that." It took him a full ten seconds to pull himself together. They were the longest ten seconds of his life.

"Harrison, I think I'm getting ready to have it. My back's been aching all day. I started having these pains, and when I got up—" She looked as if she expected him to tell her what to do.

If I were a praying man, this would be a good time to give it a shot. "Are you sure? Maybe you just pulled a muscle or—"

"Harrison? I'm sure."

They were standing in the doorway, speaking softly. He didn't know whether to carry her to his bed or head for the hospital. "I'll get Marla. She'll know what to do."

"It's probably not an emergency, only I thought—

since it'll take a while—maybe we ought to get started. Would you drive me in?"

"Harrison? Cleo? What's going on?" Marla had joined them. "What are you two standing here whispering about?"

"I think I'm having my baby," Cleo said, looking miserable and a little frightened.

"Has your water broken yet?"

"Has her *what* done *what?*"

Ignoring him, Cleo nodded. "When I got out of bed."

"If it's your first, you still have plenty of time." Marla turned to Harrison. "Why don't you go wake Nick while I help her get dressed?"

"What does Nick have to do with anything?"

"Just do it," she said. Gesturing for Cleo to follow her, Marla led the way to the north wing. "I suppose you've got a bag packed, but there might be a few last-minute things you'd like to include."

Cleo caught her breath as another gripping pain began gathering low in her belly. Biting her lip, she waited for it to pass. Marla, several feet ahead of her, turned back and waited, too.

"Better now? Good. We'll have time to get a few things done before the next one hits. I'm surprised you didn't schedule a C-section so you wouldn't have to go through with all this, but then, some women prefer pain to a scar. Is there anything special I can help you pack? I can do that while you get dressed. Brush your teeth, too. It might be ages before you can do it again, and don't forget your moisturizer. Hospitals are so dry."

"Marla, would you do something else for me? There used to be a box of stationery in the wooden box on the end table in the living room. Would you look and see if it's still there, please?"

"Darling, I doubt if you'll be there long enough for that."

"Please?"

Marla shrugged. "Of course. Stationery. No woman should go into labor without it. Don't forget your bedroom slippers."

They made it to the hospital in thirty-three minutes. At that time of night there was little traffic, and Nick was an exceptional driver. Harrison sat in back, holding her hand. Now and then he snapped out a terse instruction. "Curve coming up—watch it. Take a right on 37. Once you cross the bridge, look for 32 and take a left. Easy, easy—no, not you, Nick. Here, let's get your feet up on the seat."

He resettled her so that she was lying against his chest, supported by his arms. When the pains came she dug her fingers into his shoulders. He winced, but he only said, "Easy, sweetheart, it won't be long now, you'll be just fine," and things like that.

Cleo couldn't believe it was finally happening. That in a matter of hours she'd be holding her baby daughter in her arms. Or her son. She didn't care which. Hadn't wanted to know because knowing would have made it too real, and after the shock, the pain and sadness of losing Niles, even though they'd been on the verge of another separation, she'd been afraid to hope.

It would be a girl. She had a really strong feeling about it. With a girl, Henry Barnes might not even be interested. He'd talked so much about the sons she and Niles would have to carry on the family law tradition, as if a daughter couldn't possibly make the grade. But then, that was Henry. And to a lesser extent, Niles.

"Harrison, do you think you can find me a stamp when we get to the hospital?" she asked, and then shut her eyes tightly as another wave of pain closed in. "Whoo! I didn't know it was going to be like this."

Harrison cradled her, stroked her back and shoulders and murmured, "Shh, it's going to be all right, everything's going to be just fine."

"But the stamp?"

"The stamp. Right. Whatever you want. Now, stop worrying."

"Easy for you to say," she scoffed. Then she laughed a little and gave in to the next surge of pain.

James Robert Niles Barnes was born just after 5:00 a.m. Six pounds, eleven ounces, twenty-two inches long, he had to be the most beautiful baby ever born, despite what the nurses all assured her were a few strictly temporary flaws.

His face was as red as a tomato. His eyes were swollen shut. Both conditions, she was promised, would clear up in a matter of days, if not hours. The fact that his head was a tad pointed was only a temporary effect of the birth process. Before she knew it he'd be looking every bit as perfect as the baby in the toilet tissue ads.

Cleo didn't care what he looked like. He was hers and he was the most precious thing on earth. Puffy-eyed or not, he recognized her. The moment she took him in her arms, he quietened down. "You and me, sweetheart. Jimmy and Mama. We're going to have a wonderful time taking care of each other, aren't we?" she whispered.

Harrison had stayed with her until after it was all

over, and then he'd raced back to the house. When he returned a few hours later in his own car, he told her he had his people working on securing a cook-housekeeper.

His people. Nick or Marla? Nick, she hoped. Cleo trusted Nick's judgment where people were concerned. Any servant Marla chose would probably be one of those starchy, upper-crusty types Mrs. Barnes was so fond of, the kind who'd always made her feel inadequate. She was working on her inadequacies, but things like that took time.

Nick sent a huge bouquet of gloriosa daisies, which made her cry. And then two orderlies came in bringing enough flowers to stock every florist between Manteo and Williamston, and she cried so loud Harrison and the nurse both came rushing in, wanting to know what was wrong.

"Aw, come on now, they're supposed to make you smile," Harrison said plaintively.

"They're b-beautiful! So many— So much— Nobody ever— I don't know why you d-did it," she wailed.

"Just say thanks, and I'll say you're welcome, and we'll call it even, all right? Now, tell me about this son of yours."

So they talked about Jimmy, and she told him about her father, James Robert Larkin, who had made a name for himself in art circles back in the sixties before he'd become a victim of multiple sclerosis.

She cried a little, and then gloated while he admired her son, and then she gave him a letter to mail. "I wrote to Jimmy's grandparents. I thought they ought to know."

Harrison said, "Somehow I got the impression that you weren't too eager to get in touch with your in-laws."

"I'm not. I hadn't planned to tell them at all, but Niles was their only son. When it came right down to it, I couldn't *not* tell them. They might not even be interested, and that's just fine."

From the few things she'd let slip, Harrison had formed his own opinion of her in-laws. It wasn't a particularly flattering one, not that she'd said anything openly critical, either of her in-laws or her late husband. But Harrison was good at reading between the lines. To his way of thinking, she'd be a lot better off without them than with them.

He figured there wasn't much chance of that. Her late husband had been the only child of a successful father, just as he had. Successful men tended to think in terms of sons, grandsons—dynasties. King Lawless had died before it had become an issue, but Henry Barnes might be a different matter.

Cleo was obviously strapped for cash, watching every penny, counting on the sale of the lodge to give her enough to live on. He took a calculated risk. "At least now that I'm buying the lodge you won't have to worry about finances."

She pokered up, just the way he'd known she would. Pride was a funny thing. Hers had evidently taken a beating at the hands of these people, yet her innate sense of integrity had made her do what she considered the right thing. That took courage. At a time like this, when she was physically and emotionally exhausted, it wouldn't hurt to remind her that she had what it took to be a warrior.

So he did.

She sighed and said, "I know. I'm tough as old boots."

Right. Sure she was. Acting on impulse, he leaned over and brushed her lips with his. "For luck," he whispered.

She smiled that lazy, drowsy, guileless smile that had kicked the props out from under him more than once, and then, just like that, she fell asleep.

Some warrior, he thought, feeling a warmth in the region of his heart that was a symptom of something he didn't care to examine too closely. For a long time he watched her, thinking she looked tired but oddly content. The first time he'd laid eyes on her, he remembered thinking she looked tired. Tired, wary and far too defenseless for a woman living alone. Since then he'd come to know her a lot better, but some things hadn't changed.

"I didn't realize we'd be going home so soon. I've got all these books and leaflets, but, Harrison—I don't know how to take care of a baby. I've never even been around any babies."

They were approaching the turnoff. He slowed down, glanced in the mirror at the car seat, remembering what a fuss she'd made when they'd told her she couldn't hold her baby in her arms while riding in a car. "You can do anything, I'm convinced of it. You're invincible."

"I know. I'm woman, hear me roar," she said dryly.

"Is that what you call it?"

She laughed, but he heard the break in her voice. He'd never known a woman who could cry so easily over nothing at all. But then, he'd never known anyone even faintly like Cleo Barnes. While they were waiting for the orderly to bring the wheelchair after she'd been released from the hospital, he'd told her about seeing two logging trucks and several cars come to a complete stop near the foot of the bridge while a young opossum crossed the highway. He'd laughed. She'd cried.

Go figure.

"By the way, Nick and the Kanes left this morning."

"Oh, no," she wailed. "Didn't they even want to see Jimmy?"

"They saw him. Nick drove by the hospital on the way north. You were asleep and they didn't want to wake you, but they went by the nursery. Nick says send him a picture when his eyes open. Marla said it was lovely meeting you. Rip says you're going to have the devil of a time finding a bicycle helmet to fit that head."

This time she laughed. "If Rip's an example of what little boys are like, I'm not sure I'm going to survive the next few years."

"You'll do just fine," he told her, and meant it. He'd watched her with Marla's son. There'd been no pretense, no adult condescension. She'd been great with the boy. Rip had liked her for the simple reason that she'd liked him, had treated him as an individual, not as someone's kid.

Harrison could only hope that when he finally found his stress-free wife and got started on his two-point-whatever offspring, he'd have as good a relationship with them.

Watching Harrison carry her son into the house she and Niles had built in the early days of their marriage, before things had gone so terribly wrong, Cleo tried to smile but couldn't quite bring it off. At least she didn't cry. She was determined to skip the depression stage entirely. The baby blues everyone had warned her about. She'd been on an emotional seesaw for so long, all she wanted now was to ease back into her nice, comfortable rut and stay there with her baby for the foreseeable future.

But first she had to locate another nice, comfortable rut.

Well. She'd worry about that tomorrow.

When Harrison suggested she might want to lie down while he put together some lunch—it seemed he had bought out the deli counter at the supermarket—she smiled and said she thought that might be a good idea. She felt weepy again for no reason other than the fact he was being so wonderful when he was under no obligation at all, but she smiled.

And then she saw the room. The brand-new crib, complete with an array of crib toys. The bicycle, the baseball glove and bat, the fishing rod. And the flowers.... This time he'd bought out every florist east of Raleigh.

Her chin wobbled. The tip of her nose turned red. Her throat thickened until she couldn't have spoken if her life depended on it. And so she did the next best thing. She turned, baby in arms, and buried her face in his chest.

As if it were the most natural thing in the world, he embraced her. He held her there—held both of them, because she was holding Jimmy—and murmured more of those sweet, meaningless words that felt like a healing balm poured over raw wounds she hadn't even realized she had.

"I'm sorry, I'm sorry," she whispered.

"Shh, it's all right. Everything's going to be all right now, you're home."

Well...she wasn't, not really. They both knew it, but it was what she needed to hear at the moment, and so she didn't argue. Tomorrow—next week—soon, anyway, she'd be strong enough to make plans. If she had to send out a second barrage of résumés, she'd do it. If she had to storm the employment office, she would do that. There were parts of the world where women had babies and went right back to work in the fields. The

least she could do was decide on where she wanted to
live and set the wheels in motion.

It was late when she sank down onto the sofa, exhausted from trying to make Jimmy stay awake long
enough to nurse, and then trying to find out why he kept
crying. Maybe he wasn't getting enough to eat. Maybe she
wasn't doing it right. If so, it was not from a lack of trying. Her breasts were enormous, her nipples were tender,
and she almost wished she'd decided to bottle-feed him,
but there were problems with that, too, or so she'd heard.

He'd finally erupted in a noisy belch and fallen asleep
in her arms. She'd put him down and stood watching
him sleep for twenty minutes before going out to the
kitchen to find something to eat.

Oh Lord, Harrison had restocked the freezer. Gallons
and gallons of ice cream in every imaginable flavor, and
not a single one of them tempted her the least bit.

She could hear him in the living room talking on the
phone. He sounded different—edgier. More like the
man who had first turned up at her front door and announced that he intended to buy her house. She waited
until he hung up, then picked up her plate of cold pasta
and fruit and wandered in to join him.

With his shirt unbuttoned, a dark stubble shadowing
his jaw, he looked almost as tired as she felt. He reached
over and picked a few grapes off her plate.

"All settled now?"

"Harrison, what if I'm doing it all wrong? I wish
babies came with a set of instructions."

"I bet you've never read a complete set of instructions
in your life." He'd taken the chair. The sofa was hers by
unspoken agreement.

"How could you possibly know that?"

"What, that you don't read instructions? Oh, I dunno, just a shot in the dark."

"You mean because I don't read contracts, either?"

Instead of answering, he asked if there was any more pasta in the kitchen. She shoved her plate across the coffee table. Suddenly, she wasn't hungry.

Over the next several days, clocks and calendars were useless. James the Despot, as Harrison had taken to calling him, ruled the household with an iron hand. Or rather, with an iron set of lungs.

Cleo was exhausted but secretly proud. Her son might be small, but he knew how to make his presence felt. "Sorry about last night. And the one before that. If you'd like to get out of our agreement, it's not too late," she offered one morning when they met, bleary-eyed after another sleepless night.

He could have closed his door and not heard a thing. Instead, he brought her cocoa and sandwiches in the middle of the night and lingered to see that she finished the last drop and crumb.

"Well?" she challenged.

"No way."

Which was just as well. She'd given her word he could have the house. Besides, she didn't know what she would do without him. Him, not his rent money. She hadn't cashed a single check, partly out of pride, but mostly out of something else. It wasn't his money she wanted, it was the man himself.

And if that wasn't postpartum dementia, she didn't know what to call it.

"Fine. Just thought I'd ask."

"Fine." He crossed his arms over his chest. "Take as long as you need. I think I've finally located a cook-housekeeper. She's a Mrs. Davis, widow—worked at a bed-and-breakfast on the beach until it closed down at the end of last season. I think you'll like her."

Cleo murmured something to the effect that it hardly mattered whether she did or not, she wouldn't be here much longer.

"Oh, and by the way, I'm expecting a delivery in the next few days."

She nodded but didn't comment. Why in the world should she resent the fact that another woman would be moving in? It wasn't even her house any longer. At least, not completely hers. Besides, she really was getting tired of dusty floors and deli food, and as wonderful as he was, Harrison was not a domestic creature. "That's nice," she murmured, feeling every bit as cheerful as a lost lamb.

Harrison narrowed his eyes, shook his head and left to go feed her crows. It was another of the duties he'd taken over since she'd come home from the hospital.

Three days later a truckload of equipment and office furniture was delivered. Cleo knew how to use a computer. Hated the things—hated the jargon that went with them—but at least she'd learned to find her way around a keyboard.

Harrison's new computer was no simple PC. There was also a copier and an old-fashioned metal file cabinet. The fancy device in his hand was in case of a power failure or a terrorist EMP attack, he told her, and then had to explain what an electromagnetic pulse was and how it could affect all electronic equipment. He went on to describe a weapons system under development that was based on the same principle, his eyes lighting up like a kid with a brand-new toy. She stopped listening about halfway through the description and contented herself with watching the way he used his hands when he talked.

They were beautiful hands. Strong, nicely shaped, with just the right amount of black hair. Sexy hands.

He was saying something about targeting and directing radio frequencies, and she wondered what kind of businessman would be interested in something like that. Someone in the business of corporate espionage? An international spy?

Although why any spy would be interested in monitoring snowbird traffic on the sleepy old Alligator River was a mystery to her.

But then, so was Harrison. A mystery. Had been from the very first, only she'd gradually gotten used to him. Come to depend on him. Come uncomfortably close to falling in love with the man, if she was honest with herself, and that was the scariest thought of all.

"Do you have anything to do with the bombing range?" She'd been watching him set up his equipment, listening to the rich sound of his voice, not the words he spoke, and keeping one ear open in case Jimmy woke up.

"The what?"

"Bombing range. At Stumpy Point. Or any of those other places like—you know. Camp LeJeune? Cherry Point? There are a lot of military establishments in the area."

"Don't tell me, let me guess. We're past the crying stage, past the ice-cream binges, past the sleeping stage.

We're now entering the stage of—what? Postpartum paranoia?"

"Oh, for heaven's sake, ask a simple question... Well, what was I to think with all this talk about electromagnetic gizmos that can shut down the whole civilized world?"

Maybe he was right. Maybe she was paranoid.

"I'm not a spy. Neither am I an international terrorist, nor a science fiction writer. I have a Ph.D. in electronics. I also have a liberal arts degree and a masters in business administration."

"Oh."

"Satisfied? I assure you, I'm perfectly harmless."

Harmless? Not in a million years. However, she was too embarrassed to apologize, much less ask him what a man in his prime with all those qualifications and no visible means of support was doing in a place like this.

He continued to hook up his fancy gadgets, rearrange various pieces of furniture and crawl around plugging various pieces of equipment into various strips and mysterious boxes with blinking red and green lights.

Cleo continued to admire his shoulders, his neat behind and his long, square-tipped fingers. She continued to tell herself it was time to leave, even if she had to move in with Tally again, heaven forbid. Tally's tiny apartment was scarcely big enough for one, much less two adults and a baby.

The resonant sound of the newly installed doorbell echoed through the house. Actually, it was a brass ship's bell beside the door, something Harrison had acquired while she was in the hospital. The lodge was gradually taking on less and less of Niles's personality and more of Harrison's.

"Probably our new housekeeper," Harrison muttered. He backed out from under a massive new desk and dusted off his hands, further indication that the woman was desperately needed. Cleo had meant to run the vacuum, she really had, only she hated the clumsy machine with a passion, and Jimmy hated the noise.

"I'll go," she said. "I need to look in on the baby, anyway."

Ada Davis was a godsend. Small, neat and competent, she was a wealth of information, which she kept to herself unless asked, about everything from colicky babies to diaper rash to keeping rat snakes out of the house by cleaning the mice out of the utility room. Things, she stated in her no-nonsense manner, a body learned when they lived in the country.

She didn't live in. She had her own home in East Lake across the bridge, with five cats and a garden that needed her care. Dietary restrictions didn't faze her. She was a plain Southern country cook who could manage quite well, if she had to, without the enhancement of either butter or bacon grease.

After the first week, things were going so smoothly that Cleo came dangerously close to drifting back into her same old pattern. Putting off today anything that could be put off until tomorrow. Or the next day. Or the day after that.

She looked after Jimmy, celebrated each new accomplishment, snapped beans, peeled potatoes and made a stab of reading the classifieds in the newspapers that came for Harrison. Not that she particularly cared what jobs were available in New York or London.

The London *Times?*

Mercy. She'd never known anyone who actually subscribed to the London *Times*. And she'd thought Niles was sophisticated.

Actually, it was Niles who'd thought Niles was sophisticated. She had finally reached the conclusion that a large part of his problems stemmed from the fact that he'd been told all his life he was designated by birth for greatness. And greatness hadn't happened. Instead, he had barely scraped through law school and then married a woman his parents considered socially inferior, partly because she happened to think he was wonderful, and partly to escape marriage to a woman just like his mother.

He'd been a disappointment to his father, who hadn't failed to let him know it. Frustrated because there was no real substance to sustain his exaggerated self-image, Niles had taken it out in various forms of meanness and self-destruction.

Harrison had a satellite dish installed. From habit, Cleo started to object to his high-handedness, but then, the house was as good as his. The fact that she was still there meant only that they weren't yet ready for closing. Which was all very convenient for her, but all the same, she felt guilty. She kept asking about it. He kept coming up with reasons why they needed more time.

"Look at it as joint custody," he said with the teasing light in his eyes that was more and more in evidence lately.

To think she'd once compared his eyes to ice on granite.

"Yes, well…I've been looking. Mrs. Davis brought me a copy of the *Virginian Pilot* and the *Raleigh News and Observer.* Just as soon as I find a job opening and a decent, affordable place to stay, Jimmy and I will go check it out."

"Don't rush into anything." Harrison was hanging a wall shelf in Jimmy's room. Marla had sent a monogrammed sterling cup from Tiffany. Nick had sent an autographed baseball. Tally had sent an enormous teddy bear. The shelf was slightly crooked, but Harrison was so proud of his newfound carpenter skills, Cleo didn't have the heart to mention it. Evidently, it took more than three degrees to master basic household carpentry.

He had bought a flock of rocking chairs, one for each deck, one for the living room and one for her bedroom.

"Harrison, this has got to stop!" she'd told him. "Have you lost your mind? I can't accept all this—this—"

"Furniture? I happen to like rocking chairs. Are you trying to tell me I can't have rocking chairs in my house?"

Of course she wasn't telling him that. She didn't know what she was trying to tell him, any more than she knew what he was trying to prove. Honestly, it was as if they were playing some crazy game and neither one of them knew the name of the game, much less the rules.

Jimmy loved the chairs. She rocked him and nursed him and sang to him—he was too young to realize she couldn't carry a tune. Harrison was too polite to mention it. Wherever they happened to be, he was usually somewhere nearby if he wasn't in his office doing whatever it was he did with all that equipment.

As it happened, all three of them were on the front deck when Cindy Minter arrived.

They heard the car long before it drove into the clearing. "You expecting anyone?" Harrison, kneeling beside the front steps, was setting out tomato plants. She could have told him that his plants were too leggy and droopy, and it was too late in the season to be setting them out anyway, but he'd just discovered gardening and now he was on a tomato kick. He ate tomatoes three times a day, claiming some sort of newly discovered health benefit.

The next thing he was likely to discover would be a skin rash from too much acid, but you couldn't tell the man anything. Oddly enough, his stubbornness and bossiness no longer bothered her.

"It's probably another stray." There'd been two people just last week who'd shown up, wanting to know if the road went any farther, and if not, why not. She'd told them that it was a private road, but they were welcome to get out and explore on foot, and of course when Harrison heard about it, he insisted on calling a security company to come out and give an estimate.

The small red rental swerved into the clearing in a spray of pine straw, coming to a stop within inches of Harrison's Rover. Even with all the windows closed, Cleo could hear the loud bass beat of the radio.

Harrison rose, dusted off his hands and waited. "Get in the house," he said quietly. There was something distinctly make-my-dayish in his attitude.

Clutching Jimmy protectively to her breast, Cleo was almost at the door when she glanced back over her shoulder in time to see a petite redhead in wraparound sunglasses stumble out of the car.

"Cindy? Cindy Minter?" What in the world was a secretary from Barnes, Barnes, Wardell and Barnes doing here?

Ten

"You come back here, Cleo Barnes, I want my deed!" the woman screeched. Wearing a royal blue, body-hugging dress with a skirt that was barely decent, she wobbled her way toward the front deck, her high heels sinking into the dirt with each unsteady step. Harrison wondered if she was drunk or simply demented.

She was crying. Hysterically. Damn it all to hell, not another one, he thought. If this was an example of stress-free living, he might as well be back in New York.

Cleo moved warily to the edge of the deck, the infant cradled securely in one arm. She looked more concerned than alarmed. "Cindy, what on earth is wrong? What are you doing here? Are you hurt?"

"No, I'm not hurt! Yes, of course I am, what did you expect?"

Harrison's gaze ricocheted back and forth between

the two women. He wondered if what he was witnessing was some bizarre Southern female rite of passage.

Reaching out with her free hand, Cleo helped the other woman up the last two steps. "Watch the cracks, they're rough on heels. What are you doing here, anyway? How did you know where to find me?"

"Is this Niles's baby?" The redhead removed her sunglasses, dropped them, stepped on them, staggered and peered at the small bundle in Cleo's arms. "Aaw, Ni-iles," she wailed.

"I think you'd better sit down. Are you sick? You look awful."

That was his Cleo, Harrison thought, amusement diluting his irritation. Tactful to a fault.

As it turned out over the next several minutes, Cindy Minter, legal secretary with the firm of Barnes, Barnes, Wardell and Barnes, had come in search of a deed to a house she owned and wanted to sell.

"But why on earth would your deed be here?"

"He never gave it to me, that's why. He kept promising he would, but he never did."

"Who never gave it to you? Who kept promising to do what?"

"Niles! Who do you think? He said it was with his papers somewhere, and he'd give it to me as soon as he ran across it, but he never did, and then you came back, and then he died, and they put everything under lock and key. Old Henry wouldn't even let me in his office, and I w-w-*worked* there!"

Harrison extricated the baby from Cleo's arms, ushered the two women into the living room and left them to hash things out while he put Jimmy down for a nap. The sound of female voices, one increasingly calm, the other increasingly shrill, followed him into the north wing.

Ada Davis poked her neat gray head out the kitchen door as he passed. "What's going on? Sounds like raccoons fighting over a garbage can."

"Pretty close. How about making a pot of coffee. I think we might need it."

"Real, fake or half and half?"

"Real."

Cleo drank decaf. Because he was still in the process of "decaffeinating"—down to a one-third, two-thirds mix and holding—he still had both kinds on hand.

Jimmy was fretful but having trouble keeping his eyes open. "You've got a lot to learn, son. No matter how much you think you know, there's a whole other universe out there waiting to blindside you. Yeah, I'd fuss about it, too, if I were you." Gently, Harrison lowered the drowsy infant to the crib, then pulled the sheet up and waited to see if it was going to get kicked off again.

He tilted the lamp shade so it shone on Cleo's vast bed instead of on the crib. The bed looked inviting. He pictured her curled up in the middle of the king-size mattress and thought, What a waste.

It wasn't the bed he was thinking about.

He was tempted to hide out in his office until things settled down, but he figured it was about time he took control. When it came to scouting out the enemy in a purely social setting, he was among the best. Hell, he *was* the best.

Poor Cleo. Either she was dumb as a post, or she didn't want to admit what had been going on right under her nose.

She wasn't dumb. A little naive in some respects—

more than a little—but never dumb. He was coming to believe she had a bone-deep kind of wisdom that was rare among the people he knew.

Minter and Barnes had obviously had an affair. Either a quick, hot one or a long-term one. No man who'd ever had an affair could miss the signs. And Harrison had. Several. One at a time, and with varying degrees of satisfaction.

The redhead was trouble. She obviously didn't know how the game was played. She could have her damned deed—she could have the deed to a dozen houses—but one thing she couldn't do was hurt Cleo.

"Want me to take it in?" Mrs. Davis inquired when he stopped by the kitchen again.

"Thanks, I'll do it. Better set another place for dinner."

Her expression spoke volumes.

As did the look on Cleo's face when he carried in the tray. Things were obviously no closer to being resolved. As the redhead had taken his chair, he turned toward the rocking chair, but Cleo reached up and caught his hand, drawing him down onto the sofa beside her. She didn't say a word. Didn't have to. Her eyes said it for her. *Please—I need you. Stay by me.*

He hoped his own message was as clear. *Relax, I'm here now.*

The familiar scent of soap, shampoo and baby powder threw him off course for only a few seconds before, calling on his rusty negotiating skills, he tendered the first question. "Ms. Minter, is there any particular reason why you'd expect to find your deed here instead of with Mr. Barnes's other personal papers?"

She blinked several times. The woman had truly remarkable eyelashes and knew how to use them. "We were here when he gave it to me. I thought maybe he just forgot."

Cleo leaned forward, looking puzzled. "When who gave what to you?"

"When Niles gave me the house."

At the soft sound of Cleo's indrawn breath, Harrison forced himself to press on. Better a clean, deep cut than a series of smaller, ragged ones. "Am I correct in assuming the late Niles Barnes gave, sold or otherwise deeded you a house, yet he failed to give you the actual deed?" He didn't allow her time to answer. "And you believe Mrs. Barnes might know where this deed can be found? Is that it?"

Nice going, Lawless. Why not just hit her over the head with it?

"I don't understand, Cindy. Why would my husband give you a house? Was it something you two were involved with at work?"

Harrison intervened. Covering her hand with his, he said, "I think we can agree that it was an involvement, but not necessarily confined to work, am I right, Ms. Minter?"

"Cindy? Is there something you're not telling me? I know you worked for Niles—"

"Actually, for Niles and Pierce both, but Pierce was seeing that woman from accounting."

"Yes, but…a house?"

"Let it go, Cleo," Harrison murmured. He'd changed his mind. He would pay the woman off and get rid of her. Anything was better than watching her undermine, brick by brick, whatever was left of Cleo's self-respect.

Cindy sneezed. Watery streaks of blue mascara seeped onto her cheeks. She sneezed six times in a row, and Cleo got up and found her a box of tissues.

"Thank you. It's those adibals. They always bake be sdeeze."

The animals made her sneeze. She was allergic to the trophies. According to Cleo, her late husband, the philandering bastard, had removed the trophies from the master bedroom when he'd developed an allergy to them.

Or rather, when his mistress had started sneezing at the wrong time. Bloody hell.

"How did you know where to find me?"

"Cleo," he said, wanting to head her off. If she didn't get it by now, she wasn't going to. Some women could look the truth in the eye and still refuse to accept it. He'd wanted her to face it, get over it and move on, but she seemed determined to do it the hard way.

"Pierce told me you were here. He talked to that woman you worked for in Chesapeake, and—"

"I know, he called. But Tally wouldn't have told him where I was. She knew I didn't want—that is, she wouldn't."

"Pierce is smarter than most people think. One of these days he'll be a partner. Now that Niles is gone—"

"But why would Niles give you a house in the first place? I mean, I know Henry Barnes had a few rentals, but—"

"Henry? He's a slumlord. Niles would never have offered me one of those awful places."

"Yes, but—"

"Cleo, just let it drop, okay? If Ms. Minter thinks there's a deed here that belongs to her, why don't I look through a few of those boxes and see if I can find it?"

"Yes, but—"

Until this moment, Cleo hadn't realized that in spite of everything, she'd still clung to a few illusions. Niles

had been weak. He'd been cruel, both verbally and physically, but somewhere deep inside her she'd held fast to
the fragile belief that at least he'd been faithful. He had
sworn as much when he'd begged her to come back after
the first time she'd left him, otherwise she never would
have agreed. Promiscuity these days was too dangerous.

"Well…shoot," she whispered. No wonder whenever she suggested spending a weekend here he'd
claimed he'd invited clients down for a few days.

With every shred of dignity she could summon, she
said, "Niles was my husband. I don't believe I care to
discuss this matter further."

"You walked out on him. What did you expect him
to do, join a monastery? And I'm not going anywhere
until I find my deed." The redhead was sulky, angry and
beginning to sober up. It was not a happy combination.
"Niles promised me that house, and anyway, who're
you to talk? You're living here with another man. I bet
Niles isn't even your baby's father. I bet—"

Under Harrison's piercing regard, she caught her
breath and snapped her mouth shut. CEOs had quailed
before such a look. Entire boards of directors had been
routed by such a look.

Cindy Minter faltered. She didn't surrender. One
quick, calculating look and she began weeping again,
but he was an old hand at dealing with weeping women
by now.

Cleo, looking hurt but dry-eyed, was twisting her
fingers. Harrison covered both her hands with one of his
own. He waited. From the kitchen came the sounds of
dinner preparation. From outside came the sound of a
whippoorwill and the distant popping noise of a small
outboard motor.

Leaning back against the deep cushions, he drew Cleo closer against his side, feeling strong, feeling protective—not to mention somewhat curious as to how she was going to handle today's revelation. Hard to believe she hadn't known, but then in some ways, she was far too trusting for her own good.

Cindy sniffed, sobbed and mopped, tossing the damp tissues onto the floor. Harrison waited, unmoved, curious as to what she would try next. Minter's tears didn't faze him. A single one from Cleo could turn him inside out. Emotions, especially the feminine variety, had been a mystery to him ever since he'd first discovered that girls were different from boys, but he was beginning to catch on to a whole new dimension.

They searched. Cleo couldn't remember exactly where she'd put the things from Niles's safe, so they went through all the cartons, and then went through them again. Harrison and Cleo did. He refused to allow Minter to join in the search. Relegated to the chair he had come to think of as his own, she watched, alternately sneezing and weeping.

"That security outfit I called had damned well better get on the ball," he muttered, carefully folding a patchwork quilt and two pillow shams.

"People like to explore along the river. There aren't all that many roads they can use."

"Cleo, you can't invite strangers onto your property these days. Not everybody's going to admire the view, thank you for your hospitality and leave."

"So far they have. No, I've already gone through that box. It's only old books."

"Give up. All we have to go on is her word. There might not even be a house."

"Yes, but if there is, and it belongs to her and she needs to sell it…"

"Did anyone ever try to sell you a bridge in Brooklyn?"

"I've always wanted to own a bridge. Why, do you have one to sell?"

Cleo watched as his fist approached her face. Two months ago she would have flinched. Now she smiled. He touched her chin with his knuckles, his eyes crinkling in that way he had of not quite smiling. One touch and she was reduced to a puddle of melted candle wax. Not even Niles in the early days had affected her this way.

"Haven't you found it yet?" came a plaintive whine from across the room.

"Not yet," they chorused, and then their eyes met again, this time in shared amusement. Cleo told herself not to be so darn gullible. Bridges were one thing. For a woman in her situation to fall in love with any man, much less a man like Harrison Lawless, was terminally stupid.

The deed still had not been found by dinnertime. While Cleo nursed Jimmy and settled him in his crib, and Mrs. Davis put the finishing touches on the evening meal, Harrison entertained their guest. Cleo wondered what on earth they found to talk about and was ashamed to feel a vicious little twist of jealousy.

After dinner, she wandered out onto the front deck. To think she had driven down intending only to pack, put the house on the market and find herself another place to live before the baby came.

What had happened to her? She'd never had trouble making decisions before. Other than the decision to leave Niles that first time and, later, the decision to go back to him.

This was different. There was nothing holding her here. No vows, no promises. No more hopes, much less dreams.

The truth was, there was only Harrison. Wealthy, arrogant, sweet, klutzy, impractical, bossy, mysterious—she could think of several other adjectives, but the one that worried her most was…sexy. With a brand-new baby, the last thing any sane woman should be thinking of was sex. If her body didn't stop pumping out all these crazy hormones, she was going to do something really, really stupid.

Sex. Great Scott, she hadn't even thought this much about sex when she was married. It was simply something that happened several times a week—mostly pleasant, sometimes not. Usually "not" after Niles had been drinking.

Or after he'd started sleeping with his secretary, she thought with a quiet sort of bitterness, but surprisingly little hurt. She was way past the point when anything Niles had done could hurt her. The knowledge felt good.

She supposed it had been her fault, the fact that sex had usually been disappointing, for her at least. Niles said it was. She'd thought it was just another of his taunts designed to make her feel inferior but perhaps he'd been right. Perhaps she simply didn't have it in her to satisfy a man. She was an artist. At least, she'd once had ambitions to be one. Maybe artists sublimated their passions in order to translate them into their work.

Ha. Any latent artistic impulses she still harbored had to do with nude models. Male nude models. Male nudes with wide shoulders, long, lean limbs, square-tipped fingers and crinkly smiles.

The screen door behind her slammed. Ada Davis

said good-night, and that she'd see if she could find some fresh peaches on the way to work tomorrow.

"That would be lovely," Cleo murmured, still caught up in a dream of seeing Harrison sprawled across a model stand wearing a loincloth and her dressed in a smock and nothing else.

Ada's rusty pickup truck rattled off into the dusk. Cleo leaned her head back, closed her eyes and tried to recapture her dreams, but the soft murmur of voices from inside the house kept interfering.

She had invited Cindy to stay the night. What else could she have done? She'd lent her a nightgown—a granny gown, white cotton with eyelet trim—and tried to ignore her look of disdain. Mrs. Davis had made up the room Nick had used. There were several trophies there, but darned if she was going to take the things down.

Harrison had accused her of being a pushover. He was probably right. She was getting better, but she still had a long way to go. There'd been a time when she'd had the gumption to fight for what she wanted, but most of the fight had been knocked out of her, first by dropping out of school to take care of her father after her mother had run off and left him. Then by falling for a charmer who could talk the devil into giving up his horns.

After years of sharing a three-story mansion with the in-laws from hell and with a husband who beat her—who kept promising to get help, but who never did—she didn't have a whole lot of gumption left.

"What a jerk you were, Niles," she whispered. "What a fool I was to have loved you."

But she had Jimmy. Without Niles, she would never have had Jimmy. And as much as she might wish things could be different, life was what it was. Deal with it, her father would have said.

After another largely sleepless night, Harrison showered, dressed and went in search of breakfast. Ada was a gem. The woman had more common sense than most CEOs he'd known. Business smarts was one thing. Plain old common sense was...entirely too uncommon.

"Is that bacon and eggs I smell?"

"Nope. Same as yesterday. Oatmeal. Got you some fresh peaches, though."

"With cream?" Cleo appeared in the doorway, looking about sixteen years old, except for her eyes. One of these days he was going to lift the shadows from those clear amber depths.

"If the good Lord had wanted cream on peaches, He'd a made 'em that way."

"Right. And his pigs would be swimming in a sea of barbecue sauce. I detect a conspiracy here." He grinned at Cleo. "Where's your friend?"

"If you mean Cindy, she's probably still sleeping. I expect she'll have a headache."

"That's putting it mildly. Have some oatmeal. You're still eating for two, remember."

The phone rang. Mrs. Davis said, "Barnes-Lawless residence," and handed it across the table.

Harrison spoke his name, listened briefly, then excused himself. "I'll take it in my office."

"Sounded important. We used to get some o' them tycoons at the bed-and-breakfast. Lot of 'em around these days. What's yours do? Real estate or politics?"

Cleo choked on her coffee. "He's not mine, he's only staying here until we close on the sale."

"Fine. None o' my business."

"Mrs. Davis—"

"Folks these days don't live like we did in my day, but that's all right. Things always evens out in the long run."

Before Cleo could think of a response, Cindy stumbled into the kitchen. "My head's killing me. Would somebody please turn off the sun?" She'd made a stab at applying makeup, but it didn't cover the shadows under her eyes, the furrows between her brows or her red and swollen nose. "I told you not to put me in that old room. I sneezed all night long. I hate those old heads! Why would any man want to decorate his house with dead animals, I ask you?"

"You want coffee or tea?" Ada Davis asked. Demanded was more like it. "Tea's better for what ails you."

Cindy sent her a malevolent look. "Lady, you don't have the least idea what ails me, so don't go giving me any of that holier-than-thou crap."

"Like I said, things always evens out," the housekeeper sniffed.

Cleo said nothing. Her breasts were aching. It was time to nurse Jimmy. She wondered if she would ever get enough of nursing him, holding him, gazing down at that eager little face, watching him clench and unclench those tiny hands. His appetite had practically doubled since he'd left the hospital. At this rate, he'd soon be joining them at the table, demanding his share of oatmeal.

She rose, rinsed her dishes and put them in the dishwasher. "If anyone needs me, I'll be on the back deck."

"Don't you let them mosquitoes bite that boy."

"I won't. If they're bad, we'll come back inside."

"You might as well know, I broke one of your stinking old animals. I threw blankets over the ugly old things so I could get some sleep, but one of them came loose. It's probably fallen to the floor by now."

Cleo sighed. She hated the wretched things, too, but if anyone was going to destroy them, it wasn't going to be some sniveling little husband-stealing bimboette. She'd trash them herself. Or maybe she could claim they were fixtures—like the kitchen appliances—that went with the sale of the house.

It was Harrison who discovered the hidden safe. Not the one in the master bedroom. Cleo had already emptied that. It had been practically empty anyway, only a few dollars, a tiny key she couldn't identify and an old address book.

After breakfast he'd gone to the guest room, surveyed the damage and intercepted Cleo on her way to change and feed a hungry baby. "You want it up or down?"

"The bear? You can take it down and throw it away for all I care. Or give it to some poor fellow who needs dead animals to boost his male ego."

Harrison was grinning when he headed for the utility closet to collect a ladder and whatever household tools he might need. Interesting take on the male ego. She might be onto something.

Or maybe she was still in the process of reappraising her late husband. God knows, she had grounds to despise the jerk.

Five minutes later he charged into her bedroom, came to a dead stop and stared. "I'm sorry—I should've knocked. I'll just…"

He swallowed hard, wondered fleetingly if this was another of those dreams that had been plaguing him lately. He hadn't had *that* kind of dream in nearly twenty years.

Their eyes met and held. The light from the window was at her back, casting one side of her face in shadow. The dress she was wearing—it was yellow, with flowers—was open from the waist up. Never in his life had he seen anything so beautiful. Even in the indirect light he could see her nipples. They were large, dark and proud. One was still wet where it had slipped from the sleeping baby's mouth.

God knows, there was nothing even faintly carnal about the scene. It took him nearly a full minute to realize there was nothing carnal about what he was feeling, either.

At least, that wasn't all he was feeling.

"I found—I brought—"

She glanced at the sleeping infant, pulled the edges of her dress together and rose. "Shh, let me put him down."

He waited, rocked by feelings he'd never expected, didn't know how to handle and sure as hell didn't welcome. When she took his hand to lead him from the bedroom, it was all he could do not to jerk away, but he didn't.

It wasn't electricity. It wasn't one of those tired old clichés songwriters wrote about in ballads. It was more like recognition. As if he were meeting for the first time someone he'd known all his life.

Harrison had a feeling he was in way over his head.

Cleo turned away from the crib and said, "Now, what's the trouble? If the thing's broken, just throw it away. Drop it in the river—or no, I don't reckon that's legal. How do you dispose of a dead bear, anyway?"

"The bear's not the problem. It's what the bear was hiding. Maybe you'd better come check it out."

Eleven

Cleo picked one of the envelopes from among those scattered about on the table. "C.M. Do you suppose…could that be Cindy Minter?"

"Open it and see."

"I'm almost afraid to find out."

Harrison didn't much blame her. A wall safe was one thing. A secret cache was another. He had a bad feeling about this.

They were in his office. When Harrison had pried the flat metal case from where it had been wedged behind the trophy, Cleo had remembered the tiny key she'd found in the wall safe. It had taken her nearly half an hour to recall which carton she'd dropped it into.

Cindy was in the living room, nursing her headache and polishing her toenails. The radio droned softly in the kitchen, where Mrs. Davis was brisking around, making lunch. *Brisking* was a new verb Cleo had coined to describe the way the woman moved. Old Noah Webster couldn't have done better, Harrison had told her the first time he'd heard it. They'd both laughed. It occurred to him that he'd laughed more with Cleo Barnes than he'd ever laughed with any other woman he'd ever known.

Neither of them was laughing now. "Well? Are you going to open it, or are we going to go on playing guessing games?"

"Here goes." She opened the manila envelope and cautiously peered inside. "It looks like a deed of trust. Commonwealth of Virginia, township of—"

She glanced up, her look both puzzled and injured. "He gave her a house," she said plaintively. "I had to live with his parents. They hated me. And he gave her a house."

For long moments there was only the rustle of paper and the sound of two people breathing. Out in the kitchen, a George Strait ballad gave way to the weather and news report. *"—percent chance of showers, clearing after midnight, meanwhile, the search for William Clayton, who escaped from—"*

"Poor Cindy," Cleo said softly.

Poor Cindy? If Harrison had thought he was beginning to understand the way her mind worked, he'd been dead wrong.

"At least now she can sell it."

"May I?" He slid the document across the table and scanned it quickly. As far as he could see it was a simple, straightforward deed from Niles H. Barnes to one Cynthia Wells Minter. "Do you want to give it to her?"

Cleo glanced up, and he was struck all over again by the feeling that had come over him when he'd seen her nursing her baby. Something larger than lust, and a great deal harder to cope with.

"It's hers. We have to give it to her. What I can't understand is why Niles didn't give it to her before."

"What's beginning to concern me even more is why the thing was hidden. A man keeps important papers in a safe or in a bank vault. I imagine he had both. What kind of papers would be kept in a place where no one would ever think of looking for them? Any ideas about that?"

She shook her head. The wariness was back again. As much as he hated to see it, he couldn't much blame her. He had a nasty feeling about where all this was leading. The seven initialed manila envelopes they'd found. The ledger that was with them—he'd thought at first it was an address book, but a cursory glance had revealed only initials with a string of numbers beside each one.

It was enough. More than enough, if what he suspected proved right, to destroy the lives of at least six people.

"You want to see what's inside the other envelopes?" It was her call. Barnes had been her husband.

She sighed. "I guess we'd better."

But it was obvious she was every bit as reluctant as he was. It felt a bit like sifting through a dead man's garbage.

"Did you ever have one of those days that seemed to last forever? I haven't accomplished a single thing all day, yet I'm as tired as if I'd hung a whole gallery and then run a marathon."

Harrison chuckled, relieved that she'd come through

it as well as she had. They were both stretched out on the back deck, watching storm clouds roll in from the southwest. The hammock was back in place. He was in it.

"Never having done either, I wouldn't know. I'd say looking after Jimmy would be enough to exhaust a platoon."

Not to mention dealing with the mistress of a late husband and learning that that same husband, aside from being an abusive, two-timing sot, had been a blackmailing bastard who had held the deed to his mistress's house over her head in case she should ever decide to reveal a few of his dirty little secrets.

To put it politely.

"I feel sorry for her."

He twisted around to stare at her. "You *what?*"

"Cindy. I really do. I didn't know any of those other people—the man in the newspaper clipping or the ones in the negatives or any of the others."

One envelope had held a strip of 35 mm negatives, black-and-white and hard to interpret, but Harrison had no doubt they were incriminating. Another envelope had held an audiotape, which they hadn't yet been able to play. The other four had held letters, memos, a bank statement and a photo taken in a night club showing a couple in a fairly intimate pose. An older man and a woman who looked barely out of her teens.

He wasn't sure even now that Cleo fully understood the significance of what they'd found, but a cursory examination of the ledger had made it pretty clear that Barnes had been bleeding the poor devils for months before he died. Years, in a couple of cases.

"What are you going to do with it?" he asked her now.

"With the letters and pictures?" They had already

given Cindy the deed. She'd been embarrassingly grateful. She'd ended up bawling again, and Cleo had held her, comforted her.

Harrison had stalked off in disgust. Kindness was one thing. There was such a thing as taking it too far.

"I'll burn them."

"Want to tell me why?"

"I don't know—maybe because it's the easiest thing to do. I just want it to be finished. It's not as if I knew any of these people."

Harrison didn't, either. However, he had an idea they'd appreciate knowing the sword of Damocles no longer hung over their collective heads.

He nodded. It was her call. And she was right—there was no point in digging up old skeletons. "Rest in peace," he murmured.

"I know you think I'm crazy, but I really do feel sorry for her. For Cindy, I mean. She was in love with Niles when he married me. She wanted to marry him, but his folks wouldn't let him. They had this other woman picked out for him to marry."

"You?"

"Mercy, no. I was nobody. That's why he married me, to get back at them."

"People don't marry for revenge."

"Niles did. He told me so, once when he was—when we were having a—a disagreement. My family isn't even from Virginia. They were from the western part of North Carolina. You know what they call North Carolina, don't you?"

"Land of beginnings?" He'd seen the motto somewhere.

"That, too, but somebody said once it was a vale of

humility between two mountains of conceit. I don't know about South Carolina, but it's true about Virginia. At least about people like the Barneses, who've been there forever. They were English. My folks were Irish. I think my granddaddy was a blacksmith. My parents were both artists. Late hippy generation—free spirits, free love, antiestablishment—Woodstock and all the rest. Mama played guitar and dabbled, but Daddy was a good painter. He was doing really well, with shows and sales and all, but then in my junior year at VCU, he was diagnosed with multiple sclerosis. Mama couldn't deal with it. She left him, and then she died when her van ran off a mountain on her way out to California to a folk festival."

"I'm sorry," was all he could think of to say. It was the most she'd said about herself in all the time he'd known her. He had an idea there was a lot more that was every bit as painful. The lady was nothing if not resilient. Tough as old boots, as she put it.

"What about you?" she said, her smile only slightly tremulous.

"What about me?"

"Well, I've told you the whole story of my life, so now it's your turn."

He was tempted to tell her, damned if he wasn't. Not that she'd believe him.

On the other hand, she just might. For a young widow who'd endured more than her share of the world's woes—some of it Cindy had revealed, the rest he'd only guessed at—she was far too gullible.

"Well now, where to start," he mused. "Shall I tell you about my parents? No, they're nowhere near as interesting as yours were. How about my great-grandfather, the moonshine magnate. Or about my cousin, the felon, or—"

"Be serious," she chided, laughing. She had an infectious laugh. He didn't think he would ever tire of hearing it.

"Right. Seriously, I grew up in Connecticut, lived in New York for the past fifteen or so years."

"What do you actually do?"

"You mean besides changing tires and planting tomatoes?"

"Whatever it is, if you aren't any better at it than you are at gardening and tire changing, you can't afford to buy my house."

They hadn't mentioned the sale recently. In an unspoken agreement, they'd postponed winding things up, even though there was no longer any reason to delay.

He'd already told her about his degrees, and that he was a retired businessman. "I was in electronics. Manufacturing, that is, not servicing."

She grinned that sassy grin of hers. "Now, that I can believe. I'm still not quite convinced you're not some kind of a spy, but I can't see any company hiring you to service anything."

"Gee, thanks for the vote of confidence."

"You're welcome. What about marriage? I mean, have you ever been?"

"Married? No."

"At your age, isn't that a little strange?"

"I don't know, is it? Maybe I never had time. Actually, I came close once—fairly recently."

"Who? I mean, what happened? No, I mean, I'm really sorry, Harrison. It's none of my business. You don't have to tell me if you don't want to, but why didn't it work out? I mean, I'm just curious, because if you want to know what I think, I think the woman must be crazy. For all your faults, you'd make a wonderful husband."

He didn't know whether to laugh or take umbrage. "All my faults, huh? Would you care to enumerate them?"

"No. Not really. Most of them are pretty minor, anyway. I've sort of gotten used to them by now."

"Then maybe you ought to snap me up before some other lucky woman puts in a bid."

"You're laughing at me, aren't you?"

"Would I do that?" he asked in mock disbelief.

"Absolutely. I didn't used to think you had a sense of humor, but you do. You're not as bossy as you used to be, either."

"That sounds encouraging."

"And you catch on fast. You're willing to learn, and you'd be surprised at how many men aren't. I mean, before you can learn something, first you have to be willing to admit you don't know it all. Some men would rather eat live bait."

The shadow was back in her eyes. She was thinking about Barnes again. If the bastard hadn't taken off in a drunken rage and driven into the side of a building, Harrison could have cheerfully wrung his neck.

But then, if Barnes hadn't died, neither of them would have been here now.

He knew about the wreck. The family had made a stab at damage control, but now that he was back online and had a clue as to what he was looking for, it had been easy enough to fill in the blanks.

"You were in the electronics business, weren't you? You could have said so."

"I thought I had."

"I'll bet you were part of management. No man could get that bossy working on an assembly line."

"Don't count on it, honey. Personality traits are as much genetic as acquired."

"I'm going to make sure Jimmy grows up in the right environment, with the right influences."

She didn't say it, but he knew what she was thinking. Between her folks and his old man, the kid had a pretty unreliable gene pool to draw from. She was going to have her work cut out for her, raising a boy in today's climate without a strong male role model at her side.

Thunder rumbled in the distance. Harrison became aware of the intensified scent of mud, river and forest. Swarms of mosquitoes came out of the woods. All at once, Cleo started slapping her arms and Harrison started swearing. They collided in the doorway, laughing, swatting, trying to escape the droning horde of insects.

Claiming exhaustion, she left him soon after that. Later, sprawled in the big leather-covered chair, Harrison stared unseeingly at the massive empty fireplace and thought about heat loss and hot dogs. Once when he happened to be home on the Fourth of July, rain had canceled the party at a friend's house. He'd asked if he could invite Timothy over and roast hot dogs in the fireplace.

His mother had told him not to be absurd. He'd ended up having lunch in the kitchen with the staff while his parents had gone to the club.

He seldom thought about his childhood, seeing no reason to dwell on what had not been a particularly memorable portion of his life. Nor did he now. Instead, he turned his thoughts to Cleo. By now, she'd have finished nursing Jimmy and doing all that nuzzling stuff new mothers did. At least, she did. He seriously doubted if his own mother ever had.

Cleo would be leaning over the crib, watching to see if Jimmy was going to go to sleep or fret awhile. Harrison knew the exact way her face would soften, her eyes would get that molten amber look, her lips would part. She'd touch the baby, maybe adjust the covers. She was an inveterate shoulder-patter, an arm-clasper, a hand-toucher. He couldn't count the number of times she'd done it to him. Nothing sexual about it. She simply didn't have her emotions under control yet. He'd even seen her squeeze Ada Davis's arm when the woman had stood beside her watching the baby sleep.

Come to think of it, he seldom missed a chance to touch Cleo, either. The casual brush in passing. Lifting her hair when it fell over her brow and her arms were full of Jimmy. Totally nonsexual. Even in the old days, he would never have considered having an affair with a woman like her.

Not that he was thinking about it now.

All right, so she was warm, lush, even desirable. She was far too impulsive, far too unsophisticated—far too unmanageable.

Hell, she'd even cried when Ada discovered that nest of mice and insisted on hauling them outside in a bucket. She'd been going to drown them, but Cleo had put her foot down.

"Mice invite snakes. You want to wake up one day and find the whole house full of rat snakes again? I'd almost sooner clean up after mice than after one o' them big old rat snakes. They splotch all over the floor. Hardest thing to scrub up is snake splotch."

Cleo had been teary but suitably chastened. Harrison

had been amused at the time, but in this case, he was on Ada's side. No snakes. No mice. No varmints of any kind, and as soon as the deed to the house was in his name, that damned flea-bitten, wall-hung menagerie was out of here, too.

He heard the sound of a door opening and closing. By now she'd probably wandered into the bathroom, shedding her clothes along the way. She was not exactly the world's neatest person.

Neatness was important. No man could function efficiently amid chaos. To that end, he'd always had a small army working quietly behind the scenes, both at home and at work, to insure his orderly, serene way of life, leaving him free to devote his energies to far more important matters.

Although, come to think of it, he'd relaxed his standards a bit lately. Lately, he'd relaxed, period. Not only that, it had been weeks since he'd felt that old tightness at the back of his neck—the throbbing at his temple.

With a half-smoked cigar and a half-empty cup of coffee beside him, the latest edition of *Forbes* and an untidy stack of newspapers on the floor by his chair, he turned his mind to the past—to a way of life that was slipping further and further into the distance.

Expecting to feel the usual pain, the usual sense of loss and frustration, he felt only a vague sense of release.

"God, what if it's communicable," he muttered. If he didn't watch himself, he'd be turning into a beach bum.

Cleo. Without even trying, the woman was starting to undermine a lifetime of hard-earned self-discipline.

Cleo... By now, she'd be stepping into the shower. Fine-tuning the mix. Reaching for the scented soap she used, which invariably triggered a whole range of erotic images. He pictured her soaping her body, head tipped back, eyes closed, water trailing over her breasts, her hips....

Snatching a paper off the top of the stack, he rustled through to the business section, scowling at the fine print. LLI was up two points since Monday. It had dropped six immediately after the buyout, recovered the loss and was courting record territory.

She slept in cotton, not silk. With her hair in a braid that was always coming apart by the time she woke up in the morning. He even knew what it looked like in the middle of the night, when she roused to nurse the baby.

"Get a grip, Lawless," he muttered. Standing, he stretched, tried to convince himself he was tired enough to sleep, and then swore softly. There was no way out. Either he sat up and thought about her, or he went to bed and dreamed about her. Neither option figured into his carefully made plans.

But then, what else in his life had worked out the way he'd planned it? Lately, too damned little.

Items one and two? He had trouble even remembering what they'd been. Somewhere around item three—or was it four?—things had completely fallen apart.

They ate dry cereal for breakfast the next day, with Jimmy fussing in the bassinet Harrison had driven all the way to Manteo to purchase.

"He'll outgrow it in no time." Cleo warned him again. She'd said the same thing when he'd first brought it inside.

"So? Save it for the next edition."

"There won't be any future editions."

"I wouldn't bet on that. You're a natural."

"I'll leave it here when I go."

It was the first time in weeks either of them had mentioned the inevitable parting. He added another spoonful of sugar to his already sweetened cereal and scowled. "Do that. It'll be a handy place to keep kindling for the fireplace."

"Marla might want to have another baby."

He looked up so quickly the sugar spoon missed the bowl, fell to the table and tumbled off onto the floor. "You want to run that one by me again?"

"That's why she came here, isn't it? To look the place over? Rip will love it. I'm not sure Marla will, but at least you can spend part of your time here. You can fly into Norfolk from anywhere in the world and drive down in only a couple of hours."

"And you call me bossy? Lady, I might be bossy, but at least I'm not trying to plan your life for you."

"You said you'd seriously considered marriage once. It was Marla, wasn't it?"

He felt around on the floor for the sugar spoon, brushed it off with his fingers and dropped it back into the bowl. Ada Davis's floors were clean enough to eat off. "I might have considered it at one time or another. Not recently, though."

"Then why did you invite her down here?"

"Did it ever occur to you that one of the reasons a man buys a place like this is so that he can invite his friends to visit?"

He knew he'd blundered before the words were even out of his mouth. "I'm sorry, Cleo. Another fault of mine you forgot to list is a total lack of tact."

"That's not a fault. If it is, it's only a minor one. But, Harrison, what went wrong? Was it because of me? My being here, I mean? If I'd thought about it in time, I would have explained to her, but what with the baby and all, it never even occurred to me until a few days ago that anyone would misunderstand. Maybe if I called and—"

"Forget it. Honey, I've known Marla for years."

Honey? Well, hell. When in Rome...

"We've had a—well, I guess you could call it a low-level involvement for some time, but there's been nothing between us other than friendship in more than a year."

"But you were hoping to start it up again, weren't you? Else you'd never have invited her down here before you'd even signed the final papers. I have a feeling she was hoping, too, until she got a look at the lodge. I don't think she liked it very much. Not that she said anything, but then, she's too well mannered to insult her host."

"Not to mention her hostess."

To his great delight, she blushed. Sounding flustered, she said, "I'm hardly that. Maybe next time—"

"There won't be a next time."

"Oh. Well—at least you have good taste in women. Better than some men I can think of."

He had to smile. "Oh, I don't know about that. If you're talking about Barnes, he showed excellent taste at least once, I can vouch for that."

Her smile was more rueful than amused. "If you mean what I think you mean, then thank you. That's one of the nicest things anyone's said to me in a long time."

After breakfast, Cleo scraped the leftovers from the previous night's dinner into a pan and took it out for the crows. As Jimmy was still awake, she banged on the pan with a spoon. Harrison teased her about her bird-feeding habits, but she liked watching the huge things collect, swooping from branch to branch, waiting for her to go inside. She would like to think someday they'd be tame and trusting enough to come while she was still outside.

Well, of course, that would never happen.

"You need a dog," Harrison said quietly from the other side of the screen door.

"Not many apartments allow dogs."

"I'm talking about now. Here."

"I won't be here much longer. Harrison, that's something we need to talk about. Do you have a few minutes?" Dusting the crumbs from her hands, she opened the door and then stepped back when he didn't move away.

With the morning light slanting down on his lean features, she found it almost impossible not to stare. If she'd brought her paints with her, she would have been tempted to do a portrait of him to take with her. To remember.

As if she could ever forget.

"I just heard another bulletin. Your friendly neighborhood convict's still on the loose."

"He'll be miles and miles away from here by now. Yesterday they were saying he'd been seen in Georgia."

"Last week he was reported in Virginia."

"So there, you see? Like I said, he's miles and miles from here."

"About that dog—"

"I'd rather talk about seeing Mrs. Dunn and signing whatever we have to sign so you can send for the rest of your things and start getting settled, and I can decide where I'm going to move and get started on that. I've given up on sending out any more résumés. Somebody, somewhere, is darned well going to hire me. I have a good feeling about it."

"A good feeling," he said, his face totally unreadable.

"A really good feeling," she emphasized, trying hard to shore up her crumbling resolve.

From the kitchen came the plaintive strains of a somebody-done-me-wrong song. From the woods came the sounds of the crows squabbling over bread crusts and the remains of last night's casserole.

"Close the screen door, you're letting in mosquitoes," Harrison said quietly.

She moved the necessary few inches for the screen door to shut. He didn't. She was so close she could smell the scent of his aftershave, see the faint dark mask of his freshly shaved beard. No power on earth could have prevented her from lifting her face. By the time his lips brushed hers, her eyes were closed tightly, shutting out all but the reality of his arms around her, his hard, warm body pressed against hers—the feel of two hearts gone wild.

The kiss was everything a kiss could be and more. Hungry. She was starved for the touch, the taste of him. Tender. It was that, too, in the way he held her, taking care not to crush her sensitive breasts too tightly against his chest.

Feelings rioted through her body. Half-formed thoughts tumbled about in her head, thoughts of what was happening and shouldn't be. Of how a thing could feel so inevitable and yet be so impossible.

He lifted his mouth and stared down at her, looking every bit as dazed as she felt. "This isn't—" he started to say.

"We can't—"

"I know, I know," he groaned.

He was fully aroused, there was no disguising it. No

way either of them could pretend it hadn't happened to both of them. "I didn't know it was possible—I mean, it's been so long—it's too soon."

He nodded as if he knew exactly what she was trying to say. One of his hands sloped over her hips, holding her against him. She reacted instinctively, moving against him, aching for more.

He touched her hair, tugging out pins, fingering her braid until it tumbled down around her shoulders. "I've been wanting to do that since the first time I saw you," he whispered.

"You can't have. I was big as a cow. I was all puffy and ugly and cross."

"You were beautiful and frightened and I thought you were a complete flake."

"I was. I am. Oh, Harrison, this doesn't make any sense at all. We're nothing at all alike."

"It makes perfect sense to me. My timing might be a bit off, but that's nothing a little patience won't take care of."

Cleo forced herself to move out of his arms. Telling him no was probably the hardest thing she would ever have to do, and considering her past, that was saying a lot.

But then, her past was precisely the reason why she had to say it now, while she still had the willpower. Backgrounds counted. Where a person came from, how they were raised had a lot to do with who they were and what they expected from life.

She had loved the wrong kind of man once and lived to regret it. She and Niles had come from totally different backgrounds. It had been a disastrous match. She was just now recovering her feeling of self-worth. For the sake of her son, she couldn't afford to risk losing it again.

He was a highfalutin Northerner, for heaven's sake! At least Southerners, regardless of social status, had certain references in common, yet even that hadn't helped with the Barneses.

She opened her mouth to speak, but he laid a finger over her lips. "Shh, don't say anything now. But think about it, will you?"

Think about what?

As if she didn't know.

As if she could help herself.

Hearing Ada's firm step on the wide pine floor, they moved farther apart. Cleo felt shaky—hot and cold at the same time, as if she were coming down with something.

"Comp'ny coming!" the housekeeper sang out.

"Oh hell, not again," Harrison muttered.

"My sentiments exactly." But secretly she was glad of anything to dilute the tension between them.

Twelve

Even covered with dust, there was no mistaking the late-model Seville. Cleo felt her shoulders begin to sag. Forcefully, she squared them and stepped out onto the front deck. Thankful for the steady strength of the man behind her, she murmured, "It's Niles's parents."

"I take it you're not too thrilled to see them."

"No, but I'm not surprised, either. I wrote and told them about Jimmy, but they'd have found out, anyway. Henry has…ways of knowing things. Things he wants to know, at least."

Henry Barnes had lost weight, but he was still far more formidable than any short, paunchy, red-faced man had a right to be. "Where is he? Where's my grandson?"

"Hello, Father Barnes, Mother Barnes."

Cleo wondered, not for the first time, how it was possible to be intimidated by a woman wearing pearls, sensible shoes, an ugly hat and a shapeless flowered dress. It had to be Vesper's attitude, that inborn assumption of superiority that she was far too refined to mention.

"Where is Niles's son?" Henry Barnes demanded.

"Jimmy's asleep. Would you like to look in on him?"

For a single moment, Vesper looked almost as if she were wavering on the verge of thawing. Hastily, Cleo made the introductions. "Mother Barnes, Father Barnes, this is Harrison Lawless, my…houseguest."

Vesper's lips thinned disapprovingly. Henry's small eyes narrowed. It was Henry who pronounced their joint disapproval in two words. "I *see*."

Cleo didn't ask what he thought he saw. Didn't have to. She opened her mouth to explain that Harrison was in the process of buying the lodge and then snapped it shut again. She didn't owe them an explanation. Didn't owe them a darned thing. She'd been under no obligation to tell them about the baby, but she'd written, anyway, knowing they'd probably act as if they had a greater right to her baby than she did.

We'll just see about that, she thought grimly.

Ada Davis chose that moment to elbow through the front door with a tray of iced tea. Four glasses, tinkling with ice cubes, irresistible when both the temperature and the humidity hovered somewhere in the low nineties.

"Let's go inside where it's cool. Mother Barnes, would you like to—"

"I'd like to see my grandson. That's why we're here. I believe Henry has a few things to say to you if your *houseguest* will allow us a moment of privacy." Vesper's head wagged self-righteously at the word *houseguest*. White purse clutched in her white-gloved hands, she picked her way across the freshly swept deck as if it were a chicken yard and she were wearing house slippers. In all of five years, the only time Cleo had ever seen the woman looking less than flawlessly groomed had been the night Niles was killed. She'd aged since then, but some things hadn't changed. She would go to her grave wearing hat, gloves, stockings and corset, a circle of rouge on each dry, withered cheek.

Harrison held the door and Ada followed the two women inside, still holding the tea tray. Henry paused just inside the door and favored Harrison with another of his speculative looks. "Lawless, hmm? From around here? I understand the name was once known in the area."

"According to old records, I believe it was fairly well-known," Harrison allowed.

"Hmm. Have we met before?"

"I don't believe we have. I'm sure I'd have remembered."

"Hmm."

"I demand to see my grandson," Vesper Barnes announced, wattles trembling self-righteously.

Cleo started to respond, but Harrison beat her to the punch. "Shall I bring him out? I'd better change him first." He'd held the boy a number of times, even changed his diaper once or twice. The first few times he'd been scared stiff, but he was getting the hang of it. Infants, he'd discovered, for all they were greedy, uncivilized little hedonists, had a way of slipping under a man's guard.

Right on cue, Vesper began to huff. "Well, I never."

Henry said, "Now, see here, young man—"

Ada plopped the tray down on the coffee table, saying, "I'll change him and bring him out. Better'n having him wake up in a room full of strangers."

"I'm sorry, I forgot—Ada, these are Jimmy's grand-parents, Mr. and Mrs. Barnes. Mother B, Father B, this is our friend and housekeeper, Mrs. Davis."

"*Our* housekeeper? Would you mind telling me just what is going on here, Cleopatra?"

Harrison nearly strangled on his tea. The woman was a walking, talking stereotype. "Cleopatra? You want to explain, or shall I?" he taunted softly, gray eyes gleaming with wicked amusement.

Cleo shot him a stern look. Evidently she failed to appreciate the humorous aspects of the situation. She was holding up pretty well, but he could tell she was weakening. Damned good thing he was here to protect her interests. He wouldn't put it past these two over-stuffed vultures to whip out an agreement, force her to sign the thing and then drive off with her baby, leaving her to grieve herself to death.

No way. Not on his watch.

"Thank you, Mrs. Davis," he said as Ada marched out of the room. He turned back to the elderly couple. It hadn't taken him long to size them up. Barnes was easy. Ambitious, pretentious, more than willing to cut corners as long as he could get away with it. His wife was straight as a stick, but maybe not quite all she pretended to be. He'd lay odds her lineage wouldn't bear too close scrutiny.

But then, that pretty well summed up his own back-ground, he thought, amused. "You're probably wonder-ing what I'm doing here. I'm thinking of buying Cleo's house when and if she decides to sell. We're still dis-cussing terms."

Mrs. Barnes looked suspiciously from one to the other, almost as if she expected them to fall to the floor and start tearing away each other's clothing.

Damned if he wasn't tempted to oblige.

Henry, however, was off on another tack. "Lawless. Don't tell me, don't tell me. *Prominence* magazine, January issue, right? That semiconductor thing. The merger. My God, you're not *that* Lawless, are you? Vesper, shut up a minute, will you?"

Vesper was rattling on about housekeepers, appearances and the importance of early enrollment in the proper school. Cleo was uncomfortable. That panicky look was back in her eyes. Any minute now she was going to come out with one of her off-the-wall remarks and blow things wide open.

Harrison glanced uneasily at Henry Barnes, who was gaping like a beached fish. When Vesper said, "Niles was always a good student," he took the opportunity to deflect the man's attention.

"I'm sure he was, Mrs. Barnes. Jimmy's already showing signs of advanced intelligence." How intelligent did a five-week-old baby need to be to process milk? At least he did it efficiently, Harrison could personally vouch for that.

"Vesper, for God's sake, shut up! Do you know who this man is? Do you have the slightest idea who our Cleo's been keeping company with?"

"*Our* Cleo?" both Harrison and Cleo echoed.

Harrison thought, *Their* Cleo? When hell froze over.

It was left to Cleo to say, "I'm not keeping company with anyone, and if I were, it's nobody's business but mine, but thank you for your concern."

"Henry, do something. I'll not have Niles's baby exposed to—"

"Here he is, folks, clean drawers and all. Grandmaw, you want to hold him a minute before he starts kicking up a fuss for his breakfast? It don't take him long once he wakes up." A beaming Ada presented the small bundle as if he were the crown jewels on a satin cushion.

"Oh my goodness," Vesper murmured, twisting her head sideways to peer down at the tiny face. "Wait a minute…" She peeled off her gloves, tossed them aside, then held out her arms. "Oh, you precious thing. Henry, he looks just like Niles did at that age. Henry, look, doesn't he look like Niles? Oh, my blessed land, would you look at those eyes. They're the exact same shade of blue."

Harrison watched as the woman, who could probably flash-freeze an upstart with a single glance, morphed into a doting grandmother. He watched Jimmy's slightly cockeyed gaze try to focus on the unfamiliar face.

And then he turned his attention to Cleo, cataloging the array of emotions flickering across her mobile features. Surprise. Relief. Guilt—and something almost like fear.

And sympathy?

Yeah, sympathy. Now, why didn't that surprise him? For a woman who'd managed to survive five years with this pair of piranhas, not to mention the abusive bastard she'd been married to, she was still far too soft for her own good.

Barnes was staring at him with a look of increasing awe. Harrison recognized the symptoms. Ever since he'd let himself be talked into giving that interview to *Prominence Magazine,* he'd been fawned over by people who ought to know better. As if what he'd managed to accomplish somehow set him apart from the rest of humanity.

He had a feeling Cleo was about to get an earful before he could put things into perspective. He should have explained before now, only he was afraid it might change their relationship.

Hell, he didn't even know what their relationship was.

He knew what he wanted it to be, though.

The Barneses stayed for lunch and then stayed for an early dinner. Cleo reluctantly offered to make up the south wing for them. Vesper said yes, please. She'd lost a lot of her starch in the process of getting acquainted with her grandson.

Henry overruled her, but then, that was nothing new. Now that she'd been away from them for a while, the pecking order was obvious. Living under their roof, Cleo had been aware only of the constant flow of criticism directed her way. First there was the way she dressed and the way she spoke. Next, the friends she chose and the books she read, not to mention the worthy clubs she refused to join.

When Henry was home, there wasn't a single doubt as to just who ruled the roost. The minute he left for the office, Vesper took over. Her style was different, but she was every bit as ruthless.

Niles had been no help at all. Working for his father by day, dealing with his mother at night, he had various ways of boosting his own battered ego, none of them very pleasant.

God, she wished they'd go! Henry was obviously dying to linger, but she heard him tell Harrison they were the guests of close friends at their cottage in Duck.

"Cottage, ha! Place cost a cool million if it cost a dime, but Tom likes to call it his little beach cottage." Henry went on to mention the name of a congressman who was under indictment on a number of charges concerning money laundering and fraud.

"I'm considering representing the man. Bad business—don't believe a word of it myself. All the same, it's going to be a big suit, plenty of publicity, big settlement. Did I happen to mention I'm being urged to run for office in the next election?" His expression was a masterpiece of coy self-deprecation. "But then, campaigns take money, even with reforms. Still, there are ways and means, am I right?" He removed his glasses, polished them and replaced them on his florid face. "Yessir, ways and means, but then, what's good for politics is good for business and vice versa, I always say. Tit for tat."

Cleo could almost find it in her heart to feel sorry for the man she'd once hated with a passion. He was pathetic. More despicable than hateful. Poor Niles. Poor Vesper.

She watched the interaction between the two men, not at all surprised to see Harrison take quiet control of the conversation.

Henry mentioned a certain stock deal. Harrison glanced at his watch.

Henry said, "I could get you in on this. A phone call to my broker—no trouble, glad to do it."

Harrison smiled with his lips, not his eyes, and said, "Mr. Barnes—"

"Henry. My friends call me Henry."

"Henry, I believe I'll pass, but thanks anyway."

"Now, son, you don't want to do that. As it happens, I have inside information—"

Harrison glanced at Cleo with growing respect. To think she'd lived in their cave and survived. With a little more savoir faire and a different accent, he thought, the man could have been his own father. Feeling the old familiar tension begin to gather at the back of his neck, he flexed his hands, willing himself to relax. This poor jerk wasn't worth another coronary.

He glanced at Cleo again and let his gaze linger, appreciating the way the light played over the side of her face. It reminded him of the watercolor of the reading woman hanging on his bedroom wall. What was the reader reading? What was she thinking?

What was Cleo thinking? So far he'd managed to direct the conversation away from the danger zone, but he had a feeling something was going to hit the fan as soon as the Barneses left.

Finally, holding the drowsy baby in her arms, Cleo went out onto the deck to see her in-laws on their way. It was nearly nine o'clock, but not quite dark.

Harrison braced himself, but she came inside and settled into the rocking chair without saying a word. He told himself he'd been worrying over nothing. She obviously hadn't been listening to Barnes, she'd been too busy standing guard to see that Granny didn't abduct her baby.

Cleo rocked Jimmy and ignored Harrison. When the silence began to eat at his nerves, he said, "I think they both took it pretty well, don't you? I'm surprised Henry didn't show more interest."

"Mmm-hmm." She began to hum with no regard at all for the melody.

"Jimmy was at his best."

"Jimmy's always at his best."

"But his best," Harrison observed, "would be even better if he could figure out the difference between night and day."

"There's nothing wrong with being a night person."

"A night person. Right." He gave up. Maybe she hadn't caught on to the fact that Barnes had been hinting around for a backer. That on recognizing him, he'd done everything but genuflect. That her father-in-law was a petty sycophant, and that Harrison was slightly more than a retired businessman.

Or maybe he was just that. Oh hell, he didn't know who he was anymore, much less who he was trying to become. Next time he picked a midlife crisis, he might just try out for a motorcycle gang.

Distracted by a vision of lamplight on soft skin, of hollows beneath flawlessly sculpted cheekbones, Harrison waited in growing frustration. It was the single emotion he'd never learned to handle successfully. Probably because he'd seldom been forced to handle it. He'd had staff for that.

"So?" he said finally.

"So what?"

He wondered if she was being flippant. "So what do you think? Anything in particular on your mind?"

"About the visit? Not really. Vesper said they're going back to Richmond tomorrow."

Harrison shook his head slowly. One of them wasn't connecting the right dots. "She'll be back. I give her a week."

"Jimmy and I won't be here."

Tension slammed back full force. "What do you mean, you won't be here?"

"For heaven's sake, what's wrong with you tonight?"

"Nothing's wrong with me! What do you expect when you come out with a crackpot announcement like that?"

"Crackpot? And I didn't *announce* anything. I've never made any secret of my plans."

"Don't try to wiggle out of it. You weren't in any great hurry to leave before, so what's changed? Are you afraid Granny's going to bring reinforcements next time? What about this Holmes fellow? Is he friend or foe?"

"Holmes?" she asked. "Ooh…you must have been listening in on my phone messages. He's neither. Pierce tried to find me, but it had nothing to do with Henry or Vesper. He and Cindy are now involved. They wanted the deed to the house, that's all. Cindy assured me they weren't interested in me or Jimmy."

"And you believe her?"

"Cindy has little reason to lie to me. Yes, I believe her."

"Great. Then why run away?"

"I'm not running away. I always planned to leave once we closed on the house, you know that."

"Don't hand me that. You've been blowing hot and cold about giving up this place ever since I talked you into selling it."

"You didn't talk me into anything. I just—needed a little more time to think things through."

Harrison slowly shook his head. "Lady, you are a piece of work."

"Shh, don't wake up Jimmy. I'm going to put him down, and then if you want to talk about it, we'll talk about it, but I won't change my mind."

Witchery, he thought, watching her walk away. She'd kicked off her shoes. She had anklebones again. Nice ankles. Superb ankles. Underneath that slow, sexy smile and that slow, husky drawl, the woman was either sharp as a pawnbroker or a genuine, certified flake. Damned if he could figure out which, and the scariest part was, he no longer cared.

Waiting for her to return, he got up and started pacing, and then he started swearing. So much for his new stress-free life-style. He'd set out with a plan, a backup plan and a contingency plan. He hadn't got where he was without learning the importance of careful planning.

The trouble was, not a single one of his plans had worked out. And if that wasn't hard enough to swallow, there was the fact that he no longer gave a damn. Somewhere along the line, his priorities had changed radically. He wasn't sure just when, much less how, but he knew precisely where to lay the blame.

So the woman was sexy. Even pregnant she'd been sexy. So he was finding it impossible to keep his hands off her. That didn't mean...

Yeah, it did mean. It meant exactly what he was afraid it meant. That now, instead of being addicted to the adrenaline high that came from the fierce cut and thrust of the business world, he was addicted to a woman.

And not just any woman. This one wasn't going to fit neatly into one of his careful plans. In the first place, she was an artist. Everybody knew artists and engineers didn't mix. Hell, he wasn't even sure they spoke the same language.

He knew now who had painted those watercolors. Even if he hadn't finally made out the signature, he'd have figured it out, because they were just like her. All muted, flowing colors, hazy, merging images, with hints of something just beyond the line of sight. Taken literally, not a one of them made sense.

Taken literally, neither did she half the time. And yet, the paintings spoke to him the same way she did.

Both were light on structure, heavy on substance, the sum greater than the parts.

His life had been about structure. Seldom, if ever, had he given a single thought to substance. He'd been founder, CEO and chief stockholder of an international corporation. What more substance did a man need?

The titles no longer applied. What remained? What if she looked inside him and saw only emptiness? His money wasn't going to impress her. The fact that he was considered one of the world's most eligible bachelors wasn't going to matter a hill of beans. He could plead poor health and throw himself on her mercy, but he'd rather die than see pity in her eyes.

The plain truth was, he didn't know how to deal with a woman like Cleo. Hell, she even knew more about cars than he did.

He wandered outside, waiting for her to finish nursing, changing and bedding down the baby for the night. Or at least the next couple of hours. After a while a soft drizzle began to fall. He stood on the deck, letting the rain soak his hair, plaster his shirt to his body. It made about as much sense as anything else he'd done recently.

Ada Davis came outside and raised her umbrella. "Need a good rain. Garden's dry as a bone."

He murmured an agreement. If she'd said the house was on fire, he'd have had the same reaction, which was no reaction at all.

"If you're waiting for Cleo to join you, she's holed up in her bedroom with yesterday's paper, going over them help wanted ads. I told her she was going to ruin her eyes, reading in bed like that."

"Help wanted— Thanks, Mrs. Davis. I'd better get in out of the rain."

She shook her head, muttered something about some folks and hurried out to her truck. Soaked to the skin, Harrison took time to shower and change, and then he made cocoa and sandwiches. As a peace offering, it wasn't much, but then, it wasn't peace he was after, it was a showdown.

Standing just outside her door, he balanced the tray and took a deep, bracing breath. He was no good at this. Management problems he could deal with. If he had to. He'd seldom had to, because his was a well-run organization. He'd dealt successfully with mergers and buyouts and thwarted a few attempted hostile takeovers. What he was about to do now was scary as hell. Mainly because he wasn't certain of his goal, much less how to achieve it. Much less what he was going to do when he succeeded.

That he would fail never entered his mind.

He rapped lightly. "Hey, open up. I know you're awake in there."

"It's late. Go away, Harrison."

"I've got hot cocoa," he called softly through the door.

"Cocoa and what?"

"Peanut-butter-and-jelly sandwiches."

"What kind?"

So far so good. She'd taken the bait. "Chunky and fig, respectively," he called through the door.

By the time she opened the door, his confidence was soaring. "Oh, for goodness' sake, come in before you wake the whole household."

Trying not to look too much like a well-fed tiger, he followed her inside. As the household consisted of two adults and one sleeping infant, he thought he could handle it.

A few minutes later, he wasn't so sure.

Thirteen

Not even the scent of peanut butter and scorched cocoa could defuse the tension as Cleo stepped back to allow Harrison to set the tray on her dresser. The very air seemed to tremble.

This was a mistake.

A bigger mistake had been leaving him out on the deck without settling matters between them once and for all.

The biggest mistake of all had been letting him in her house that very first day, when she'd opened her door to see a stranger with cool gray eyes, a beard-shadowed jaw that was aggressively square, his fist lifted to knock again.

No it hadn't. Her worst mistake had been falling in love with another control freak. The only difference was, Harrison was strong where Niles had been weak. Harrison did his controlling—or tried to—in the nicest possible way.

Nor had Harrison made any effort to sweep her off her feet, the way Niles had done. But then, Niles had had another bride all picked out for him and needed a foolproof excuse not to marry her.

Cleo had been that excuse, and she'd paid the price for it.

"Is he asleep?" Harrison's low-pitched voice undermined her determination with no effort at all. She nodded, tightening her robe, wishing she hadn't undressed. Wishing she'd pretended to be asleep. Wishing all sorts of things she had no business wishing.

"I was waiting for you to come back. We were going to talk, remember?" Leaning against the oak highboy, his legs crossed at the ankles, he could easily have been a male model—one of those sexy, classy, older men who wore sexy, classy, understated casuals and made every other man in the world look like an overdressed juvenile by comparison.

He'd been in her room countless times before. He'd brought her warm milk when she'd wakened in the night to nurse Jimmy, and stayed on to keep her company.

He'd nailed up shelves for Jimmy's treasures. He'd rocked in her rocking chair and read to her from the Sunday papers while she lay in bed with Jimmy sleeping beside her. Read her pieces on gardening and on child rearing, when she knew very well he was dying to turn to the business section.

Tonight he'd brought cocoa and PBJ sandwiches. So why did that serving tray remind her so much of a Trojan horse?

"Now, what was this about leaving?"

"It's time. Jimmy will be six weeks old next week." Did he know the significance of that? Probably not.

"You don't have to rush off," he said, and she laughed.

"I'd hardly call it rushing. But the lodge is yours if you still want it. I—I appreciate your patience."

"Dammit, it's not patience! You love this place. Why are you so eager to get rid of it?"

She threw up her hands. "I can't believe I'm hearing this. Look, we've had this discussion before. I like it here, but even if it were closer to town and I could find work in the area, it's too big, too isolated, and besides, I need the money."

She'd switched on her bedside lamp, determined to find something—a single lead, a direction. A goal. Instead, all she could think of was what she'd be leaving behind. "If you're offering me more time, Harrison, then thanks, but it won't work." Unless he was offering the rest of his life, time wasn't what she wanted from him.

Silence lay like a seductive pool between them, deep and calm, rife with hidden dangers. She tightened the sash of her robe and then loosened it again, conscious of the way she must look. Her waist still wasn't back down to its old measurement. Her breasts felt as if they weighed a ton. She'd never felt less desirable in her life, and never regretted it more.

"Cleo?"

"Oh, for heaven's sake, if you want the house, then tell Mrs. Dunn. If you've changed your mind, and I certainly couldn't blame you, then I'll just wait for another offer. But stop looking at me that way," she snapped.

"I like to look at you. I'd like to do more than—"

"You said you wanted to talk? Then say what you came to say and leave. It's late. I need to get some sleep before Jimmy wakes up and wants to nurse again."

Her breasts throbbed, and it wasn't from thinking about Jimmy, it was because of the way he was looking at them. At her. As if he'd never seen a woman's breasts before.

The first time he'd barged into the room when she was nursing, they'd both been embarrassed. He'd blushed and backed out, and for days after that, she couldn't look at him without remembering the expression on his face.

The next time, too, had been accidental. They'd both pretended a nonchalance neither of them had really felt, but after that he'd seemed to find one excuse after another to join her while she nursed. He seemed to take such pleasure in the small ritual that she'd let him stay. Besides, she'd liked the feeling it gave her, as if they were sharing something special.

After a while it had come to be a habit. The late-night feedings. The snacks he'd brought, which they'd shared once Jimmy fell asleep. She'd read about new mothers looking forward to the time when their babies slept the night through.

She wasn't one of them.

"Where will you go? What kind of job are you looking for?"

"One with benefits, including an on-site nursery. One I'm qualified for, which sort of limits the possibilities," she told him with a rueful smile. "Without a degree, I can't teach. I'd make a good gallery manager—I can do everything from hang shows to keep books. Show hanging is an art in itself. But the benefits, even if I could find an opening, are lousy."

"Ever think about marketing your work?"

She looked away. "It wouldn't sell. Some of the best

watercolorists I know can't make a living at it. Besides, mine's too…personal."

He looked as if he were going to say something else but changed his mind. "The Barneses would take you in."

"Thanks, but they took me in once before, and I swore I'd never be taken in again. I know Vesper. She'd start out wanting to take Jimmy around and show him off to her friends. Next she'd tell me I looked tired. Then she'd hire a nanny, and next thing you know, she'd have him enrolled in Niles's old schools, all the way to choosing his university—and probably his major. No, Henry would choose that. Law." If she sounded bitter, it was because she felt bitter. And defensive. And vulnerable on far too many fronts.

"She lost her only son."

"And I lost my only husband, so stop trying to make me feel guilty! Even if you're right and she's not trying to take him away from me, I can't let her and Henry do to Jimmy what they did to Niles. I'd sooner pitch a tent in Monroe Park than move back into that house and allow them to raise my son."

At a sound from the sheet-draped crib, they both turned. Harrison quietly crossed the room to gaze down at the sleeping infant. With a sigh, Cleo joined him.

Jimmy smacked his lips in his sleep. His little knees were bent, his tiny hands flung over his head. His head was perfectly shaped now, but he was still bald as a gourd.

"He's just so beautiful," she whispered.

It seemed the most natural thing in the world when Harrison slipped his arm around her waist. She let her head rest on his shoulder. Because she was tired, she told herself. Because her head was beginning to ache from a wearing day and too many unanswered questions.

"Tired?" he whispered.

She nodded.

"Your head hurts, doesn't it?"

"How did you know?"

"That little pucker between your eyebrows. Your eyes are darker when you're hurting."

"You see far too much," she said dryly.

"I see why you don't want to move back with your in-laws. What I don't see is why you can't stay on here."

Pulling away from his side, she dropped down onto the foot of the bed and pressed both hands against her temples. "Harrison, I can't go on drifting forever. I know you think I'm a—a flake. I'm not. Honestly, I'm as practical as a doormat, but—"

"Interesting choice of words."

"Don't go looking for hidden meanings. I've got things under control, I really have." The way a meteorologist had the weather under control. Watch what happens and then report on it.

The mattress sagged as he sat down beside her. She tilted toward him, struggled to resist the temptation to stay there and tried to think of something sensible to say. About the job market. The stock market. The hog market, for goodness' sake!

Lifting his hands, he slipped his fingers under hers and began to massage her temples while his thumbs circled gently over her cheekbones. Magically, the pain began to ebb.

She sighed. "That helps."

"I used to have a lot of headaches," he murmured. "Haven't had one in ages."

Who had massaged away his headaches? Marla? A streak of jealousy shot through her.

"Lean forward so I can get to the back of your neck. We'll ease the tension."

Wrong. In case he wasn't aware of it, the tension had tripled in the past two minutes.

He toppled her forward so that her forehead rested on his shoulder. His strong, incredibly comforting hands continued their steady pressure. "Better?" he murmured.

"Mmm-hmm."

Outside, the rain continued to beat down, emphasizing the seductive intimacy of the softly lighted room. His hands worked their way down her spine, stroking, pressing, easing tension. Creating tension of an entirely different sort.

Cleo thought, This isn't smart. I know exactly where this kind of thing can lead. And, oh Lord, I wish it would!

Dredging up her practical side, she said, "By the way, why was Henry so impressed? He seemed to think he knew you from somewhere."

"Shh, don't tense up again. How's your headache now?"

"Better. Almost gone, in fact." She wanted to take back the words in case he stopped doing what he was doing. Honesty fought a battle with sensuality and lost. "Hmm, yes—right there. That feels so-o-o good."

His thumbs worked their way up her spine. If this was supposed to be an exercise in relaxation, it wasn't working. *Earth to Cleo—wake up, you silly pigeon!* "What was I saying?" she murmured.

"Were you saying something?" His hands eased down her back, around her sides until the tips of his fingers brushed against her breasts. He was breathing through his mouth. Audibly. Rapidly.

"Oh, yes—about Henry." Anything to take her mind

off what was happening to her. "The only thing that impresses Henry is money or power. I know you're not poor. Are you very rich, or maybe powerful? Poor Henry was practically groveling."

His hands grew still. Cleo told herself she was glad and tried to believe it, but he didn't remove his arms, and she didn't pull away.

"Would it make a difference if I were?"

"To Henry? You heard the way he was dropping the names of all those politicians. If you are—rich and famous, I mean—then he's probably dropping your name right this very…" His hands began to move again. "Ooh, right there. Yes, like that." She snuggled closer to allow him better access to all the places that ached for his touch.

Well, perhaps not *all* the places….

"Forget Henry," he said, his voice low, rough, almost unrecognizable. "Would it make a difference to you?"

His hands stopped moving again, and she sighed, realizing she was practically sitting in his lap. Reluctantly, she attempted to move away.

He refused to let her go. "Answer my question, Cleo. Would it make a difference if you knew I could afford to support you and Jimmy so that you wouldn't have to work at all?"

"Harrison, I'm hardly stupid. That car you drive didn't come in a box of Cracker Jacks. You're paying me five hundred dollars a week, which is way too much, and—"

"And you have yet to cash a single check."

"Because I haven't needed to! You keep feeding me! You've practically bought out every furniture store in two counties, and you haven't even moved in yet, at least not officially. I have a feeling you don't just work for that electronics company you mentioned, you probably own it."

"I did. Not anymore."

"You lost it? You lost everything, and that's why you're down here trying to start over?" Did he hesitate, or was it only her imagination?

"It's one of the reasons."

"Another one being?"

"Maybe I found something down here I value more than anything I left behind."

"Did you?" She held her breath. It was crazy to hope. Crazy to feel what she was feeling. Crazy to think he might be feeling it, too. Now that she finally had her hormones back under control, she refused to allow them to run her life again.

He was going to kiss her. She licked her lips nervously and waited. Carefully, he lowered her onto the bed, never once breaking contact with her eyes. The kiss began slowly, almost tentatively. She lifted her arms around his neck, and he groaned, and then he was lying half on top of her, his weight almost painful on her full breasts, but not nearly as painful as the ache his kiss—his tongue—his hands—triggered deep inside her.

Somehow, her robe fell open to her waist. Somehow, his shirt came unbuttoned. Cleo had seen his chest before. Now she explored to her heart's content, from the patch of hair in the center to the tiny tufts surrounding his nipples to the narrow streak that trailed downward to disappear under his belt. She traced the course and was tugging at his belt when he covered her hand with his.

"It's probably too soon," he whispered hoarsely, holding her hand, dragging his lips to her throat, where a throbbing pulse echoed the wild beat of her heart.

"No, it's not."

"I wouldn't want to—"

"I need—"

Broken sentences, broken promises, broken hearts. She'd been down this road before. It led nowhere, and yet...

His hands cupped her breasts so tenderly, relieving the weight. He kissed the blue-veined slopes and she wanted to tear off her wretched old nursing bra and bare herself to his kisses. Of all the deplorably, embarrassingly unsexy things she might have been wearing, it would have to be a heavy-duty, flannel-lined, snap-open nursing bra.

And she had stretch marks. And flab. She had never in her life wanted to be more desirable to a man and never felt less desirable. She should have known better.

"Wait," she whispered, "let me turn out the light." She reached for the lamp, but he caught her hand and brought it to his lips.

Harrison's heart was thundering. He was scared, but not too scared to notice that not even fear had a dampening effect on his fierce arousal. He reminded himself he was no longer the man he'd once been. With his genetic history, he couldn't—shouldn't—be doing this. What if he died in the act? It would be awful for her.

In spite of the doctor's assurances that there was no real reason why he shouldn't resume his sexual life, he kept thinking about all the stories he'd heard about men who'd died in their lovers' beds. Sometimes it was a mistress, sometimes only a one-night stand. It occurred to him that he'd never heard of a case where a man died in the arms of his wife after sex, which might indicate that guilt was a factor.

There was no guilt involved here. He wasn't sure just what was involved, which was one more reason for caution. He knew one thing: he'd never come close to feeling this way about Marla, or any other woman he'd ever slept with. How the devil was he supposed to control his emotions when he couldn't even understand them?

They lay there, his face in the curve of her shoulder, his arm resting across her waist. She smelled of soap, talcum and warm, aroused woman. It was all he could do not to risk it and let nature take its course. There were worse ways to die.

For her sake, he couldn't do it. She'd blame herself, and guilt was a hell of a legacy. She deserved better.

"Harrison?" she murmured. "I'm sorry."

He lifted his head, focusing on the face mere inches from his own. She looked flushed, damp, puzzled. "No, I'm the one who's sorry. I didn't tell you everything. I guess I didn't want you to think I was a complete crock."

"It's been almost six weeks." She watched him, her gaze moving over his face.

"Cleo, did you hear me? Honey, I let you down, and I'm sorry. I shouldn't have started anything like this. I only meant to talk things through so we knew where we stood."

She laughed, but there was no joy in it. "I guess now we know."

"We do?"

"Well, I know one thing—a nursing mother carrying about ten pounds of flab is not very seductive."

He swore softly and lifted his head so that he could look down into her face. "You can't believe that. Honey, I've never wanted any woman as much as I want you right now. If you need proof…"

When she went on looking up at him, it slowly dawned on him that she wasn't blaming him, she was

blaming herself. "Ah, no, Cleo. You've got it all wrong."
He had a feeling Barnes had played hell with her ego,
but surely she knew how he felt about her. The proof was
damned hard to conceal.

"You don't believe me?"

Silence. Could her self-confidence still be that fragile?

There was one way to convince her, and recklessly,
he took it. Covering her hand with his, he guided her to
the only hard evidence he could offer.

Her eyes widened. He shut his. When her fingers
closed convulsively around him, he nearly died. Heart
pounding in his chest, he waited for the crushing pain.
It didn't come.

"Then why…?" she whispered.

"You're not ready," he managed to say. "Are you?"

"Not quite—near enough."

"I don't have any protection."

"They say nursing mothers hardly ever conceive, at
least not right at first."

He bit the bullet. For her, he could do no less. "Cleo,
I've had a coronary."

He waited.

"So?"

Her hand was still on him, which was probably just
as dangerous as if he were inside her, only he couldn't
think of a way to remove it without increasing the risk
of making her feel unwanted.

Unwanted! That was a laugh!

Against his will, he began to move his hips. Not
much, but enough so that he knew he had to get out before he embarrassed himself at best and killed himself
at worst.

He reached down and covered her hand with his, fully

intending to remove it. Instead, he found himself guiding her, unable to resist the mindless drive to completion.

"I…can't…do…this," he rasped.

"Let me help you. Let me give you this much, at least."

And she did. Lord help him, she did. Explosively, embarrassingly, he came to her touch and cried out, something he had never before done.

Eventually, when he could catch his breath, he tried to frame an apology. She whispered something, but the words were lost when Jimmy, startled out of his sleep, began to wail.

He thought she said, "Wait," but he didn't hang around to find out. When the door shut behind him, he was clutching his shirt, clutching his pants, wondering how far he'd have to drive to outrun his embarrassment. Alaska sounded like a good place to start.

Breakfast was awful. It was Saturday. Ada didn't come on Saturdays. There was only Jimmy and Cleo and Harrison, and nothing to dilute the awkwardness.

"Coffee?" he asked. "You haven't had any yet."

He felt his face burning and hoped she didn't pick up on the double entendre. It was purely unintentional.

"I'm not hungry."

"It's the weather."

It wasn't the weather, and they both knew it. It was the knowledge that he had come apart in her hands last night, had screamed out his pleasure, waking the baby, and then left her to deal with the crying boy while Harrison slunk away to shower and spend the rest of the night brooding.

At least, he'd expected to brood. Much to his surprise, he'd fallen asleep and hadn't roused until the birds tuned up outside his window.

"My father died at the age of forty-seven of a massive heart attack." Cleo's habit of uttering non sequiturs was rubbing off on him.

"I'm sorry, Harrison. Mine was two years older than that when he died. I told you he had MS, didn't I?"

"You don't understand what I'm trying to tell you, do you?"

She nodded and stirred her untouched cereal. "You're afraid of dying."

"Well…hell. Wouldn't you be?" He didn't know how she did it, but she managed to make him feel like a kid trying to avoid a shot in the doctor's office.

"Did what we did last night cause any—you know, problems?"

"You mean, other than terminal embarrassment?"

She reacted to the wry touch of humor with one of those slow, sweet, sexy smiles that never failed to play havoc with his brain.

Not to mention a few more body parts.

"You think you were embarrassed?" She chuckled, and the husky sound streaked through him like lightning. "What about me? Acres of flab, a heavy cotton harness designed to keep me from leaking. If you think any woman feels desirable under those conditions, you're flat-out wrong."

"If I was too afraid and you were too embarrassed by your underwear, what the hell happened? You want to take a shot at explaining that?"

"I guess we forgot."

"I guess we did," he said dryly.

"I guess we'd better not forget again?" It was clearly

a question. He knew what his answer was, but he wasn't certain of hers. The last thing he wanted was pity.

"I'm driving into town this morning. Want to go?"

She shook her head. "I've got things to do here."

"Then give me your list, and I'll stop by and pick up anything you need."

Cleo nodded, stirred another spoonful of sugar into her coffee and shoved it aside. The minute he was gone she intended to call Mrs. Dunn at the real estate office. The sooner she cut her ties here, the sooner she could start the process of healing her heart.

At least this time the wound would be a clean one. With Niles, it had been ragged, ugly, messy.

This time she would simply bleed a lot and hurt like the very devil, and after a decade or so it would be over. She'd forget all about Harrison and maybe even find someone else. A boy needed a father. A woman needed a husband. Someone to love, someone to share her life with. Someone to turn to in the night when the loneliness got too hard to bear.

Yes, and a woman needed another hole in her head.

Fourteen

The line was busy. It stayed busy. Between busy signals at the real estate agency, Cleo opened drawers, cab-
inets and closets, stared helplessly at the few remaining
contents and left them where they were. There was no
law that said you had to take every shred of personal
property with you when you sold a house.

At least, she hoped there wasn't.

Jimmy was good as gold, but then, he usually was.
Sometimes she woke him from a sound sleep to rock
him because she needed it, even if he didn't. At the moment, however, she needed to finish packing.

She wrapped a set of mugs that Niles had bought for
her from a street fair the first year they were married. A
reminder of the best part of her marriage might help her
eventually to forget the worst parts.

Her watercolors. Keep them? Glassed work was so
hard to pack.

Leave them behind? She would if she thought they would keep Harrison from forgetting her. But then, his preference in art, if he even had a preference, would be something bold and angular, full of sharp edges and hard lines. He was that kind of man. Bold, angular, full of sharp edges and hard lines.

The trouble was, he was so much more than that.

For one thing, he was patient. She thought about their daily walks, with her trudging along like a gravid turtle, when he was so obviously dying to break into a run.

He tried so hard to be helpful. His crooked shelves. The botch he'd made of her yard when he'd insisted on pulling up all her lovely weeds and replacing them with neat little squares of vegetables. A whole package of squash seeds in a single bed two feet square, and those poor, spindly tomato plants.

And all the tools he'd scattered around when he'd tried to change her tire. A tire tool and a jack would have sufficed, but not for the world would she have punctured his masculine pride.

So many things to remember. Their first trip to the supermarket. His gradual "decaffeination," and the resulting headaches he never complained about. The impatience he tried so hard to hide. How could a man be so impatient with himself and so patient with someone else?

Wandering out onto the back deck, a forgotten crib sheet in her hand, Cleo thought of all the ways he had changed since he'd first shown up on her doorstep. All the reasons why she loved him. All the reasons why it would never work.

"Well...shoot," she muttered, flinging herself onto the hammock.

His coffee cup was still on the rail where he'd left it that morning, his newspaper was tossed aside, still opened to the business page. If she tried a little harder, she could probably detect the faintest trace of his aftershave lingering in the hot, still air.

She was still there, still daydreaming, when she heard the crows squabbling and opened her eyes to see the man gobbling down the scraps she'd put out for them.

Armed with a fistful of brochures and a map, Harrison set out early. He'd been dragged to more champagne openings in more posh galleries than he cared to remember. This time it was voluntary. Before the day was over he intended to visit every gallery from Duck to Hatteras. There had to be one that was just right for her. If not, he'd damned well build her one.

His plan was simple. Inquire about job openings and study the available art to see how it compared with hers. He happened to think hers was special, but he'd be the first to admit he was no expert. While he'd never questioned his social obligation to support the arts financially, his interest had been philanthropic, not personal.

By the time he'd crossed Oregon Inlet Bridge and headed south for the next gallery on his list, his plan had undergone a few revisions. In the first place, there were no job openings. At least, none in the galleries he'd visited so far.

In the second place, it was possible that her work might not be commercially viable. She didn't paint pretty beaches with waving sea oats. She didn't paint lighthouses or dilapidated old buildings with rusty roofs. She didn't paint oversize tropical fish or seashells or wharves lined with fishing boats.

Not that he had any particular bias against those subjects. Most of what he'd seen so far appeared reasonably competent. The trouble was, none of it excited him. None of it bore the slightest resemblance to Cleo's simple, understated watercolors.

So he was prejudiced. So be it.

If she wanted to support herself with her painting, he'd buy everything she turned out and consider himself lucky to have it. For all his exposure—the tax value of his corporate collection alone ran well into the millions, and that didn't include his personal collection or the commissions he'd paid his decorator to acquire it—he'd never before realized how personal paintings could be.

Hers were pure Cleo. Deep. Quiet. Deceptively unassuming. He was determined to have them.

He was even more determined to have her.

It was late afternoon by the time he crossed the inlet and headed north again. He'd had one more mission in mind when he'd set out. Nothing concrete, just a vague idea. All he'd needed was a phone book and a few answers to questions such as, Where do I find something or other? Where's the nearest whatchamacallit? Don't tell me I have to drive all the way to Norfolk to locate a whatsit?

His mind teeming with fresh ideas, Harrison was already making mental lists by the time he crossed the Alligator River Bridge. Conclusion: in an area like this, near a national park, with a more or less captive audience, any man with capital, imagination and business savvy—and Harrison modestly confessed to an abundance of all of the above—could write his own ticket.

Cleo knew who he was, because there were still one or two places where the original orange color showed through the filthy tattered remnants of his coveralls. Even so, there was no way she could chase him away or turn him in, not until she'd fed the poor wretch and done something about his eyes. He'd been eating her crow's food, for heaven's sake. No wonder the poor crows were upset.

"More tea?"

"Please, ma'am." He held out his glass, his hand shaking so hard she had to take it from him to pour without spilling. She'd brought him a bar of soap and a towel and made him wash up at the hose outside before she'd let him into the house, but there was a limit to what even soap and water could do.

"You might as well finish up the chicken, there's only one piece left."

He pounced like a duck on a june bug. In just under a minute another bone was added to the pile on his plate.

Leaning against the refrigerator, she studied him. It was hard to be sure, considering the shape he was in, but she didn't think he was more than eighteen. Twenty, at most. He was certainly no hardened criminal. Someone had taken the time to instill a few old-fashioned manners in him, for one thing. "What were you in jail for?"

At first she thought he wasn't going to answer. Not quite meeting her eyes, he muttered, "Got caught driving the wrong car."

He was a car thief. Grand theft auto, as they said on the police shows on TV. At least it wasn't murder.

"Why on earth did you break out? They've been hunting you for weeks. You knew you couldn't get away."

"I had to go to the bathroom."

"Oh, for heaven's sake, if I'm going to help you, I need you to tell me the truth!"

"Ma'am, it's the honest God's truth. We was working on cleaning up that there patch of woods that burned last month, and I had to go, and the man, he said to wait, only I couldn't wait, so when Buck said something real ugly about Ambrose's old lady, Ambrose, he busted him one and Buck, he gut-punched Ambrose, and the guard, he went over to pull 'em apart, and I snuck behind some bushes."

"And?"

"And did it."

"No, I meant, what happened then?"

"Nothing. The guard, he pulled Buck and Ambrose apart and told 'em—well, you don't want to know what he told 'em, ma'am."

She was tempted to call the sheriff's office and tell them to come collect the poor wretch. If it wasn't for the fact that he was all scratched up and his eyes were swollen nearly shut—poison ivy, from the looks of it— she'd have done it, too. But before he'd even got as far as the deck, he'd tripped twice and nearly hanged himself on her clothesline. How could she turn in something so pathetic without first taking time to feed it?

"What did he say to you?"

"He didn't say nothing to me. Casey—that's his name. The guard, I mean. Casey ain't real smart. He ain't mean, not like some I could name, but he ain't too bright, neither."

She took a deep breath and then wished she hadn't. "So you went back, and Casey didn't fuss at you—so what then? How did you get away?"

"That's just it, ma'am. I never went back. I just stayed there behind the bushes, and after a while I snuck away and just kept on going."

"That's incredible."

He ducked his head. "Yes'm, I reck'n it is."

"What happened next?"

"I run. They was dogs and all, so mostly, I waded. Them dogs can smell on water. Most folks don't know that, but a dog, he'll sniff the air over the water and he can smell where a man's been."

"Then how on earth did you manage to elude them?" Dogs weren't the only ones who could smell. She was going to have to fumigate her kitchen after he left.

"I don't know nothing about 'luding, but I only waded in water that was moving. That way, my smell went downstream and I went upstream and then I come ashore on the other side."

"That was clever."

"Yes'm," the escaped convict said dolefully, "I'm real clever. Ma said I took after my pa that way."

"Well. What is your name, anyway?"

"I was named after my pa, Billy Junior Clayton, but I was called after my uncle Al."

Cleo sorted it out, and then she said, "Well, Al, we're going to have to do something, you know that, don't you?"

"Yes'm, I reck'n I do. You're a-gonna turn me in, ain't ya?"

"It probably doesn't seem like it right now, but it's the best way. You can't go on running for the rest of your life. You need medical help. Once the swelling goes down and you can see again, I expect there's some kind of school program available for a clever man who wants to better himself and start fresh."

"Yes'm, I reck'n."

She was running out of patience. Jimmy would be waking up any moment now, and she didn't want the boy, no matter how harmless he seemed at the moment, to know she was here alone with an infant. "Stop saying, 'Yes'm, I reckon.' If you truly mean it, say, 'Yes, ma'am, you're absolutely right!'"

She waited.

"Well?"

"Yes'm."

"Yes'm, *what?*"

"Yes'm, what you said."

The sound of a car door slamming out front cut short her prayer for patience. Her prisoner jumped up from the table and promptly ran smack into an open cabinet door.

"Ma'am, you promised," he accused.

"I didn't call the authorities. It's probably a friend of mine. He lives here. He's perfectly harmless, I assure you."

"Cleo? I'm home!"

"He don't sound harmless."

There were degrees of harmlessness. Harrison Lawless fit into a category all his own. "We're in the kitchen," she called out, and then had to reassure her uninvited guest all over again when he tried to bolt through the back door.

She plopped him back down in the chair. With his swollen eyes, the poor boy looked more like a tattered, pink-skinned bullfrog than a desperate criminal. "Now, stay there and try to look calm, even if you're not. Mr. Lawless is a reasonable man. I promise, he'll hear you out."

But *reasonable* was another word that didn't begin to describe the man who burst through the door with a fistful of brochures. "Cleo, I've got a brilliant—" He broke off, staring. "What the devil is going on here?"

Colorful scraps of paper fluttered to the floor as Harrison moved swiftly across the floor and snatched one of the utensils from the knife block. Unfortunately, it happened to be a sharpening tool, but he was too busy glaring at the poor wretch cowering before him to notice.

"Harrison, this is Al. Al, this is Mr. Lawless. Al has been—well, he's been, um, camping out in the woods for a while, but we've decided he'd be better off going back to his, um—"

"He's the escaped convict. For God's sake, Cleo, listen to me—"

"No, you listen to me. This poor boy needs help, and he's already agreed to go back and turn himself in, haven't you, Al? He's going to get his eyes taken care of—he has some bites that are infected, too—and then he's going to get into one of the educational programs and get his GED, and when he's paid his debt to society, why, then we'll see if we can help him get a job."

Harrison closed his eyes and started counting. The only thing that kept his blood pressure from shooting through the roof was that "we" business. It was the first indication that she might have changed her mind about leaving.

He looked from one to the other. From a fiercely protective Cleo to a cowering shred of human debris huddled over a plate full of chicken bones.

"Lady, one of us needs a keeper," he said, slowly lowering his weapon. "At this point, I'm not sure which one it is."

A few hours later, Cleo and Harrison stood on the deck and watched a three-quarter moon emerge from behind a veil of iridescent clouds, turning the shadowy woods behind the lodge into a place of magic. Jimmy had finally gone back to sleep with his little belly full, his bottom dry and a brand-new skill. While she was changing his diaper, he'd managed to get his foot in his mouth.

Poor, pathetic Al had gone back to the correction facility, but not before both Cleo and Harrison had spoken at length to the superintendent.

"He'll be all right, won't he?" Cleo asked now. She'd endured a lecture from Harrison earlier about self-defense and common sense. She'd come back with one of her own about charity and civic responsibility. They'd called it a draw.

"He'll do added time for breaking out."

"He didn't break out, he was already out. He just… stayed out."

"He also drove a getaway car after an armed robbery."

"Well, at least he was law-abiding enough to stop for a traffic light." She'd made it her business to learn the details of Al's criminal career. "I'll bet anything his friends didn't even tell him they'd just held up a convenience store."

Now that the matter was safely resolved, Harrison was amused at her staunch defense of the young hoodlum. He'd been less than amused when he'd barged into the kitchen, full of plans, eager to enlist her help. His first impulse had been to throw himself between Cleo and danger—which he'd done, but not before making a fool of himself by arming himself with that damned knife sharpener.

If he'd needed something else to bring home to him just how he felt about her, that had done it. He'd have taken on a pride of lions bare-handed before he would ever let anyone harm a single hair on her head.

Not until after it was all over had it occurred to him that he'd just undergone a pretty stressful hour and a half without so much as a single twinge. He took a deep breath and flexed his left arm to be sure.

He felt fine.

Feeling the warm, soft body beside him, he felt better than fine, he felt…

Oh, boy. He wasn't up for a repeat of last night's performance, but he was sure as hell up. Randy as a goat. They stood there side by side, staring out at a sky so bright that not a single star was visible. His arm was around her waist. Her head rested against his shoulder. Whatever awkwardness they'd started out with that morning had been swept away by subsequent events.

Once they'd got rid of their uninvited guest, they'd cleaned and aired the kitchen and then headed for their respective showers. Standing under a needle-spray of cold water, he'd tried his damnedest to concentrate on the clever plan he'd formulated on the way home, wherein he laid out his idea for three separate, but related, small businesses and then tactfully lured her into agreeing to give him her input. While she was distracted, he'd planned to pop the question.

Instead, he'd spent the whole time picturing her under her own shower, wishing she was sharing his. Sharing his bath, sharing his bed, sharing his table— sharing his life.

He cleared his throat. "I did some research while I was out today. Came up with some ideas I'd like to run by you."

"Harrison, I'm leaving behind a lot of stuff. Anything you don't want, feel free to dispose of."

"Sure. Uh, Cleo? As I was saying, I—"

"I'm not sure if there's a Goodwill around here, but there's bound to be something."

"Listen, about what I was saying—oh, hell. Cleo, would you marry me?"

She tipped her face and stared at him, her eyes enormous. "Would I *what?*"

"Marry me? Now, don't answer off the top of your head, take your time and think about it."

"Harrison, you just asked me to marry you. Are you crazy?"

"Would it help my case if I were?" He was tempted to use her compassionate nature against her. "I'll be honest with you—I'm not always as easygoing as you might think."

"You're not? Does that mean you can be bossy? Hardheaded?"

He nodded. "I won't deny I've been called stubborn, persistent, domineering, not to mention a few less flattering terms. On the other hand, I'm extremely, um, solvent. I was named one of the world's twelve most eligible bachelors."

"Oh, Harrison, I—"

"Wait, hear me out. I told you I'd had problems with my heart. Genetically, I'm probably a lousy risk, but I'm working to improve the odds. Diet, exercise, no stress. You know the drill."

"No stress. You mean, like this afternoon?"

"Touché." His smile was a masterpiece of self-deprecation. "It might help to know I've got a whopping life insurance policy."

She socked him in the arm. "I don't want to hear this!"

"But you're far too softhearted to walk away when I'm trying my damnedest to propose. At least, I'm hoping you are." With the soapy, powdery scent of her infiltrating his senses, he was finding it increasingly hard to concentrate. "Let's see, where was I? I'm better at working with my brain than with my hands. You've probably noticed that I'm not much of a handyman, but you're too polite to mention it."

She covered his mouth with her fingertips. "Just hush up a minute, will you? It's my turn to talk."

"You're going to say no, aren't you?"

"No—" He winced. "I'm not going to say no, at least not right away. First, I want to know why you asked me to marry you."

"Because—well, hell, after last night, it's no secret how I feel about you."

"You asked me to marry you just because we had sex?"

"One of us had sex. One of us didn't."

She felt her face flame. "Harrison, this is practically the twenty-first century. The sexual revolution is ancient history, for goodness' sake! My parents helped usher it in, so even using the most conventional standards, you're under no obligation—"

"I'm not talking obligation, dammit! Look, do we have to discuss what happened last night? It's embarrassing as hell."

"You don't have to be embarrassed, and you certainly don't have to marry me. I know I'm not the kind of woman you usually have—well, whatever it is you have with your women." A sound emerged from his throat, sort of like a rumble. Cleo wasn't sure if he was swearing at her or laughing at her. "Well, anyway, you know what I mean. I'm nothing at all like Marla."

"Marla!" Grabbing her by the shoulders, he turned her to face him.

"I know, I know—you're just friends, but you can't deny you were going to ask her to marry you. Another thing, and this is for your own good. If you backed out last night because you were scared of what might happen, I understand. But, Harrison, I know what the experts say about sex after a coronary. I've been reading all kinds of health publications lately, not only about child rearing but about hypertension and cholesterol. I know the statistics say that married men live longer than—"

"Hold it right there. Do you think that's what this is all about?"

"Well, isn't it? Just tell me the truth. My feelings won't be hurt."

He shook her, and then he crushed her in his arms, his face buried in her hair. "Hell, no, it's not! All right, I admit that I considered getting married."

"But not to me."

He hesitated. "Maybe not right at first."

She laughed, but it was a muffled, shaky sort of laugh. "What changed your mind? You discovered I'm not quite as flaky as you thought?"

"Don't ask. Not after what you did today." His arms tightened around her.

"I'm not stupid. I knew I could easily outrun him or whack him over the head if I had to. The poor boy could scarcely see."

"So you took in an escaped convict, fed him and set out to plant his feet on the path of righteousness."

"It worked with you, didn't it?"

He rocked her from side to side, trying to ignore a condition that was becoming increasingly apparent. "Do you have any idea what you're doing to me?"

"Driving you up a wall?"

"That's too obvious. What else?"

"Well, speaking of obvious..." She pressed herself

against him, shifting her hips for a closer fit. "Sex is probably aerobic, if that helps."

"All depends on the way it's done, I suppose."

She leaned back in his arms, taunting him with an impudent grin. "We could go slow until we found out how you were going to react."

"Slow, huh? Sweetheart, I don't think that's an option."

"What if I did all the work?"

"You'd do that for me?"

Wordlessly, she nodded. God, he loved this woman! If he had a pedestal handy, he'd have put her on it. Come to think of it, the idea presented a few interesting possibilities.

"How long before Jimmy wakes up hungry?"

"Hours, if we're quiet."

"Now, that I can't guarantee," he quipped, chuckling at the memory of last night's shout. He'd never done that before.

But then, he'd never proposed to a woman before, either.

Thank God he hadn't carried out his original plans.

Hours later, sprawled on the hot, rumpled sheets, a warm breeze from the ceiling fan playing over his damp body, Harrison listened to the soft purr of the woman beside him and thought about what had just happened. Happened, in fact, three times.

So this was what love felt like, he marveled. Lighter than air, deeper than space, richer than the assets of all the Fortune 500 with change left over.

Euphoria. That was how she'd described the way she'd been feeling when he'd first met her. Content to drift, to dream—to go with the flow, as her parents would have said.

Not his. They had bucked the flow, considering it a social obligation.

He'd learned a lot from this woman. He had a lot more to learn, and a lifetime to learn it, no matter how things turned out.

"Harry," she murmured. Her hot little hand found his navel. One finger began to explore.

Harry. His father would have gone ballistic if he'd heard his son called Harry. How the devil could his mother have called a squalling infant in wet diapers Harrison?

There might come a time when Jimmy would prefer to be called James. Nothing pretentious about that. James Lawless, he sincerely hoped, but that could wait. At the moment, he had other things on his mind.

"Harry, are you awake?"

"You have to ask?" Parts of him were wide-awake, all but sitting up and begging.

"I was thinking…"

"You were thinking?" he grated, his teeth clenched as her hand strayed farther south.

"I was thinking that if I decide to marry you—"

"If?"

"All right, when," she said, and continued to toy with his personal, his very personal, his *most* personal property.

"When?" he said in an agonized whisper.

"Next month?"

"When?"

"Next week?"

"How about today?"

"Harry, it takes longer than that."

"I can't wait any longer. If you don't stop doing what you're doing, you're going to find out just how impatient I can be."

With a soft chuckle that stroked every ragged nerve ending in his body, she mounted him. Hovering there, she brushed back and forth against him while he stiffened convulsively and waited for the end.

With agonizing slowness she took him in and settled into a gentle rocking motion, her head tipped back, her full breasts swaying. Other than gasps, moans and sharply indrawn breaths, neither of them made another sound.

Later, as daylight began to filter through the white cotton curtains, Harrison felt a tickling, featherlike touch on his face.

He twitched his lips.

"Harry," she murmured drowsily. "Are you awake? You do realize that marriage is about more than sex, don't you?"

"Hmm. Harry. I like the sound of it. New life—new name. What could be more appropriate?"

"Yes, but do you? I mean, I fully intend to try my very best to be a good wife, but I can't promise to change. I tried once. It only made everyone miserable."

"You're serious," he said, amazed. Rolling over onto his side, he propped his head on his fist and studied her features as if he'd never before seen a stubborn, pointed chin, a wide, full mouth—reddened now from his kisses. Eyes that were almost too clear, too expressive. Eyes that looked out on the world with an understanding heart. "Cleo, I love the woman you are now. If a dozen years from now—two dozen years—you turn into someone else, I'll probably love her, too. Living together, we'll both change. For whatever it's worth, you have my heart in your keeping. It's yours now and always. Yours and Jimmy's. And if we're lucky enough to have more children, then it'll just have to stretch."

Seeing the moisture seeping from her lowered lashes, he shook her gently. "Don't clog up on me now, sweetheart. Do we have a deal?"

The slow, gentle way she smiled at him said they had a deal.

Outside, a chorus of bullfrogs tuned up. The wren nesting on the back deck began to scold. From a distance came the muted putt-putt of an outboard motor as a fisherman headed out to tend his crab pots. While in the next room, Jimmy experimented with a few sounds.

Harrison whispered, "My turn. I'll dry him off, bring him in, and he can have breakfast in bed." Life in the slow lane, he mused. Thank God he'd come to his senses in time. If he ever started racing his engine again, mistaking structure for substance, all it would take was one of Cleo's slow, sexy smiles to put things back into perspective.

"You're spoiling me," she murmured sleepily.

"Is it working?"

"Hmm…I guess time will tell."

There was a definite cat-and-canary quality to his smile. "That's what I'm counting on, love."

* * * * *

Everything you love about romance...
and more!

Please turn the page for Signature Select™
Bonus Features.

Bonus Features:

BONUS FEATURES

LAWLESS LOVERS

EXCLUSIVE BONUS FEATURES INSIDE

The Writing Life
by Dixie Browning

It's been a whirlwind. I could never have
imagined twenty-nine years ago when my first
two books were published where it would lead. At
the time, I knew less than nothing about writing,
having been a painter practically all my life. As a
painter, I specialized in watercolor, the one
medium I'd never studied. See, I knew that if I
took classes in watercolor, sooner or later
someone would tell me I *couldn't* do this or that,
and I absolutely *must* do...well, whatever.

As a writer, I was eventually forced to do a bit
of preplanning. It's called a proposal, and I
wasn't required to do them at first. But then
things changed, and I had to figure out what I
was going to write before I ever started writing.
Worst still, I was supposed to follow my own
recipe, or in this case, proposal. The trouble is
that invariably, I'd forget and follow my characters
when they veered off course. They were so much

more interesting than any staid, paint-by-numbers proposal I'd concocted.

As a painter, I tried—I really, really did—to do compositional studies, value studies—all the rigmarole you're supposed to do before you launch on the real painting. Trouble is, once I'd done those, the creative part of my brain had had enough. Been there, done that, not again, thanks. I used to make jewelry, too, but when it came to earrings, not a single pair ever matched. Once I'd done the first earring, the second was just a copy, and copying bored me stiff. I have several pairs of earrings I made all those years ago, but no two are alike.

Back to writing. Let me admit something now, in the twilight of my writing career. Once I struggle through a proposal and mail it off to my editor, I start writing. No waiting for the proposal to be approved, much less a contract to be signed. In the heat of the moment, I simply have to create!

The thing is, I forget to re-read the proposal. I have enough momentum to launch my story, and just enough on the ball to remember the names I've assigned to my characters. But that's it. If they catch the wrong train and end up somewhere I never foresaw, I go with it. If they're accosted by a mysterious stranger, how can I walk away without finding out who he is and what he wants? Dangerous? You bet. Fascinating? Irresistible? Oh, yeah.

If I drop a big splash of water in the middle of a wet wash and it suggests something that has no business in the middle of my watercolor, do I try to erase it? Blot it up? Heck no, I fool around and see what other "accidents" I can cause to happen, see where they lead. See, the thing is, with art—my kind at least, whether it be painting or writing—the subconscious mind knows so much more than the conscious mind. It's so much more fun to follow where it leads than to stick to a well-marked highway that leads to a safe, known destination.

6   Does that tell you anything at all about the proper way to write? Or to paint? Nope, it tells you only how I do it. My way is right for me, but maybe not for you. But you know what? My way is probably lots more fun—that is, if you like walking a tightrope without a net.

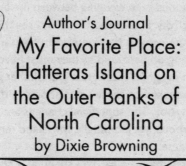

Author's Journal
My Favorite Place: Hatteras Island on the Outer Banks of North Carolina
by Dixie Browning

I was reminded just yesterday of why this place is known worldwide as the Graveyard of the Atlantic. On our daily beach walk, we came upon a newly revealed shipwreck—dozens of enormous worm-eaten timbers still held together after more than a hundred years by iron bolts now little more than clumps of rust. Soon it will be covered by sand again, like so many others that appear and disappear each year. When I look at Hatteras Island on the Outer Banks of North Carolina with its historic old villages, its miles of beautiful, untouched ocean beaches and the rugged, marshy sound shore, I try to see it objectively, but my view is distorted through the lens of the past. A past that includes my own experiences as well as tales told and retold by earlier generations, events that have been immortalized in song by local bards. Shards of memories keep wedging between me and my objectivity. I look around me and see things as they are now, as they were when I was a child growing up here, and as they must have been when my great-great-great grandfather was shipwrecked on these same shores in the mid-1700s. The superficial changes are enormous, yet essentially, the island remains the same.

How many hours did I spend as a child swimming alone in the ocean? Surfing alone on my homemade surfboard? Now there are surfers from all over the world with their fancy store-bought boards. There are even lifeguards at designated beaches. How many hours did I spend walking the shore of the Pamlico Sound in search of whatever treasures could be found there? A feather, an arrowhead or a bit of ancient pottery...a chunk of logwood that originated in the forests of South America, called dyewood because when it washes ashore from a shipwreck, it stains the sands around it pink. Those things are still to be found as the constant erosion uncovers bits of the past.

There was a time when the mail was delivered by boat and "called off" at the mail landing where people gathered to claim any letters. Later the mail came in by truck, a rough ride on an unpaved and often flooded road, but now and then I still hear someone—an older person—ask at the post office if the mail has been "called off." We still collect our mail from the post office, as there's no home delivery.

There was also a time, not so many years ago, when leaving the island meant driving for fifty miles through deep sand. Having to get out and push. Having to wait until the engine cooled when the radiator steamed dry. This was before the age of four-wheel vehicles. One alternative was to catch one of the few freight boats, none of which had any passenger accommodations other than a fish box to sit on and a bucket for whatever. The boat trip to Elizabeth City took about eight hours, depending on the weather. The only other option was calling for a plane to come from Morehead City, land on the beach (before the airport was built) and carry you wherever you needed to go. I've done it all.

A highway, often flooded and occasionally breached, now runs the entire length of the island, where once there were only countless ruts in the sandy beach. At low tide we drove the wash, zipping along at nearly twenty miles an hour. Now fishermen and sightseers plow countless ruts in our sandy beach with their four-wheel-drive SUVs, searching for a promising fishing spot. Continuity...

Nearly half a century ago a bridge was built on the north end of Hatteras Island. Before that we relied on a ferry to cross Oregon Inlet. There was no ferry landing, only a wooden ramp that was lowered onto the beach. I remember the ferry captain, Toby Tillett, a man who had known my family since before I was born, telling me the first time I came home with my infant daughter that the older a child grew, the more pleasure and the more trouble they were to their parents. I told my daughter when she was old enough to appreciate the prediction. We laughed together and years later she repeated the story to her own children. Continuity...

The National Park Service now claims miles of open beach between the villages, but in and around the villages themselves, fancy eight- and ten-bedroom "cottages" line the beach, each with its own swimming pool and paved parking area. (The term cottage industry has a different meaning here.) With progress came a chain supermarket. When I was a child living in Hatteras village there were three stores, all of which carried a bit of everything from canned goods and kerosene to lanterns and hip boots; from sewing thread to homegrown collard greens and salt pork. Now two of those stores, including one that was established in 1866, are operated by descendants of the original founders. Continuity...

There was a time when the island fishermen built their own boats and their own houses and raised their children to follow in their footsteps. No more. Whether that's a good thing or not, it is an inevitable part of evolution. Now, along with a few remaining commercial fishermen, we have sports fishermen with varying needs to be catered to. We have honeymooners and families who come year after year to enjoy the matchless beaches, and celebrities who think they "discovered" this unique island hideaway. Small planes come and go from our tiny Billy Mitchell Airport, named in honor of the man who proved to our government that planes could sink ships when he bombed a derelict battleship within sight of our beach.

Billy Mitchell was not the only historical figure to visit the Outer Banks. Reginald Fessenden sent the first musical notes ever transmitted by radio from this very island. A few centuries earlier in the late 1500s, a ship bringing the first English colonists to America paused briefly to ask directions of the island natives. A few years later, long before the Pilgrims landed on Plymouth Rock and even before the Jamestown settlement was established, the survivors of that ill-fated first colony retreated from Roanoke Island after alienating all the native Americans surrounding them. Many believe they retreated to Hatteras Island, called Croatoan at the time, and threw themselves at the mercy of the only remaining friendly natives in the area, the Hattorask people.

They left word of their destination carved in two places in the settlement they deserted. Further proof came a century later when the English gentleman John Lawson, first surveyor general of North Carolina, described finding on Hatteras Island "natives with blue and gray eyes, who value themselves highly for their affinity for the English." Thus it is logical to believe that many, if not most, of the oldest families carry the blood of those first colonists as well as that of the native Algonquins, the Hattorask Indians. Continuity?

A drive through the villages, both on the highway and on the back roads, reveals old houses that have withstood long years and fierce weather without losing their essential dignity. Often they can be recognized by the dainty gingerbread trim or by the chimneys—one or two for the front, one for the kitchen that was usually built off the back of the house. Often there's a cistern near the back door where rainwater was collected for household use. Now they're overshadowed by newer and larger buildings. Some might see them as ruins sitting on potentially valuable land. I see them as the homes of people I remember, many of them my kinsmen. Family graveyards are still visible throughout the villages, although many are so overgrown they've all but disappeared.

Oh, and did I tell you that when I grew up here, neither drivers' licenses nor license plates were required because there was no state highway? As often as not there was no doctor, either. Babies were delivered by a midwife or a Coast Guard pharmacist mate who married a local woman and for many years, served three communities in lieu of a doctor. There was a single hotel in Hatteras Village with bare, unheated, uninsulated rooms. There was rumored to be a deputy on the island, but there was no jail.

Now we have it all. Doctors and deputies, rentals and shops catering to the tourists who've replaced commercial fishing as the chief livelihood. The shops can be found scattered throughout the several villages, as zoning came so late as to be ineffective. I can see both sides of the zoning issue. What person who inherited a parcel of land from his father's father wants to be told what he can or can't do with it? The natives, whose roots go back for centuries, tend to be extremely independent, probably an inherited trait. Forgotten by governments, colonial British, Federal and Confederate, their forebears survived entirely by their own efforts, living off the land and the sea. Some who return to the island after years spent on the mainland (myself included) come from that same stock.

To sum it up, the island of Cape Hatteras, the nation's first National Seashore Park, is neither the most glamorous nor the most picturesque place to live. Objectively speaking, it's probably a mixture of both, a community in flux, as are most. It's far from the most convenient, yet after living on the mainland for so long, I knew when it was time to come home. My roots, too, go centuries deep in this sand. I've seen mountains many, many times higher than our highest dunes; forests many times more impressive. I'll take our hardy maritime forest and our modest ridges, many of them hidden deep in the woods.

A hundred or a thousand or ten thousand years ago, these same ridges, called Great Ridge, Middle Ridge, Flowers Ridge, Dark Ridge, Indian Ridge—all grew from a few grains of sand that collected on a clump of grass, a fallen branch or perhaps the wreckage of a ship. As time went on, they were gradually covered by wild grasses. Eventually a maritime forest took root and managed to thrive in the poor soil despite repeated lashing from storm winds and flooding by sea tides. In the deepest woods, protected from wind and tide, one can find enormous pines, some standing, others dead of old age. The spreading live oaks and laurel bay, cedars, holly and wax myrtle, are laced together with all kinds of vines including the wild grape vines described by the very first explorers who set foot on these banks. In less protected areas, one can easily pick out the ghosts of hurricanes Emily and

Isabel. Soon they'll be joined by the ghosts of Alex, the first hurricane of 2004.

For as long as history records such things, fierce storms have consistently swept the coast. Yet the island survives. The island people, those who identify with this rugged, barren place either genetically or spiritually, remain. As I'm writing this I can look out my window and see live oak trees that were here in the time of my grandparents, perhaps my great-grandparents. On one of my favorite walks, where only a few years ago there were huge, spreading oaks and cedars, I see dead cedars, dying oaks. Yet even now, beneath the leafless, lichen-covered branches, acorns have sprouted and are already growing.

Continuity.

THE LAWLESS FAMILY

A Family Tree

16

THE LAWLESS FAMILY: A FAMILY TREE

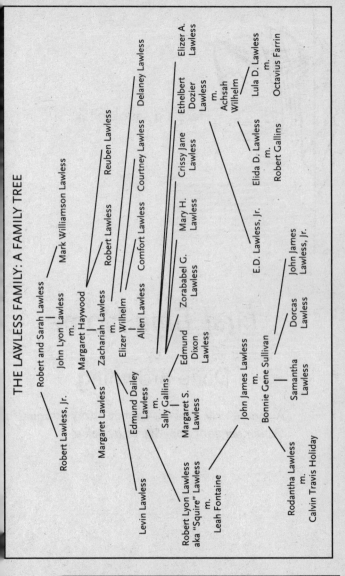

Here's a sneak peek...

First Time Home
by
Dixie Browning

*A brand-new Lawless family story coming in
September 2005 from Signature Select*

CHAPTER 1

Laurel raced up the two flights of stairs, fumbling for the keys in her tiny purse even as her heavy tote banged against her hip. Today she was twenty minutes early, which gave her time to change shoes, do something with her hair and be seated at her desk looking cool, efficient and ever-so-subtly tempting by the time Jerry arrived.

She'd sprayed a whiff of Tea Rose cologne on her bare midriff after her shower. Nothing blatant, but as the day wore on and her body warmed up, it would offer a hint of what tomorrow held in store.

A weekend in the Hamptons. Possibly even a *house* in the Hamptons. She could hardly believe it, but Jerry had hinted that they might look at a few houses as long as they were there.

Not that he'd actually proposed, but a hint here, a hint there and pretty soon a woman might start dreaming herself a future.

He knew her weakness all right, she thought with

a rueful little smile as she unlocked the front office of JB Associates, affectionately known as Jay-bass. If he'd offered her a tiny fixer-upper in Outer Suburbia she'd have been just as thrilled.

Okay, maybe not *quite* as thrilled, but all she really needed was some place to put down roots and eventually start a family. Small was good. With a small house they could do most of the fixing up themselves. A home was more than a house.

She was still lost in thought when she heard the clatter of feet racing up the stairwell that opened onto the third floor offices. Immediately, she tried to look intelligent, industrious, sexy and temptingly kissable as she waited for Jerry to pop in to say good morning.

Not that they usually indulged at the office, but before anyone else showed up, one kiss wouldn't hurt. She couldn't think of a better way to start the day, especially when she was running so far behind schedule.

The door burst open and a stunningly handsome, if rather wild-looking man stared at her. "You're already here? God—!"

Her temptingly kissable mouth fell open as she stared back at the man who had started out as her employer, recently become her lover and was hopefully her soon-to-be husband. "Jerry? What's wrong?"

Jerry Blessing raked a slender, manicured hand

through his normally flawlessly groomed hair. His dark eyes raked over her cubbyhole office, moving from the filing cabinet to the computer, to the stack of newspapers she hadn't had time to clip for her files. "Look, I don't have time to explain, but I want you to go home. Now! I'm expecting—"

"Go *home!* Jerry, I've got three appointments this morning alone, and this stuff's due at the printers no later than noon today." She waved a hand at the mock-ups she'd done.

He was sweating. Jerry Blessing *never* sweated. From some distant Mediterranean ancestor he had inherited olive skin and the darkest of brown eyes, only now his face was the color of wet plaster and his eyes kept darting around her office, never once making contact with her own.

"Look, will you just do this much for me? Oh, and one more thing—" He held up a staying hand as he backed out her door and swung into his own corner office.

Laurel waited for several minutes, almost afraid to move. What was going on? From the office next door she heard the slamming of several drawers and what sounded like a chair striking the wall. Jerry's precious ergonomic dark green leather roll-around?

Heaven forbid.

She didn't move a muscle, hardly dared breathe. And then he was back, carrying what looked like the smallest of several paintings that hung on his linen-covered walls. "Mama's watercolor," Jerry said tersely. "I want you to take it home with you."

"You're giving it to me?" Totally at sea, she stared at him.

"For safekeeping. Look, you might as well know, we're being audited. I don't want to take any chances on some government goon damaging Mama's painting."

Government goon? Who, the IRS? Aggressive accountants, maybe—nosy, obnoxious nerds, quite possibly, but government goons?

She waited for more of an explanation. She waited for some word of…well, something. A reassuring embrace wasn't too much to ask, was it? She started to ask about their weekend trip when he cut her off with a flap of his hand.

"Go, go, go! For God's sake, Laurel, leave before they get here. It's only a fluke that I had this much warning."

Before she could move he wheeled away and the next thing she heard was the slamming of his office door, followed by what sounded almost like the click of a lock.

Laurel stared down at the amateurish watercolor in her hands. Not only was it not very good, it was poorly framed. Any value had to be the sentimental type, which said a lot about the man. He owned far more impressive art, both in his office and his upscale apartment.

Moving toward the door Jerry had slammed on his way out, that had bounced open again because the latch never held, she stared across the intervening few feet to his closed door.

"Well…shoot," she whispered. Turning away, she reached for her tote. Not bothering to change shoes again, she slipped the small painting into its commodious depths and scooped up the papers she'd placed on her desk only moments ago. If that was the way he felt, the heck with it. The posters would get done when they got done, and if that was too late, then too damn bad!

She was hurting inside as she waited for the ancient elevator to rattle its way to the third floor. No way was she about to tackle those stairs wearing five-inch heels.

On the way back to the apartment she shared with a friend, she stopped in her neighborhood bodega for something rich and sweet to hold off the jitters. She had a lot of thinking to do and food always helped. While she was there, she perched on one of the few chairs and changed into her walking shoes while she exchanged pleasantries with the proprietor, an elderly man with snow-white hair and coal-black eyebrows who called every woman younger than sixty-five *nieta*. Granddaughter.

She only wished she were. Life would be much simpler if she had grandparents. Any family at all, even an aunt and uncle and a few cousins whose big noisy home she could visit on holidays. Right now she needed someone honest and objective to tell her what the devil was going on, because she hadn't a clue.

The next day she was summoned for questioning. It had to be the scariest moment in her life, even though neither of the men who appeared at her apartment door with a polite request that she accompany them downtown was particularly scary. If anything, they were almost too polite. For some reason it gave her cold chills. She asked a few questions of her own, which were ignored, so she shut up and huddled in the back seat, thinking she didn't know these men from Adam, despite the fact that they had identified themselves as from some branch of government.

Which branch? Homeland Security? IRS?

Oh, God, she was hyperventilating. What if she opened the door and jumped out? Would they come after her? For all she knew, the doors might be locked. She didn't dare try them to see.

Maybe she could leave a trail of…of what? Lipstick? Comb? Social Security card?

Not until they parked in an underground garage did the tall one—he looked a little like what'shisname, the old Western movie star?—offer her an answer to one of her questions.

"It's about finances, ma'am."

With his hand on her elbow, she had no choice but to follow him onto an elevator. "But I don't have anything to do with the financial end of the business. I don't even buy postage stamps." Jerry handled that by himself, serving as both CEO and CFO.

She was offered a drink of water and then the inquisition began. It was polite—she'd give them that much. But afterward, she couldn't remember a fraction of what they'd covered. The tall one, whose name was Galanos, offered to drive her home. She declined but quickly wished she had accepted the offer when she stepped outside to face at least two film crews and several reporters, two of whom she knew personally.

All she needed was a pair of orange coveralls. Before she could signal a cab she was hit with a barrage of questions, reminding her of the coverage she'd seen and dismissed so many times on the news. People surrounded by men in dull suits, the perps—that was what they were called—laughing and trying to pretend they weren't scared out of their Gucci loafers.

Recovering her wits, she remembered the standard response. "No comment."

For the next few days whenever she ventured outside, one or two flashbulbs had gone off in her face, a few microphones were poked at her. "Is it true, Ms. Lawless—?" "What can you tell us about—?" "Is there a direct connection between Jerry Blessing and Al Qaeda?"

Crazy. The world had gone absolutely bonkers, that was all she could conclude. Thankfully, it hadn't lasted long. There was always another scandal to take her off the hook.

She had expected to hear from Jerry if only to find out what she'd been asked by the authorities and how she'd answered, but no such luck. A brief phone call—was that too much to ask? Laurel checked her cell phone battery. If he couldn't get her on her cell, surely he would call her other number.

So she waited. And waited.

26

A week later she was still waiting; almost too stressed to settle down to any task more demanding than folding laundry. She had tried several times to call Jerry, leaving messages which he never returned. With her salary on hold and her bills piling up, she needed answers, and she damn well needed them now!

And she knew where to get them. At least it was a starting place.

By the time she reached the old renovated office building that housed JB Associates and two other small businesses, she was steaming, and not just on account of the weather, which was the typical mid-summer, mid-Manhattan steam bath. Her hair was sticking to her face and she'd just reached up an arm to brush it away when someone called her name.

She turned her head just as someone stepped in front of her and poked a microphone in her face. "What—who—get that thing away from me!"

"Ms. Lawless, is it true that—"

She darted up the steps, ducked inside, slammed the heavy door and leaned against it. What in the world had happened now? Jay-bass, the downfall of, was yesterday's news.

"Is *what* true?" she muttered to the dark, dusty-smelling entrance hall.

She took out her cell phone and punched in Jerry's cell on her quick dial. Nothing. Not even an invitation to leave a message. Maybe he was upstairs. She considered using the cranky old elevator that took forever to groan its way up two flights, but then she thought, maybe this wasn't the swiftest idea she'd had. Wearing a white cotton shift and red sneakers, minus any makeup and with her hair looking like a hawk's nest, she was in no condition to confront anyone. She certainly didn't want Jerry seeing her in this condition, even if he happened to be here.

Okay, so it had been a really lousy idea. What had she hoped to accomplish?

Improvisation wasn't her long suit.

Once she was certain the reporter was gone, she let herself out and hurried away, wondering what to do next. She had to do something, only what? Nothing she tried was working. Nothing even made sense any more.

Later that evening she was comforting herself with a chocolate éclair and a glass of wine while she watched the evening news coverage of parents picketing a local school. Three commercials later, she watched as a vaguely familiar looking woman hurried along the sidewalk. She was wearing red sneakers and a white shift, carrying a familiar envelope-size shoulder bag.

Laurel watched herself spin around, saw her own lips moving, but no sound emerged. At first it didn't quite register, but then it did. Oh, God—this morning! The camera didn't flatter her at all. She looked angry and scared and hot and sweaty, not to mention frightened.

"Oh, no," she whispered.

"D' you say something?" her roommate Peg called from the kitchen.

Before she could answer, another talking head appeared. The camera cut away briefly and she saw Jerry hurrying across the same section of sidewalk, followed by the same reporter who had cornered her. Time must have elapsed. Jerry couldn't have been there when she was, or else she'd have seen him.

He turned to face the camera and she read his lips when he said, "No comment." Then he said something else, only the remote was on the other side of the room with the volume turned all the way down.

"Isn't that Jerry?" Peg appeared in the doorway that separated the small living room from the minuscule kitchen.

"I think so." Laurel knew so, she just couldn't talk about it. Even without seeing his face, she'd have known his walk, his build. She even recognized the tie he was wearing, a limited edition designer model he got from the tailor who fitted his suits.

What was going *on?* If he was still considered a person of interest after all this time, it had to be more than a simple accounting glitch. She retrieved the remote while she watched Jerry's lean backside disappear through the front door. The spokesperson was saying, "Blessing has been accused of funneling money to terrorist organizations. According to a spokesman for—"

Furious, Laurel snapped off the sound.

"Wow, no wonder you're pissed." Peg stared at her as if she'd never seen her before.

"I'm not pissed, and that's not what's going on."

But was it? Could it possibly be true? Jay-bass raised funds for worthwhile causes that were too small to rate celebrity telethons. Jerry had lost friends in 9/11. He would never, ever help any terrorist group. Not knowingly, at least. "You know the gutter press. These people build their reputations on other people's misfortune. Believe me, they never let the truth get in the way of a good story."

Peg eyed her with open sympathy. "Have you talked to him lately?"

Laurel only sighed. Could it be possible that her future husband was a thief? Not possible. This was the man with whom she wanted to build a life—a home...or so she thought.

...NOT THE END...

*Look for the continuation of this story in
FIRST TIME HOME by Dixie Browning, available in
September 2005 from Signature Select.*

If you enjoyed what you just read,
then we've got an offer you can't resist!

Take 2 bestselling love stories FREE!

Plus get a FREE surprise gift!

COMING NEXT MONTH

Signature Select Collection
LOVE SO TENDER by Stephanie Bond, Jo Leigh and Joanne Rock
Why settle for Prince Charming when you can have The King?
It's now or never—Gracie Sergeant, Alyssa Reynolds and Ellie
Evans can't help falling in love...Vegas style! Three romantic
novellas that could only happen in Vegas.

Signature Select Saga
SEARCHING FOR CATE by Marie Ferrarella
A widower for three years, Dr. Christian Graywolf's life is his
work. But when he meets FBI special agent Kate Kowalski—a
woman searching for her birth mother—the attraction is
intense, immediate and the truth is something neither Christian
nor Cate expects. That all his life Christian has been searching
for Cate.

Signature Select Miniseries
LAWLESS LOVERS by Dixie Browning
Two complete novels from THE LAWLESS HEIRS SAGA.
Daniel Lyon Lawless and Harrison Lawless are two successful,
sexy and very sought-after bachelors. But their worlds are about
to be rocked by the love of two headstrong, beautiful women!

Signature Select Spotlight
HAPPILY NEVER AFTER by Kathleen O'Brien
Ten years after the society wedding that wasn't, members of
the wedding party are starting to die. At the scene of every
"accident," a piece of a wedding dress is found. It's not long
before Kelly Ralston realizes that she's the sole remaining
bridesmaid left...and the next target!

Signature Showcase
FANTASY by Lori Foster
Brandi Sommers doesn't know quite what to do about her
sister's outrageous birthday gift of a dream vacation to a
lover's retreat—with sexy security consultant Sebastian Sinclair
included as the lover! But she soon discovers that she can do
whatever she wants....

SAGA

USA TODAY bestselling author

Dixie Browning

A brand-new story in
The Lawless Heirs miniseries...

FIRST TIME HOME

Reeling from the scandalous ruin of her
career and love life, Laurel Ann Lawless
escapes to North Carolina and turns to
relatives she's never met. She soon feels
a strong sense of belonging—with her
newfound family and her handsome
new landlord, Cody Morningstar.

*Available
in September.*

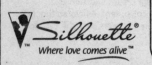

Silhouette®

Where love comes alive™